SOMETHING SO BEAUTIFUL

LEE DAWNA

LeeDawna Books

First edition

Cover design by Premade Ebook Cover Shop
www.premadeebookcovershop.com

ISBN 978-1-949192-01-8 (paperback)
ISBN 978-1-949192-00-1 (ebook)

Published by LeeDawna Books www.leedawnabooks.com
leedawnabooks@suddenlink.net

~

This book is dedicated to my husband,
a man whose essence lives within these pages.

~

~1~

The worst parts of our lives are the things we never see coming. The things we can't prepare for because our nightmares aren't made of them. Like my mother dying when I was nine and my father abandoning me six months later. Or being widowed by thirty. I never imagined any of those things, yet they all happened.

Then there's the insanity. I never saw it coming. Never planned for it. And not once dreamed of it. Yet, here I am. Mary Williams. Thirty-two years old and slipping slowly into madness.

Probably. I feel sane. But the noises in my head say otherwise. Ones that sound like the old screen door on the back of my house creaking open when the hook is tightly latched. Or the echoes of footsteps crossing empty rooms. I've stopped running from those. My house is small enough that even with rubbery legs I can check all eight hundred square feet faster than dragging my wobbly legs to a neighbor's house. The only thing I can't seem to do is force away this fear. It's always here. Scratching at the edges of my mind. Clawing at my spine. It writhes against my intuition until running is all I can think of. And I would run. If I knew which way to go. It's kind of hard to get away from yourself.

I haven't always been a mass of paranoid delusions. Kim, my best friend since fourth grade, used to call me *strong*. A survivor capable of finding a way to cope with anything. Now, she and her husband Kevin have decided I'm having a grief-stricken mental break. At least, that *was* their opinion. One they didn't hold their tongues about. Too many times pamphlets about mental institutions were slipped to me when I was walking the floor of my store, never mind that it's already hard enough being the manager of a top clothing retailer without customers who happen to distantly know my friends reaching out as if it's their duty to aid the poor grieving widow who's slowly going mad.

The embarrassment would have been magnified if my employees ever found out what the whispered conversations were about. But Kim doesn't promote her theory anymore. Not since I stopped talking about how I feel inside. Since I started smiling and saying everything is fine. One small victory now replaced by an equally disturbing proposal. She's filling the vacancy in our standing Wednesday lunch with babble about a blind date. It's no wonder she thinks it's the best idea she's ever had, she thinks all her ideas are Pulitzer-worthy. But after all these years and everything we've been through, she could at least pretend to hear me when I say I'm not interested.

Two can play this game. I'll just ignore *her*. "How is Kevin adjusting to his new job?"

"He loves it." Her bright blue eyes sparkle, hands rubbing wildly together, sending her blonde bob bouncing over her shoulders. "Just like he loves me setting you up with his friend, John. The four of us are going to have so much fun this weekend!"

One surefire way to pump her brakes is telling her about the noises still plaguing me at night. Casually mentioning the footprints in the soft earth under my window, the random flowers on my porch, or maybe even my jittery repulsion to the darkly twisted words of a poem I found plastered on my windshield yesterday. But I'm not the only person at a busy mall driving a silver car, and I'm sure neighborhood kids are responsible for the flowers. Probably the footprints, too. So I'm not stirring up trouble for myself *or* putting her through worrying about me again just to get out of a date.

Kim may have broken my trust and embarrassed me, but it was done out of love. "I'm glad Kevin likes his job and that he made a new friend. Didn't you tell me Jenny isn't seeing Rob anymore? I bet she'd love to double-date with you."

"She can triple with us. But only after our double, because this weekend is a special occasion." Stars dance in her eyes. "Wait until you meet John. He's this six-foot-tall god. Body chiseled from pure stone. And I'm telling you, bring a bib. Because the first time I met him, I nearly choked on my drool!"

"I'm sure Kevin appreciated that. And…"

This time it's me who's checking out, words trailing off as my attention is drawn to the old wooden windows of LaTerra. Today, the yellow brick building with its glass front feels like a jail cell. A jail cell inside a display case. Me the bauble on exhibit. Intuition screaming. Bleating. Someone is watching. Cataloguing my every move. All the usual ridiculous nonsense.

The hair on my neck rises, telling my every fiber to be afraid. But no one would waste time putting my boring life under a microscope. I barely socialize enough to have friends. Outside of Kim and her family, customers and co-workers during business hours are the extent of my connection to the world. Still, what I feel seems so real. It has for years. While cancer ravaged my husband, I began looking over my shoulder. Only occasionally then. Now that Mike is gone, it's constant. Even when I'm visiting his grave.

~2~

My petite friend's bubbly yammering isn't enough to distract me from the paranoia. I try focusing on what Kim is saying but my eyes won't leave the windows. As if someone would actually be out there in these thick sheets of rain. "This thunderstorm has been hovering over Huntington all day. Do you know if it's going to let up soon?"

"Who cares?" She slaps the table, jolting my attention to her. "Do you know how you're going to wear your hair Saturday? Oh, I do! Wear it down. Everyone loves those long, dark, luscious locks of yours. John will want to dig his hands right in!"

"I realize you don't need me for most of the conversations we have, but watch my lips." I lean forward. "Replace me, or cancel the date. Because I don't care how hot John is or what he thinks of my hair. I. Am. Not. Going. Saturday. Or any other day of the week."

I cover the bases and give her what I'm told is a million-dollar smile. She's immune. "John's so excited to meet you. Did I mention how hot he is? I'm talking lava hot. Which is the whole reason I set you two up."

"Hello?" I snap my fingers, waving a hand between us. "Remember me?"

"I remember how Kevin swooned over you the first time he saw you. And that's how I realized John isn't the only person I know hot enough to live in the land of volcanoes."

"Flattery isn't going to get you anywhere. But thanks for trying. And for picking someone based completely on looks."

"You're welcome." She giggles. "You and that man together will be a full-out eruption."

"Mt. Vesuvius or not, I'm not going."

"Yes, you are." She grins. "And I can't wait."

I'd scream, but she wouldn't hear that either. I'd be angry, but she's like a sister to me. An annoying, scheming sister. The kind you can't live without because, for all the trouble they cause, they somehow manage to make life better. Still, she went behind my back to set up this date. And picked the wrong time to do it. "Try me again in a year. Or seven…teen."

"I will not." She hits the table hard enough this time to bounce a fork off her plate. "I know you aren't going to stand this man up. He's more excited than he's ever been in his whole life. How can you even think about leaving him hanging?"

How can I feel guilty about not going on a date I never asked for? "Just tell him I can't make it but you're setting him up with someone else. Then choose someone else. *Anyone* else."

"No!" Her body heaves across the table. "It's been more than two years. And the one thing Mike didn't want was for you to be alone. So for a few hours this Saturday night, don't be. Please, Mary? All I'm asking for is a few hours."

"It isn't as simple as you're making it out to be." My eyes rest back on the windows, the periphery catching her tiny arms folding over her chest as she pushes back into her seat.

"All you're doing is having dinner with Kevin and me, and John will be there, too. There's nothing simpler than that." Her pout twists the knife of guilt deep. "I'll be there with you the whole time. Like a girls' night. With Kevin and John."

So nothing like a girls' night. Yet I hate myself for making her bottom lip stick out. Even if the pout is more to do with her weekend plan being ruined than concern for my widowhood. "You'll never leave me alone with him?"

"Never." She smiles. "See? Nothing to worry about."

Except a psychotic break. But I've sworn to myself that unless someone walks right up to me and gives me a reason to be afraid, I won't be. I only wish that resolve lasted for more than five seconds. "Fine." A shiver traces up my spine. I swallow it down, uttering syllables I've dreaded since she first opened her mouth. "I'll go."

I put my hand up to stop her theatrical squeal but it's too late. The transition from joy to horrified shriek unfolds with a crash. Terror plasters her face. I throw my arm back, straight into the path of the shattering window.

Glass shards penetrate my flesh, raining down in a watery mix. I turn away. A dark figure dives over me, its greedy hands twisting and pulling, cracking my skull off the chair on our way to the floor.

~3~

The waiter did his best to shield me from damage, the scene inside LaTerra unfolding so fast I'm not sure I screamed. Kim did. A lot. "What happened? Is she okay?" I can't see her around the waiter's burly frame.

"She's fine." He keeps me pinned to the floor. "This hailstorm just hit a line drive at your head, though. I saw that baseball coming from across the room!"

"Hail did this?" I eye the rain hammering the floor a foot away. "Ice?"

"A *big* chunk of ice." His fingers graze my cheek. "And you turned your pretty face right into the glass. I only see a few nicks, though."

Edging away from his touch, I peer into the storm's darkness. Maybe it did fling hail. Or maybe it's the fictitious character my imagination believed was there the whole time. "It was the storm? No one threw anything?"

"It was the storm." His hand finds its way into my hair. "The next time one slings hail, I hope it's at lunchtime on Wednesday."

"What about me?" Kim jerks his collar. "I nearly died and all you're doing is lying on her like it's your third date."

"Kim!" I scramble out from under him, grabbing my purse from the bits of glass while she demands a free lunch. "Neither of us is hurt, that's the important thing."

I want out of here. Away from him. Away from the storm. "Thank you." I stuff all the cash I have into his hand, it's enough to cover the bill and tip, albeit barely. Especially considering the lengths he went through to try to help me. The knot on my scalp proof of that *help.*

I hook an arm around Kim, turning her toward the door. "This is a sign. I can't go on that date."

7

"Hush." Her hand launches to her forehead. "I can't think about any of this now. I'm too shaken. We nearly died, Mary. *I* nearly died."

"Come on." I slip my raincoat around her shoulders. "I'll walk you out and give Kevin a call so he knows you're upset."

The type of man who likes to exaggerate almost as much as his wife, Kevin takes the rest of the day off from work after hearing Kim's hysterical recounting. I do the opposite. Even though the concentration of glass was on my side of the table and I actually have blood to prove what happened.

Worse, neither of them lets me use the incident as a reason to call off the date. The dread of which forces me to work longer hours all week. A lame attempt to keep my mind too occupied to fret. Not one grueling second of the last two days has tapered the building anxiety of going on the first date I've been on since Mike died. Nor did scrubbing the floors of my tiny house this morning until my fingers were raw. The clock is still ticking down. And Kim is still texting me every five minutes with suggestions on what I should wear tonight. I know fashion. And am plenty old enough to dress myself.

Boycotting every single dress she suggests, which happens to be every dress in my closet, I select the new arrival I picked up that won't be unveiled at Scarlets until next week. It's a black, mid-knee, cap-sleeve sheath she can't take credit for dressing me in. I give her the hair, though. The dark locks cascade down my back, the silhouette framing my olive complexion. Now to get through this date as painlessly as possible. *Just show up, be pleasant, and in a few hours this whole thing will be over.*

FRONT DOOR OPEN—my alarm announces Kim's arrival. I gave her a key the day I moved in. The alarm code the day it was installed. "I'm back here!" Silence answers. I step into the hall. "Did you hear me? I'm in the bedroom." The house is deadly quiet. "Kim?"

~4~

There are enough things going bump in my world without Kim sneaking into my house, thinking it's funny to hide and jump out at me. "One of these days, I'm going to take your key away."

"Take the alarm away instead." She laughs. "Remember last Halloween when Kevin set it off trying to sneak in?"

"I'm still combing fake spider web out of my hair." I shiver. "Why do you two get a kick out of hearing me scream?"

"I get a kick out of how good you look." She motions for me to twirl. "John's socks are going to fly straight off his feet and circle the moon!"

I didn't consider dressing to impress. Only dressing like an adult who doesn't need to be told what to wear. But it *is* a nice dress. "You'll knock Kevin's socks off after I give you this dress in your signature color."

"I might not be curvy in all the right places like you, but in blue I'll give you a run for your money." She heads for my room. "I'll go change and we'll see who wears it best!"

"It's at Scarlets." I turn to the door. "And if we don't leave right now, I'm going to go put on sweatpants."

My alarm set, I drop into the passenger seat of her ice-blue Jag. Nerves churn my gut. Every mile away from home adds another layer of dread. "Where are we going?"

"The Charleston Club."

"That's the club where you and Kevin go dancing, right?"

"It's a favorite haunt of anyone who knows anything about the downtown nightlife."

"You know I don't go clubbing." I watch behind us in the side mirror. Just in case my malfunctioning intuition is right this time and we're being followed. "I thought we were having dinner."

"We are." She turns onto the highway. "It's a swanky little restaurant that happens to have a dance floor. And there's a live band tonight."

The noise of music could be a good distraction. From my head *and* my date. "I'm not dancing. So don't ask, and don't beg."

"You have to! With Kevin. That way I get to take John for a spin." Now I know why she wanted to set *me* up instead of Jenny. Jenny wouldn't share.

I brace as she pulls into the crowded parking lot, the old stone building towering over us. Gripping the door handle for strength I climb out of the car. There's no turning back now. "Remember, you promised not to leave me alone with him. That means no running off to dance with Kevin. If you go dancing, take John."

I follow her eye-roll inside, immediately swallowed up by the Roaring '20s atmosphere. It's loud. And busy. Two things that will come in handy if this John character and I have nothing to say to each other. "Come on." She grabs my arm to keep me from lingering in the foyer. "They're already here. Kevin got us a table in the back."

"Great." My teeth clench as I step to her side, simply walking through the room instead of putting on a display the way she is. She's a beautiful woman and her steps demand everyone notice. Her legs sling out, hips swaying, head moving just the right amount to catch the light. There should be a wind machine and paparazzi in front of her.

"Mary!" Her hand circles my trailing wrist, pulling me back to her side. "You're a leggy, raven-haired beauty. Act like it!" Her painted nail points ahead of us, lips purring. "Don't waste what God gave you. Your date is watching. Give him a show."

~5~

It's bizarre to lock eyes with a stranger. Weirder still to be drawn to him. I try to look away, but from across the room I can see his eyes are green. They're like homing beacons, calling to me as his steady stare studies every intricate move I make. A shiver slithers along my spine. An all too familiar feeling. "Kim, have I ever met this man?"

Her head shakes. "Kevin met him about the time you were, well, you know, *struggling*."

I break his gaze. "Did you tell him I was having mental problems?"

"No way." She laughs. "I want you *in* his black book, not on his blacklist."

I don't want to be on any list. But he seems familiar. Like I've known him for years. And he's every bit as handsome as she described. More. Not even stained jeans stretched over his thick legs in a room full of date-night-bests takes an ounce of attraction from him. Or from the confidence pulsing in the air around him. His jaw is firm. Shoulders wide. Arms muscled. They flow out of his t-shirt giving a preview of what lies beneath, and I don't need the full show to know he's pure, head-to-toe, glorious man.

At the table's edge, nerves shoot my hand forward. "Hi, I'm Mary."

"Hello, Mary." His voice rolls over me, rumbling along every nerve. The dread shatters. Crashing around my feet while his eyes pull me closer. "I'm John. It's nice to finally meet you." His hand floats to mine, fingers lightly gripping then delicately cradling, tilting my palm down to hold my hand instead of shake it. The feel of him races over my flesh. I can't move. If I do, I might jump into his arms.

A smile slides over his lips. His free hand pulls out my chair. "I'm looking forward to having dinner with you."

"Me, too." I let him guide me into the seat. Sitting only because he's putting me here, my body uncharacteristically willing to follow wherever he leads. "More than I expected to be."

He sits next to me, bringing my hand to his lips. "Then, we're off to a good start."

"A galloping start!" Kevin pipes up, reminding us we're not alone. "See? I told you I had your back. You have to start trusting me, Johnny Boy."

His expression changes. Eyes finally leaving mine. But not to respond to Kevin. "What happened?" His fingers slide over the back of my hand, gently tracing a cut from Wednesday's storm. His caress plasters my tongue to the roof of my mouth.

"It was terrible!" Kim doesn't suffer from any ailment of the mouth. Ever. "We were having lunch and the window next to our table exploded. I thought I was going to die right there on the spot!"

"It wasn't that bad," I admonish, my voice small.

"A baseball-sized piece of hail crashed through it." Kevin puts an arm around Kim. "Yeah, it was bad."

I can't stop either of them from giving a highly dramatized version of the event. John listens, eyes searching mine. I breathe in slowly, getting a grip on my body while he looks for whatever he lost.

"Of course *you* don't think it was terrifying." Kim isn't having her trauma downplayed. "You were too busy with the waiter on top of you to notice anything else."

"Kimberly!" My face burns. "The server shielded me from the glass. And from the storm blowing through the broken window afterward. That's all."

"Those servers fight over who gets our table every week." She crosses her arms. "That man was so ready to pounce, if I wasn't there he'd have knocked her up on the spot."

"That isn't true! He didn't…I didn't…we weren't…" I babble like a guilty spouse. "It was just a freak accident."

John lets go of my hand, gets to his feet, and breaks our gaze with such force it rattles my heart. Which is stupid. I really am losing my mind. "John, you don't have to leave. I'll go. This was a mistake anyway."

"Tonight isn't a mistake." He offers me his hand. I accept. He lifts me from my seat, moving me to the warm chair he just vacated. "I'm not leaving. Or giving anyone else the chance to be your hero." He nods toward the windows.

"The glass is on the other side of the building."

"Like I said, I'm not taking any chances." He brings my hand to his lips, caressing my knuckles. "Not on windows breaking, or on overeager servers pouncing before I do." Color slams into my cheeks. He chuckles, throaty and deep. "Don't worry, no matter where I'm sitting, freak accidents coming from *any* direction aren't getting by me."

Despite being touched by how ridiculously sweet he is, I glare at our snickering friends, slipping my fingers from his and standing. He stands with me. "Oh. I was just going to see if Kim would go to the ladies' room with me."

As if he's in charge, he motions for her to get up. She shakes her head. "All she's going to do is tell me to stop embarrassing her. Which is practically impossible."

"Then you're not trying hard enough." I sit back down. He sits down, in a strange old-fashioned way, and with an amused grin on his face. I want to fade into the background. "Let's order." I pick up the menu. "Let's just order."

~6~

I study John through dinner. Meeting his ever-waiting eyes whenever I'm brave enough to take on the emeralds. He never shows a twinge of nervousness. Not even a stutter or simple flinch. Usually everyone is a ball of nerves on a first date. Well, these days I'm a ball of nerves, period. But John's calm. And it's peaceful being with someone so naturally sure of themselves. I'd like to rest my head on his confident shoulder. Just for a little while.

"Did you like the food?" I keep my head to myself.

"I did." He nods at my empty plate. "And you didn't leave any doubt as to how you feel about the chef."

Him taking note of me polishing off an entire fourteen-ounce prime rib by myself, including sides, is embarrassing. But he ordered the exact same thing and his plate is as clean as mine. "Maybe I should have curbed my appetite for a first date, but men do know women eat. Right?"

"We do." He grins. "Which is why I meant my comment as a vast compliment. If you'd only picked at your food, I'd be worried about your vanity instead of about what to feed you next."

"My vanity is in check." I set my napkin aside. "And I'm completely full."

"Then it's dance time!" Kim drags Kevin from the table, winking as she dodges my attempt to grab her.

"It looks like she's in a hurry." John's palm extends to me. "Would you like to dance?"

I'd like to not do something seriously stupid. Which is difficult with his smooth voice rolling over my flesh like fog, making my head cloudy. "If you're not dying to get out there, I'm happy watching the dancers instead of being one."

Of course, I can't just say no. I'd feel bad for ruining his night if he's secretly a dance fanatic. It isn't his fault I can't control my body. "Is that okay?"

"I'm definitely not dying to get out there." He brushes a lock of hair from my face. "But my dad always told me not to deny a beautiful lady the chance to dance, and you're beyond beautiful."

I can't keep the flush off my face. I haven't been able to squelch it all night. I turn away. His hand slides along the back of my chair. "I wish Dad was still alive. He would have loved seeing the way you came in here tonight. Moving through the room and giving out those polite smiles of yours without ever once noticing people were purposely going out of their way just to cross your path. It was quite a vision."

"Thanks for laying it on thick, but no one walked by me on purpose."

"They did." His thumb strokes my shoulder, sending my flesh into a tailspin. "If you hadn't already been coming to me, I would have done more than cross your path."

~7~

I've never been one to move fast. Mike and I knew each other for a year before we ever had a date. So to me, holding hands with a man I only learned existed an hour ago is the very definition of fast. I need to stop being goo-goo eyed over someone who has all the charm, and equipment, to bring my entire gender under his spell. John's the type to amass a harem, while we're all too occupied with his abs to notice.

I bite the inside of my cheek, fighting the urge to lean into him rather than pull my shoulder from his touch. "Tell me about yourself." I move clear of his caress. "If you can manage to do that without unnecessarily flattering me."

His hand slides over my shoulder, eyes staring as if he's etching every inch of me into his soul. I sit forward, color running deep. A wince shoots across his brazen face. "Sorry." He lifts his palm, making a show of removing it from my chair. "I'm only being so forward because I'm captivated by you. And dumbfounded you don't realize how absolutely stunning you are while I'm sitting here battling how to soak all of you in without staring at you like a buffoon."

"I think you're losing that battle."

"I'm losing badly." He chuckles, stretching tall to tower over me. "Let's turn our chairs around. Maybe I'll get distracted by the dance floor."

He spins our chairs and moves them a little closer together than they were before. "There." I point as he takes my hand and lowers me back to the seat. "Plenty of beautiful ladies for you to fix your eyes on."

"Really?" His continue to rest on me. "I hadn't noticed there were any other women here tonight. But you feel free to watch the dance floor, then maybe you won't notice me watching you."

16

"Clever." The charmer. "Which is surprising for someone so handsome."

"You think I'm handsome?" His fingers brush my chin.

I turn his palm to his own face. "Me and all the other women I was just talking about. If you want to dance, they'll form a line and be glad to wait in it all night."

"Too bad for them I have tunnel vision." He lowers his hand. "The only lady in my sights tonight doesn't want to dance."

He notices my fidgeting. "Sorry. I just thought you should know I'm a one-woman man. And tonight, you're that woman."

"Don't worry." I smile to convince us both I'm okay, noting his admission that I'm only *that woman* tonight. Which unfairly makes me angry. "No one else in my place would dare eat the way I did on a first date, and most women like to dance. So your next date will give you plenty of chances to worry about her vanity while you grope her on the dance floor."

"I hope not." His emeralds close in. "I'm enjoying the fact that you aren't like any other lady I've ever met. I'll be disappointed if that changes on our next date."

"Hi, John." A lace miniskirt shimmies by, auburn locks and red lips turning back with a provocative wink that makes my body temperature cool despite how high the vixen sends my blood pressure.

"She's pretty. Maybe your next date will be with her." My snappy tone is uncalled for.

He scoops up my hand. "Allow me to explain the difference between pretty and beautiful."

"There's more to life than looks." I yank my fingers free. "How about you explain why your hands are so rough. Manual labor?"

"That depends." He grins. "Do you think manual labor is sexy?"

~8~

I think John is sexy. It's all I can do to angle my body away from his so I don't end up on his lap. Where miniskirt clearly wants to be. "The only work Kevin does with his hands is typing. I thought you did the same kind of work. Isn't that how you met him?"

"Nope. I met the clueless man at the gym and took pity on his lanky limbs." He shrugs. "Somewhere along the way we became friends."

"He's so funny it's hard to resist liking him."

"I believe I could resist."

He isn't as close to Kevin as Kim let on. "So, what do you do?"

"By trade…" He points to his stained clothes. "I'm a carpenter. I like working with my hands. Unless you don't like the roughness? Tell me now and I'll change professions tomorrow."

"Just like that?" I smile despite feeling sad that, in reality, miniskirt has more right to be sitting here than I'll ever have.

"Exactly like that." He waits for a real answer to a question I thought was a joke.

"What woman doesn't like a working man's hands?"

"I only care what you like." He leans in, tentative and slow, watching my expression as his fingers glide through my locks. "I like building things, Mary. And already have some idea of what we could form together." I swallow. Hard and unsteady. His lips turn up. "I'd feel a lot better about my shot at having a second date if you'd relax a little, despite the fact I'm an unrepentant buffoon." He moves away. "Better?"

I nod, anxious energy kicking up from my depths. This man unnerves me. And he's doing it while giving a comfort I've never felt. Not even with Mike. Each minute, I find myself more impressed with the hunk of man beside me. I wouldn't have pegged John for a creative type, though. "What is it that you build with your rough carpenter hands?"

"Furniture." He smiles. "High end custom work."

"How high end are we talking?"

"I travel the world for unique inspiration and to hand select choice woods. So high enough to cover that cost."

He'd be appalled to know most of my furniture came from Goodwill. "Do you build for a particular brand?"

"I'm my own brand." I should have guessed he wouldn't work under anyone very well. "I sell through private networking. Or trade shows when they interest me enough to go."

Hopefully they interest him enough to keep his other bills paid. "I manage Scarlets, the big retailer at the mall. I want to own my own boutique, but it's expensive to start. So rather than take on the debt I stay at Scarlets, where I know there's a paycheck." His face twists. "Sorry. I didn't mean to imply you're being careless or that your work isn't good enough to make a living. I'm sure it's very good. I'd love to see it next time you have it displayed at a trade show."

"I didn't mistake your words." His throat bobs. "My mind just wandered off. And I'd be happy to show you my work *any* time. Trade show or not. We can go right now if you want."

I bite my lip to keep from saying yes. What I need to do is figure out how to hold his attention. At least for tonight. "I've never made anything before. Unless you count snapping together pre-made furniture pieces. That's the kind of carpentry I know how to do."

"Then I'll make you something and deliver it in pieces." He grins. "Because there's nothing like the feeling you get when all the pieces come together."

I should be flattered. But an all too familiar shiver slithers down my spine. "What I build from your pieces might be different than what you plan."

He moves closer, hands smoothing down my arms to rub away the chill that isn't from being cold. "I make sure things always turn out exactly the way I plan."

"Then I hope you planned for the night to end on a sweet note." I stand to break his caress, moving my chair back to the table. "I hear this place is famous for a decadent triple layer chocolate fudge cake."

"One look at you," he motions for the server, "and I planned for this night to end exactly the way you want it to."

~

Before I arrived at the Charleston Club, I wanted this date to end with a polite goodbye and never another thought about the man. Now I can't even finish eating my share of the cake. John and I are both picking at the slice, while Kim and Kevin polished theirs off long ago.

"This is the best cake I've ever tasted."

He nods his agreement. "Do you want to box it up and take it home?"

"I've proven my lack of vanity enough tonight." I smile. "You take it. And I'll split the dinner bill with you."

"It's sweet of you to offer, but I don't let my dates go Dutch." He smiles back. "Plus, I've already paid the bill for the table."

"For all of us?" Kevin beams. "That's why you're my best buddy! You always pick up the tab."

"You're only saying that because he's driving you home tonight." Kim forces a yawn. "I wish I had someone to drive me. I'm so tired."

Her plan is obvious, and John takes the bait. "May I drive you home? Then Kevin can drive Kim."

"That seems to be what they had in mind. But I'll call a cab." I might have avoided finishing the cake, but time is up. This pumpkin has to get home. So I can remember why I can't have the prince. And with the way my nights have been lately, I'll be fully aware by dawn.

~9~

John is a persuasive man. And after miniskirt approached him again, stroking her hand down his bare arm while asking him to dance, I can't say I'm not enjoying the fact that she witnessed him leaving the restaurant with *me* on the very arm she dared touch.

It's silly to be jealous. And John was already overly stern in his rejection of her offer. But letting him drive me home instead of jumping into a cab where she'll see he's alone now somehow seems fair. After all, I'm the crazy one who can't ever see him again. She'll have plenty of other opportunities.

"Are you sure my house isn't too far out of your way?" Guilt gets the best of me and we're not even in the vehicle yet. "I can call a cab if it is. Or if you want to stay here and dance."

"I don't know that girl." He sighs. "I mean, I know her a little. We had coffee. Once. Eighteen months ago. I've had her number blocked ever since."

"You don't owe me an explanation." But I'm glad he gave it. "It really is fine if you want to stay."

"I don't." His hand rests on the small of my back, guiding me farther into the parking lot. The dark part. Away from the other cars and onlookers. Icy fingers claw at my nerves. I squint into the night and focus on the warmth of his hand.

My gaze fixes on the one thing I *can* see. An oversized white behemoth in the back row towering above all the other trucks. The jacked-up brute has snow camouflage trim decking out the windows, mirrors, and fenders. "Look how pretty!" I head toward it, feet on autopilot.

"You like trucks?" He follows, studying me as I inspect the masterpiece.

"I like this one." I catch his expression. "Women are allowed to like trucks just as much as they're allowed to eat what they want."

"Yeah." His guttural chuckle tickles my insides. "But it's going to take me a minute to reel up my jaw because this is my truck and I've been sweating bullets over it the whole time we've been walking out here."

"Why?"

"Because most women are appalled by having to climb up into it. Which is why I drive it on dates. It's a test." He gives his stubbled cheek a hard scratch. "Tonight, well, no man likes his truck to be called *pretty*, but I'm more concerned with whether or not you like *me*. If this truck earns me a strike, I'll go drive it straight off a cliff."

"That's a bit dramatic."

"What you call dramatic, I call necessary."

His fingers brush over my cheek. "Before tonight, I felt like the right woman for me should at least appreciate this truck for the one-of-a-kind work of art that it is. But now I feel like an idiot for driving this instead of my car." His hand waves over his clothes. "Especially after showing up dressed like a bum. I can't lie and say I'm not normally dressed like this, but on dates I do typically clean up." He pinches the bridge of his nose. "Today's just been an off day. I didn't come properly prepared to meet you."

"There's nothing wrong with what you're wearing." His humble side compels me to slip my hand into his.

"Except I'm way too casual to be standing next to you." His grip tightens, arm bending to bring me closer. "I never knew what the hype of a little black dress was all about until tonight. You're elegant. And so absolutely stunning."

"Mostly, I'm just excited about getting to ride in your truck." I withdraw. "Are you ready to go?"

Opening the passenger door, he guides my step onto the running board. I slide into the seat, reclaiming my over-held hand. He leans on the frame. "If you don't want to go home yet, I'll be happy to ride you around all night. Because I'm still trying to figure out how such a perfect creature exists, yet in all my years I've never met you."

"Thank you for following Kim's coaching and embarrassing me as much as possible in one evening." I turn pink. "You've thoroughly explored the depths of how red my face can get. Now, I'd like to go home."

"Kim didn't tell me a thing." He straightens. "I'm embarrassing you all on my own. I hope that isn't earning me a strike? I'm not doing it on purpose."

"Could have fooled me."

"Well, mostly I haven't done it on purpose. But you're making it easy. Now hold on tight and I'll take you straight home, sweetheart." His incredibly inviting grin deepens, heating my flesh. "Unless you want to make it easy for me not to."

~10~

Riding home in John's decked-out truck includes the unexpected perk of being endlessly grilled about my social life. Not that I mind him wanting to know how I spend my free time. It's just that the truth of my plain existence is boring. My social life is restricted to time with Kim and her family when someone is having a birthday, wedding, baby, or any other general life get-together. Outside of that, I don't get out much.

"Do you like to attend parties? Or host them?" He's asking the same questions, only worded differently.

"No. I prefer a low-key life."

"Kim doesn't. She loves the high life. So why are you friends if you don't have anything in common? What am I missing here?"

"How opposites attract." I smile. "She pushes me not to live in a box. And I, hopefully, push her toward living in a more level-headed one. That's the way we've always been, ever since we were kids."

"I wish I'd known sooner her best friend wasn't like her." He sighs. "They've mentioned your name before but I never paid any attention. Kim's nice enough, and I can see why Kevin likes her, but I'm not into theatrics."

I wonder if he's into crazy. "That's a funny statement coming from a man who threatened to drive his truck off a cliff if some woman he met *once* didn't like it." He shrugs. I point up ahead. "The next house on the right is mine."

"You're not *some woman*." He pulls into the driveway, shifting into park and bringing his grin back out to play. "You're the first real lady I've met in a long time. So sit tight, sweetheart. I'll help you down."

His big hands encircle my waist, guiding me to the ground in front of him. A whistle escapes his lips. "You're a vision. You make getting in and out of this truck graceful. In that dress. With those shoes—"

"Because you lifted me out." I pull away. "Thank you for the ride. And for dinner. I had a nice time."

"Me, too." His hand centers on the small of my back, a nod telling me to lead the way. "I'll walk you to the door."

I move forward, his eyes leaving me to study the house, yard, and surrounding houses. "This is a cute neighborhood. Do you like it here?"

"It's close to work. Only having a fifteen-minute commute is nice after a long day."

He takes another look at the house. "The place isn't extravagant, but you're doing well for yourself."

"Are you trying to insult me in a polite way?"

"I'm trying to compliment you." He chuckles. "Even if I wanted to insult you, I couldn't. You haven't said or done one single thing tonight that could be used against you. And trust me, I've been looking. But you've been perfect."

He must not be looking as hard as I thought. "In spite of you scrutinizing me—and testing me—I had a good time."

"I'm sorry." He sighs. "If I offended you, I sincerely didn't mean to. Tonight has been an honor and a pleasure." He runs his hands over my arms to warm me up. But the cold is still not why I'm shivering. A twinge of fear creeps over me. Maybe because he's leaning in to kiss me. I turn, avoiding his lips.

Unlocking the door, I step inside to shut off the alarm before it blasts the neighbors awake. He follows me inside. I meet his eyes. He smiles. My throat tightens. He presses the door shut behind him. One long stride, and the distance between us disappears.

~11~

The only man I've ever spent the night with is my husband. And only after we were married. I'm not going to start being immoral now. Especially with a stranger. One who is ten times bigger, stronger…and not interested in me.

There's no need to grab my gun when John's eyes aren't on me. They're roaming over the living room the way they scoured the outside, landing on the shoulder mount of an eight-point white tail deer. "That's something you don't normally see in a single woman's house."

"Been in a lot of women's houses, have you?" I slap a hand over my mouth.

"Not nearly as many as that sounded." He chuckles.

I lower my hand, swallowing the embarrassment my tongue insists on inflicting. "It isn't a world record, but that's my very first buck, so I had to get it mounted."

"You shot that?" He playfully falls against the wall. "You hunt?"

"I don't know why that shocks people. A lot of women hunt."

"Not when they look like you." He comes toward me wielding his grin, his complete focus now on me. And there isn't much space to put between us in this house.

I retreat the few steps to the eat-in kitchen. "Would you like some water? I don't have anything else but I can make some tea. It wouldn't take long."

"I'll have water." He's closing in fast.

"Are you sure? Tea wouldn't be any problem." I back into the counter.

"I'm sure water is fine." Amusement flashes across his face. I spin away, pulling two glasses out of the cabinet.

To retrieve the water pitcher, I have to slide by him. He enjoys the encounter. I do my default move and babble nervously. "More women would hunt and fish if they were exposed to it. We're led to believe those are men's sports, so we stay away without experiencing it to see if we like it."

"Does that mean you fish, too?"

"I do." I hand him a glass of water. "Lots of women do. That's a fact, and you're big on facts."

He nods. "It's a fact that there aren't as many outdoor-loving women as a man would like."

"And here I thought you said you were a one-woman kind of man. Were you lying about how many women take you home with them, too?"

I'm mortified. I've never been jealous in my life. "Sorry. That was uncalled for. And none of my business."

"No, you're right." He laughs. "I can't complain about there not being many women like you out there when all I need is one of you. It's just that," he sips the water and sets the glass aside, landing all his focus back on me, "I've been under the impression you were extinct. So I quit hunting you. Then here you are, making me fight to not bend a knee right now."

My next default is to turn away. Into the counter. Like I have a reason to fiddle with the dishtowel folded there. "I'm not flattering you for flattery's sake." His warm body slides behind me, lips whispering over my shoulder, "I'm genuinely enamored with you, Mary. I have been all night." His fingers trace along my arm. "You're beautiful, intelligent, and dripping with pure sweetness. Mix in a love of the outdoors that'll have you by your man's side all the time, and part of me really wants to get down on one knee this very minute."

Part of me would say yes if he did. My temperature rises. "Want some fruit salad? I made a fresh bowl this morning." I move away from his embrace, head pounding. I should be asking him to leave, not offering to feed him a twelve-course meal. "It's mainly berries and a few apples." I open the refrigerator. Maybe stuffing my face will keep me from jumping into his arms the way his eyes beckon me to. Maybe.

~12~

John's brazen. Forceful, even. But the fear I've been feeling is not because of him. It can't be. It's been a part of me for a lot longer than only tonight. And somehow, he manages to subdue it. Lure me into his sea of tranquility. When I'm not fighting the urge to undress him.

"I never considered hunting or fishing until I met Mike." John has no idea I'm disappointed he backed off and took a seat across the table from me, seemingly happy with nothing other than conversation between us. "While I was falling in love with him, he taught me the basics of both."

"Mike?" he snaps.

"Did Kevin not tell you I'm a widow?"

"No." He takes a deep breath. "He didn't."

"I should have mentioned it earlier." My hands shake. "It's just that, this is a brand new experience for me. You're the first date I've been on since Mike died, and I'm not sure what's expected."

"There are no expectations outside of you being yourself, and you're nailing that part." His kind smile is followed by the usual pity grimace. "I'm sorry for your loss. How long has it been?"

"Last January marked two years."

"And you haven't dated in all that time?" His eyebrow shoots up. I shake my head. He blows out a puff of air. "It's hard to believe you've been able to stay single so long."

"Hard to believe I've been *able* to? Are you one of those men who thinks a woman can't possibly take care of herself? That alone in the world with no man a woman is hopeless?" I sit forward. "I haven't been looking for your flaws, but if that's one, it's a big one."

"Good thing I'm not one of *those* men." His chin dips. "I think a woman can do anything she puts her mind to. Not all women have a mind to use, but that's a different topic. And, to be fair, all men don't either."

"Well, at least you're fair about your sexism."

I can't help but smile over the way he laughs. He's so charming. Especially when he leans over the table with that mischievous grin. "I'm not sexist. I'm just doing a terrible job delivering compliments to you tonight. What I meant, Mary, was to point out the fact that I would expect a lot of men, maybe all that have ever crossed your path, to be vying for even the smallest bit of your affection."

"Then what I meant to say, John, was regardless of how others perceive me or what they desire, I've stayed single because I'm not ready to date. I only met you tonight because Kim guilt-tripped me into it. If I could have gotten out of the date, I would have."

"That makes two of us then."

"What?" My mouth falls open.

"I only found out about this date an hour before I was supposed to show up at The Charleston Club. Before that, I was under the impression I was having a guys' night at a sports bar with Kevin."

"They told me days ago you were expecting to meet me."

"Nope." His eyes narrow. "And trust me, I let Kevin know exactly what I thought about his blindside. Had I known you weren't a willing participant either, I would have *shown* him where to shove it."

They duped us both. "I hope the disappointment of your plans changing didn't put you out too much."

On his feet, he circles the table and pulls a chair as close as he can to mine. Cradling my hands in his, he searches my face. "I'm not put out in the least. And you're looking at a man who is the exact opposite of disappointed. Please tell me you feel the same."

I don't want to. "I do."

"Good." He runs his lips over my palms. "That means this date will end on an even better note than it started on."

"Agreed." As long as that note isn't hit in my bed. "Want some crackers? I might have some cheese to go with them."

~13~

I had a few days to get used to the date idea. But from the way John's describing chewing Kevin out, I don't think a few days would have mattered for him. "At least it's over now. You survived. And it sounds like Kevin won't try this stunt with you again."

His fingers softly glide along my wrist, a stark contrast to the bite in the air when he talks about Kevin. "I wish I had known I was meeting you, because I'm happy we're getting to spend this time together. It's just the principle of the thing, how they went about getting us together, that bothers me."

It bothers me, too. "Why did Kevin intervene for you? I know why Kim bullied me, but you're clearly open to dating and don't have any problems in that area." I saw that for myself tonight. Miniskirt was all too willing to hit any notes he wanted. Anywhere he wanted. And he didn't look surprised by it.

His hand withdraws and he sits back in his chair. "I'm thirty-five and have never been married. People act like that's a travesty against all things holy. But I can think of worse scenarios."

"Like being widowed by thirty."

"Absolutely." He shifts. "I didn't mean to sit here complaining when you've been through something so hard."

"You weren't complaining." I smile. "You were being upset on principle."

He chuckles, leaning forward and tightening our hands together. "Now you know why I'm off my game tonight. I was so mad I didn't even bother to bring you flowers."

"Oh, how terrible. I'm so upset."

"It gets worse." He smiles. "I planned to bolt soon after dinner started." He waits a beat to let his grin sink in. "Then you walked in and it took all of one second to change my mind. You absolutely blew me away. And have continued to do so ever since."

I feel the same about him. "I imagine first dates have gone much worse. So we can't hate Kim and Kevin too much. Especially since they were just trying to help us out."

"You're letting them off the hook too easily." He leans closer. "I may owe them for the introduction, but they're not getting my gratitude for free."

"I don't like the way they did things either, but I'm not going to torment them over it since their motives were pure."

"I'll torment them for both of us, then." He shrugs. "Good motives don't mean getting away with bad behavior."

"Why do I feel like someone has said that very thing to you?"

His chuckle brings light to his emeralds. "I might have learned it from living it."

I hope *I'm* not learning a life lesson tonight. Like why you shouldn't let strangers into your house. Incredibly sexy strangers. "I'm going to put the dishes in the sink." I snatch my hands from his and grab our empty plates. He follows me, brushing so near I feel the heat of his breath.

"Do you have speakers?" His voice vibrates through me.

"What?" My head is fuzzy.

"Some way to play music? A radio? Anything like that?" The words rattle me. My body wants to turn to his. To stop the quiver by pressing against him. But I can't do with him now what I'll regret in the morning.

I dig my fingers into the sink edge, anchoring my unruly body. "In the living room. Under the television." *And you need to leave!* One more minute to compose myself and I'll say those words out loud.

~14~

"One In A Million You" by Larry Graham is a song I've danced to many times. Alone. Inside the comfort of my own home. That isn't going to change now just because it's belting out of my living room. Whatever John thinks is happening, the only reason I'm letting go of this sink is so I can tell him to leave.

Feet like bricks, I move to the archway between the kitchen and living room. His smile and outstretched palm stop me dead. "May I have this dance?" I weld my mouth shut. He crosses the room, hand still reaching out. "Mary, may I *please* dance with you before this night slips away entirely?" I feel my arm rise. Rough calluses slide over my hand. Carpet moves under my feet. He cradles me delicately against his chest, our bodies swaying ever so slightly as he moves us to the music. "I've been longing to hold you." His lips fall to my ear, tingling nerve endings all the way down to my toes. "On our first date, dancing is the best way to feel you against me."

Shockwaves crash through my core. On a first date, he shouldn't even get to hold my hand. It might be old-fashioned, but without boundaries I've always feared becoming prey. Like now. When I'm losing the battle with my own body, melting against him to leave no lines as to where I end and he begins. His cheek caresses mine. His hand runs down my back. "You fit so perfectly in my arms, I never want to let you go." I meet his eyes. His lips dive toward mine, hovering just above so I can taste his breath inside me. "I want to inhale you so deeply you become a part of me."

His words remind me of the dark poem left on my windshield. I tense. His mouth changes trajectory, lips landing against my cheek. His hand eases my head back to his chest. "Lust isn't what's talking for me

32

tonight. I'm not throwing out lines trying to land in your bed." I don't know him well enough to know if that's true. Neither does my body. Still, my shoulders relax with every breath he takes. His heartbeat a steadying drum.

My eyes close, fully enjoying being warmly curled in the slow spin of his arms. His lips find my ear again. "I'm having some pretty intense feelings for you right now. I'm expressing them because, with you in my arms, my world finally feels complete."

"Mine, too." I don't mean to encourage him.

He cups a hand under my chin, tilting my face to his. "Then let's make this song never end." His lips cover mine. Warm. Opening. All my vulnerabilities displayed as my mouth follows where his leads.

He separates our lips, reconnecting our gaze. He wants me to want him. I see it in his eyes. Feel it as his heart bounces off mine. I also feel the guilt. Mike and I never had this kind of attraction. We barely had enough heat to consummate our marriage before the cancer ravaged his body. But he *was* my husband. And a good man. Even if he only spent a few nights in this house, it was our home. Now I'm standing in it kissing a complete stranger in the middle of the night. Worse, I want to be. I want John to hold me. Kiss me until the entire world falls away.

Tears threaten my eyes. He pulls back. "Mary…" I wrench from his arms. "Wait!"

I break for the hallway, disappearing into the darkness before the floodgates open. It's bad enough he can hear this downpour. I don't want him to watch.

~15~

Being the gentleman he's proven to be all night, John isn't beating on the bathroom door. He isn't begging or trying to fix anything. He's giving me space to cry in peace. He could also be gone. A smart man would have bolted as soon as I did. These emotions are mine and *I* don't even want to deal with them. Plus, things are not supposed to get this heavy on a first date.

Slowly, I open the bathroom door and peek out. He's sitting on the sofa, head in his hands. I get closer. "Idiot," he mumbles. "Stop messing everything up."

"Are you talking to me?"

"No!" He surges forward. "Never." Arms fly around me. "I'm trying to get myself to stop scaring you. To stop saying creepy things like *I want to breathe you in*. I don't know where that came from. I… I…" He's nervous. Finally.

"It wasn't that creepy. If I grade on a curve."

"A big one." His hand strokes my freshly washed face. "I've been acting on impulse instead of reason. I know better. And I usually don't attempt a kiss on the first date. I like to wait until I know just how many tongues have been in my potential partner's mouth."

"Is that a vaguely disguised question?"

"No." His arms envelop me again, head resting on mine. "Please forgive me. I'm grasping at what little common sense I have left. I've told myself to keep my hands and lips to myself, but clearly my body has a mind of its own."

I understand his struggle. My body isn't taking orders very well either. "It's okay. Neither of us meant for things to go this way."

"No." His lips rest against my temple. "See? My plan is shot all to hell and I've only had you back for thirty seconds. But I swear I won't make a play for your lips again. Just, please forgive me. I want a chance to make up for the tears I caused."

If the tears were his fault, I'd forgive him. But I'm the one at fault. And I have more reasons than sorrow over Mike to keep me single. If it weren't for the shabby state of my mind I'd be open to finding love again. Especially now that I've met him. "Since we're both flying by the seat of our pants..." And I can't breathe for how tight he's holding me. "How about we take an actual seat?" I motion toward the sofa. He ushers us there, sitting down with his arms still wrapped around me. Any closer and I'd be on his lap.

"Thanks for letting me cry in peace." I pull away to gain air. "You weren't obligated to stay. You could have left."

"I would never leave you like that." He brings me back close. "You were crying because of me, and you're still trembling." His lips brush across my cheek. "No matter what my head is yelling at me to do, I can't force myself to let go of you. I swear I'm not trying to scare you, though. And I do have sense. I just can't find it right now."

I shouldn't laugh. But he's clearly not used to being nervous. In the course of one evening I've managed to destroy his confidence. The man's entire foundation is on shaky ground. "I'm not scared, and your good sense can stay on vacation; I wasn't crying over anything you did. You're off the hook."

"Hardly." His arms cinch tighter. "I've been sitting out here trying to decide what to do, but nothing seems right. My first instinct is to hold you, so that's what I'll do."

As much as my instincts want him to hold me, I might pass out. "How about I sit over here," I slide away again. "And we just talk."

$$\sim\!16\!\sim$$

John rebounds quickly. His demeanor is back to that of a man in control. One who *can* take a hint. He's staying far enough away to not accidentally anaconda squeeze me, but close enough to keep a hold on my hand as we fall into the easy flow of conversation we had at dinner, touching on everything of a lighter nature. Movies, music, food and travel. Everything and nothing. Until the wee hours of morning.

My heavy eyelids beg to close. I nod off. He runs a thumb over my cheek. "I would leave, but it wouldn't be right to run out on you so late." I'll never say the words out loud but I'm glad he's staying right here, with his warm hand holding mine. If this is a dream, I never want to wake up. But reality beckons, and a familiar sound is rocking my peaceful world.

I focus on his face. His eyes are closed. A gentle rise and fall in his chest as he sleeps through the sound of my back door creaking open. It slams. He doesn't move. Maybe because the noise is only in my head.

The fear of an actual intruder isn't as scary as the fear of hearing imagined noises. Unlike real people, psychotic episodes can't be kept out with an alarm. The alarm! Expecting him to leave, I never reset it after we came inside. I never even locked the door.

Running across the room, I jam my finger against the buttons. SYSTEM ARMED lights up the screen. Tears threaten to unleash. I never leave the alarm off. I'm too afraid to be without it. And too afraid to *not* know if someone is actually breaking in this time. I have to check the door. If someone is in the house, at least John is here. If I'm imagining the noise, at least he's sleeping through it.

Arming myself with the nearest object, a foot-long blue glass dolphin, I ease through the living room toward the kitchen. The tormenting door is to the right of the refrigerator, behind the windowed wooden door that at this moment is closed. Which doesn't mean much.

Tiptoeing, I inch along to the door. Trembling fingers reach for the lock, pounding heart blocking all sound from my ears. My fingertips graze the metal. "Mary!" blasts from behind me. I whirl around, throwing myself against the door. John approaches slowly. "I didn't mean to raise my voice and scare you, but I said your name twice." He eyes the dolphin clutched like a weapon in my palm. "What's going on? Is someone out there?"

Few things have embarrassed me more. "I, um…was just looking to see if the sun is up and forgot you were here for a minute."

"I'm still here." He stalks closer. "Sorry I keep scaring you."

"I'm not scared."

He settles in close, gently removing the dolphin from my death grip. "I can see in your big doe eyes how not scared you are."

"I was just lost in thought and didn't hear you." I look away. "So that part scared me."

He rolls the dolphin in his hands. "What were you thinking about?"

If I explain the sentiment behind the dolphin, maybe he'll buy it as a black hole of thought. "Mike bought that dolphin at the beach where we had our first and only vacation. The sea air agreed with him so much I looked into buying a house on the beach, but he refused to move. He said all he needed was to bring that dolphin home for good luck. Looking back, I'm sure he knew then he would never beat the cancer."

"I'm sorry." He places the smooth glass back into my palms. "I can tell it's painful for you to talk about."

"Especially since his refusal had more to do with me than him." I sigh. "He didn't want me to be alone after he was gone. So he made sure I stayed in Huntington with Kim."

And now I'm making sure John doesn't press for a truth I selfishly want to hide. It's bad enough I kept him here all night just because his presence is comforting. "Would you like coffee? Or something to eat? I make pretty good omelets."

"I look forward to trying one sometime." He smiles. "Right now, I have to go."

"Of course. Here, let me at least wrap up a bagel for you."

"The only thing I want before I leave is your number." He stops my hands short of the breadbox. "And since I've already spent the night, would you be willing to go out with me again?"

No. As this morning has proven, crazy people should *not* be dating. "Yes. Even though I'm not sure why you want to go out with me again. Not after the way this date went."

"I've been on a lot of dates." His strong fingers lace through mine. "And even though there were bumps in the road, this was by far the best date I've ever had. So thank you for your sweet hospitality and for the pleasure of your company. I promise I'm leaving just as soon as I get that number."

I write down the digits and hand them to him with a smile. He slides the paper into his pocket, lifting my hand to his lips. "You have such a beautiful smile. I hope to see it often." Then there were other words. I didn't hear them. I got lost in emeralds that eventually left, taking part of me with them. A part I miss even more now that night has set in again, and big hands are dragging me from my bed.

~17~

The last thing I remember before waking up in the midst of being dragged out my bedroom window is getting a text from John at the end of the day, after what had to be the longest first date in history: *Didn't want to call in case you were sleeping, heard you had a late night. But I can't let the day end without telling you I'm still overjoyed to have met you. I'll talk to you soon.* After that, I closed my eyes and let dreams of him carry me away. Until two strange men actually carried me away.

"Carbon monoxide?" a familiar voice asks from beyond the curtain of my tiny space in the emergency room.

"Carlos?"

Dr. Redmond's head pops in. "Mary?"

"It's me." I smile. "Apparently there's something wrong with the sensor on my alarm system."

"Really wrong." He flips through my chart. "The levels the fire department reported are fatal."

"It was a close call." By the time the alarm sent the alert, I was already out cold. The firemen busted one window in each of my two bedrooms, unsure of exactly who was inside. They pulled me out just in time.

"I told the doctor who came by earlier I'm feeling fine now. I was a little woozy at first, but that passed and I haven't seen her in hours. Can you get me discharged?"

"I can get you transferred into my care." He pulls a stool over to the bed. "As soon as a room opens upstairs, we'll move you."

"I have to be at work in two hours." I'm not staying here. "Before that, I need to find someone to replace two broken windows."

"I'll call the contractor who's doing some work for me. He can take care of the windows." Carlos closes my chart. "As for work, you'll have to miss a day. Maybe more. You might feel fine now, but side effects can show up later."

The doctor I saw earlier mentioned hallucinations as a side effect. That could be what's been wrong with me this whole time. A carbon monoxide leak driving me insane. "How about I just come back if anything happens? You know how I feel about hospitals and why I'd rather leave the beds open for people who actually need them."

"You've spent a lot of unhappy time here." He frowns. "But that doesn't override the need for you to be here now."

"Does today's arrival of the new wardrobe you ordered for you girlfriend override it?"

While Mike was sick, Carlos and I became friends. He wasn't part of Mike's medical team but our paths often crossed in the cafeteria. He always took time out of his day to explain any confusing medical jargon in terms I could understand. When he started shopping at Scarlets, I made it my mission to repay him with extraordinary service. It isn't much, but he's such a snazzy dresser he requires a lot of attention. He lavishes gifts on his girlfriend, too. But never lets her outshine his flare. I haven't met her, but I'm sure she appreciates the less colorful wardrobe.

"The last time I let someone else box up her gifts, you said they weren't packaged right."

"They were messy," he agrees. "This time I'd like to bring you a new set of alligator-skin luggage. If I let you go to work today, could I drop those by later and have you pack the gifts in them?"

"I'd be happy to pack the suitcases for you." I slide off the table. "Though this feels partly like a ploy for you to also come check on me."

"It is." He stands. "But the timing is perfect. She and I are in need of a vacation. I'm ready to whisk her away."

"What will she love more? The surprise vacation or the surprise of a new wardrobe with enough clothing to last her for years?" I pick up the nightshirt I came here in.

"I'll let you know." He slides behind the curtain so I can change. "Let me admit you. Just for a day? You can pack the luggage tomorrow."

~18~

Dr. Redmond caved, not making me stay in the hospital. Before I got home from work, his contractor had the two broken windows replaced and even fixed the carbon monoxide leak. Which is great, because I can't hold my eyes open any longer. I need sleep. It's coming fast and hard. With every hope for dreams full of a green-eyed charmer.

A bang pries my lids open. "At least I know I'm not being poisoned again." I sit up, listening. A thud sounds from the crawl space, plunking against the floor like a jackrabbit. I jump off the bed, stomping to scare away the rat. I haven't seen them here since I bought the house, but I remember well the mess they left behind.

The rodent thumps again, rattling the floor beneath my feet. I stomp harder. "Go away!" I bang my heel down. "Get out of here!" A thud shakes the baseboard three feet over. "That's it." I grab my robe, pulling the flashlight off the dresser, and beat a path to the security pad. I turn the alarm off and head straight out the back door.

Darting around the corner of the house, I stop at the crawl space door. It's ajar. A shiver runs up my spine. I shouldn't be out here. "Please be a rat." I bend toward the wooden hatch, trembling fingers pulling the door open wide. "Not a big rat. A baby one."

Shining the light inside, the beam betrays my fear, quivering over the darkness and making it impossible to see anything. I lean in, toppling over the frame. The flashlight bounces away. My hand lands in moist earth, my head in a spider web. And something is touching me. Sticky and wet sliding up my arm. "Get away!" I jerk. It laughs. I fall backwards, kicking free of the door and sliding through the grass. Whatever is in there, it isn't a rat. "What are you?" I wipe slime from my arm. "Did you *lick* me?"

Nothing, and everything, moves in the dark underbelly. A knot creeps into my throat as a shadow drifts deep within, darkness on darkness. My fingers dig into the grass, ice building in my veins until the chill consumes my flesh. I lunge forward, slamming the door shut and threading the twist lock back into its slot. Crickets rise up in shuddering song. The hair on my neck electrifies. My flashlight bounces off the inside of the door, its light shining through the cracks, coaxing my panic into overdrive. *Run.*

Chills chase each other down my spine. I slam the back door behind me, the repulsive laugh replaying in my head. *Calm down.* I fumble with the lock. *Whatever it is, it's out there now.* Unless it has a friend. Because I left the door wide open.

Petrified, I force my rubbery legs forward, stepping into the archway between the kitchen and living room. "Hello? If someone is in here, I have to warn you I have a gun. Even if you're just a really big rat, I'll shoot." The house is silent. And my gun is in the bedroom.

Counting to three I push into a sprint, grabbing the derringer from the nightstand. "Now I have a gun. And I know how to shoot, so just say you're in here and I'll let you leave without hurting you."

The gun wobbles in my unsteady grip. I flip on the bedroom light and open the closet. It's empty. Lowering down, I check under the bed. Nothing but a few dust bunnies. I turn toward the door. "I'm going to come back out there now, and I intend on checking every nook and cranny. So if you're here, this is your last chance to leave without getting shot."

Counting to ten between long, steadying breaths, I slip into the hallway. Moving slowly, I search the rest of the house, flipping on lights along the way until the place is lit up like Christmas. I'm alone. But the hair on my neck still isn't convinced.

You're reacting to the carbon monoxide. I reset the alarm, willing the explanation to sink in. *Delayed hallucinations from long-term exposure. Tomorrow, I'll get my flashlight out of the crawl space.* My heart thuds. *After I call the exterminator.*

~19~

Attention on the backyard, making sure my hallucinations stayed out there and not inside with me, I found myself still at the back door when the sun came up. Exhausted. And without seeing a single leaf blow across the yard last night.

Heading to Scarlets, I stop for coffee. Like yesterday, today is going to be a caffeine-fueled day. Being the manager, I arrive thirty minutes before the rest of the staff and am accustomed to the empty employee lot behind the mall. Today, the hair on my neck stands on end, the same way it did all night. I scan the few cars around me. None of them look occupied.

Wrapping my fingers around the door handle, I ease it forward. A cold shiver commands me to run. I scramble out of the car, feet pounding over the pavement, not stopping until I burst through the employee entrance and put a steel slab between me and the outside world.

I check the peephole. Nothing is moving out there. The dew-covered vehicles have been here all night. Which means I've completely lost touch with reality. *Are people suffering from paranoid delusions supposed to know they're suffering?* I pull away from the door and plod toward my office. I officially can't ever go out with John again. Not when the only person I need to make a date with is a psychiatrist. And an exterminator.

It's been forty-eight hours since I saw John's face. Thirty-six since his one and only text. Points of simultaneous joy and anguish. But without him in the picture, I'm free to make the exterminator my first priority. No sense rushing to the psychiatrist when it benefits no one other than myself. Besides, if John hasn't forgotten about me already, he will soon enough. The divine man has options. And enough of my crazy showed the other night to remove me from his list.

43

Dialing the exterminator I used before, I give him an account of the plausible parts of my night, conveniently leaving out getting licked. If there *was* something under the house last night, in the light of day I'm pretty sure it didn't lick me. Or laugh.

A few hours later the gangly exterminator stands in my office, waiting for me to sign my name to his check. "I'm glad there's nothing in the crawl space now."

"Me, too." He scratches his chin. "But something's been in there. Something big."

"Bigger than rats?"

"Rats wouldn't pull down the ductwork like that. My guess is it's the handiwork of raccoons." He wiggles his fingers. "Their crafty little hands can't be kept out by a simple twist lock like what you've got on that door."

Those same fingers could pick up a flashlight. And whether or not they licked me, I don't care. I only care I didn't hallucinate the whole thing. "I'll stop at the market on my way home and get a padlock." I hand him the check, fifty extra dollars added since he put the ductwork back up while he was under the house. "Pest problem solved."

"Let's hope so." He gives me a wink and bumps into my assistant manager on his way out the door.

"Did he get the rats?" Pam fingers a stack of invoices, pretending she has a reason to when really she only wants to snoop.

"He declared my house to be rat free." I swat her away from my desk. "Now if I can only get our resident cat to stop being so curious."

~20~

My weekly supplies secured in two brown paper sacks, I hurry back out of the market, anxious to get home before nightfall. I don't like to drive after dark and I also want to secure the padlock before raccoons decide to invade my crawl space again.

Cradling the sacks, I stop short of my car. A stargazer lily stands out against the windshield. Tucked under the wiper. The way Mike used to leave them. "Excuse me." The voice behind me sends my bags bobbling. The store attendant grabs them, keeping the contents from spilling across the pavement. I meet his eyes. I know him. He's worked here for as long as I've been shopping at this store.

"Sorry. I'm a little jumpy lately." I reclaim the bags. "Thanks, I've got them now."

"Are you sure?" He smiles. "I can load them up for you. That's your car, right?"

If he knows my car, he could have left the flower. "Um, did you see who put the lily on my windshield?"

"No." He studies it. "Maybe if we sold flowers as pretty as that, I'd think to leave you one." A car horn blows behind us. My bags go flying again. He grabs them.

"I think I might need to give *you* flowers." I reclaim the sacks for the second time, moving out of the way of the passing car. A familiar laugh hits my ears. I stretch for the flower, tossing it down and kicking it under my tire. The last thing I need is Kevin revving Kim up about a secret admirer. "Wait until I tell your wife you've been out scaring little old widows."

"Only the ones blocking traffic." His lopsided grin makes me smile. "I'm in a hurry. I have a hot date with John tonight. Jealous?"

Yes. "You can have him. And don't bother giving me dibs on any of your other friends. I'm *at* the market, not on it."

~21~

While Kevin enjoys time with John, I enjoy another lonely dinner. Sitting in the same chair at my dining table where I was the night the green-eyed stranger charmed his way into my heart. I can't let go of the hope he might be in my life one day. Or the fear I might be the one who put the lily on my windshield today. It could be a symptom of grief. My mind having me recreate things Mike used to do. Acting them out unconsciously, only to be shocked by them later. It could also just be a coincidence. Someone running around doing random acts of kindness. And I repaid them by throwing the flower on the ground.

My phone rings. Noise in my tiny house automatically makes me jump but this sound is welcome. I place my plate in the sink and pick up the source of my excitement. I can't help wanting it to be John. "Hello?"

Silence meets my eagerness. I glance at the number. It's private. "Hello?" No response. I hang up, slipping the phone into my pocket. *It's better if John doesn't call anyway.*

Tempering my disappointment, I yank the phone back out again when it rings. The number is still marked as private. "Hello?" No answer. "If I'm not who you want to talk to, please stop dialing my number." I hang up, yawning while flipping on all the lights in the house-my new preemptive routine. Better to light the place up now so I'm not forced to later.

The last switch is in my bedroom. My fingers flip it up in time for the phone to ring. Try as I might, I can't stop my heart from wanting it to be John. It isn't. Unless his number is blocked. "Hello?" No response. "Is anyone there?" Only creepy silence. I hang up, take three steps, and it rings again. I jam my finger against the screen, "If you aren't going to speak or at least breathe like a normal prank caller, then please stop calling." I hang up. One step deeper into the room it rings again. I swipe to ignore the call.

Grabbing my nightgown, the small rectangle rings again. I undress and step into my gown, hoping it will stop but the blaring ring is unrelenting. *They'll lose interest soon enough.* I pull the decorative pillows off my bed. *Prank calling kids always do.* Except when they don't. One call after another keeps coming. I turn the phone off and get into bed, snuggling down into the soft sheets with my eyelids already sinking. A car horn blows. The single beep turns into a long, drawn-out blare. It stops. Then restarts seconds later. And sounds like it's directly in front of my house. I tighten myself in the sheets. No one I know would sit outside and blast their horn like this. But if it *is* someone for me, the neighbors are going to kill me.

Shaking, I drag my tired body to the living room window. The driveway is empty. So is the street out front. The entire neighborhood is quiet. "Figures." I turn back toward the bed that's calling my name. The blare of a horn stabs my ears. I whirl around, fast enough to catch a glimpse of the car zooming by, headlights off, blowing its horn only while in front of my house. It continues down the street silently, taillights giving away where the shape turns before racing by again, horn blasting. Then it turns around and does the same thing, continuing the crazed routine over and over. I clutch my chest. *This isn't happening. This **isn't** happening.*

The streetlight has been out for months, leaving it too dark outside to see what kind of car it is, let alone who's driving. *If* anyone is driving. My eyes dart from house to house. No lights are on except mine. *No one hears this but me.* The car speeds by again. I close my eyes. If I'm imagining this, it isn't because of Mike. He never did anything remotely close.

The only way to know for sure if I'm hallucinating is to go out there. To stop the car. Touch it. Look into the face of an actual person. But I'm too afraid to open the door. *I don't want it to be real.* Tears slide down my face. *But I don't want to be crazy either.*

The blaze of darkness speeds past. I scream, willing my words to bounce off the hood and into the heart of my nightmare. "Stop! Please! Just stop and let me have peace!" Tears fall hard and fast. "For one night, give me peace!"

~22~

The only thing worse than being too afraid to go outside to stop a ghost car is turning my phone back on to call someone, only to have it ringing before I have a chance to dial. Last night, whenever the car disappeared, the phone rang. When the car was outside blowing like a maniac, the phone was quiet. "Apparently my mind can only have one hallucination at a time."

"What was that?" Pam asks.

"Nothing." I yawn, wishing I had a sofa in my office. I could sleep through lunch. "Here's the sales list for the day. We need to move the gray suits that came in yesterday. Let's put them up front."

"You've got it, boss." She takes the list, laughing when I jump out of my seat over the desk phone ringing.

The blinking light stops. Someone else picked up the line. But the jolt reminds me I need to turn my cellphone back on. I finally took the battery out for good, opting not to call anyone because saying out loud that I was scared because someone gave me a flower and blew their horn sounds ridiculous. Especially the part where I admit it could all just be me playing tricks on myself.

Waiting for Pam to leave, I turn the phone on. It beeps right away. Shaking fingers punch in the voicemail code. "Hello, Mary. It's John. Sorry to call so late, but I'm hoping you'll go to lunch with me tomorrow? I'll be in town near your store, so give me a call or drop me a text to let me know either way. I'll be waiting to hear from you. Goodnight, sweetheart." Pressing the phone against my ear, I listen to the message again, his smooth voice a lozenge for my nerves.

"What's that big grin about?" Pam pops her head back through the door.

"Nothing." I would tell her about him, but she teases me enough. Calling me to the men's sales floor every time any unwed man happens to walk in. Then there's the fact I can't actually date John. Last night proved that.

She eyes me. "You know you're not a good liar, right?"

"Yep." I nod. "Which is why our energy is better spent focusing on the work we have to do."

"Okay." She sighs. "I'll get to work setting up your runway. I mean, the men's sales floor." I frown. She shrugs. "Not my fault you're so stunning men come in hoping to catch a glimpse. But I have standards. I only call you for the ones not wearing a wedding ring."

"You shouldn't call me for any of them. Not when I can't reciprocate anyone's advances."

"But you can." She smiles. "We just have to find the right one. Or did you already? That grin sure looked promising."

The way I'm feeling about John after only one date is enough to promise my heart many things. But talking about him will only prolong the pain of telling him I can't ever see him again. News he deserves to hear face-to-face. "'Bye, Pam."

She reluctantly leaves and I text John: *I can meet you around noon if you're still free for lunch.* I have to look into his eyes so he knows he isn't the problem. I am.

I'm free! How about Sweet Lou's? Have you been there? he texts straight back.

Good choice. They have excellent food.

I'll see you at twelve sharp then. Can't wait! Where should I pick you up?

I'll meet you there. I swallow. *And I'm buying this time.*

~23~

Pulling into the parking lot of Sweet Lou's, a small family-owned Italian restaurant, John's handsome face waits for me at the entrance. Pain traces through my chest. I underestimated how hard telling him goodbye is going to be.

I park in the shadow of his beautiful truck and take a deep breath. Like magic he's beside the car, trying to open my locked door. I hit the latch and he swings it wide, hand enveloping mine and helping me out. "Hi." His lips stroke my cheek, his free hand passing me a bouquet of sunburst roses before moving around me, his strong arms pulling me deep into a hug. I retreat, pressing against the car and meeting his eyes. He grins. "Sorry. I've just really missed you. Thanks for meeting me on short notice."

"Thank you for asking." I shift away from the cool metal. "And for the flowers. They're beautiful."

"Compared to you, they're not even close." The intensity of his gaze throws me off balance. So does the way he makes jeans and a t-shirt look like he's wrapped in a million-dollar suit. I drink him in. One final gulp before cutting myself off.

"You're the one dulling the roses."

"I dressed up for you." He winks. "These jeans are stain-free." I laugh. A car two spaces over blows its horn. My laughter turns into a bloodcurdling scream, fingernails burrowing into his forearm. He steadies me, grip tight. I can't answer the questions swimming through his eyes.

"Sorry." I remove my nails and rub his arm. "Loud noises make me a little jumpy."

"A byproduct of living alone." He watches the car drive off, then slides his hand to the small of my back, turning us toward the restaurant. "I don't fly into a panic when I hear them, but as a fellow loner I get it. When I'm not sawing, hammering, or chucking wood across the building—"

"Basically, you don't get it at all." I smile at his attempt to act like my hysteria is no big deal.

"I do." He grins. "In theory."

Pulling out my chair, he sits beside me without ever letting go of my hand. He also does the one thing I don't want him to do. Pay attention. "It was loud Saturday night, especially with the live band. I never saw you jump then."

"I must have hidden it well." I clear my throat, changing the topic. "I have yet to open a door or pull out a chair in your presence. Does this gentlemanly behavior continue? Or are you just really good at first impressions?"

"I'm looking forward to *showing* you the answer to that question." His emeralds extend an invitation I want to accept. "I'm sorry." His hand slides to my burning face. "Clearly I'm an idiot who can't stop being too forward with you. I swear I'm not trying to embarrass you, though."

"Really? Because it feels like you know exactly what you're doing."

"I don't." He chuckles that beautiful sound of his. "Not with you. I can't even get myself to keep distance between us."

"You want distance?" This comes out as an accusation instead of the relief it should be.

He tucks against my side. "Not an inch. Which is why I'll have to beg for forgiveness and plead for all the patience you have because I'm trying to do this right, but restraining myself around you is proving to be impossible."

My gaze rests on our entwined hands, one truth beating through my soul. "You don't have to beg or apologize for anything. I'm nothing but happy sitting here with you." This is everything I want. Everything I need. Just a little more time with him.

~24~

I hate myself for not daring to utter the words I know I have to say. I even toasted with John to us having more time together. An oath I'll have to break now that he's walking me to my car. Fantasy world is over. I owe him a huge apology for the way I've behaved the past forty-five minutes.

"John?"

"Right here." His hand tightens on mine, eyes forward instead of on me. "I've never had anyone do that to me before, Mary. I can't believe you went behind my back."

This is why he's quiet. "You're miffed I paid for lunch?"

"Yeah." He turns to me. "I texted you back and told you no. *And* I told you the other night I don't let my dates pay."

"And I told you twenty minutes ago that I don't care." I meet his glare head-on. "I called you right. Your male ego—"

"This isn't about ego." His hand juts up. "It's about me *inviting* you. Which by definition means I'm paying."

"So if I invite you to lunch, I can pay?"

His smile builds slowly. Giving him away. His ego wouldn't be okay with the woman paying no matter what. "It's nice to see a real, true gentleman in the flesh. But I do have a job. And a responsibility to myself."

"I heard." His emeralds roll back in his head. "Kevin told me all about your pride issue."

"If being a responsible adult is prideful, then I'm guilty as charged." I withdraw my hand. "What else did Kevin tell you?"

"That you have a heart of gold." His soft voice coaxes my hand back to his. "And that you'll do anything for anyone. Which is why you're

52

going to unlock your door now. So I can open it for you. I don't want you to think my good manners are faltering just because you tricked me."

He swings the door open but pulls me against him. "Instinct takes over when my hands are on you, and I'm not going to apologize for it." His lips press into my cheek. "In case this is out of line, let me tell you how it took all the strength I have not to land on your lips just now. Hopefully you can be as proud of me for that as I am."

"I appreciate your struggle." My arms want to hold him. "And appreciate you understanding mine."

His arms read my mind, wrapping tightly around me. "Last time I didn't stop myself from tasting your lips I upset you in a way I never want to upset you again. So, despite having broken every other rule I set for myself today, that's one I'm not breaking. Today." Light dances across his face. "We'll wait until you're ready for more than just a hug."

Pulling away before my mouth tells him I'm ready now, I swallow. "Despite breaking them, it's the fact that you're sensitive enough to make rules that counts. And I really wish things were different." I bite back tears. "But..."

"I can be patient." His hand cups my face. "As patient as you need. If taking you out again Friday night is patient enough. Which is what I'm going to ask when I call you later. Do you think you can say yes? I promise to do nothing more than what I've done today."

The difference between my head and my heart is on syllable. One bitter syllable that my mouth refuses to say. "I doubt anyone you use that grin on has ever said no to you. Like them, I'll be waiting by the phone." And hating myself for it. "I need to go, though. I can't be late getting back to work."

He keeps a hand on me while I slide behind the wheel. "Sweetheart, when I call, I'll be grinning the whole time. Keep that in mind."

"If you know what's good for you, you'll trust me when I say you need to stop grinning."

He kneels by my door. "If you know what's good for you, you'll trust me when I say pride isn't a flaw I'm scared of."

~25~

I doubt John is scared of anything. And the promise of his grin was enough to get me through the rest of the work day without another drop of caffeine. His face has been front and center in my thoughts. Until now.

Sorting the day's mail, a small white envelope is tucked among the rest. Hand-delivered to my mailbox. The only marking is my name printed neatly across the front in block letters. It's bumpy, like confetti is inside. I slide the letter opener under the flap and shake the contents onto the counter. Out falls a card. Surrounded by dead lily petals. *Something so beautiful shouldn't have to die.* The phone rings, the noise rising out of my purse to shake the air around me.

"It's John." I whisper, convincing my hand to ignore the icy chill and retrieve the phone from my bag. Sliding inside, my fingers move over the smooth surface of the phone. I lift it slowly. The display comes into view. Private number. Exactly like last night. I turn the phone over, take out the battery and quiet my world. Until the sun sets, and the first car horn blows.

~

Yesterday, I blew off lunch with Kim for John. Now, I wish I'd blown him off instead. The result of spending yet another night curled on my bed, praying the locked door and gun by my side are protection enough. Even though I know they can't save me from myself. Just like I know this rain-check lunch isn't long enough to get Kim to agree it's selfish of me to keep seeing John. Not when I can't confide in her about the true state of my mind.

"Yes, I like him. But that's irrelevant." I glance at LaTerra's boarded-up window. "A lot of things are complicating the situation and I don't

54

want him wasting time on me when he can be out there with someone who will add real value to his life."

"I'm adding value to that man's life," she winks at our heroic server, "so he'll save *me* next time."

"Kim! I'm serious."

"So am I." She's annoyed. "You need to stop downplaying what a catch you are. No one has ever seen spending a minute with you as a waste."

"Then they haven't spent the right minutes with me."

Her glare would be scary if she wasn't so tiny. "John isn't going to be single forever. And you clearly have feelings for him, so stop refusing to see him."

"It isn't fair to date him when I know it can't go anywhere."

"What's unfair is you not dating him in spite of the feelings you have for him." She softens. "You owe it to him, and to yourself, to see where this might lead."

"Where it might lead is what I'm afraid of."

"Why?" She grins. "Word on the street is you have him all revved up and ready to bust."

"The street corner of Kim and Kevin isn't public opinion."

"The news is straight from the John Beller Highway!" Her eyes glitter. "Kevin came home exhausted the other night because John grilled him about you for three hours straight."

"What did Kevin tell him?"

"I have no idea." She shrugs. "He's been too tired to even talk about John."

John had lunch with me afterward, so it couldn't have been that bad. Outside of the allegation that somehow I'm prideful. "I don't know why John has any interest in me. I'm an idiot most of the time I'm with him. I sit there and blush, and cry, then blush again."

"Maybe that vulnerability is why he likes you." She breaks off part of her taco bowl. "Kevin's never seen John give a single woman the time of day, and there are throngs of them coming after his cute butt. Now he's walking around with his tongue hanging out. He's crazy about you. Just like I knew he'd be."

I'm crazy about him, too. Emphasis on the crazy. "Every time he touches me, or looks at me for that matter, my temperature rises a hundred degrees. I keep wondering if I'm imagining him."

"He's real, honey." She giggles. "I say go for it!"

"What if I hurt him?"

"The only thing he's in danger of is getting cavities, because you are way too sweet for your own good."

"Dating him when I know for sure it isn't going to work out isn't sweet."

"Why do you think it won't?" She crunches her tortilla. "How do you feel when you're with him?"

"Happy." Tears sting my lids. "When I'm with him, the only thing I feel is happy."

"Then don't rob yourself of that happiness." Her hand reaches across the table. "Let go of the complications you think are there and just go with the flow. Because the flow might take you to a terrific place. One that releases you from whatever is keeping you up at night. Yeah, that's right. I see the bags and dark circles. You look terrible. So sleep. And be happy you get to date Mt. Vesuvius!"

~26~

Still contemplating how to consider John's needs over my own in a world where I date him instead of let him go, I'm not thrilled my office is filled with people. "Did something happen while I was at lunch?"

Moving aside, my staff exposes the vase of flowers sitting on my desk. "They were just delivered." Pam speaks for the group. "We're dying to know who they're from."

"They're from a green-eyed charmer." My smile threatens to crack my face. Everyone in the store finding out about John now, even if he isn't in my life for long, is a small price to pay for the comfort his words will hold.

I open the card. *Appreciate there being no lilies this time, and maybe you'll get some sleep.* The words rip air from my lungs, the unsigned card slipping from my fingertips. I seize the vase from the desk and slam it into the trash. Petals fly up in a poof, scattering across the floor. "Whoa!" Pam grabs me. "I know you haven't gotten flowers in a while, but that's not where they go. What's going on with you this week?"

"Nothing." I clutch my chest.

"It doesn't look like nothing." She reaches for a chair. "Here, sit down."

"I don't want to sit down!" I snatch the card off the floor before anyone picks it up. "All of you need to get back to work. Now!"

They file out, murmuring among themselves. My trembling fingers rip the card to shreds, tossing it into the trash. I get on my knees, meticulously picking every last flower petal off the floor. I want no trace of this evil remaining. Not even the trash can.

I *can't* be doing this to myself. I push the back door open, stomping toward the dumpster. *I'm not crazy! I didn't send myself flowers!* I throw

57

the whole lot in, trash can and all. "Other people saw the flowers. I didn't make it up!" I yell at the dumpster. It answers with the sound of settling trash. I turn on my heel, padding back toward the building. Crazy or not, I have to apologize to everyone. Starting with Pam.

I reenter the building and she's already heading my way. I meet her in the hall just beyond my office. "I feel horrible for snapping at you. I'm so sorry."

"You were upset." She waves off the apology. "Want to talk about it? In all the years I've worked with you, I've never heard you raise your voice. Not even in the hardest of times."

I wish I could have kept it that way. "Right now, I'm not ready to talk about what's going on. All I can say is those flowers were not sent in kindness. That's why they upset me."

"I see. Well, there's a man here asking for you. And he has flowers, too." She slides her hips left, giving me a view of the waiting visitor. "Do you want me to tell him you're busy?"

All I want her to do is move. "No, he's fine."

"Yes," she whistles, "he is F.I.N.E."

Moving around her, arms desperate to throw themselves around John, I wish to be as bold as him. "You're a nice surprise." I stop short, arms remaining steadfastly at my side. "In here looking for another pair of unstained jeans?"

"I just happened to be in the neighborhood." He hands me a flower bouquet larger than the one he gave me yesterday. "Thought I'd stop by."

"Lucky me." I draw in the scent of the roses. "You're in town, *and* just happen to have flowers in hand."

"Busted." His chuckle warms the ice-cold fear. "I admit to planning this chance encounter. Friday is too far away to be the next time I see you. And I can't see you tomorrow unless I ask today. So Mary, may I please take you to dinner tomorrow night?"

Go with the flow. "I'd love to have dinner with you."

"Wow, more flowers. You're popular today." A sales clerk passes by, ruining the moment. John's face falls. I curl my fingers over his, the contact sending heat waves quaking up from my toes. "The other flowers weren't actually for me. These are, and they're beautiful. Thank you for thinking of me."

"All I do is think of you." He folds our palms together. "Which is why I'm here. I had to see you. Now, tell me the truth about who's sending you flowers." His free hand cups my face. "All I need is their name. I'll take care of the rest."

~27~

Standing with John's fingers grazing over my cheek, I'm heaven-bound. Outside of not being sure if he's dropping the flower issue I'm jumping right over. *And* the fact that we're being watched by the same employees I snapped at earlier. He's aware of them. He meets their stares. "I can shop for the few minutes I'll be here."

"You loitering isn't their problem." I take his hand from my face. His eyes float back to mine. "Even if it was, anytime you stop in I'll spare the few minutes you ask for."

"I don't want just a few minutes." His body moves close. "I want you to take the rest of the day off. Can you?"

I force my lips to say no. "It's been a rough day. I need to get back to work. But I *am* glad you came. Really glad."

"I had no choice but to come here." He turns us toward the front entrance, our pace slow. "I called you last night, but you weren't waiting by the phone like you promised."

"Sorry." I completely forgot about the torture device formerly known as my phone. "I turn my cell off sometimes and forget to turn it back on."

"It's okay." A sly smile turns up the corners of his mouth. "I did call last night, but decided long before that to stop by today. It was a slim chance, but one I'd rather take than never know if today could have been spent with you."

"You'll have to settle for tomorrow night. I get off work at six. What time do you want to meet?"

Stopping at the front entrance leading into the mall interior, his eyes are on mine. "It's a proper date, so I'll pick you up. Will six thirty be too soon? I don't want to rush you; I know women like to take their time.

But I'd like to be there as soon as possible." His fingers trace the spot along my jaw that seems to fascinate him. "I'm happy to wait outside your door for as long as you need. I just want to be where you are."

I wish he'd never leave my side. Never let go of my hand. "I'll be ready at six thirty. And to avoid the tiff we had at lunch, we'll go ahead and include the rule that this half of our proper date will pay for her own meal."

"Not on your life." His lips brush my cheek. Lingering. If it wasn't for the warmth racing through my core, I would put up more of a fight. As it is, my head is cloudy. "Expect me to be in here a lot more," he whispers, lips pressed against my ear. "And anytime you get a day off, or even a minute, call me. I want to spend it with you."

"Careful, I might take you up on that offer." His breath snakes over me, weakening my knees.

"Careful." He holds me up, lips moving back to rest on my cheek. "I might buy this whole store just to make sure you do."

"That's a hefty price to pay for a date."

His shoulders straighten, fingertips running the length of my face. "For the right date, I'll pay any price. And you're the right date. So turn your phone on and keep it on. You never know when I might call."

I'll at least turn it on periodically to see if he's called. "If I don't answer, leave me a message and I'll call you back."

"That'll do." He sighs. "For now."

"You're not good with not having your own way, are you?"

"I've never had the misfortune." He plants one last kiss on my cheek and strolls down the mall corridor toward the main exit. My eyes, Pam's, and everyone else's are glued to him.

"So *he's* why you've been grinning? Mmm-hmmm. I do *not* blame you." Pam coos over my shoulder as a group of women do some cooing of their own, trying their best to get his attention. He doesn't miss a beat. Not even a single flinch. His feet walk their path as if no one else exists in the world.

"You mean that poor, handsomely afflicted man who can't fathom anyone saying no to him? Yeah. He's the one making my head spin." And I'm already in the middle of a cyclone.

~28~

Love never dies. Unless you do. The end red when astray you're led, reads the note plastered on my windshield. "Hi, Mary!" Andy calls. He's by the dumpster where he takes breaks from his mall security job.

Jerking the lame attempt at poetry off my car, I head his way. He puts his cigarette out. "I know you don't like the smell of these things."

"No, I don't." I eye the dumpster, wondering if he saw me throw the flowers inside earlier. "Um, have you seen anyone hanging around my car today?"

"No, I've only been out here a few minutes. Why? Is something wrong?"

"I've just had some weird things left on it." I crumple the note. "Nothing bad. Just…*poems.*"

His eyebrow rises. "From a stalker?"

Is it possible to stalk yourself? "Probably from no one. Just let me know if you happen to see anyone. Okay?"

"Okay." He nods. "He's got black hair."

"Who? You've seen someone?"

"Nah." He laughs. "My uncle told me once…I told you he was a police officer, right? He's helping me get a spot in the academy."

"So you can follow in his footsteps." I give him a smile. "I remember. But you were saying you saw someone with black hair at my car?"

"I didn't see anybody, but my uncle says all the crazy ones have black hair."

"I have black hair."

"Yeah, but you're not crazy." He beams. "You're real pretty, though. My uncle says so, too. When he comes to see me, I always walk him down by your store. He thinks it's real nice."

I think talking to Andy is a waste of time. Unless his uncle is right. "Thanks, Andy. Tell your uncle I might dye my hair. You know, just in case."

The drive home feels like a death march. Vigilance doesn't quell the knot in my stomach. I check the mirrors and look at every car. No one is following me. No one is in my driveway. And no one left notes in the mailbox today.

Inside the house, every door and window is locked. I check all of them twice, then barricade myself in the bedroom. Night is coming. I feel sick. I'd love to talk to John. But the battery is staying out of my phone. I'll call him tomorrow if I miss his call tonight. *If* I make it through the night.

"Who's there?" I rub sleep away, adjusting to the dark room. I don't remember falling asleep. I do remember locking the door. The one that's wide open. My hand flies to the derringer. "Stay away! I have a gun!" The shaking starts in my fingers, racing like wildfire until the rest of my body convulses. My alarm isn't going off. If someone broke in, it should be blaring. And I know I set it. Just like I know I locked that door.

A shadow moves across the bedroom floor. I grip the tiny handle of the gun with both hands. "I don't want to shoot. Just leave!" Darkness closes in. The gun wobbles. "Don't make me do this." A flash of light. Blinding me. I roll left, fighting the sheets. Kicking until they untangle and throw me to the floor. The gun comes loose, bouncing off the wall. I duck, hand fishing for the unfired gun as it spins underneath the bed. Light flashes in the hall. The cold metal of the derringer graces my fingertips. I pull it to me, flat on my stomach as movement slides by the door. The shadow races toward the living room, quiet as butterfly wings.

Pressing my shoulder to the wall, I pull my knees under me, crawling on all fours to the door. I should just lock it. Call the police. But locking myself up won't help. They've already gotten in once. And they could reach me before I get the battery back in the phone.

I poke my head around the jamb. A shadow floats across the living room floor. Disembodied. My knees tremble. "All I want is for you to leave. Just go, and leave me alone."

Silence builds. I ease up the wall, letting it hold my weight. Two deep breaths fill my lungs. Light flashes from the kitchen. I slink toward it. It flashes again. From outside the back door.

Moving fast, I press against the window's cool glass, checking the knob. It's locked. A shadow runs across the yard. Then another. The wind picks up. Lightning flashes. Another shadow. A *cloud* shadow. "It's a storm." My legs give out, tears hitting the floor harder than my body. "Mary! Stop doing this to yourself. It's only a storm!"

~29~

I'm not only deliriously delusional, I'm sleepwalking. It's the only explanation for how the locked bedroom door opened, the house lights were all turned out, and the alarm was disarmed. The sleepwalking also means my tired body got no rest. Again.

Checking the mirror, my eyes scream how long it's been since they've seen the back of my lids. I pray the magic of makeup is kind to me. Tonight I'm pulling out the whole bag of tricks. John liked my look the night we met, when I wasn't trying to impress him. This time, I'm trying. I owe him that much. Especially after not answering his call last night. Or his text. Both of which I responded to this morning, only to have him call *and* text again…to test my response time. That's when I decided to wear my magenta wrap dress. It's old, but hands down the one I get the most compliments on.

Fifteen minutes isn't a lot of time to get dolled up for a date. I promised to be ready at six thirty, though. And he isn't giving me a second longer. The clock just struck and he's simultaneously knocking on the door and calling me. "Very funny." I open the door, disarming the alarm.

"I had something witty to say." He slides the phone into the pocket of his blue button-front shirt. "Now I can't remember anything. You are absolutely stunning."

I like the way his eyes admire me. And the way he looks in a good pair of jeans. "You're stunning yourself. And those flowers are gorgeous."

"I thought so." He extends the oversized bouquet, a grin flirting on the edge of his lips. "Before I saw you. Now I know they aren't even close to expressing how much I want to take you out."

"They express your feelings pretty well." And must have cost a fortune. "Come on in while I put them in water."

Closing the door behind him he follows me toward the kitchen, eyes scanning every inch of my house the way they did that first night. This time he veers left, taking a few steps down the hall. "Are you looking for something?"

"Flowers." He nods. "I don't see any outside of the ones I gave you this week. Unless there are some in your bedroom?"

"You're serious?"

"Deadly." His eyes meet mine. "If another man is making a play for you, I want to know."

Detaching from his gaze, I take a water pitcher out of the cabinet since I don't have a vase large enough to store even the small bouquet he gave me, let alone this one. "Another man making a play for me would be my business. I'm the judge and jury on who I do, or don't, go out with." Except when Kim guilts me into dating perfect strangers, and those perfect strangers tempt me into doing what I know I shouldn't.

"The choice on who you date *is* yours." He circles behind me, hands moving around my waist to help guide the bouquet into place. "But," his lips fall to my ear, "I still feel exactly the way I did the night of our first date. And you seem to like me, too. So letting another man slip in before we've had a chance to explore what's between us simply isn't going to happen." His breath moves over my neck. "I'll be confronting any man who approaches you until we know our path. Is that going to get me in trouble with you?"

I don't think anything will get him in trouble with me. Not even his arms sliding around me when I'd normally mace a man for doing this. "When you cover your aggression with a sweet justification, I can't be angry. So, congratulations. You and Kim officially have something in common. Manipulation."

~30~

John backs away from me, leaving a void against my skin. "That's strike one for me tonight. I'll take it. Only because I'm planning to hit more than a few home runs before this is over."

"Is that so?"

"Definitely." His hand comes back to comfort my void, cradling my shoulder this time. "I'm also planning for you to like it."

This heat says I will. "If I don't, you'll have a sweet justification at the ready?"

"Probably." He smiles. "But I promise I won't need any more tonight. Unless you don't want to ride in my truck? I was going to bring my car but the draw of seeing you in my truck is too strong. Strike two?"

"If I had given you any strikes," I slide my hand onto his arm, "your truck would erase them."

He covers my fingers with his. "Then let's get out of here, sweetheart. I've got more than my truck waiting for you."

I set the alarm and we walk arm in arm to his behemoth. Anxiety builds. I shouldn't be doing this. I shouldn't be *wanting* to do this. "Don't feel like you need to bring me flowers every time you see me."

"I was hoping tonight would end with me getting the promise of seeing you more." He opens the truck door with a broad smile. "Those words sure sound like I can go ahead and plan on it."

I let him run his hands around my waist. He hoists me up to the seat. "Instead of exploiting my words, why don't you tell me where we're going?"

"Someplace I can earn the right to hear you say yes to our next date." He steps on the running board, pressing his lips to my hand. I want to tell him not to. That we should just stay here because I can't see him anymore. But the words won't form. He sees the turmoil. "Sweetheart, whatever you're worried about, don't be. I'll take care of everything."

~31~

Marsalas is an upscale gourmet restaurant so exclusive I've never even driven by it. Now, I'm sitting inside the velvety palace in a warmly lit private dining room hung with intricate tapestries of cream and gold. Next to a king. Whoever John Beller is, it's clear he's the guest of honor here tonight. And clear I've completely fallen for him. I can't pull myself out of his orbit. I want to feel his hands. The heat of his body. The warmth of his smile. He calms the storm, the space next to him an island of peace in an ocean of chaos.

Our chairs are side by side, his unyielding fingers stroking lightly over mine, both of us managing to eat without ever losing body contact. "This place is amazing. And formal. I feel like I need to address you as *Mr. Beller.*"

"You deserve only the best, sweetheart." He gives my hand a squeeze. "But I prefer to hear *John* roll off your lips."

I prefer to hear *sweetheart* roll off his. "John, burgers and fries sitting on the tailgate of your truck would have been good enough. I don't need anything fancy."

"I love burgers, fries, my truck, and your company." He grins. "So I'd love to have burgers and fries on the tailgate anytime you want. I brought you here to show how thankful I am to get a second chance. Our first date was good, but I wasn't prepared, and there were too many hiccups. I plan to make that up to you tonight."

"I'm the one who needs to make it up to you." The hiccups were my fault. "You were perfect. And though I've thought more than once that I dreamed you up, you kept showing up all week still being just as perfect."

"I'm mirroring you then." He sweeps my chin to his. "Because a more perfect creature was never created than the one I'm looking at right now."

I brace for his lips. He doesn't come closer. Not physically. It's the intensity of his surety that engulfs me. "Hold on tight, sweetheart. I'm going to make this long ride a fast one."

"I'll try to keep up."

Maybe tomorrow I'll be strong enough to snuff out the attraction. Tonight, I'm letting him have what we both want. Whatever may come, I want this memory. "Are you ready to go?" He paid for our dinner before we arrived. His way of one-upping me.

"I'll have them get the truck." His smile is intoxicating.

"I'll leave the tip."

He confiscates my bag and waves over a server. "Trust me when I say they've been well compensated for the food and for the service."

"I find that hard to believe. The service has been akin to worship."

"I'm sorry you noticed."

"Kind of hard not to." I smile at the man obediently awaiting orders. "Can you tell me where the ladies' room is?" Sequestered in our little chamber, I haven't seen much of the place.

"Yes, ma'am." He pulls out my chair. "Right this way."

John stands when I do. Every time. "I'd like to tell you to take your time, but I'd rather you hurry back."

"Of course you would." His honesty is cute. "If there isn't a line, I'll be quick."

"She isn't to wait," he orders.

"John! You can't say that!"

"We have private facilities for you, ma'am." The server motions for me to go with him. "Right this way, please."

"See?" John grins. "I can say whatever I like. So hurry back, there are quite a few things I want to tell you."

~32~

Using private facilities just beyond the common ladies' restroom, let through the locked door as if I'm more important than anyone else here, is awkward. Checking the mirror to make sure there's no food stuck in my teeth like I'm a schoolgirl ready to be kissed for the first time is even more awkward. I scurry back out into the hall like a normal person. A kissable normal person. If John unleashes his lips tonight, I'm not stopping him. And I'm absolutely *not* crying.

Call it women's intuition or just the ability to read body language, but the tall brunette tromping down the middle of the hall is on an intentional collision course with me. The closer she gets, the angrier she looks. "Watch where you're going." she snaps, but I'm already stepping to the side. "Excuse you." She spins toward me.

"Excuse both of us." I toss up my hand, not breaking stride.

She follows me, swerving in front, towering over me in her six-inch stilettos. "Are you the woman who was with John Beller tonight?"

"I'm the woman who *is* with John Beller tonight. And he's waiting. So, excuse me." I step around her, continuing on my path. She isn't following this time. I'm curious as to who she is and why her demeanor is so hostile, but I'm more curious about what kissing John is going to be like. This is our last night together. I want it to mean something. I want to leave him with a better memory than our last date offered.

"No crying," I whisper, catching my first glimpse of him at our table, standing when he spots me. I smile. "That didn't take too long, did it?"

"Depends on your perspective." He reclaims his grip on my hand, leading us toward the valet. "I'm happy to wait for you any time, any place. But not having to makes me a lot happier."

"At least you're honest."

He chuckles as the valet trots off to get his truck. "I'm honest because the truth always comes out in the end. And—"

"It does! And I've *truly* missed you." The brunette from the hallway latches on to his arm, her lips heading for his. I almost slap her. But his head jerks, making her lips fall short of any mark on his flesh. His arm yanks from her grip, hand tightening on mine as his body moves closer to me. For an instant, she lets her eyes show me the warning her pursed lips want to give. Then they twinkle, bringing their focus back to him. "It's so good to see you. You look as wonderful as ever. Better even. We have that in common, you and I. Don't I look fabulous?"

Facing me, he blocks her out of our space. "Susan and I have nothing in common."

"Who's your little friend, John?" She glares over his shoulder. "Don't be rude. Introduce us."

"Hi." I sidestep the tension flying off him. "I'm Mary. And I've gathered already that you're Susan. It's fitting we at least know each other's names after nearly colliding in the hallway earlier."

"After what?" A growl snaps from his throat.

"After she stumbled across the hallway earlier." Susan heaps attention back on him now that he's squared up to her. "I hope she isn't a drunk. I know how you hate that sort of thing." Her fingers slide over his shoulder. "Better yet, I know what you like. I know *every* way you like me. And it's been far too long since we were together last. Let's change that."

"Unless I'm reading my date wrong," I move into the path of her gaze. She removes her trailing fingers from him. "He's interested in me tonight. Drunk or not."

She steps away, blowing him a kiss, words dripping with invitation. "John, honey, I'll be in touch. So finish up with your plaything and then come play with me. The way you used to."

"Stay away from me!" His voice booms, silencing the restaurant.

"Better?" She turns, winking at him over her shoulder. "You always did like the view from this angle." She walks out the door, timing her parting words perfectly. The valet opens a suicide door and she zips away in a flashy car. I turn to John. His green eyes are menacing.

I've never been in a fight in my life, but the way his chest heaves makes me wish I'd pulled Susan's hair out. It's probably fake anyway. Like her chest. "Are you okay?" I cover the spot on his arm where she grabbed him.

"Are *you* okay?" He shifts. "What happened in the hall? What did she say to you?"

"Nothing happened outside of us passing a little too closely." I force a reassuring smile. "She didn't touch me. And I didn't touch her." I only have an uncharacteristic desire to punch her.

"But she talked to you?"

"She spoke," I shrug. "But didn't really say anything. I'm guessing there's a lot of history between you two?"

"Too much history." He releases a deep breath. "I..."

"No need to elaborate." I run my hand from his arm to his back. "We all have a past. And I'm not intimidated by her, which is clearly what she was trying to do."

"Which is what I shouldn't have stood to let her do." His hands cup my face. "I'm sorry. I was just so shocked to see her—"

"It's okay." I smile. "There hasn't been any harm done. So let's get you calmed down, because there's still a little bit of time left in our date."

Pressing his forehead to mine he exhales, his emeralds slowly returning to their natural state. "I don't want to waste a single second with you."

~33~

It's selfish to want John's lips when he's upset, but they're all I'm thinking of. Susan is a mystery I don't deserve an answer to. Though the idea of him with her turns a knife in my gut, she's a part of his life that has nothing to do with me. A part he can go back to after me.

"Mr. Beller?" The portly manager waddles up in his gray suit the same way he did when we first arrived. "Could I speak with you, sir?"

"It had better be important." John seethes. "Otherwise, I know you aren't interrupting my date."

"No, sir. I mean yes, sir." The man makes a gesture with his arm, wanting us to go ahead of him. "It's important. Please, step into my office."

"*No.*" John bites. "I've been waiting for my vehicle longer than necessary and I'd like to get my lady home at a decent hour tonight. Tell me what you want, then see why we've been made to wait so long."

The man's throat bounces. "Mr. Beller, that's what I want to speak with you about. There's been an incident. Your vehicle is damaged."

Insisting we be taken to his truck immediately, John has the manager moving as fast as his squatty legs can carry him. We follow, his grip on my hand firm but gentle as I match his stormy pace. Outside, a valet joins the manager and takes us to where the truck is parked—in the back of the lot because of its monstrous size. Where the lighting is dim.

"There's damage on two sides, neither of which were visible to the attendants coming in and out." The manager points to the driver's side where deep, scribbling scratches run down the length. Then he motions toward the tailgate where the words STAY AWAY are etched. "The lot is fenced, as you can see. But someone gained access and we simply couldn't see them over the size of your truck." Sweat forms on his brow.

73

"I can't express how sorry we are. The restaurant will take care of the damages, and we'll have extra lighting and security cameras installed by the end of the week. We'll also reserve a spot for only you, and I'll have it monitored the entire time you're here on every future visit. You can rest assured this will *never* happen again."

The man grovels. John stands unmoved, until I shiver so lightly I barely feel it myself. His hand instantly lets go of mine, tenderly moving around my shoulder with a gentle pull into his side. I feel guilty for enjoying the moment, tucked against his warm body, his musky scent enticing my mind to wander a tantalizing trail. But at least being cold saves these two men from John's wrath. "I know who vandalized my truck. I'll take care of it myself." Their mouths open but his hand flies up to silence them. "I need to get her home."

"Yes, sir." The manager's eyes dart away, then meet mine. "Please let us know if we can be of assistance."

John's body stiffens, arm sliding to my waist. He moves me to the passenger door, this time only taking my hand to help me up into the seat instead of lifting me the way he did earlier. Circling the truck, he snaps at the manager one last time before sliding behind the wheel. I give John a smile to ease the mood. He doesn't glance my way. He starts the truck, throws it into gear, and drives.

~34~

The ride from Marsalas back to my house is quiet. John and I are never quiet together. I don't want our date to end on this note. I want to pave the road to a smoother goodbye. One that gives me the memory of his lips on mine. One that leaves hope of him being a part of my distant future, should I ever manage to get what lies between my ears straightened out.

"You want to get your lady home at a decent hour, huh?" Humor seems fitting. A jab at the way he sometimes sounds lifted from the pages of a Jane Austen novel. "If I'd known you had a lady, I wouldn't have agreed to go on this date. No matter how much you grinned."

"The lady sitting next to me is the one I was referring to as mine, but I'm not having much luck making that a reality." Tension twitches his jaw. "Every time we're together, something goes wrong."

"Maybe the universe is warning you about me."

"Tonight wasn't the work of the universe." The steering wheel protests under his grip. "I'm sorry I dragged you out of the restaurant. I'll never forgive myself if I hurt you."

"You didn't." I wiggle my fingers. "Not even by sounding antiquated and calling me *your lady*." His shoulders drop, distant eyes taking in more than the road. He looks like a man who just lost his best friend.

With boldness born of compassion, I slide across the bench seat. My lips press against his flexed jaw. "I'm sorry about the truck. I know it means a lot to you."

"I don't care about the truck. I care about you." His hand slides to mine, lifting the fingers to kiss them one by one. "Don't let me off the hook just because you're the sweetest lady in all the land."

75

"My hand is fine. And I know you love this truck. It's okay to admit you're upset over the damage. Do you think Susan did it?"

Swinging into my driveway, he shifts into park and brings his body around to mine. "Mary, the only thing in this world I'm upset over is our date being tainted. Again. I desperately wanted this night to be perfect for you."

"It was."

"Far from it." He swings back around, opening his door and jumping down, reaching his hands up for me. "But if you don't give up on me, I promise I'll show you what perfect is."

My body takes its place between his palms. "Outside of what happened to your truck, the night was perfect in my eyes."

Lowering me down in front of him, his hands run around my waist. "Despite how miserable I feel right now, those words make me happier than I've been in a long time."

"Finally." I pat his cheek. "There's that grin. Good boy."

He rests against my forehead. "Let's get you inside before you have me out here seeing just how far this grin will get me."

I wait under the soft glow of my porch light, eyes on his, bracing for the moment his head will dip and his lips cover mine. He seems to want it. And I'm giving him all the signs of being open to it. But he only strokes my jaw. "I'm going to stand right here while you go inside. Then I'm going to leave so you can get a good night's sleep. Because I'm hoping to see you again tomorrow. And when I ask please say yes, because I'm not prepared for no."

"I have a feeling you're prepared for everything."

"Except rejection." His grin deepens, tugging dimples into his cheek. "May I please have another date with you tomorrow?"

No. Firmly, solidly, no. "Since you're grinning, I have to say yes. But check with your lady first to make sure it's okay with her."

"A yes from you means it's okay. Now get inside and I'll call you in the morning." His lips land on my cheek. "Good night, sweetheart. Sleep tight. And for the love of all that's holy, answer your phone when I call!"

~35~

I'm used to the sound of the creaking screen door out back. Tonight it's different. *Congratulations, Mary.* I drag myself out of bed. *Your imagination has variety.* An actual person could be out there banging it shut. Or it could be the wind. But history tells me it's in my head. "Ouch!" I pinch myself. Definitely not dreaming. Or sleepwalking.

Picking up the derringer before leaving my bedroom, just in case, I creep slowly toward the sound, flipping off lights along the way so I can see outside. The noise stops the instant the kitchen light goes out. "Is anyone there?" I call to the back door, shivering at the thought of getting an answer.

Moving one step closer, I reach for the knob. It's locked. But the latch on the screen beyond dangles loose. "Hello?" I open the main door, frost settling into my veins. I slam the hook through the loop, securing the door, the night separated from me only by the flimsy screen. Cold air presses in. I rub my arms, the hair on my neck electrified. Because my alarm isn't going off! I fling around. I never disarmed it before opening the door. It should be blaring right now.

Shoving the backdoor shut, my frantic fingers fumble over the lock. Clicked into place I dash to the alarm pad, it's unarmed. *It can't be.* I blink hard, forcing my trembling hand to steady long enough to punch in the code. My phone rings. The phone I took the battery out of. The one on the counter, tauntingly lighting up its space in the dark room. The number is private.

I'm not playing this game with myself. I rip out the battery, tossing it across the room. The screen door opens. Slow and steady, stopping my heart. Dipping below the counter, I flinch when it slams shut. But scream when the lights flicker.

The door screeches open, slamming with vengeance while lights dance to life around me. "Stop it!" I run for the bedroom, locking myself inside, pointing the derringer and watching the knob. The screen door beats wildly against its frame, alarm system announcing, BACK DOOR OPEN. "Don't come in here!" I shout, tears racing down my face. "Please don't come in here."

The house falls silent. No footsteps move toward my door and the knob hasn't moved. Still, the last thing I want is to leave this room. But I have to check the alarm. The door. *Be brave.* My hand touches the knob. *No one is out there.*

Icy fingers claw over my body but I open the door, anyway, leaning on the wall, letting it support my unsteady steps. The back door is closed. I turn to the alarm pad. It's unarmed. I rearm it, the last button pressed to the sound of the slamming screen door. My knees go weak. FRONT DOOR OPEN. I whip my neck. Staring straight at a closed front door. BEDROOM TWO WINDOW OPEN. I scramble down the hall. The window is closed. Pushing back to the alarm pad, fighting myself all the way, I punch in the code, watching the system arm and disarm right in front of my eyes. "Stay on!" I pound the buttons. Rearming. Only for it to disarm. BACK DOOR OPEN. *No, it isn't.* I jam the code in harder. It disarms just as fast.

"Stop!" I order, wiping my face. *No more crying. It's just a glitch.* BEDROOM ONE WINDOW OPEN. *The contractor probably rewired the windows wrong.* FRONT DOOR OPEN. *Just a small, technical—* The screen door slams. *Wind.* Lights flicker. *Old wiring.* Fear seizes my trembling limbs like a virus. *Paranoia.*

I crumble, my body hitting the floor as the back door beats wildly against its frame, the slamming drowned out only by the barrage of window and door alerts. Lights around me pulse with the thud of the door. "Stop!" I can't hear the sound of my own screams. Hands over my ears, eyes shut against the torrent of tears, I scream louder. "Just Stop!"

~36~

Morning finds me still in the hallway with tears that have long run out staining my face. I punched my code into the alarm pad for hours last night, while the house around me screeched from every direction. On the few occasions I heard footsteps, I couldn't see through the blur of tears to know if anyone was actually there. No one touched me. So it's safe to say I was alone.

The full force of my mental break hitting the week I meet a man so charming I've been lovestruck since he first touched my hand is a cruel twist of fate. And my carelessness in not saying to John what I should have said from the start is why I'm not letting him pick me up for this lunch date he's called to ask for. He wants to. But I can't obligate him to then drive me home after the face-to-face conversation I should have had with him during our last lunch. Today, I tell him how sorry I am to have wasted his time. And how grateful I am for his time being wasted on me. He's been my only peace this past week. My only hope for brighter tomorrows. A gift I'll always cherish. One I might have unwrapped had I listened to Kim long ago. She said I needed professional help, and I do.

"I'll come to you. Just text me your address," I whisper, glad my phone still works after I threw it last night. "What can I bring?"

"Just yourself." His voice spreads out of the phone and washes over me. "I've taken care of the food. The only other thing needed today is sunshine, and the forecast is looking good. We can get to enjoying it faster if you let me pick you up."

"Thanks, but I'm looking forward to the drive. I'll see you soon."

Unlike last night, today I'm dressing to un-impress. Jeans, a pale-yellow t-shirt that I usually clean house in, and an old brown jacket on top. It's the

79

exact opposite of how he's used to seeing me. Hopefully he'll take one look and change his mind before I even have to tell him I'm insane.

The thought-provoking twenty-minute drive to his house ends with me navigating his tree-lined drive. I wind upward from the road, cutting through a lush green lawn that rolls outward to the edge of a thick wood.

Coming out of the last gentle curve the view opens, revealing a sprawling estate. The grounds are meticulous. Natural elements showcase the landscaping, highlighting the modern ranch whose front entrance has layers of stacked stone framing solid mahogany doors that rise all the way to the roofline. There's an intricate ivy pattern carved along their edge, and large bronze handles grace their center. The home's oversized windows are tinted, and a two-story, four-bay garage stands next to the house with the entryway stone repeated on its face.

A second drive cuts off the main, leading to yet another large building on the lower part of the property. It mimics the architecture of the home, with the same stacked stone finish on the front. Every inch of the massive grounds, from the structures to the wooded acreage beyond the expanse of open land, are worthy of admiration. Just like John.

I watch him on his way out to where I parked my car. Faded jeans and white t-shirt. He's going to be hard to say goodbye to. I close my eyes. *Remember last night, and with all the strength you have, let him go.*

His lips press against my cheek as if they have to be there in order for him to breathe. I savor the feel of him on my flesh. "I should have picked you up." His arms surround me. "You drive way too slow."

"I drove the speed limit." I push away from what I can't have.

He grins. "Those signs are suggestions. Especially when I have someplace important to be. Like at your door." I fall silent. His big hands run down my arms. "You're here now, and looking perfect. A little tired, though. Did the critter under your house keep you up again?"

"What?" My tongue fishes itself out of my throat. "How did you know about that?"

"I talked to Kevin." His brow cocks. "He said you had to call an exterminator. A raccoon tore down your ductwork?"

"Something tore it down." I still my heart. "It's gone now."

"I'll come over and put the ductwork back up."

"The exterminator took care of it." I move away from his hands "But since you brought it up, exactly what did Kevin tell you? Outside of this alleged pride issue."

"Only what I already suspected." His fingers trace along my arm. "That you're someone worth having in my life."

"That's debatable."

"Only with you." He leans in. "Which he also told me would be the case. But it's okay you're not bragging about how great you are. I like finding that out all on my own."

Not until this moment did I consider what a man's intentions are when he asks a woman to his house. His eyes are sparking with life. "I can't wait for all the things we're going to find out about each other today, Mary. I've been looking forward to this all week."

"I'm not sleeping with you." I spin away. "I've heard of the three-date rule—"

"You can stop," he groans. "I didn't ask you here for sex. And I don't use date numbers to pressure women. I should have made that clear this morning."

The *manners* he keeps displaying already made that clear. I think. "Sorry. I'm just still kicking myself for letting you stay at my place that first night. I don't know what got into me." He inclines a grin my way. "Never mind. Now I remember."

"You have nothing to worry about." He urges me forward with a chuckle. "But I do. You could easily persuade me to make the sort of plans I don't have for today."

"I'll be doing the opposite of persuading you." I lean away from him. "If I can bring myself to."

"What's that supposed to mean?"

"Nothing." I turn around and head back toward my car. "I have something in the backseat for you."

"My present giving me presents!" He takes my hand, coming with me. "A man can get used to this."

"Please don't."

"Too late."

~37~

A fruit salad isn't much, but I hope John appreciates the throwback to our first date. Even though he said not to bring anything, I didn't feel comfortable not contributing. Especially to a lunch that's going to end with a forever kind of goodbye.

Standing in his entryway, tension builds in my neck and shoulders, running down to where his hand rests on the small of my back. "So, what do you think?" he asks as my eyes roam over the wood-lined cathedral ceilings towering above the main living area, dropping to take in the kitchen, dining room, and living room; all of them open to one another, the whole of every room displayed from any vantage point. Not even the double-sided glass fireplace blocks the view. I trace the length of its chimney down to the waiting crushed leather furniture. "Warm and cozy?" He smiles. Anticipating.

"Exquisite." I satisfy his curiosity. "I thought the outside was stunning but this, it's beyond warm and cozy. It's beyond everything."

"I was hoping you'd think so."

He urges me farther inside, around the kitchen's L-shaped bar, sliding the fruit salad onto one of the stools and navigating us to the back of the mahogany dining table. I eye the long slab of wood. "Do you host a lot of parties?"

"No. I like privacy. But I figured if I ever do need to host, I'd better have all the pieces in place."

"And a small table would get swallowed in this room."

"Right." He nods to the door. "Now, tell me what you think of this."

He leads us through two floor-to-ceiling glass doors that open to a patio of large flat stones. "All the stone came from this land," he narrates as I walk ahead, fingers grazing along the three-foot-high stacked stone wall surrounding the patio.

"This is the same stone that's on the front of the house? And all of it came from this land?"

"Even the stone for that did." He points out the firepit rising from the center. "Crews were here for months, but there was plenty of rock to go around. It just took a while to get the right pieces together."

"You like making pieces fit."

"You have no idea how relentlessly I'm willing to work on every single piece of my plan." His voice is velvet. Caressing. Electrifying.

Moving away, I look over the various chairs and tables adorning the space. "I made all of these." He steps to my side, watching my expression.

"Really?" I look more closely at the detail in the chair nearest me. "It's beautiful."

"Now do you believe I can make a living being a carpenter?"

"I never thought you couldn't." I wince. "I just—"

"I know." His fingers slide down my arm and into my hand. "I'm just showing off a little."

"You have a right to." I swallow. "Even your décor is perfect. It's nothing like I expected a bachelor pad to be."

"That's because I'm an unmarried man. Not a man looking for an excuse to live like a child." He turns us back to the house. "I can't take credit for the decorating, though. My sister did it. And with very little of my input."

"She has impeccable taste."

"So do I." His eyes land on mine. I fidget. He chuckles. "Come on, sweetheart; I'm dying to give you the full tour."

I resist going back inside but he tugs me gently forward, keeping me at his side as he moves through the glass doors. "Relax, sweetheart. Nothing is going to happen here today that you don't want to happen."

"I don't want a tour of your personal space, but you seem pretty set on that happening."

"Only because I want you to tell me what you think about the rest of the house." He pauses, bringing my hand to his lips. "And because I want you to so badly, *and* because I'm not accepting any no's today, I'm going to insist you take this tour with me."

"John…" I should end things now. Before I lose the will.

"One foot in front of the other, sweetheart." He moves slowly forward. "There's a bedroom I need you to see."

~38~

John's adorable apology for taking advantage of how easy it is to tease me earns him my cooperation in this tour. He leads me through all the rooms on the left side of his house. Three bedrooms, two full baths, and a guest bath. The largest bedroom is directly at the end of the hall and is set up as a mini master suite. The second is used as an office, and though not as large as the other, it's still big enough to house a double bed and other normal bedroom furniture without any hindrance to the office space. The third is an ordinary guest room, just as large as the second but with a sitting area in place of the office furniture.

To the right of the home, on the other side of the main living space, where he continues to urge me along with a grin and a wink, is one massive master suite. The entire room is serene blue and a mahogany king bed graces the center. A sitting area is off to the right in front of a large shaded window. The wood of the furniture matches the bed, and the plush red and green throw pillows pop against the cream fabric. I let him lead me farther inside, where two floor-to-ceiling glass doors just like the ones in the dining room come into view. Outside of them, a majestic vista of rolling hillsides.

I never thought to give him a tour of my place. Now I'm glad I didn't. His home is otherworldly. "Nothing about your house disappoints. You have to love living here."

"I designed the place myself." He brushes against my chin, bringing my eyes to his. "I waited, hoping one day I'd build a house with my wife, but eventually decided to just go ahead and do it on my own. This is what I came up with." He watches me closely. "I've been here five years now. Still without having the dream wife to go with the dream house."

Too bad I'm not her. "Tote a picture of this place around and you'll find a wife real quick." The offhanded comment falls out. "Sorry. Material possessions aren't the reason a woman will marry you." I give his hand a squeeze. "She'll marry you for who you are. This house will be secondary. I mean, not even second…it's—"

"I understand." He cups my cheek. "And I'm glad you like the house. Because if the lady of my dreams doesn't, then I have to build another one. And I'm pretty attached to this one."

I wish I were his dream, because he's mine. "What's in there?" I head for the first of two sets of doors in the suite, nervously trying to get away. He pulls me to his side as the doors open into an enormous tiled room. The creamy brown stone has intricate mosaic running through the middle. To the left, a nine-foot walk-in shower holds two sets of body sprayers, two rain shower heads, and a handheld wand shower head—all controlled by a touch screen. "My entire house can fit in your bathroom. Maybe in the shower alone." He laughs. I wander over to the large tub encased in a tile cocoon all its own. "Nice to see you love bubble baths."

"I put that in for my future wife." His voice drops low. "Do you like bubble baths?"

One slip of his grin and I might take one with him right now. "I'm starving. What are we having for lunch?" I bolt for the door, dragging him with me since he's sewn himself to my flesh. "It's a nice day. We should eat outside."

"It's funny how you think being somewhere else will be a safe zone." He grips my hand and twirls me into his arms. "It won't. But by all means, lead on." I freeze. He releases me. "I'm talking about you blushing every time I get personal. And how I'm not going to stop, because getting personal is the whole reason I asked you here today."

"So you do believe in the three-date rule?"

"By my count, this is our fourth date." He steps away with a sigh. "*Personal* as in getting to know each other better through *conversation*. In a place where there aren't any distractions to interrupt those conversations."

I smooth down the hair on my neck, that unfamiliar tone rising from my throat again. "Like beautiful women in stilettos?"

"You were so calm about her last night I was beginning to wonder if I should worry." His grin sparks to life, hand slipping to my waist. "You have no reason to be jealous of anyone. Now, let's go eat, and *talk* about where this is going. Do you mind taking a little ride?"

Yes. Because Stiletto might get to be with him again once he knows I can't. "I'll go if you stop trying to embarrass me. It isn't as cute as you think."

"I'll have to be cuter then." He winks. "Come with me, sweetheart. I have a surprise for you. It involves water, bubbles, and a bed."

"Then the only place I'm going is to my car."

~39~

John's jokes are getting worse. But I'm giving him plenty of material. I'm not only nervous, I'm jumpy and maintaining a permanent shade of crimson. I'm also clumsy, tripping into the garage after landing my eyes on his gunmetal-pearl Viper. "I bet you're glad you weren't driving this last night."

"I don't take it out much." His arms encircle my waist, keeping me upright. "Not even when I *should* be driving it on dates with you."

His pretty white behemoth is parked two spots over. "Your truck is fancy enough. Last night you said you knew who was responsible for the damage?"

"I did say that." He turns us toward the UTV. "Let's get on with our date, because I have a hungry lady on my hands and I promised her a nice lunch."

"Is the vandal's identity a secret?"

"It's a mood killer." He rubs my side. "And I don't want any distractions today."

Like everything else he owns, the UTV is oversized and decked out. He places an equally oversized picnic basket into the bed and lowers me into the passenger seat. "Comfy?"

"Yeah, but I've never been in one of these before."

"Then hold on tight, sweetheart." He slides behind the wheel. "I'll make your first time memorable."

Taking off with a grin, he laughs when I grip his thigh. "Well, now you're just asking for more."

"I'm trying not to die." I jerk my hand away. "Slow down!"

"I'd rather make you hold on to me." He brakes hard, sliding the machine sideways. My fingers clench the seat, not the place he wants them buried. "Don't worry." He chuckles. "I don't do reckless. I do calculated risk. There's a big difference."

I hold my heart. It's popping out of my chest. "The difference isn't as big as you think."

Sticking to a slower pace, he steers us through the rolling hillsides I saw from his bedroom. We climb to the top of the steepest point along a well-worn path that leads to a pine thicket. He parks beside one of the bristling trees and grabs the basket out of the bed before hurrying around to take my hand. "This is my favorite spot. I hope you like it."

The wood opens into a clearing that scrolls toward a scenic overlook. A tranquil valley lies below, limestone cliffs standing tall across the way. "It's breathtaking."

"Most people have no idea views like this exist around here." He smiles. "I'm proud to own this one. And glad you like it because this is where we'll eat lunch today."

I thought his house was the most stunning thing I'd ever seen, but he's topped it. "I love the peacefulness." He spreads a blanket from the basket over the ground and lowers me onto it. "This view is the reason I chose to build here."

"Then I agree. You really do have good taste."

I kick off my shoes. He does the same, sitting beside me to unpack the rest of the basket. I reach in to help. "Nope." He moves it away. "This is my treat. Just relax, and I'll do my best to pamper you."

"Sharing this view with me is pampering enough. And you've already done all the work."

"I haven't even gotten started." He winks. "But I'm about to. Which is why I brought you up here. It's a nice quiet place to talk, and we need to get on the same page about a few things."

My heart aches. This is the part I've been dreading. But it has to be said, no matter how much my resolve slips every second I'm near him. "John, however this lunch ends, I want you to know I'll never forget you."

~40~

John refuses to hear me say goodbye. Every word is ignored. He offers me chicken salad sandwiches with my choice of three cheeses. Taking one, I pile some of the vegetables from the tray onto my plate, adding a little of both the dips he brought.

"Is that lemonade?" I point to the glass pitcher with a red plastic lid.

He pours us each a cup. "There's ice water, too. And peanut butter no-bake cookies for dessert."

"Homemade cookies?"

"It's all homemade." He sighs. "Even the vegetable dips. I didn't know what you'd like, so I tried to give you options."

I take a bite of the sandwich. It's good. He isn't just a handsome face. "Your culinary talents are impressive."

"That's nice to hear." His lip ticks up. "Because I've been doing my best to impress you."

"The job is thoroughly done. Since day one."

"Hardly." He sets his own food aside. "I'm doing something wrong, because you're not even willing to have a serious conversation with me."

"You're the unwilling one. All because you don't want to listen to what I have to say. So, go ahead. You talk and I'll listen." With a topic change. "How much land do you own?"

"I hear every word you say." He points to the pine where the UTV is parked. "I own two hundred acres. There's a good number of deer and turkey running through here, so I usually set a ground blind at the base of that tree. I've harvested some nice bucks there."

"Then ask me for a date during hunting season!" The words fall out. My face scorches. "I didn't mean that. Or mean it to sound so...so..."

"Perfect?" He smiles. "I'd love nothing more than to sit in a ground blind with you. So count on the fact that I'll be asking."

I'm usually not the type to give mixed signals. "John, I…" My voice shakes. "I'd never use land, or anything material, as a reason to date someone."

"I know." He rearranges the food containers on the blanket so there's nothing between us. "What I don't know is what you're wanting from this. I know what I want. And I know if what you want doesn't line up, I need the reasons why. So I might have a chance at changing your mind."

I wish he could change my mind. Literally. "It's kind of hard to say what I want."

"It isn't hard at all. I'll go first." His fingers slide to mine. "I like you. More than a little. That should be obvious by now. And what I want, Mary, is to be in a relationship with you."

"What do you mean by *relationship*?" If all he wants is a date here and there, maybe it won't hurt.

"I mean, you and me committed to each other." He moves closer, breath tickling my lips "You're already the only woman in my life, and I want the same from you. Can you commit to me and only me?"

"No." Shock strikes across his face. I summon my courage and press on. "I can't commit to you."

The wind is out of his sails. So forcefully it's heartbreaking. "Please don't be upset. We could date occasionally. Maybe every few months or so have an evening out?"

"What's going on here?" His hands slide away. "Now that you've had a taste of the dating life again you want to play the field?"

"I'm not blowing you off to keep my options open." I swallow. "I didn't even *want* to taste the dating life to begin with. And I never expected you to want anything serious with me."

"Well, I do." He turns away. "Is that why you haven't answered my calls or bothered to call me? Because you never thought about being with me long term?"

Even though I've only known him a week, I've definitely thought about it. "Sitting here, knowing I can't be with you, hurts. Because I really like you, too. Much more than a little. So I'm not rejecting you as a person or saying being exclusive with you is a problem. What I'm saying is…I'm scared. Confused. And have so many things going on in my life right now I can't let anyone in. Especially you." He turns back, hope unhidden in his eyes. "John, I want *you* to be the one with options. Find someone who can make you happy. Because no matter how much I wish it were me, it isn't."

"It is." His hands are back, claiming mine. "It's always been you."

"You don't know that." I pull away. "But *I* know you do *not* want to go down this road with me. I have too much baggage. Too many issues to work out." Last night proved there's no hope for me. "You deserve someone better."

His hands sweep up this time, cupping my face. "I've got who I want. And honestly, since you said you really like me too, I haven't heard much else. This is a done deal. I'm just waiting for those lips to stop moving so I can kiss my girlfriend."

"I'm begging you." Here in this place with him, swimming in tranquility and basking in his emeralds, I can't be trusted to do the right thing. "For your own sake, be reasonable."

"I am." He closes the space between us, hands guiding my face to his. "I've been dying to try this again." His lips lower. "It's time we get this right."

~41~

I'm not running from John and he isn't slowing down. He pours into me, hands sliding through my hair as his lips slide over mine. "I can't fight the urge to kiss you like a fool unless you make me." He groans, mouth dragging to my neck, moving over inches of skin begging for his touch. "Tell me to stop, sweetheart."

"I can't." My arms run around him. "Not when all I want is you."

"Then kiss me." He drags back to my mouth, laying us down on the blanket. It feels good to give in. To have his lips trace along my jaw. And terrible to think about what it will do to him when he finds out the truth.

"I'm scared, John. Scared you'll change your mind about me."

"Never." His eyes blaze. "I'm as sure about you as Mike must have been."

If Mike lived long enough to see me lose my mind, he would have stayed with me. "That's pretty sure."

"It's more than sure." He rolls, cradling me against his chest. "So let's cool things off while you tell me about him. I'd like to know more about the man who was lucky enough to marry you. Mainly because I'd like to not break seven thousand promises in one day." He nuzzles my ear. "I keep trying to behave, but you're not making me."

"Even if I wanted to, I can't." I rest against him. "Believe me, I've tried to *leave* seven thousand times. But you're not making me, so here we are."

With his hands staying well within respectable zones, a comfort considering I'm not likely to stop him from groping me, I open up about Mike. "When he finally worked up the courage to ask me out, he was so nervous he was dripping in sweat. His hands were shaking so badly that even if I didn't want to go, I would have felt too sorry for him to say no. But I was glad he liked me enough to want a date."

"Trust me when I say it was he who was glad *you* liked him enough to say yes." His laugh is deep, our bodies connected as I sit between his outstretched legs and look over the view with him. "It's a feeling I can relate to."

"As if you've ever had a woman say no to you. And he was the same. I can't imagine anyone ever turning him down. He had an enormous heart, always ready with kind words or helping hands. His tenderness was as natural as breathing."

"Kevin said he was too good a person to be taken out of this world so young."

A truth that never fails to fill my eyes with tears. "He was the best person ever brought into this world. Which is why I'll never forgive myself for missing all the early warning signs. I should have known no one gets sick as much as he did unless something is seriously wrong."

"You couldn't have known he had cancer." His arms hold me tight. "Mike didn't even know, and his body was full of it."

"But he was my partner. I should have…sensed it."

"You did. You took him to the hospital instead of on your honeymoon." His lips rest against my temple. "Kevin said Mike called, begging for help. He wanted to overlook how sick he was, but you didn't let him."

I'll never forget leaving our wedding and driving to the hospital. Three long days later, our lives changed forever. "When the probing and prodding was done the doctor walked in, announced it was advanced stage bone cancer, then walked straight back out the door."

"You're serious? He didn't offer help? Or give advice?"

"We never saw that man again." I wipe my face. "The worst part was having to stand by uselessly as the cancer wasted Mike away. He fought, but it had too much of a hold. He even died months sooner than his team of doctors expected."

"I'm sorry both of you had to go through that." John's big hands brush aside my hair with utter tenderness. I feel guilty. I shouldn't be taking this comfort from him.

"*I'm* sorry I'm not strong enough to tell you goodbye. That we can't ever see each other again." He deserves the truth. "That's why I came here today. To break things off. For good."

"Why?"

"Because I'm selfish." I get up. "And not just right now. I've always been this way. When Mike died, I prayed every day for months that I'd wake up and his death would only be a dream. I prayed for him to be well, too, but the doctors said that would never happen, so I was praying just to have him alive at the hospital so I could see him."

"There's nothing wrong with that."

"Everything is wrong with it!" I move away from his outstretched arms. "I was praying for my husband to have to suffer longer. I never knew how selfish I could be until then." Tears trickle over my cheeks. "I didn't want him to be in pain. I just didn't want to lose him either. I wasn't ready to lose him."

John grabs a napkin from the basket and dabs my eyes, coaxing me into his arms. "Mike was your husband. Of course you wanted more time with him. And I know he wasn't ready to leave you any more than you were ready to lose him."

I close my eyes at his words. He delicately kisses each lid. "Nothing can ever take away the pain of what you've experienced, but I'm going to do everything within my power to ease it."

~42~

I don't deserve John's kindness. Yet he pours it out, and I don't stop him. "Mary," he lifts my chin. "I'm going to be here for you, through anything. And in a way Mike would be grateful for because if I were the one with his fate, my dying wish would be for you to have happiness in every possible way. If that included another man, I'd want it to be someone who would take care of you and adore you as much as I do."

"You don't even know me."

"I do." His lips tug into a smile. "So don't worry your beautiful head about emotional scars. Your baggage isn't anything I can't carry."

I touch his face. "I'm so selfishly glad you're not a reasonable man."

"And I'm so selfishly glad you're mine. *All* mine."

Lounging on our picnic blanket, taking in the picturesque view between kisses that have me feeling like a teenager on make-out point, he sparks another conversation. His delectable mouth choosing a terrible topic. "Last night at dinner, I told you about my family. But you didn't tell me about yours and there's something I need to know." He sits up. "I'd like to discuss what Kevin told me about your immediate family situation."

"What made you go to him instead of asking me in the first place?"

"I'm not a man who leaves things to chance." He smiles. "I confirmed who I thought you were and got the information I so desperately needed before pursuing you *too* aggressively. I didn't want to make you run in the opposite direction." He pulls me up and into his arms, lips brushing mine. "I was worried, but today feels like I got things right."

"It doesn't feel like you're wrong."

His hand slides down my cheek, consoling the blush. "You're beautiful. Red-faced or not."

"Flattery doesn't get you off the hook for pumping one of my best friends for information. For three hours."

Annoyance ticks his jaw. "I took Kevin to his favorite sports bar to ask a few questions. It was the never-ending supply of cheeseburgers I paid for that kept him there for three hours."

"So it was a date?"

"And he didn't even dress up for me." He winks. "Seriously, though, I talked to him because days went by without you calling me once. When I called you, you never answered. So I took the initiative to figure out why. I've never experienced that before, it's usually the complete opposite."

"Sorry I bruised your ego." I sigh. "I wasn't missing your calls on purpose. It's just been…a taxing week."

"I can see that in your face today." His fingers glide along my brow. "And since Kevin told me you're so independent you never complain—or boast, for that matter—my ego is back in check."

"Good boy."

His chuckle rumbles from his gut. Right into my heart. "The oracle also told me you don't like pity or sympathy of any sort. So I'm struggling with how to make you relax after a taxing week."

"You're doing just fine." I look away. "And no one likes to be pitied."

"You're so innocently naive." He brings my face back to his. "A lot of people are happy to take all the sympathy they can get. But not you. One whose life has been so hard it breaks my heart, because if there's anyone who actually deserves an ounce of hard, it isn't you."

"You don't know that."

"I've seen enough already to know it's true." His smile presses softly against my palm. "And I'm glad Kevin told me about your childhood, because this strong-willed independence of yours makes a lot more sense now. Which is what I want to ask you about. What made your dad abandon you after your mom died?"

Talking about my dad is taboo. Kevin knows this. So do John's searching green eyes. "Please, sweetheart. I want to hear the story from you, to know whether or not Kevin exaggerated the facts. Have you really lived alone since you were nine?"

~43~

My mom died only a few months after my family moved from West Virginia to Pennsylvania. After that, Dad and I were alone. With no family nearby and too short a presence in a new town to have friends, Dad was in a bad place. He did the best he could for me.

"The situation with my dad wasn't ideal, but I appreciate him keeping a roof over my head."

"You appreciate him keeping a roof over his *daughter's* head?" John scoffs. "He abandoned his child. Right after she lost her mother. And that child was you!"

"I'm not immune from having hardships just because you think I'm cute."

"I don't think you're cute. You're gorgeous. But more than that, I think you're the best person I've ever met." Anger floats under his surface. "Your dad is a piece of dirt and I'm going to make sure he knows it."

"You're not allowed." I pull out of his arms. "It's my life. Not yours."

"It's my girlfriend's life, which entitles me to an opinion on it. And my opinion is that he's pathetic." His eyes narrow. "You have a tendency to brush things off way too easily."

I don't dwell on things. I pick up my feet and get on with life. "What I've lived through has nothing to do with you. So no, you're not entitled to an opinion on it."

"I'm entitled, and so are you." He grips my fingers, pressing my palm to his heart. "You were a kid who just lost her mom, and he left you to fend for yourself."

"I was fine on my own." I remove my hand. "I didn't need him reading me bedtime stories."

"What you needed was for him to be there. What did the man you're letting off the hook think? That a growing girl was sewing her own clothes from wool she spun from the goat she sheared? And that a magic lawnmower kept the grass in check? And what about when you were sick?"

"The odd jobs I did gave me valuable life experience, right along with all the money I needed to buy clothes. So it doesn't matter what he thought any more than it matters what *you* think."

His big hands run along my face. "Sweetheart, it matters because I'm disgusted someone would treat you that way. And they get away with it because you're too nice to not let them." He smiles. "But you go ahead and be nice. I'm mean enough for both of us."

"I don't need anyone being mean on my behalf." I remove his hands. "The situation isn't as black and white as you're trying to make it."

"Mourning his wife or not, the man let his kid down. That's pretty clear."

"Not if the kid is happy to not have put any extra burden on him. I'd rather be the one disappointed than know I disappointed him."

"Only you would feel guilty for being a child who needs a parent." His arms surround my waist, forehead resting on mine. "Maybe you were better off without him. And I know you are now. Which I can't wait to tell him."

"I'm not letting you talk to him."

"You're not *letting* me?" He laughs. "Sweetheart, I already know where he is. I only asked about the situation to make sure what Kevin told me was true. Now that I know it is, I'll be doing more than just talking to him."

~44~

My dad was never mean to me. He hit a bad patch and dealt with it the best he could. Yes, his way of dealing left a nine-year-old virtually alone. It left me knocking on every door within walking distance looking for work. Some kids opened lemonade stands while I cleaned houses, did laundry, and mowed lawns for all the people around me who thought my tenacity was *cute.* That grit prepared me for life.

While Kim's family looked after me so I didn't end up a ward of the state, and helped with all the things it was impossible for me to do alone, like drive to a store, I always took care of my own responsibilities. And still do. And Mike never once complained. He accepted me for who I am. A woman capable of fending for herself.

"By eleven, I had steady enough work to send back the food allowance Dad mailed every month." Kim and her family called it stubborn. I called it competence. "He did pay the house payment and utilities, though." All things I made sure I could afford on my own before ever agreeing to marry Mike. He was fine with me paying the bills. "So Dad didn't orphan me on a street corner. I had a home. And you have no right to nose into who he is or where he lives."

"We'll have to agree to disagree, because I don't feel it's ever acceptable to deal with things the way he did. He didn't even come to your wedding. Or Mike's funeral. You're all grown up and he's still abandoning you."

"You can't abandon someone who never expected you to be there in the first place."

He sits quietly for a while. "Tell me something, sweetheart. Have you ever been angry? Really angry? Are you even capable of it?"

"Threaten to talk to my dad again and we'll find out."

"That would almost be intimidating if you weren't smiling." He laughs. "But you are. And so beautifully I can't remember what the warning was. Only that I want to kiss you. So pucker up."

He's right. As fine a job as he's doing making me angry, it's pointless. I can't stay mad at him any more than I can say a bad word against my dad. And smiling is apparently a reflex. "I don't need you defending me. For anything. Especially something that happened so long ago."

"I hear what you're saying." He settles us back on the blanket, making no promises. "You and Kim grew up a couple of streets apart?"

"We were thick as thieves. Does something about that bother you, too?"

"No." His arms slide around me. "But I was pretty mad when Kevin told me about George."

Stories from my childhood have different versions based on if I'm telling them or Kim is. "Her brother never liked me in a romantic way. She made that up to annoy us."

"Then why does he turn beet-red every time she brings up his lifelong dream of landing you? Kind of like you're doing right now?"

"It's embarrassing to have his reputation tarnished all because he helped me keep an old clunker running."

"A clunker you bought with your own money at sixteen. A whole hundred dollars, right? Kim's dad helped with the paperwork, and George worked on it?"

"Kevin was a plethora of information."

"I didn't give him a choice."

My life story as told by Kevin via Kim's exaggeration. I can only imagine. "George is a mechanic, it's what he does for a living. He still works on my car today."

"And instead of payment," his nostrils flare, "you make him cookies."

I'm surprised that tidbit was divulged. "It stems from my teenage years when we worked out a deal for me to cook for him in lieu of payment, since I could barely afford to keep gas in the tank."

"When a twenty-five-year-old man regularly drops by the house of a sixteen-year-old girl who just happens to live alone, the meal he's looking for isn't coming off the stove." A growl vibrates from his chest. "And in case he still wants that payment, he's on the list of men I need to talk to. Right up there with your dad."

"Do that, and I *will* tell you goodbye. No matter how much it hurts."

His eyes close, a muscle ticking in his jaw. "If I'm the only one it hurts, it'd probably be worth it." His emeralds flash open. "Losing you isn't part of my plan, though." His fingers graze over my cheek. "I'll lay the stars at your feet. Hand you the world on a silver platter. The one thing I won't do is let someone disrespect you. Past, present, or future."

"The past is none of your business. The future is unpredictable and, at present, the only person disrespecting me is you."

~45~

John says he isn't jealous. Only factual. And yes, it's fact that George asked me out sometimes. But I always thought he was joking. "I wonder if he ever told his wife about you ripping his heart out with laughter every time he asked you on a date."

"I hope not." I swallow. "I mean, I really thought he was only trying to be funny. And in all these years, he hasn't ever said anything different."

"It still hurts, then."

If what he says is true, it might. "I'll talk to him."

"Nope." He rolls us over on the blanket. "If I'm not allowed, you're not either. And I'll be taking care of your vehicle from here on out anyway, so you don't need him."

"I'll take care of my car. Even if it means finding a new mechanic."

"You don't have to handle things on your own anymore. We're together, and I'm devotedly yours. I'll help you with everything. Even something as small as an oil change."

An oil change isn't the kind of help I need. "I'm used to doing things on my own. And I won't be a clingy girlfriend, you can have all the space you need."

"This is all the space I need." His lips fall over the skin at the base of my neck. "We both sentenced ourselves to lives of solitude, and that ends today. Past hurts aren't dictating to us anymore." He slides over me. "And I'm going to make sure you know exactly how I feel. I'm not letting you be oblivious with me the way you were with George."

His mouth swallows mine, getting no resistance from me. He groans. "I hope you're falling as hard as I am, sweetheart. Because I'm ready to completely lose my mind over you."

"I've been trying really hard not to fall for you, but losing my mind is my specialty."

"Those kinds of words are going to make my manners evaporate." He grins. "Are you scared?"

"The only time I'm not scared," I sober, "is when I'm with you."

His mouth lowers back to my flesh. "Then remember how badly I hate to be told no."

I would, but we're off the blanket and loading back into the UTV before he gives me a chance. "Where are we going?"

"A less romantic atmosphere." He sighs. "If such a place exists with you around."

~

The house-mimicking building on the lower part of John's property is his workshop. It's just as large as the garage, with every inch of space utilized for his trade. Long tables line the main room, holding furniture in various stages of completion. Torturous-looking hooks dangle from chains anchored in the ceiling. Saws, stacks of wood, boxes of nails, glue and, if I had to guess, every tool known to mankind is within reach.

Bins of brackets are neatly organized in their respective places, and the oddly delightful smell of stain mixes with freshly cut wood to hang in the air. He walks me through, educating me on the art of furniture-making while answering my many questions. "Sorry for the inquisition. I've just never seen anything like this before."

"Asking means you're genuinely interested." He smiles. "And I like that you're asking intelligent questions."

"Have a lot of non-genuine, unintelligent ladies in here?"

His head shakes. "They don't ever make it this far. Which is why I'm so excited to finally meet someone who has."

I give his hand a squeeze. "Maybe if you stop testing the ladies you go out with, more will make the cut."

"I was looking for the one who would pass with flying colors." He winks. "And I found her."

"You read my test results upside down." I wait as he opens the door to an enclosed glass room. "Mine really said, you should run."

"Maybe you're the one who should run." He circles my waist from behind, lowering his mouth to my ear. "I promise I'll catch you."

Of all the times I've wanted to run lately, this isn't one of them. I don't even want to pull out of his arms as we walk through the showroom. Everything from wardrobes to wooden game boards are on display. "What are these?" I stop at a table along the front wall where portfolios are sprawled.

"Pictures of past projects. I take these to trade shows and individual buyers so clients can give me a better idea of what they like. Then I customize." He looks around. "Sometimes I let buyers come here, which is the whole reason for this room. But I like privacy, so I rarely invite."

I flip through the pages. "Your craftsmanship shows the love you have for each piece."

"I'm passionate about everything I do." He smiles.

I sense the double meaning. It sends horses stampeding through my chest. "Passionate enough to let your girlfriend be one of the special buyers who gets an invitation?"

"You're already here." He spins me to his chest. "And you can have anything you want, anytime you want it. *Anything. Anytime.*"

"All I want is a bed." I jerk free of his arms. "I mean...I want to know about that bed. The frame...over there." I point. "It's the same as the one in your bedroom, right?"

"I don't make any pieces the same." He grins. "I'll take you back inside so you can get a closer look at mine. And maybe, if we're not too distracted, you'll notice the subtle differences."

~46~

I need sleep. Then maybe I'll stop putting my foot in my mouth. "How many pieces of furniture did you make for your house?" I ask as John leads us back to where I will *not* be entering his bedroom.

"All of them." He opens the front door. "If it's made of wood, I crafted it."

"Everything?" My eyes land on the massive dining table. "Even that?"

"Everything." He nods. "Right down to the cutting boards. Does that impress you?"

Turning his hand over, I run my fingers across his callused palm. "Who knew *my* man was so talented."

"Call me yours again." He steps into me, a smile dancing on his lips.

"Mr. Impressive, you're mine." I meet his eyes. "Until you come to your senses."

"You're mine *because* I came to my senses."

Bracing for another long kiss, I'm met instead with one of those distractions he said we wouldn't have today. His phone rings. I jump out of my skin. He smooths down the hair on my arms with a groan. "I meant to take a page out of your book and turn that thing off. Especially since that ringtone is my mom's. I'll have to call her later."

"No, talk to her now." I move to the sink. "I'll wash up the lunch dishes."

"We'll do these together." He takes the cup I picked up out of my hand. "Just like an old married couple."

"Except we're not." I push him away. "And you should never ignore your mom's call."

"There are a lot of reasons to ignore her call. Like being with you." His hand lingers over the phone, finally dragging it off the counter with a huff. "Hello, Mom. Is this important or can it wait?"

I can't make out every word, but not even the sink's running water drowns out her bellowing voice. Or his. Making it hard not to eavesdrop. "I don't care who her father is." More grumbling from the phone. "You're calling me in defense of Susan? You, of all people?" The other end of the line falls silent. "I love you, Mom. But there's no changing my mind. It's done. And I have to go. I have company." He hangs up, slamming the phone onto the counter. I reflexively jump, a little squeak passing my lips. "Sorry." He rushes around the island. "I didn't mean to scare you."

"I'm not scared." I'm embarrassed. And worried. I slide into his arms. "Are you okay?"

"I was." His head rests against mine. "Until that call came. Now our perfect date is tainted. Again."

I have experience with phone calls spoiling things. "The day is only messed up if we let it be."

"You may not feel that way in a minute." His anguished sigh shivers over me. "I didn't want to do this today, but after what just happened, I have to go ahead and explain my history with Susan."

"I've known since last night she isn't someone you want to talk about."

"She's a thorn in my side and the last person whose name I want on my lips." He motions for me to go ahead of him into the living room. "But since she tried to speak to you last night, and without me present, I need you to be aware of who she is. There's a strong chance she'll contact you again."

"Why?"

"Because I almost married her."

~47~

It's silly to be jealous of John's past with Susan when I actually *was* married. But no sillier than him blaming a long family history of love stories on an urgency to marry that led him into Susan's web.

"We're not normal people. Love doesn't come easily for us." He plops onto the sofa, hands dragging down his face. "But after you grow up hearing the stories and watching your parents and grandparents act them out, it makes you want love for yourself. And…there's a lot of pressure to carry on the legacy."

"Love doesn't come easily for anyone." Except a crazy person like me who falls for strangers. "When you listened to the stories, I'm sure they weren't telling you to rush down the aisle."

"I wanted to, though. I would have been married the day I turned eighteen if I found the right person." He meets my eyes. "Only you weren't around back then."

I'm glad I wasn't. I would have been fifteen. Too young not to get in trouble with him. And from the way he's describing those early days of adulthood, I wouldn't have been alone in my reckless abandon. "It sounds like you dated the entire east coast. In all that time, no one other than Susan ever made you bend a knee?"

"I didn't bend a knee for her." His jaw ticks. "All I did was put a gaudy ring on her finger. Because all she cared about was the price tag attached to it."

"I'm sure that's not true." I rub his arm. He's really upset about this whole quest for a wife thing not working out.

"I heard her say it with my own ears, Mary." His eyes fix on the wall. "And long before I ever bought the ring."

His confession shocks me. He doesn't seem like the type to stand for anything less than absolute devotion. He's only known me a week and is demanding it. I don't mind. I expect it from both of us. "You still wanted to marry her after hearing her talk about you in terms of dollars, not affection?"

"That's what I was hoping to tell you later." He blinks. "Much later."

"You can wait." I'm not telling him I'm seconds from being institutionalized. We can each have a secret.

"By the time I was twenty-six, I was *desperate* to marry. Susan's family and mine have been in the same circles for years, so I decided it would be enough of a legacy to unite our families. It wouldn't be the great love I wanted, but I thought that in time, I'd love her."

"You settled?"

"She's attractive enough." His throat clears. "And cooed at me all the time. So I approached her about us dating. She said she'd been secretly in love with me for a while. That's all it took. I made up my mind then and there to overlook every single thing I didn't like about her." He hesitates. "Remember when I said I'd buy Scarlets to get time with you?" I nod. He sighs. "Well, I can actually afford to. Another thing that traces back through a long line of Bellers is money. I have a lot. As in I could buy that entire mall and never flinch."

I don't flinch now. His head drops. "Mom warned me. Said that Susan only loved my money. But Susan acted like every other female I'd ever met, so I didn't see a reason to end things only to have to go through the dating process all over again, still finding another just like her."

As terrible as it is, he has a point. I see women like Susan in Scarlets all the time. All too willing to use every penny of their husband or boyfriend's spending power. And if the cash runs out, they move on to the next willing bank account. "She loved you, too, though. Right?"

"What Susan loved was the idea of a financially rewarding divorce." He stands, pacing the room. "After dating for a year, the next logical step was to propose. I went to her townhouse unannounced, with the intention of sweeping her away on a romantic weekend that would end at a jewelry store. I let myself in, and got the surprise of my life."

~48~

John descends into the memory of what happened on the day he was committed to proposing to Susan. The pain in his voice brings tears to my eyes. "You don't have to go on."

"I do." He sits beside me. "Because I don't want you led to believe something worse of me than what I'm actually guilty of. I know I was wrong to ever date her and that I got what I deserved for wanting to marry someone for all the wrong reasons. But I would have been good to her. I would have treated her with respect and done everything within my power to make her happy. I just didn't get the chance." His teeth clench. "She was on the phone that day, talking to her friend. I stood behind a wall, listening to her brag about how she'd be a Beller soon and about how much easier it was to marry *her* rich man because I happened to be cute, versus her friend who'd just married a balding, older rich man."

"You're serious?" My arm wraps around his shoulders. "She said that?"

"Worse." His eyes close. "She hoped I'd get put in an early grave, sparing her from the tediousness of a divorce."

My body slides to the floor in front of this man who overheard his girlfriend say she wouldn't even mourn his death. On my knees, I cup his face. "How dare she say something so horrible."

"How dare this world have so many Susans and only one of you." His fingers linger on my cheek. "But the truth is, I deserved every single thing that came from her."

"Don't say that." I press my face to his. "No one deserves such evil."

"I did, Mary." He takes my hands off his face. "I wasn't just dating her. I was sleeping with her. And she wasn't the first."

I'm not promiscuous, but I have no delusions about being rare in that regard. "Pre-marital sex doesn't condemn you to be devalued."

"It condemned me to get her pregnant."

My breath hitches, the thought of *her* carrying his child is devastating. "You and Susan have a child?"

"No, sweetheart." His thumb traces just under my eye. "When she couldn't sweet-talk herself back into my life, she played the pregnancy card, going straight to my mom to break the news because she knew Mom wouldn't stand for her grandchild being born out of wedlock."

"Your mom was going to force you to marry her?"

"I was going to force myself." His shoulders straighten. "I held off for three months even though Susan wanted to rush down the aisle. Then I got smart enough to set up my own doctor's appointment. She never let me go with her before, saying I made her too stressed. But it was my child and I wanted to see an ultrasound."

"There was nothing to see?"

"She confessed in the parking lot." His eyes glint. "I made her go inside to take a pregnancy test so I could see the negative result for myself, then drove her home and told her to keep the gaudy ring I bought her the month before. It didn't mean anything to me."

Relief floods through me. I run my hand over his knee. His muscles tighten. "The hardest part was having to confess to Mom that Susan's lie was possible. I wasn't careful, and I learned the hard way that my parents were right about sex, and about choosing a partner."

My mom didn't live long enough to teach me that. I just inherently knew I only wanted to be with the man who would marry me. That's why I have to watch myself with this one. My flesh wants to give him everything, compliments of my heart. "What's important is you're free of her now. And you won't ever make that mistake with her again." Flashes of her seductive innuendos slam into my brain. "Unless you want to see how truly angry I can get. You can dump me for a lot reasons, John Beller. But not for her."

~49~

John says Susan couldn't fully land him back then and she isn't going to now. That her money-hungry brain is just working overtime again. "Her being at Marsalas last night and my truck being vandalized are not coincidences. After we broke up, she harassed me for a year. Coming at me from every angle and showing up every place I went just to intimidate other women. The relentless devil even threatened to reveal I had an STD. That's when I decided I'd been punished enough. I sent my lawyers after her *and* her family. Being a judge, her dad needed the problem to go away before I did my own revealing. So she left me alone and went off to find another rich man."

"Poor him."

He nods. "A few months ago Mom heard they were getting divorced. Now all of a sudden, she shows up again. But I have no intention of being harassed. Especially with you in the picture. So I called my lawyer this morning. We're getting a restraining order." His hand rests on my shoulder. "It includes you. So she can't harass you either."

"You think she'll come after me?"

"Not physically." He sighs. "But I don't even want her innocently crossing your path in a hallway. Which is what the phone call was about. My lawyer contacted Susan and she cried to her dad, who chose to call my mommy on me." His eyes roll. "They're friends, so Mom didn't appreciate being sidestepped, but I don't care. All I care about is you and what you think of me."

I'm only thinking one thing. "You have a sexually transmitted disease?"

"No!" he howls. "I have test results to prove it. And I haven't slept with anyone since her. I can get tested again, though. If you want."

"I'll take your word for it. Because I don't plan on, um…we shouldn't…you know…for a while."

"I know." His fingers caress my skin. "I'm sorry I didn't wait until marriage the way you did."

"How do you know I waited?"

"Kim told Kevin." He stands when I leap up. "She said you asked a lot of questions before you walked down the aisle. Nervous about what to expect your first time…wondering if it would hurt. She and her mom talked you through it?"

My face is an inferno. And he's making it worse. "Can I ask, did Mike have the honor? I know he was sick right away—"

"Yes!" I turn my back to him. "He managed to get the job done. But giving that part of myself to someone is still just as big of a deal as it was before."

"I was only asking so I'd know. Not because the answer changes anything." His arms slide around my waist. "I'm not the man I used to be. I've grown up. Gained new perspective on what's really important. And I'm hoping you'll let me prove that to you."

"It isn't about what you can prove." I step out of his embrace. "John, I'm not even close to being experienced the way you are. But still I know how hard it is to go without intimacy once you've had a taste. And you've had lots of tastes."

"Doing the math, it's been a lot longer for me than it has for you." He scratches his neck. "Look, I can't lie and say I'm not thinking about sleeping with you. I am. But I'll wait for as long as you want because this time around, I'm making sure I get the whole deal. If you're not it, I'm not sleeping with you. No matter how gorgeous you are."

"Right." I can't help but smile. "You'd deny me if I asked to go to your room right now?"

"I'll never deny you anything." His palm extends to me. "First, I need to know if you can handle *my* baggage."

"I can." I slip my hand into his. "And if I'd known what Susan did to you, I would have dropped my shoulder and barreled right through her last night."

"Your sweet little self actually looks serious about that." He chuckles.

"I am." I place my lips on his. A groan lifts from deep within his chest. My mouth moves over his. Slow. Tempting. He drags us to the floor, barely containing the excitement of me being the one to initiate the contact.

I still my lips. Meet his gaze. He hoists me onto his lap. "Come on, sweetheart. Tell me how big I need to grin to get you to kiss me again." His lips run over my neck. "I dare you."

<h1 style="text-align:center">~50~</h1>

Perched on John's lap, his hands tangled in my hair while our lips move over each other, *I love you* pounds so hard in my chest I'm liable to say it out loud. "I should go." I pull up for air.

"I was hoping you'd stay for dinner." His lips run to my ear, voice low and hoarse. "Will you? Please?"

I breathe him in. Salty musk. He smells as good as he tastes. "Who can say no to you?"

"I hope you can't." His lips trail over my jaw.

"You're in luck." I force myself off his lap. "I'll go freshen up and then help make dinner."

"No, ma'am. Dinner is on me." He points down the hall. "Use my room."

I go the opposite direction. He catches my hand and spins me toward his room. "When you come back, pick out a movie. That is, if you're willing to stay and watch it with me?"

"You know I like to eat. Feed me a good dinner and I'll stay." I release his hand. "I can find my way from here."

"Okay, sweetheart." He leans in. "Feel free to get as close and personal with that headboard as you'd like. Yell if you need any help."

His bathroom mirror shows the many shades of red he's managed to turn me today. But being embarrassed over how embarrassed I am helps squash my overwhelming urge to take him up on his *many* offers. I head back to the kitchen, much less aroused. "What can I do?"

"Sit right here." He lifts me to a stool. "Perfect."

"Hardly." I get back on my feet. "Does the salad need tossing?"

"I've got it." He puts me back on the stool.

I cross my arms. "Are you always like this?"

"Charming and impressive?" He grins. "Yeah, I try to be."

I slide off the stool. "I was referring to you being bossy."

"Bossy or not, today is my treat for you. So sit back down and relax."

He reaches for me. I dodge his hands, opening a cabinet. "I'll set the table since you only said I couldn't help cook."

"Next time, I'll be clearer." He pats the stool. "Sit down or I'm going to have a lot more to apologize for than having sex with some girls."

"Sex with some girls?" I clank plates on the table. "Even if they were only sleeping with you so you'd spend money on them, your eyes were wide open to that fact and you chose to do it anyway. So you're not innocent either. And they're people. Not just *some* girls. Who they are matters just as much as you do."

"That came out completely wrong." He pulls out a chair for me. "Who they are matters to me even now, because the problem was never me being unscrupulous. The problem was me rushing in, hopeful we were building our relationship only to find out later there was no chance of us being right for each other."

"Exactly like we're doing." I pour us both a glass of water, raising mine. "Cheers."

"I'm not toasting to that." He pats the chair. "I'm not rushing into anything this time. I know all about you, and that's the only reason you're here right now."

"Don't judge knowing me on the information you pried out of Kevin."

I set my glass down. He picks his up. "I know a lot. Like, you're O-negative and haven't missed a blood donation appointment in ten years. Now that's something we can toast to. Cheers, sweetheart."

~51~

John justifies his actions by twisting his desire into meaning he has a right to scour through the details of my life in order to act on his feelings. "I understand you have trust issues, John. But I like you. And I came to that conclusion all on my own, without knowing anything other than who you are when you're with me."

"I haven't cooked for a woman in seven years." He uncovers the cake platter that's been sitting on the table. "And not one has ever been in this house. Now, I'm baking cakes from scratch and falling all over myself to get you to stay for dinner so I can serve it to you. All because I took the time to be thorough." He coaxes my pliable body into the waiting chair. "I like you for who you are when you're with me, too. Which is exactly why I pried into your life. I'm infatuated with you. And not only were you never answering a single call or bothering to even send an emoji to let me know you got my texts, Kevin said he saw you and you acted like there was nothing between us."

"When?" My eyes close. "The grocery story. I was preoccupied that day."

"You seem to be preoccupied every day." He sits next to me.

If he's done as much investigating as he says, he should know why I'm preoccupied. "You're bothered by the fact I never initiated contact, but I wasn't doing it to dismiss you. I just wasn't sure if I should reach out or not."

"I wanted you to reach out. Not fade into the mist, never to be heard from again." He runs his fingers over mine, studying the way our hands fit together. "That's not the fate we're doomed for. That's why I checked into you. For us. Because without knowing who you are, we can't be here—you in my house, us spending the day together, being in a relationship. So I'm not apologizing. I'll beg you to forgive me, but I'm not sorry."

He has a lot to lose. And took precautions to ease his own mind. But I don't want his money. Or him to find out what I'm not ready to tell. "How exactly did you *research* me?"

"Google mostly." He shrugs. "I started by trying to find your social media. You don't have any. So then I looked up property records, the kind of stuff you can find online. Then I called Kevin. He told me your blood type. Which is a really weird piece of information for him to have."

"Kim." I sigh. "The two of them have some weird fascinations. Is that chocolate fudge?" I point at the cake that looks exactly like the one we shared on our first date.

"I planned for this day to end with us being exclusive and thought this would be a nice way to celebrate." He smiles. "The chef at the Charleston Club gave me the recipe. I did my best but the frosting is a little off. Which isn't going to matter if you don't forgive me."

Already his unhappiness undoes me. I tighten my fingers on his. "I understand there's a lot at stake for you, so even if your methods are ridiculous, I forgive you. It's been a good day and I appreciate the thoughtfulness of the cake." I also appreciate him not unearthing my crazy. "Do me a favor and let whatever is between us unfold naturally from here on out. Don't rush it."

If he waited to get to know me on his own, *girlfriend* is a title I'd never have. I wouldn't have today. "You're a world-class carpenter, chef and baker, while all I do is sell clothes. You're putting me to shame. Is there anything you can't do?"

"For you? No." He brings my fingers to his lips. "And there isn't anything remotely inadequate about you."

"Just you wait and see."

~52~

I slice into the cake, feeding John a bite. He rubs frosting on my lip, leaning over to suck it off. I start to return the favor. His phone rings. I jump, toppling my chair. "Whoa!" He pulls me to him. "That's the second time you've done that today. Are you okay?"

"I'm fine." I grab a napkin, wiping the smeared frosting off his cheek. And my shirt. "I just didn't expect the ring. Sorry I missed your mouth."

"That's okay." His eyes twinkle. "You've managed to hit it plenty today."

"Go answer your phone."

Sliding his cell off the counter, he waves it in the air. "Show me how to take care of this once and for all. You're the pro when it comes to ignoring calls."

"You're answering this call." I glance at the display. "I have a bone to pick with our pal Kevin."

"So do I. He told me you were a prude."

"Prude?"

"I thought it was a nice quality for a woman to have." He chuckles. "But you've been all over me today. So either he was lying, or you're just that attracted to me. Which is it, sweetheart?"

"Neither." I reach for the phone.

Keeping it away, he swipes the screen with a grin. "Kevin, I'm still not telling you about my date with Mary, but she's here with me. So *that* tells you you're wrong. I'm not getting frozen out. Now explain to me why you went the extra mile to make me think I blew my shot with her?"

~

Kevin apparently had a lot to say about what he considers prudish behavior, and blew up my comment from the supermarket, telling John I didn't think much of him. Big bruise to John's overactive ego. One I'm surprised doesn't kiss and tell. As soon as Kevin asked how far he'd actually gone with me, John nearly jumped through the phone. Kevin's apologized three times now. More importantly, Kim's been trying to reach me all day, telling Kevin to call John as a last resort because even *she* thinks I'm too prudish to be with him again after going out with him last night.

"At least I'm not the only one you ignore." John winks as Kim's voice bleats through the speaker.

"Sorry. I don't mean to ignore any of you." I kiss his cheek. "Especially you."

"Me?" Kim giggles. "I originally called to see how your date with cutie pie went last night. When I couldn't reach you, I panicked! I went by your house and you weren't there either."

"It's my fault." John pulls me onto his lap. "I've monopolized her time today. But I have some good news that will make up for it. As of today, Mary and I are officially a couple."

She screams. We hold our ears until it's over. "I'm eternally in your debt for introducing me to this beautiful lady. We'll all go out for a double date again next week. You two choose the place, just let us know when and where and we'll meet you there. Until then, we're busy." John hangs up. I gasp. He shrugs. "You know as well as I do they weren't going to shut up any time soon. In my opinion, talking to them is a mood killer."

Sadly, he's right. "Turn your phone off. It's better when you're making this imperfect world perfect."

"The world does look pretty darn perfect from where I'm sitting." He feeds me a bite of cake. "And it's going to look even better when we're kicked back in the living room. There's a whole collection of chick-flicks at your disposal."

"I thought you said you never have women here."

"Women I'm romantically interested in." He smiles at my jealous tone. "My mom and sister have an open invitation to come stay with me. And they insist on watching movies that make them run through every tissue box in the house." He points to the tall cabinet in one corner of the living room. "That's why you'll find an impressive tissue collection accompanying the movies."

He isn't lying. Half the cabinet is movies and the other half dainty boxes of tissue. I won't be needing any. With the way he and I are lip-locking today, I choose an action flick. We don't need added romance when we're curled up together in the dark. "Are you comfortable?" He nestles my head against his broad shoulder.

"Very." I yawn, falling asleep before the title appears on the screen.

~53~

John doesn't wake me when the movie ends. By the time my eyes open, the house is dark. Silent. Peaceful. The way I want all my nights to be.

"Did you have a good nap, sweetheart?" He strokes my hair.

"The best one I've ever had." I sit up, feeling the tug of wanting to lie back across him. He's sanctuary. "Sorry for falling asleep on you."

"I liked it." His fingers skim along my shoulder. "It was nice having you resting in my arms."

"It was nice resting in them." I kiss his cheek, not able to help myself. I love the smell of his skin. The feel of his rough jaw under my lips. "We can't keep having sleepovers. I need to leave."

"We can do anything we want. And I'm fond of sleepovers."

"You told me." I pat where I just kissed. "Which is why I'm leaving. My name isn't getting notched on your belt."

"I don't wear a belt." He pulls me back to him. "You're supposed to find it endearing that I told you the truth about my past."

"I do." Endearing enough to hate every woman who touched him before me. Enough to hate myself for not letting them have him. Of all the options in his world, he's placing his bet on me. *I* wouldn't even do that.

"I hate driving after dark." I push away. "I should have left hours ago."

"Hmm." His hands slide behind his head. "The pieces of this plan keep falling right into place. Which side of the bed do you want?"

"Neither." I pop up from the couch.

"Kidding, sweetheart."

He meets me at the door, claiming my hand as we go outside. "I'll drive you home."

"I didn't say I couldn't drive at night." I tug toward my car. "Only that I don't like to."

"Which means I'll drive you." He turns me to him, kissing me and sidestepping toward the garage at the same time.

"Stop! I'm driving myself." I slip away. "I'll text when I get home to let you know I made it."

"I'm driving you." He catches my waist, spinning me around. "But you can still text if it makes you feel better."

Freeing myself from his clutches, I head for my car. "I wish I'd never mentioned not liking to drive at night."

"But you did." He reaches for me. "Now I have to drive you. It wouldn't be gentlemanly not to."

"Enough." I put my hand up. "I'm driving myself, and don't you dare say anything else."

"Mary." His hand drags down his face. "I wanted to pick you up this morning knowing full well I'd be driving you home late if I could talk you into staying for a movie. So please, let me drive you."

"No." I scramble into my car before he can grab me. Or at least before he decides to.

He taps the window. I roll down the glass. "I'm capable of driving myself. Therefore, I am."

"Fine. If it's going to be an issue, you can drive yourself."

"I don't need your permission."

"I didn't say you did." He sighs. "The last thing I want is to push an issue on the first day of our relationship. We've already had enough ups and downs today."

"Mostly ups." I start the engine.

"That's true." He grins. "Why not hop in my truck and have a few more before I kiss you goodnight?"

"Tempting. But no."

"Will it be tempting enough if I drive you home in your car?" He leans in the window. "I'll stay with you until morning, then you can drive me back here."

"Despite your grin, it's still a no." I tap his nose. "Move. I need to get going."

Body fully bent inside the car, his lips fall over mine, surrender on his tongue, a reluctant goodbye in his groan. "When you get home, don't text. Call me. I want to hear your voice."

I put the car in gear. "I'll call in about thirty minutes."

"Make it twenty!" he yells as I drive away. "I'll be waiting! And you better remember how to turn on your phone!"

$$\sim54\sim$$

Turning left out of John's long driveway, my trip begins peacefully enough. There's no traffic on the isolated roadway. I'm free to cruise along at my own pace, counting the many charms of John Beller. *How on earth am I ever going to manage dating him?* Last night pricks the edge of my mind. I have to get my head together. For his sake. One woman has already ruined his life. He doesn't need another one dragging him down.

Headlights emerge behind me. Coming out of nowhere and moving fast. I blink. They're on my bumper, horn blowing. The sedan is in a hurry and there's no place to pull over. I press on the gas, navigating the curvy road as fast as I can without being in danger of toppling into the ravine. Still, their horn is relentless, conjuring its bleating straight from my memory. Shivers race along my spine, fear ripping at my seams. I clutch the wheel. *Stop being paranoid. It's not the same car.* Icy chills dig in. Clawing. My foot jams the gas pedal.

High beams shoot on behind me, blinding me. I swerve, tires bouncing off the pavement, inches from crashing head-on into the mountain. I pull left, tapping my brakes. "There's nowhere to pull over!" I yell into the rearview, the shadowy car clinging to my bumper. "Pass in these curves if that makes you happy!"

I slow to a near crawl, the angry horn rattling what's left of my nerves. I speed back up. The vehicle sticks with me. Inch for inch. A small shoulder appears on the right. I slam the brakes, swerving into the dirt. Dust billows up, not thick enough to hide the lights sliding to a stop behind me. I freeze on the rearview, the car behind me lurching threateningly.

Reacting, my body jerks forward, pushing against the confines of the seatbelt. The engine behind me revs. Their tires screech. Panic pours through my tense muscles but it's too late, my limbs are concrete as the sedan's grill collides with my bumper, filling the air with the twang of twisting metal.

They back up, ramming me again. My heavy foot slips from the brake and falls on the gas, sending dirt and rock flying as my tires spin back onto the road. My old car pushed to its limit, the hunter behind me races forward. I can't get away. The faster I go, the harder they come.

Trees pass by in a blur. I struggle for breath. The pursuer hammers my bumper, spinning my car out of control. I fight the wheel. Going with the skid. Against the skid. "What do you want from me?" I yank right, away from the rocky embankment, tires tearing over pavement while the sedan races left, turning back sharply and clipping my rear corner. I fly into a dead spin.

My front end slams into the guardrail, the momentum launching my car over the railing. The deploying airbags bust my face, the spewing blood flinging around me as I flip end-over-end into the ravine. Jagged rocks rip away metal, tossing my rag-doll body in a coat of shattered glass and crushing steel.

Coming to rest upside down at the end of a long trail of debris, smoke painfully heaves into my lungs. Billows upward. Drowns the echo of my screams. A metallic film coats my tongue. I claw at the strap binding my dangling body to the seat. My hands are numb. I'm bleeding out. "John," I whisper as a shadow crawls toward me, laughing. "John! Help me!"

~55~

I've had plenty of dreams I can't wake up from. None this long. Dark. Void. I hear John's voice in the nothingness, begging me to come back to him. But he's nowhere. I'm nowhere.

"Can you hear me, sweetheart?" The words trail across my mind, a vapor pleading for answers from stone lips. "Please come back to me. I can't lose you."

"She's not waking up." Kim's here. Somewhere.

"She is." John's voice overpowers the darkness. "I know she'll wake up."

I reach for the strength of his sound, feel it press against my flesh. Solid. Unwavering. "... brain swelling ... functioning normally." Fragments of conversations pass by. I reach for the words. They slip away. *John!* I scream into the void. Light rushes back at me, bright and sickening. I gag. Choke. "Sweetheart!" John dips into view. "Mary, you're awake!" Tears roll from his eyes. "You're really awake."

Bile rises to my throat. I cough it out. He rolls me to the side, wiping yellow goo from my mouth. I cling to the sensation of his hands, block the pain with the warmth of his palm on my back. "Call the doctor!" He shoves a tube away from my lips, cleaning the oozing liquid from my chin. "You're okay, sweetheart. I've got you."

I fight the beckoning darkness, forcing his name through lead. "John."

"I'm here, sweetheart." His tears fall harder. "I'm right here."

"We're here, too." Kim materializes behind him. "I've been so scared. Petrified! This has been a nightmare."

"One she's living through." John shoulders her out of my sight. "Can you talk to me, sweetheart? Can you say my name again?"

"She really shouldn't be talking right now." Carlos moves over John's left shoulder, reaching for the IV line. "We need to sedate her and get the feeding tube back in."

Pain permeates my flesh, the people around me rapidly fading. I try to hold my heavy eyelids open. But the nothingness calls. Demands I come back. All that remains is darkness, and phantom voices.

When John's words aren't soft and pleading, they come to me hot and vicious. He yells about sedation. About falling off a cliff. I anchor to his sound, using his voice as a homing beacon. "Anyone who doesn't like my attitude can leave. That includes you, *Doctor.*"

John! I cry out for him.

"Please wake up, sweetheart." I feel the weight of him at my side. Feel the sting of his tears dripping over my cheeks. "Please wake up. Talk to me. Squeeze my hand." His lips press against my dead palm. "Please, sweetheart. End this agony. Let me know you're here."

I can't hold onto him. Images flash before me. Of wreckage. Smoke. Shadows watching. Laughing. *You should have listened.*

~56~

"You're okay." John restrains me, his big hands and steady voice pulling me back. I blink into the present, his face hovering above mine. His tears pummel my body. "Talk to me. Please? I can't live without you. I won't take a single breath if you're not here to share it with me."

I'm helpless to stop his sorrow. I don't feel a tube in my throat but my mouth still won't work. "I need you, sweetheart." He cries. "I *need* you."

"I'll examine her now." Carlos is here. "Step out of the room."

"Be quick about it." John wipes his face. "I've timed all of you and out of every nurse and doctor, you take the longest. I highly doubt that's because you're thorough enough to warrant the extra time." His lips lower to my forehead. "I'll be standing right on the other side of that glass, sweetheart." He points to the inside wall, toward the hospital corridor where a large window with heavy shades to draw for privacy sprawls beside an entrance door. "As soon as he's finished, I'll be right back by your side."

"If you can hear me," Kim pleads, "get up! This boyfriend of yours is losing his mind, and taking the rest of us with him."

"Yeah, Mary." Kevin grins over her shoulder. "Give us all a break and let the big guy know you're still in there."

I want to. But the little I've managed is all there is to give. "You're going to show them how remarkable you are." John opens the door, motioning our friends out the room. The corner of my mouth lifts. He laughs, tears spilling on his way back to my side. "That's my lady, always smiling."

I'm not sure I smiled so much as twitched, but I'd do it again if I could, just so he'd stay beside me. The last thing I remember is his hand pressed to the glass, eyes on me. Carlos drew the curtain. Then, a nightmare woke me. One that threatens to break me.

129

~

The dreams are becoming more vivid. Twisted. And each time I wake in a thrashing fit of fear, John is here, placing a cool cloth on my head and whispering softly. "I've got you, sweetheart. You're okay."

Try as I might, I've yet to speak a full sentence. "Accident." I form the word, push it forward and startle at the sound.

"I know." His eyes study my face. "I'm never letting you drive late again. Or at all. Ever."

I press for more words. Coughing up bile instead of syllables. He rolls my head to the side. "Nurse! She's choking!"

"Accident." I latch onto his hand.

"I know, sweetheart." Tears flood his eyes. Terrified, swollen eyes. "And I'm so sorry."

A nurse with thick blonde curls rushes in. She checks my airway, then gives me an injection. I can't stop her. He doesn't stop her. And the little movement I had flees. Along with the strength to force out words, bile, or even thoughts.

The next time I push my lids open, his eyes are fixed on mine. Memories rush in. "Accident!" I scream, tearing at his shirt. He holds me down, my thrashing body powerless against his grip. "Accident!"

"I know." He lowers over me, his full weight trapping me in the very bed I'm trying to escape. "I'll never be careless with you again, sweetheart."

"I told you this would happen if we lowered the doses." Carlos comes into view, syringe in hand. He lifts the IV line. This time, I even lose the darkness.

~57~

My mind wasn't okay before the accident. Now my body isn't, either. It's a swollen mass of bruises. My left leg is casted from knee to foot. Three ribs are fractured. My nose is busted, bottom lip split open, right eye swollen nearly shut and a multitude of cuts and gashes cover every visible part of me. Not to mention the dark black imprint the seatbelt left. The bruise reaches out of the hospital gown and covers my shoulder, declaring the force with which it saved my life. And these are just the parts I can see. Or feel. There aren't mirrors, so the whole of me is a mystery as I lie inside this private hospital room, consciousness exposing the passage of time.

Two windows overlook the parking lot, the noise of the busy street beyond the parked cars faintly reaching my ears. The next wall is solid, housing charts and medical equipment. The third broken up by the door to the bathroom and the smaller door of a closet. Beside the closet there's a table, and the mobile tray that rolls overtop the bed. It hasn't moved from its spot. Much like John.

"If there has ever been a moment to heal a man's heart, it's this one." His fingers curl around mine, tears falling from his eyes.

"Then why are you crying?" The strength of my voice surprises me.

"I don't know." His smile shakes out more tears. "Because now that you're awake, there's not a thing in this world wrong." He kisses my fingers. "Your hands are so warm with life."

My throat hurts, but mostly my heart breaks over his grief-marred face. "You look really tired. How are you?"

"You're the one in the hospital and you're asking me if *I'm* okay?" His tears chase one another down his face.

"We've been telling him you're going to get him." Kim leans over his shoulder. "He won't eat. Or even go change his clothes. After I went out and bought him a brand-new outfit so I could take his smelly stuff home and wash it."

I reach for her familiar hand, keeping my eyes on him. "Why aren't you eating?"

"I've been waiting for you." He whispers.

"I'm not hungry." I swallow spit down my dry throat. Since spending more time awake, and ditching the feeding tube, my mind is clearing. Through the haze, I remember what happened. All of it. And now that my head and mouth are working in unison, I have to tell John.

Halfway through my account, Carlos enters the room, warning the trauma of the accident mixed with the medication I've been on could have me recounting a warped dream instead of actual events. It doesn't feel like a dream, but my mind *has* been powerfully hallucinogenic in the past. "Maybe I did make it up."

"I'll find the truth." John kisses my forehead, phone ripping out of his pocket. "I'll be right back, sweetheart."

"I'll help." Kevin follows him into the hall. "If someone wrecked her…" The door closes.

"You remember how things were before." Kim takes my hand. Eyeing me in that *you poor delusional thing* way. "And you weren't on medication then."

"I know." I probably did imagine it. "Someone wrecking me on purpose doesn't make much sense."

"You've never had an enemy in your life." She smiles. "Except, I was getting ready to be. You scared me to death. Don't ever do this to me again!"

"She's right." Carlos pats her shoulder. "You've had all of us in a frenzy."

My attention floats to the window where John watches, eyes glued to me as his lips give words to whoever he's on the phone with. "I have a feeling he's the one causing the frenzy. When can I get out of here, Carlos? It's the only way to make him stop."

~58~

Three hours after telling John about the car hitting me, he confirms my story is true. He's consulted with the police, the towing company that has what's left of my car, and anyone and everyone else he thought could help. There are mismatched paint chips on my crumpled bumper, and another review of skid marks near the scene confirms the likelihood of the skid being set in motion by a hit. Now he's trying to figure out if it was random or targeted.

"Does she have any enemies that you're aware of?" the elder of two detectives, Detective Beckley, asks John. He's meeting with them in the hallway, refusing to let them enter my room. Ever since evidence started piling up, he's acted like I'm glass and the rest of the world is a hammer.

Glancing at me through the slightly ajar door, he shakes his head. "She doesn't have any enemies that I'm aware of. But that doesn't matter. Work on this case day and night until you find whoever is responsible. And when you do, bring them to me."

Beckley nods. His partner, Detective Summers, takes a different stance. "We arrest people. We don't drag them off at anyone's beck and call. And we need to talk to her. Step aside."

"You *will* bring the piece of dirt to me." John's body blocks the door. "Just like you *will* do your job with the information you've been given. She isn't spending the brief moments she's awake reliving every detail of that night just because you're lazy."

"We can do our job without bothering her." Beckley steps in front of his too-young-to-know-better partner. "No need for us to question her today. Just keep passing along any new information she happens to remember."

"We don't need to be told her words in third person." Summers asserts. "We owe it to that woman in there to do our best, and that starts with talking to *her.*"

"We've got enough to get started," Beckley warns.

"What you have," John slides him aside, stepping into Summers, "is the full support of the governor. He assured me no expense will be spared in this investigation. And already confirmed he called you to say as much. He also led me to believe you two are the best. Prove it."

"Oh, I'll prove it." Summers stands straighter. Tall, but still not enough to be even with John. "What's the real reason you don't want her questioned?"

"She's tired." Beckley yanks on his sleeve, dragging him away with a nasty bark in his ear.

John watches them leave, coming back to me once they disappear around the corner. "That was terrible," I groan.

"Did you want to talk to them?" He sits beside me.

"No."

"I had a feeling you didn't." His touch on my wrist is light. "You've been through enough today."

"It's really true? There was another car? I didn't imagine it?"

"You didn't imagine it." His hand slides over mine. "I'm not sure if that's good or not."

"Is it bad if I say I'm relieved it wasn't a dream?" Tears sting my swollen lids. "To experience something so real, and then it just be my imagination…"

"It's bad either way." He wipes the tears. "With or without the other car, you got hurt. And there's nothing good about that."

~59~

I don't want to talk to the police, not only because of the night of the accident, but because I'm afraid I'll have to tell them about all the terrible nights that came before. So however atrocious he's being, John can keep them at bay. When I get out of the hospital, I'll talk to them. On my own. Without him or anyone else around. And I *am* getting out of here. I don't care what Carlos said. I don't need around-the-clock care any more than I need to stay sedated in this hospital bed.

"I'm going home before this place mutinies and has you locked up." I push my elbows into the bed and stare at John. "You ruffled those detectives enough I'm sure they'd happily drag you away."

"There you go again…" He eases the pain of me getting up by taking my weight on him. "Worrying about me when there isn't a thing in this world for you to worry about other than getting better. No one is going to touch me. No matter how much they want to."

"They only want to because someone simply breathing too heavy sets you off. You nearly tossed George out on his ear earlier. And all he did was say hello."

A growl rumbles through him. "I'm sure I'll appreciate meeting Kim's family once you're recovered enough to have company. But I don't think you're up for it yet, and Kim knew that before she let them barge in here."

"Shouldn't you ask me what I'm up for?"

"Yes." He swallows. "But you just woke up. And I've barely had a chance to talk to you. About anything."

The whole day has been chaotic. "Just as long as you didn't kick him out because you're jealous. Considering who I'm dating, you can see he isn't my type. Plus, he's married."

135

"And yet the potbelly still walked right in here and took my spot, holding your hand the way I would have been had I not been out in the hall on the phone."

"Be nice." He does have a potbelly. "He didn't know there were assigned seats."

"I *was* being nice." Fury tinges his brow. "I was even going to let him slide. Then I read the card on the flowers he brought and that pretty much sealed his fate. It was either kick him out or knock him out. I figured one would get me in more trouble with you than the other."

If he hit George, our relationship would be over. "The flowers were a concerted gift from the whole family, I'm sure he didn't write the card."

John fluffs my pillow. "Are you mad I asked them to leave?"

"You didn't ask. You ordered." He shrugs. I sigh. "I'm not mad." It was awkward having them fuss over me. "I'd rather just get through this and see them later. After I'm home."

He smiles. "Which is why I offered to host a little get-together once you're up for it."

A get-together Kim jumped all over. The chance to plan a party on his dime. "By now, Kim realizes the depth of your wealth. Whatever she comes up with is going to be extravagant. You'll have to give her limits or rescind the offer to let her plan it altogether."

"The only limit is for her to make sure it's something you'll like, not what she wants. I've made that very clear." He kisses each and every one of my fingers, savoring them. "If I see her going in the wrong direction, I'll call my sister. Sheila's good at throwing parties."

"How about you just don't throw one? There's no need to let anyone spend your money when the only thing I want is what money can't buy. I want to go home. Now."

"Which is why I called my doctor earlier." His kiss-capade continues. "He'll be here soon. Then we'll see about moving you out of here." His phone vibrates against the tray table. "That's my sister. I'll tell her to prepare, because once you're feeling better, we *are* going to celebrate. It's not every day we escape the world ending."

~60~

My stomach is growling loud enough to let everyone within a ten-block radius know it's ready for food. John's ecstatic. Hunger is another sign I'm recovering, my body regaining normal functions. I could do without my nervous system, though. Pain permeates every part of me. The more medication flushing from my system, the more I feel the agony.

"I need to get out of this bed." Pain isn't the only thing more acute. The nightmares are more real.

"I'll move you up a little." John's hands slide under my armpits, cupping the side of my body. Gently. Still, the pain is intense. "Tell me if this hurts." He slides my torso up to sitting. It's excruciating.

I point to the small container on the table across the room. "Is that applesauce?"

"Yep." He grabs it. I reach for it. He keeps it out of range, popping off the tinfoil top. "Here you go." He spoons a bite of the nearly liquid sauce into my mouth. The sweetness feels good against my tongue.

"This is the best applesauce ever."

"You haven't had solid food in far too long." He chuckles. "We'll get that fixed up real soon. Only, no chocolate cake until your stomach is adjusted. Then I'll feed you all the cake you want."

"My stomach will adjust once the medication stops making me sick." I also need to be awake. Aware. Able to control any nightmares that follow me into wakefulness. "I'm tired of sleeping all the time. You did tell the nurses I said no more meds, right? I don't want them slipping something into my food."

"I told them to check with me before each dose." He shifts. "Because you do need some of the medication. Just not the ones that knock you into a coma."

137

"Hi." I greet Carlos' perfect timing. "I'm feeling much better. Enough that John and I were just talking about how I don't need *any* more medication."

He frowns. "I'm glad you're feeling better, but you still need all the medication I've been prescribing. Which is why I'm here."

"You can examine her." John stretches over my friend. "But, like your nurses, you will *not* administer anything without my approval."

"You mean the medication she's in dire need of?"

"Medication I've been told she doesn't need. Which is why I'm making decisions for her on a per dose basis."

"I didn't realize you had a medical degree," Carlos snarks. "The medical power-of-attorney role you forced your way into isn't one, in case you're confused."

"Seeing how she's just fine *not* being forced into a medical coma, I'd say I don't need a medical degree," John bites. "This clearly isn't brain surgery."

"What you see on the outside could be completely different than what's happening inside her." Carlos folds his hands. "If the wrong thing is happening in there, it may very well turn into brain surgery."

"Which is why my family doctor is on his way to evaluate her."

"Family doctor?" Carlos scoffs. "You think a general practice doctor knows better than me? Better than the team of doctors here in the hospital working on her care?"

"That's exactly what I think." John closes distance between them. "An opinion I came to on the basis of observation and patient results."

"Enough!" I'm the one who should be making the decisions. "The medication puts me in a fog and has me missing huge chunks of time. That's why I'm not taking a drop of anything anymore. And I don't care what either of you says about it."

"Fine." Carlos turns back to the door. "But in a little while, when you're curled up in pain crying your eyes out, don't blame me."

~61~

Wanting me awake, John sent my medical records to his family's doctor and took Dr. Mansfield's absentee opinion over everyone else's, ordering the hospital to lower my doses of medication. As much as I hate the upheaval, I hate being stuck in a hospital bed more. And I *really* hate John asking me to stop calling Dr. Redmond by his first name.

"Where's Kim? I want to be alone with her. And alone means *alone*. You have to leave."

"Not on your life."

"This *is* my life." I snap. "I make my own choices. And I choose to be alone." His eyes glass over, hurt dripping from every pore. I take a breath. "I'm sorry. I appreciate everything you're doing but I need time to process what's happening. And you haven't left my side. You need to go get some food. And sleep."

"I don't need anything outside of what I have right here in this room." John's lips fall to my hand. "If you want to talk to Kim, go ahead. She's out in the waiting room. I'll call her in and stay quiet the whole time. But I'm not going anywhere."

"I want her to give me a sponge bath."

"That changes things." A slow grin creeps over his lips. "I know where there's a big tub calling your name."

Even in this situation, he manages to make me blush ten shades of crimson. He chuckles, sending Kim a text. "One day I'll have you wrapped in bubbles." His lips sweep across my forehead. "Kim's on her way and I'll go when she gets here. Do you need anything before I leave?"

"Only for you to take your exhausted self home. Not into the hall where you're going to stare at my window the whole time. But home. As in your house."

139

"As sweet as it is that you're worried about me, I'm not going anywhere." He winks as Kim opens the door. "As soon as she's finished I'll be right back here, sweetheart."

He steps outside and takes his place at the window. I meet his gaze until Kim closes the curtain. "It's impossible to reason with him."

"You don't have to tell me." She sighs. "I've been living on his unreasonable side. I've tried to get on his good side by being his invaluable resource on all things Mary, but I don't know if he has a good side right now."

"He does." I've seen it. "It's just hidden behind how much he's worried about me."

"Well, I told him what you like and what he's doing that you won't." She frowns. "The fact that he completely ignores me isn't my fault. Remember that. Because the man has a whole slew of surprises for you and none of it was my idea. I'm just doing what I'm told."

"Like what?"

She shakes her head. "I've been advised to keep my mouth shut. As hard as that is, I'm not crossing the beast."

The man I know isn't mean. Naturally intimidating. But that isn't his fault. "I'll do this." I take the sponge from her and point to his chair. "You're just as tired as he is, and that's part of the problem. So just sit down and rest."

"Nope." She plucks the sponge from my fingers. "He'd flat out have a coronary if he knew I let you wiggle a pinky. No way I'm letting you wash yourself."

"He's on edge, but normally he's gentle."

"I've seen the sweet side of him." She smiles. "He shows it to my best friend. So even if he's torturing the rest of humanity, anyone who's good to you has my vote. It doesn't hurt he's so easy on the eyes, either. When he's off on a rant, I just focus on his body and wait for the noise to stop."

~62~

Kim isn't wrong about how easy it is to get lost in John's looks. I listen to what he has to say, but most of the time I think about what else he can do with those lips. Those hands.

"Thanks for the sponging." I focus on her instead of my daydream. She's not as tired as John, but she's still worn out. "It's amazing how water and a little soap almost makes a person feel normal again."

"I was already going by your house for some clothes but your hotheaded hottie made me bring one of every type of outfit you own." She tugs a duffle bag out of the closet. "Just in case you want to throw on a dress and some high heels while you're here."

"You'd better not have heels in that bag."

"I don't." She laughs. "But he did tell me to bring everything. He's scared to death you'll want something and it won't be here." She takes out a nightshirt. "Do you think we can manage getting you into this?"

"To get rid of this hospital gown, we can manage anything."

Every movement is excruciating, but forgotten once the shirt is comfortably resting against my flesh. If only breathing wasn't painful. "Got any pants in that bag? I'm ready to go home."

"Yeah, right," she scoffs. "Even if you were in the condition to go somewhere, bossy-butt isn't going to let you get out of this bed."

"Is he still outside?" I feel guilty for wanting him to be.

She rolls her eyes. "I'm not even going to dignify that with an answer when you know good and well he's standing out there with his nose pressed to the glass."

"Stop making me laugh." I latch onto my aching ribs.

Her eyes cloud over. "I know you're in a lot of pain. Even if you would rather bite your tongue off than tell me."

"I can live with the pain, but not with staying here." I clasp her hand. "How long have I been in the hospital?" She looks away. "Kim, how long?"

"I don't know." She shrugs. "A couple of weeks."

"Two weeks!"

Squealing, the words rip coughs from my throat. John flies into the room, door crashing off the wall and narrowly missing Kevin on the rebound. "What did you do?" Green eyes bore into her.

"Nothing." She grabs water. He snatches it from her, dropping the cool liquid into my mouth via a straw.

I clutch his hand. "I've been here for two weeks?"

"Is that what you're upset over?" He slumps. "Sweetheart, you scared me to death. I don't like it when you cough that way."

"No one does." Kevin leans on the bedrail. "And it's been closer to—"

"Kevin!" John and Kim both yell.

"She's going to find out anyway." He shrugs. "Heck, if I was in a coma for nearly a month, I'd want to know."

I can't feel my heartbeat. "I've been in a coma for a month."

"A little under three weeks." John cradles my head against him. "And the time doesn't really matter. You're getting better every single day. It won't be long now and I'll take you home."

"Now." I wrap a fist in his shirt. "Take me home, now."

~63~

Fear ticks inside me. My eyes close and nightmares spring to life. I have to get out of this hospital before the bomb goes off. Before John sees me lose my weakening grasp on reality.

"I can do at home what I'm doing here."

"I want you discharged, too." He gives me a sip of water. "But not at the sacrifice of your health. We'll make a decision about moving you soon. Okay?"

"Not okay." I glance at my casted leg. "This is costing me a fortune."

"Shh," he urges. "There's nothing for you to worry about. Just rest and get better."

"I am better. And you're not paying my medical expenses." I read his mind, looking around him to Kim. "Is that part of the advice he didn't listen to?" She won't chime in. "I take your silence as a yes."

"Sweetheart, of course I paid your medical bill."

"Paid?" He's already done it. "I'll pay you back. And the hospital *will* send all future billing to me."

"You're lying in this bed, battered and bruised, because of me." His voice lowers. "I understand you're prideful, and when you're up to it we'll talk about it, but I'm taking care of the medical bills. No amount of discussion is changing that."

This is part of the reason I'm not taking medication. My head needs to be clear. So I can control what's happening around me. What's happening *because* of me. As it stands, all it takes to coax my eyes closed is the steady rhythm of his fingers gliding through my hair. "You're not paying my debt." I yawn, drifting away without giving my brain permission. And like every other time I've fallen asleep, I wake up screaming.

The only bright spot is John never pressing to know what terrors the dream world offers up. He's also getting better at figuring out when a nightmare is setting in, waking me up before the terror gets too far. I only wish I could make them stop altogether, before I scar him for life.

"I still feel groggy," I tell the sunny-faced nurse checking my vitals. "Please take the IV out." I'm afraid they're sneaking doses of sleep medication in. She looks at John. He shakes his head. "You don't need his approval. I want it out."

"Sweetheart, it needs to stay in place." He traces a thumb over my wrist. "Just in case."

"Just in case what?"

"Just in case the pain you're in gets too unbearable," she answers for him.

"A little pain never killed anyone," I counter. "It's better to feel it so I know my limits than be numb and overdo it."

He leans back, studying me. A slow grin creeps over his face. "You can't argue with that logic."

"I believe you could argue with anything," the woman snaps.

"I can." He winks at me. "But I'm not going to."

"Have you been paying attention to the screaming?" Her hands land on her hips. "The writhing in pain?"

"She's right, sweetheart." He sobers. "You're not resting and we all know you're in pain. There's no harm in having a little something." He nods to her. "Go ahead. Just make it a low dose."

"No!" I jerk free of his grip. "I'll rip this IV out myself and walk straight out that door if either of you dare put one drop of anything in that line." I glare at him. "You said your doctor was coming and then I could leave. So get him here. Now!"

<h1 style="text-align:center">~64~</h1>

John doesn't understand my need for vigilance. Not when he thinks his mere presence keeps all bad things away. Despite my protests, he still wants the nurse to give me medication.

"Look, if you and the nurses don't want to hear me scream, put me in a cab and send me home. This is *my* body. No one can force drugs on me."

"I want to respect your wishes, but there are limits to what I'll let you endure. I'm not going to sit here and watch you suffer."

"You don't have to sit here at all."

"I do." He presses into my hand. "So stop acting like I can stick you in a cab and send you on your way when I wouldn't even do that the first night we met."

"You two are as stubborn as mules," the nurse huffs. "Let me know who wins the battle, because I'm supposed to at least be giving her aspirin right now."

I'm winning. Because it's *my* body. "If I absolutely can't bear it, I'll ask for medication."

"Okay." He nods to the nurse. "Take the IV out."

"Well done." A tall, thin man with a salt-and-pepper beard claps from the doorway. "I don't have privileges in this hospital so I couldn't have helped you." His twinkling blue eyes smile at John.

"She'll have you wrapped around her finger in two seconds flat." John gets up and clasps his hand. "Same as me."

"You're probably right." He sighs, nodding to the nurse, who ignores him on her way out. "Sorry I couldn't get here sooner. One of my elderly patients contracted pneumonia."

"Mom told me." John comes back and rests his lips on my forehead. "This is Dr. Mansfield, sweetheart. Since you're well enough to argue with me, I'm going to let him examine you. Then I'll be right back by your side."

Mansfield makes quick work of his job. Examining me and reviewing my records once more before giving his recommendations to an unhappy John. The bulk of their conversation is kept from me, the men conferencing in the hall outside my room. With the door closed. All I know is since Dr. Mansfield can't order tests here, John demanded them. I've been thoroughly probed and prodded.

"When are the results going to be ready?" A new day has dawned since Mansfield was here.

"Soon." John's teeth clench.

"Do you think Carlos is mad at me for letting your doctor in here?"

"Who cares?"

"I do."

"You shouldn't," he snaps. "You never needed the high doses of medication the idiot prescribed. Dr. Mansfield said most of your injuries are superficial. And if the tests confirm the worst of them aren't as bad as we thought, you don't have to stay in the hospital anymore."

"I wasn't going to anyway."

"So you've said." His emeralds study me. "The one and only wish you've asked of me is about to be granted. So start thinking of what you want next. I need to spoil you, sweetheart."

"Home is all I want." I close my eyes. "And you partly making that happen is the only reason I'm not mad over how mean you're being to Carlos."

He leans over me. "And how absolutely wonderful you are is the only reason I'm not mad at you for continuing to use his first name after I specifically asked you not to."

Making him worry to the point he's turning this hospital into a war zone isn't very *wonderful.* "Just do me a favor and remember *Carlos* had reasons for what he did."

His eyes harden. "What I'll remember is you being willing to give him reasons."

"Fine by me." I yawn. "Just as long as I still get to go home."

~65~

While we wait for my discharge papers, John orders chicken soup from a local bistro. To appease me, he takes bites in between the spoonfuls he feeds me. I feel better having something solid on my stomach, and better having seen him eat. Something I haven't witnessed since waking in this sterile room.

"I feel bad for taking Dr. Mansfield's advice over Carlos'. Especially after all he's done for me in the past."

"You're entitled to a second opinion. He has to respect that." He lifts the spoon to my mouth. "Besides, he should be in here begging for your forgiveness instead of you worrying about his feelings."

"He's probably scared to come in here again." I eye him. "And Dr. Mansfield wasn't here from the beginning. Him thinking Carlos got my diagnosis wrong is only an opinion formed after the fact."

The vein in John's neck bulges. "You're stretching to give him an out. Because he's a friend? Kim said he's in Scarlets all the time, talking to you."

"Mostly he's there to buy clothes for his girlfriend. Just last week— Oh, no! Not last week. John! I need to call the store. I have to go back to work!"

"Shh." One big arm stops my escape while the other reaches for the water, bringing the cup to my lips. "I sent a note with Kim to Pam and gave my number so if any higher-ups need to talk to me, they can call me directly." His lips brush my knuckles. "You're not losing your job. I've taken care of everything. So just relax and get your beautiful self all healed up. The little cuts and dings are already looking better. And the swelling has gone down a lot."

"What I can see looks horrible, and I imagine the rest is worse. Which is why you and these nurses should be running far, far away."

"Far enough away to let you manage getting out of this bed?" He grins. "I'm on to you, sweetheart. I'll have none of this trying to escape. You're not getting out of my sight."

It was worth a shot. "Why don't you lie down?" I pat a spot next to me on my bed. "I'm getting tired again and we could both use a nap."

"I'd love to lie next to you. But there's not enough room and I don't want to hurt you."

"I don't think it's possible for you to hurt me any more than I already am." I sigh. "I *do* think it's possible you'll hurt other people over me."

"Without hesitation."

"There will never be a time when someone deserves to be hurt over me. Please tell me you know that."

"The world is dark without you, Mary." He cradles my hand, resting his head by my side. "Get some sleep, sweetheart. I'll be right here when you wake up."

The sound of his breathing slowly changes. For once in this long string of days, he's sleeping. "God, let him rest," I whisper. "He needs to rest before he kills someone."

~

Barely dozing while John sleeps, my hand delicately strokes his hair. This moment is peaceful. Warm. The kind of moment I'd like to stay in. If we were home. Mine or his.

"Mmm, that feels nice." He moves against my fingers.

"Sorry." I was keeping myself awake so I didn't bother him with another nightmare. "I didn't mean to wake you."

"If you're awake, I want to be." He uncurls from where he was folded over the bed, head tucked close to my side. "But awake or not, you can touch me anytime you want." I blush. He chuckles. "I'd like to know what goes on in that head of yours because I didn't say anything blush-worthy just now. Unless you're thinking of touching—"

"John!" I cough.

He leaps to his feet, grabbing water. "I'll stop teasing. Until you're able to handle it."

I reach for the cup. "What I can handle is you bringing the table over here where I can get the water myself."

"I'll keep the water where it is." He kisses my forehead, his new thing.

"I'm not your responsibility."

"You've been my responsibility since you agreed to be my girlfriend." He sits back down, head heavy. "And I've thought every day since about how one little decision could have changed everything. I should have driven you home that night."

"You tried. I wouldn't let you. And now we're in this mess."

"You saying no that night didn't matter." He sets the water aside. "Me doing what I knew in my heart was right mattered. And I didn't. I let you drive away. That's why you're here."

"You didn't *let* me do anything. I made a choice. Now I'm facing the consequences of that choice. Just like I'm going to face the consequences of leaving here." I sit up. "I'm going home. Right now."

~66~

Three hours ago I was told I'd be discharged within the hour. John insists the paperwork is being done but something feels off in his body language. He's still as charming and in control as ever, but uneasiness pulses every time he checks his cell.

"Call the nurse." I sit up, making him drop the phone in an attempt to restrain me. "The nurse can help me dress, since Kim disappeared. Does she even know I'm being discharged?"

"She knows." He hits the call button for the nurse.

"You rang?" The blonde hurries in, saluting. "Nurse Billie at your service."

"Her clothes are in there." He nods to the closet, ignoring the mockery. "Get her dressed and then pack up her room."

"Please." I squeeze his hand. "And thank you."

Clenching his jaw, he clears his throat. "Nurse Billie, please help this very special lady of mine get dressed. Then please pack her things. Thank you."

"What do you know?" She smiles. "Someone does have control over him."

"Don't tell her she wields the power." He leans close to my lips. "She'll never forgive herself."

"Very funny. Now go press your nose to the glass so I can get presentable before we leave."

"Yes, sweetheart." His lips dart to my forehead. "I'll be right outside."

Billie pulls the curtain closed on him with a smile. "Maybe I wouldn't mind how bossy he is if he kissed me the way he kisses you."

"Trust me…" My eyes close in reverence. "If he kissed you, you wouldn't mind a thing. Which is why he's the one who holds the power. And why I need to get out of here."

While Billie dressed me in sweatpants and a t-shirt, she filled me in on how many nurses tried to console John. Most with a phone number slipped into his pocket. That's when they first learned he isn't a tolerant man. I don't blame him. If someone hit on me while I was by Mike's bedside, I would have reacted the same.

I only wish John wasn't making such a fuss over me. Even the way he insisted on brushing my hair, his hands working tenderly over my scalp, trying to do the impossible task of missing every bump and cut, was too much. If I told him he banged the gash on my right side, he would have ordered himself strung up by his toenails.

"This is a little extravagant for a ride home." His Viper is parked at the hospital's back entrance.

"It's easier to get you in this than the truck." He gently lifts me from the wheelchair and into his arms. But no matter how delicately he places me in the passenger seat, it's painful.

"Extravagance suits you." He slides the seatbelt into place, lips shifting to land on mine for the first time since I've been awake. "Did that hurt?"

The cut on my lip throbs. "When you kiss me, nothing hurts."

"Good." His lips come back to mine. "I'll use this tactic a lot."

He circles the car while I pray the cut on my lip heals fast. "I was planning on taking you out for a ride in this car after our last date." He drops behind the wheel. "Today won't be remotely close to what I had in mind, but it still feels good to have you riding shotgun."

"That's because it feels good to be out of the hospital." And smells good, too. "I've been meaning to ask, do you wear cologne?"

"Not usually." He shifts the car into gear. "Why? Do I smell?"

I nod. "In a really good way. So bottle yourself up. You'll make a fortune."

"I have my fortune." His hand slides to my knee. "Take a little nap, treasure. It won't be a long drive, but I'm going to go slow to make sure I don't bounce you around."

I'd rather him go fast. "Turn here. I'll show you a shortcut." He drives past the right-hand turn. "Go back. That way is a lot faster. And hardly bumpy at all," I tease.

"No," slithers out of him. And up my spine.

"No?" I swallow, hairs on my neck pricking. "John? What's wrong with you?"

His jaw sets, eyes focusing straight ahead. "I really didn't want to do this right now." He picks up speed, passing the main highway that leads to my neighborhood.

"Didn't want to do what? Stop! You're going the wrong way."

"You're not leaving me any options." He shifts through gears, racing now.

"What options?" I grab my aching ribs. "Slow down!"

"This would go a lot better if you'd just close your eyes."

"I'm not closing my eyes. And you're not going any farther until you tell me what's going on!"

He doesn't let up on the speed. Or change direction. "Where are you taking me?" I whisper. "John, I want to go home."

~67~

Miles pass under John's tires. Tense stretches of road whizzing by in a blur. But one scene I remember. A curvy patch of highway that leads to his house. Now that we're here, he confesses to the destination. Where he expects me to stay. Not for an hour, an afternoon, or even an overnight visit. Permanently. Until I'm one hundred percent recovered.

He thinks his only mistake was underestimating how alert I'd be. He thought I'd sleep through this drive. "Stop the car!" I shout. "Let me out. I'm going home. *My* home."

"The only way I'm stopping this car is to kiss you again." He glances my way. "I'm guessing doing that right now will get me slapped. So, relax. We're almost there."

"Stop telling me to relax!" I'm anything but. "When we get to your house, I'm taking a cab back to mine."

"That's not happening." He smirks. "But when we get home, we'll sit down and have a nice conversation about why I made this decision."

"You made this decision because you think you have the right to control everyone." I cross my arms, holding ribs that ache more with each protest. "You aren't controlling me."

"This isn't about control."

"Yes, it is!"

The splitting pain of my words falls on deaf ears. He navigates his driveway. Kim's car is parked where mine was parked the day of the accident. "I should have known she'd have something to do with this."

"Don't blame her." He parks and opens his door, running around to open mine. "You're here because I want you here."

Kim prances out of his house, meeting him at my door. "You look so much better already!"

"You do." Kevin agrees, rushing in behind her.

"I'm sure I would look a lot better in my *own* house."

"I knew you'd fight us on this." Her hands plant on her hips. "Which is why I didn't tell you. But you're here now, so quit whining about it!"

"Don't snap at her." John warns. "She has a right to be upset."

"Don't snap at *her* when you're the one who caused this."

He takes the rebuke, kneeling with outstretched arms. "May I?"

My hand flies to my heart. "You're actually asking me before you do something?"

"This isn't about choices." His hands slide into place under me. "It's about doing what's best for you."

"What's best for me is to be in my own home, like I've been saying this whole time."

"I disagree." He cradles me against him. "I don't say that lightly, I know a disagreement like this could be devastating for us. But I learned the hard way to do what feels right in my heart. Whether you like it or not."

"Spoken like a true egomaniac."

"Ouch." He walks on, taking me inside the house. "You actually can get angry. And mean."

And remorseful. "I'm sorry, but you can't make me stay here."

"Sweetheart." His sigh is deep. "There are very few things I can't do. Making you stay here isn't on that very short list. So, make yourself at home."

~68~

John carries me straight to his bed, ignoring my pleas for him to stop. Kim and Kevin are on his side, and therefore not willing to give me their phones. "You two are my friends. You shouldn't be standing by letting this happen. I don't want to be here."

They look away as John kneels beside the bed, moving a blanket over me. "Are you comfortable?"

I push it off. "Are you listening to me?"

"Every word." He picks up the blanket. "Are you in pain?"

"No." I lie.

"Do you need something to eat or drink?"

"I *need* to go home."

Kim tugs his arm, fingers lingering too long on his bicep. "Can I have a minute alone with her?"

"You can have twenty. When you're driving me home." Which also conveniently gets her hands off him.

"She can have five minutes." He straightens. "I'll be right outside, sweetheart." His lips press against my forehead. "Don't you dare get out of this bed."

I would tell him I'll dare do whatever I please but that will only keep him from going out the door, Kevin in tow. I wait for his lingering eyes to disappear before I grab my tormenting ribs. "Why is he doing this? And why are you in on it?"

"Look around." She claps her hands together. "He's been barking orders at me for days. Wanting to make sure everything is perfect for his *dear, sweet Mary.* And all because he cares for you. That's why he's doing this. He's head over heels! And…" She pauses. "He feels responsible."

"Don't be ridiculous." I pull myself up to rest on the headboard. "The fault belongs to whoever was driving the other car."

155

"Mary." She sits next to me. "John is the one who found you. He literally clawed you out of the wreckage with his bare hands."

My heart stops. He can't be the man in the smoke. I stare at the door. "He wasn't there. He wouldn't laugh."

"Of course not." Tears fill her eyes. "He was devastated. He said you were supposed to call him that night and when you didn't, he decided to drive to your house. He saw the fire from the road and…" Water trickles over her cheeks. "I saw what you looked like afterward. I can't imagine what he saw. Or what he felt when he realized it was you. By the time we got to the hospital, he was covered in your blood and on his knees, begging God and everyone else to save you. Between my own grief and what came out of him…" Her voice breaks.

"I'm okay now." I take her in my arms. "I'm sorry I turned everyone's lives upside down."

"You have no idea how hard those first days in the hospital were." She chokes on a sob. "It was scary for all of us. But John, he was on a whole different level."

It's clear he cares for me. But that's what I'm worried about. I wipe her face. "He and I had a good thing going before all this happened. Which is why I need to go home. This drama will kill every bit of his affection for me."

"You can't kill love." She sniffs. "And if that man doesn't have the bug, there's never been a man on earth bitten by it. John Beller is a goner." She smiles. "And all because you listened to me."

~69~

I love John. I've given up trying to deny it. But the emotion he feels for me is guilt. And it's driving him insane. Something I know a lot about.

Looking around his room, the work he's had Kim doing leaps out. Everywhere, there's something of mine. As if I'm in my own bedroom. Even one of my favorite blankets is draped across a chair and another lies at my feet. The one I threw off me earlier. "You brought a lot of my things here."

"He wanted you to be as comfortable here as you are at home." She sighs. "I've been to your house and every store within a fifty-mile radius twenty times to make sure anything you could ever want is *at your disposal.*"

"It looks it." I can imagine him giving that exact order.

She follows my gaze and bounces across the room to the sprawling flower arrangement, the most beautiful display I've ever seen. "I told you the man is smitten!" She plucks the card from the petals.

"I don't know how he could be."

"I know how." She winks, handing me the scarlet envelope with gold threads.

I want to tell her how I feel. That I have to leave before my crazy shows. But I can't. "I made a big mistake with him, Kim."

"You slept with him!"

"No." I flush.

"Why not?" She taps the card. "I could use more than this to spark my fantasy. Do the deed and give me the details!"

Had it not been for the accident, I was on the verge. And, of course, she already read the card. "I love him. I know it's soon, but I care about him *so* much."

"When you woke up saying his name, I thought you might love him." She sits beside me. "That's why I went along with his plan to move you in here. Well, that and the fact that he didn't really ask." She taps the card. "Don't take my word on how he feels about you. See what the man himself has to say."

My dearest Mary,

You have captured my heart. And I pray with every ounce of it that you recover fully, and quickly.

Love, John.

"See?" She beams.

"I hope to one day be that lucky." I hold the card to my heart, knowing it's just a polite way to end a note.

"You're already lucky." She laughs. "But you might want to lay off calling him an egomaniac."

"I can't believe I said that."

"At least it's true." She grins. "I can think of a few more adjectives for his royal hotness."

"I'd advise against it."

She's never seen me jealous, so I hope she doesn't recognize the protective tone. "Tell him to come back. I need to apologize."

"Humph." She cups her hand to her ear. "What do you know? He must have actually taken a whole step away from the door. Otherwise he would have heard you ask for him and already busted in here like the love-struck egomaniac eruption-of-sexy he is." The door opens. She freezes. I laugh. He smiles.

"That's a nice sound to hear."

"Which part?" I hold my hand out to him. "The part where I'm not the only one who thinks you're an egomaniac?" His face scrunches. I swallow. "You weren't eavesdropping, were you?"

"I was in the kitchen, timing this talk." He glares at Kim. "And clearly gave you five minutes too long."

"Kevin and I are leaving now." She waves. "You two lovebirds have fun. Bye!"

~70~

John busies himself with everything in the room, doing his best to avoid the conversation we need to have. "It was nice of Kim to make our dinner before she left." I lure him in with small talk.

"I wish you could have eaten a little more." He straightens the blanket on the chair across the room. For the third time. "Do you want this?" He holds it up. "Is it too cold in here?"

"It's warm. But no, not too warm," I answer his next inevitable question and pat the bed. "Can you come over here? I owe you an apology."

He sits exactly where I indicate. "You don't owe me a thing."

"Except my life." I meet his eyes. "If you weren't watching the clock that night, or willing to come check on me when I never answered your call, I wouldn't be here. Would I?"

Tears run down his face in answer. "I thought you just had your phone off again. That it would be funny when I showed up at your door. Then I saw the fire in the ravine. I stopped…" His voice cracks. "I was almost too late."

"I'm sorry." I wind my fingers through his. "You shouldn't have had to go through that. But I'm glad you cared, even if it was only to tease me."

"I was watching the clock and counting the minutes." His thumb runs over the back of my hand. "Trying to be patient, but wanting more than anything to hear your voice."

I made him wait nearly a month for that sound. "You went far above what a boyfriend should ever have to do. Especially one who'd only dated me for a day."

"It feels like a lifetime," he whispers.

"Hospitals will do that to you." Suck every ounce of life out of your soul. "I'm grateful for everything you've done. And I don't expect anything else. You've given me enough, you're allowed to stop now."

"I'm not doing what I think you expect me to do. Or even what I think you want me to do." His gentle fingers glide down my swollen cheek. "I'm doing what *I* want to do. Because I can't go through that again. I can't ever come so close to losing you."

Despite the pain, I press his palm to my face. "You saved me. Now it's my turn to save you." I meet his red-streaked emeralds. "You have no obligations to me, and I don't want to be a burden."

"You're not a burden." He moves forward, a whisper on his lips. "You're the light in my world. And I *want* to take care of you. Which is why I brought you here. Now instead of resisting, can you please just kiss me?"

Our mouths slide together, his warm lips being mindful of the cut I keep forgetting about. It only hurts when he pulls away. "You told me once you were a reasonable man." I exhale. "I'm going to need you to prove that."

"I am." He picks up my hand. "You have to know my intentions have never been, or ever will be, to upset you in any way. But I brought you here knowing it would make you mad, and I didn't ask if you wanted to come because I knew you'd say no. I'd much rather beg for your forgiveness than not have you here with me because this is the one place where I know you'll be safe. I'll protect you from everything, and everyone."

"It was a random accident, John." I sigh. "You can't justify your actions with a belief that I'm in some kind of danger that only you can save me from."

"Some idiot wrecked you after ramming your car *numerous* times. They could be worried you know something that will get them caught. Which means they're still a problem." His fingers tighten around mine. "But you're safe here. I'll protect you, and you'll make a full recovery."

I also might lose my mind in front of him. "I'm no one. Nobody could intentionally want to hurt me. And the driver of that car knows as well as I do there was nothing to see that night. He kept his high beams on the whole time, and it was too dark—"

"He? You saw a man?"

"I thought there was someone in the smoke." My throat tightens. "But I'm sure I just dreamed that part."

"Maybe you saw me there?"

"Maybe." I swallow, that cold laughter echoing inside me. Such a haunting sound couldn't come out of him.

He cups my face, the feel of his hands shaking off the memory. "You're someone to me, Mary. And I'm begging you to trust me."

"I *do* trust you. But this situation *is* a burden. Mine. Not yours." I run my fingers over his. "Things were good with us before the accident. We were building something special. At least, I hoped we were. So instead of putting this strain on our new relationship, we'll take a little break until I'm better, then I'll call you and we'll see about picking up where we left off."

"There are no breaks for us." His head shakes. "We're together. We're *staying* together. So if you'd rather be at your house, fine. I'll live there with you."

~71~

John moving into my house would defeat the purpose of going there. I try explaining that us staying together will ruin what we've started but he denies the possibility. And as much as I like kissing being his solution to everything, I pull away from his lips. "We can't keep doing this. We have to face reality."

"What isn't real about this?" He moves in for another lip-lock. I dodge left.

"If you can wait for me, we'll be a couple. Someday. But I'm not *asking* you to wait because that isn't fair. And I'm not staying in your house because that forces you to put your life on hold for me. You don't deserve that." I rest my palm on his shoulder. "I told you from the beginning you deserve more, and I'll try to be more. But if you find someone else—"

"Stop!" He shoves his hands through his hair. "Wherever these feelings are coming from, stop them! There will *never* be anyone else."

"John—"

"No." He tilts my face to his. "I love you. Without one single doubt in my mind, I'm completely in love with you. And caring for the woman I love is a privilege. Not a burden. So stop ripping out my heart because I can't give you what you want, Mary. I can't let you be alone. I *can't* leave the woman I love when she's in need." His breath shallows. "I'm not entirely sure I'll be able to leave you once you're not. All I'm sure of is my love. And that I'm a permanent part of your housing arrangement for the foreseeable future."

My heart explodes, wrenching tears from my eyes. He wipes them away. "I don't mean to be bullheaded and make you cry. But I've loved you from the start. Even while you were in the hospital, without us having any interaction, I could feel myself falling more in love with you." I cry harder. His face falls. "Please don't cry. I don't ever have to say those words again if you don't want to hear them."

I clutch his shirt before he pulls away. "What I've wanted from the start is to hear them. Because it's how I feel about you. But I thought you'd think I was crazy if I told you I love you."

"This whole time…" His tears match mine. "I've been so terrified of scaring you away I've nearly bit my tongue off to keep from saying I love you. But you love me?" He swallows. "Please don't lie. I have to know how you really feel."

My fingers wipe the salty streaks from his cheeks. "John Beller, I'm so in love with you it's the whole reason I didn't want to date you, but couldn't stand not to either."

"From now on…" His forehead rests on mine. "I'm going to tell you exactly how I feel. Just think of where we would be right now if neither of us held back."

"Where we're at right now is a pretty great place." It's only been a week, outside of the hospital weeks. And they don't count. "*If* what you feel for me is love. Not guilt."

"I loved you long before I felt guilty." He smiles. "So now that you know I feel both, accept the housing arrangement. Then instead of arguing, we can make healing this cut on your lip our top priority. I want to give the love of my life a proper kiss."

I can't help but smile back. He's so wonderful. And outside of the nightmares, I haven't had any *episodes* in the past few days…or weeks. It's hard to know if I was hallucinating while in a coma. "It's late, so I'll stay here tonight. But I have a request."

"Anything you want is yours." He presses my palm to his lips. "Name it."

"Move me into one of the spare rooms."

"Anything except that." His emeralds light up. "This is the best room. And it's where you belong." I blush. He grins. "All your things are already set up in here, and we wouldn't want to make Kim mad by undoing all her hard work. Would we?"

The two of them *have* to be related. "I'll have to do something nice for her. And for Kevin, I know he got roped into helping. And as unnecessary as all of this is, you're sweet for orchestrating it. So I'll do something nice for you, too."

"From egomaniac to sweet." He swipes his forehead. "Now that's progress. Just think of what you'll be saying in another few hours." I fling a pillow at his shoulder, jolting my ribs. He slides the pillow away. "No shenanigans until you're better. Then you can give me a good wallop." He winks. "And the best gift I can get is seeing you fully recovered."

"As long as it's in your house." I sigh. "In your bed. And with special emphasis on my lip."

"I love how fast you catch on." He leans in. "Let's see what else I can teach you."

~72~

Blood courses through John's body in a whole new way now that we've professed our love. I feel the change in each kiss. Each gaze. Deep inside, he reaches out for me. And every part of me clings to him. He's my anchor. The single powerful thread holding my sanity together. One spun by a love I don't understand but feel so deeply I can't deny it.

"Stop looking at me that way." I turn my blushing face away. He turns it back to him.

"Don't be embarrassed when the man you love lets you know how attracted he is to you." His fingers trace along my jaw. "Especially after I heard the banter between you and the nurse at the hospital. Trust me when I say I like kissing you just as much as you like it."

"Stop." My face burns. "It was just girl talk."

"Speaking of talk…" He adjusts me against his shoulder. "I need to have a serious conversation with you before it gets too late."

"Tired of me already? No problem. I'll call a cab and be out of here in half an hour."

"Not while I'm still breathing." He opens a drawer in the nightstand. "Your medication is here. The sleeping pills."

"While I'm still breathing, I'm not taking any. There. That was easy."

He wipes his building grin away. "As impressive as you are, the nightmares are a growing concern. I'm worried about you."

"You don't have to be. Especially if we scrap the whole idea of me staying here. I'll go home and you won't even know if I have a single dream."

"Last night, I added up all the time you slept before a nightmare set in and it was only sixty minutes. That has to change in order for your body to heal. Not to mention the toll it's taking on your mind." He puts the bottle in my hand. "I see the pain. How the nightmares affect your mental state. There's nothing to prove, sweetheart. You don't have to suffer."

"I'm not. And I'm not trying to prove anything." I give the bottle back to him.

"Dr. Mansfield prescribed these." He pops the cap and shakes pills into his palm. "They're not as strong as the others."

"I don't want them."

"Mary." He swallows. "It will break my heart to force you to do anything, but if I have to, I *will* make you take these."

"Forcing me to take drugs is illegal."

"I don't care." He shrugs.

"I care." The fear inside me cares. "You can't drug me just because it makes you feel better."

"Aww, sweetheart." He trades the pills for my hand, wiping a lone tear off my cheek. "It doesn't make me feel better. It tears me apart. But I've sat idly by and let you have your way. And your way is tormenting you." His lips run over the trail the tear left. "As much as I admire your resilience, I have to make decisions that are right for you. Even if they aren't what you want."

"Why can't you just trust me to know what's best for me? I've managed to survive on my own for thirty-two years."

"I know." He rubs his temple. "But love means doing what's best for the other person, even if they can't see it."

"Love is also respecting the other person's wishes, even if you don't agree with them."

"Is that what you said to Mike?"

~73~

Every time Mike wanted to give up, I wouldn't let him. I made him stick with the medications. Even the ones that made him sick. I guess that means I understand where John's coming from. Except I don't have cancer.

"If nightmares set in and I don't rest, we'll discuss medication. Tomorrow." Coupled with my leaving without him in tow. "And don't ever bring Mike up like that again."

"I didn't mean to be disrespectful. I was only trying to make a point." His hand lingers on the pill bottle before closing the nightstand drawer. "Promise you'll ask for something tonight if you get to a place where you need it. I mean actually assessing the situation and understanding when a sleep aid is in your best interest."

"Deal." I yawn. "It's been a really long day. Let's stop pushing each other's buttons and get some sleep."

It doesn't take long to fall asleep, or for nightmares to set in. Every time I wake up screaming, I see the torment on his face. I fight him like he's the monster in my dreams. He manages to hold me until I'm still. Calm. Hands clinging to him until I'm fast asleep again. Then he goes back to his place across the room. To watch, waiting for the next time dreams thrash from my convulsing body.

If he wasn't scared to leave me, he could sleep in a spare room. Get the rest he desperately needs. Selfishly, I'm glad he's here. I only wish he were nearer than he is now. The dim light of dawn reveals his frame sprawled uncomfortably over the sofa. It isn't long enough for his length and his broad shoulders are too wide for the seat. The only way this man is going to get some real peace in his life is by taking me out of it. "Preferably before all my crazy shows."

"What, sweetheart?" He peels his body off the creamy fabric and zombie-clunks my way. "Are you hungry?"

My eating skills must have really made an impression on him. "I'm just sitting up. Lie back down." Sleep hangs in his eyes. "You can get in bed with me if you want. There's more than enough room and I'll be still while you sleep."

"Thanks." His smile is deceptively bright. "But it looks like you're up for the day so I'll get us some coffee and start breakfast. Anything in particular you feel like eating?"

"Shockingly, I'm not very hungry. Just make whatever you want and maybe we can share?"

"You've got it." He kisses my forehead. "I'll be back in just a little bit, sweetheart."

In the quietness of morning, I hear a shower running. He's using one of the spare rooms. "Did you have Kim move your things into another room?" My first question now that he's back and wearing fresh clothes.

"I had her move a few things." He carries one of his custom serving trays, two cups of coffee and two glasses of orange juice balanced on top. "In case you were uncomfortable sharing space with me."

"I'm uncomfortable over how this whole situation is affecting every aspect of your life." He's worn out. "I'm so sorry about last night."

"Don't worry about last night on my account." He slides the tray onto the nightstand, handing me a glass of juice. "Just remember how hard it was on you when tonight rolls around, because I'm not letting that happen again."

The pill bottle is out. Opened on the nightstand beside the tray. "Before you sleep on the sofa again, I'd rather take those."

"I'll be sleeping there regardless." He sips coffee that looks strong enough to wake the dead. "I'll never be farther away than the other side of the room."

"Then sleep here." I pat the space next to me. "We're both adults. And with the condition I'm in, there are no worries about anything getting out of hand."

"Even if you weren't hurt, there wouldn't be any worries. I stop and go on your command." He winks. "The only thing I can't control is how much you'll blush. Before. During. And after."

He's absolutely in control of *this* rosy-red blaze. "Do you remember yesterday when you kidnapped me? And later manipulated me into staying? I do. And I said I'd stay for only one night."

"What I remember best is you propositioning me thirty seconds ago. And I accept. I'll sleep with you." I hide my face. He chuckles. "Sit tight, sweetheart. I'll be back shortly with some eggs."

~74~

When John returns with our breakfast I'll be in better condition than when he left. A quick trip to the bathroom to spruce up will assure him I'm feeling better, and walking on my own is a necessity.

Sliding into a seated position, I bite down the pain ripping through my torso. Two deep breaths and I swing my legs over the bed edge. All things considered, I'll gladly take splitting pain over the waves of nausea hammering me now that my feet are on the floor. I'm upright. Head spinning. Stomach churning. The lights are going out. "John!"

He hits the doorway at a dead sprint, skidding across the floor on his knees. Too late to catch my crumpling body. My head bounces off the hardwood. "Mary!" His hands thrust under me. "Sweetheart!"

"I'm okay." I swallow the pain. "I just got dizzy."

"Dizzy?" His heart pounds, fingers frantically searching for new knots on my scalp. "You got out of bed? Why?"

"I was going to clean up."

"Clean up?" He deflates. "In the bathroom?"

"Yeah."

His emeralds steady, deep breaths returning his heartrate to normal. "Why didn't you tell me? You know I'll take you."

"I'm tired of bothering you for every little thing." I sigh. "If my head doesn't spin I can make it on my own." I'm not sure I actually can, but I *am* sure the clench of his jaw says he isn't remotely close to entertaining the idea.

"Telling me what you need doesn't bother me. Scaring me to death bothers me!"

"I didn't mean to scare you." I rest against his chest. "I had no idea I'd get lightheaded. And that's all that happened. I'm fine in every other way."

"Fine?" His head rears back. "You haven't been fine since the night of the accident. Now you're hurt even worse."

"I didn't fall that hard." Compared to falling off a cliff. "You got here just in time."

"No! I was late. Again. And it's *killing* me."

He stands, my body cradled to him. "You have to start letting me help you."

"All I do is let you help me."

"Not willingly." He stomps into the bathroom. "I have to force help on you. And for what? Just now you thought you'd hobble in here on one leg because that's easier than asking for help?"

Actually, yes. "I was going to use the wall for support. After I hopped over to it."

"You didn't make it there, did you?" His pulse rises. "Did you notice how easily I carried you in here?"

"I noticed the crutches you put in the closet yesterday. Giving me those would be easy."

"I had Kim lay out your things so you can reach them from here." He deposits me in a cushioned chair by the sink, ignoring my observation. "There's a chair in the shower, too. I have plastic to cover your cast if you want to try sitting in there."

"I would love to have a shower. And I can manage getting in there on my own if you bring me the crutches. Please. And thank you."

"Asking nicely doesn't automatically mean the answer has to be yes."

"I thought you said I can have anything. All I need to do is ask."

I love making him grin when he really, *really* doesn't want to. "Instead of letting you use my words against me, I'll go grab your clothes. Then I'll get you situated in the shower while thinking about the day I get to put you in a bubble bath."

"Get me the crutches and that will happen a lot sooner."

"Tempting." He pauses at the door. "Very tempting."

~75~

I haven't looked in a mirror since the accident. Now, the swollen and bruised thing looking back at me doesn't resemble the reflection I once knew. The cuts are worse than I imagined. And I never knew flesh could be so many different hues at once. Before, I never thought of myself as much, but at least I'd been human.

"Aww, sweetheart." John softly reenters the room, wiping my tears from where they trickle. "I know it's shocking to see yourself like this for the first time, but I swear to you, you *will* heal. You already look so much better." I can't imagine looking worse. "I'm sorry I didn't think to cover the mirrors." He kneels, wiping the tears wetting my chin. "Sweetheart, please don't cry. You're still as beautiful as you were. And more so than I ever thought a woman could be."

The blatant lie forces more tears to spill. He wipes them away. More rush down to take their spot. He straightens, putting his body between me and the mirror. My eyes hit the floor. I can't bring myself to look at him. He kisses the top of my head. "If you saw yourself only a few days ago, you would believe me when I tell you all of your wounds and bruises will heal."

Maybe. But right now, I'm unraveling. And I don't want him to see what's coming. "I want to take a shower. Alone."

"Of course." He grabs a towel, throwing it haphazardly over the mirror before taking a roll of plastic out of a drawer. "I'm going to undress you. But I've thought a lot about it and have a plan to keep my eyes off what I don't have a right to see."

With no choice, I hold on to the remnants of my shredded sanity, clinging to every fiber so I don't fall apart while his hands move over me.

I focus on stopping the tears, the flood gates begging to be released. Every ounce of pain I've ever harbored chomps to rip out of my depths. "Hurry."

"I'm trying, sweetheart." He removes the last of my clothing, hands doing the work while keeping a thick towel draped over the front of me. "Up you go." He hoists me into his arms, carrying me to the shower chair and positioning me with a shower nozzle in my hand before closing his eyes and removing the towel. "Spray the water to see if the temperature needs to be adjusted." He turns away, fingers moving over a touch screen embedded in the wall.

I hit the button. Water stings over my legs. "It's good."

"The floor is heated. It'll be warm in a minute." He hesitates, still facing away from me. "I've got a bathing suit for you. We can put you in it so I can help you in here."

"No."

"Okay." He rubs his face. "Your soaps are in the side of the chair, and I'll stand right outside the door in case you change your mind. Which I hope you do. I'm worried about you being in here alone."

"Please, just go."

Stepping to the edge of the shower, he stops again. "Do *not* stand for any reason. The tile is slick. When you're finished, call for me and I'll come get you." I don't answer. He sighs. "Sweetheart, I want to help you. And I love you. Please remember that." I'm silent. He leaves. And though I know he can still hear every gut-wrenching sob from where he stands outside the door, I'm as alone as he's ever going to leave me. All the pain is coming out. Every last drop.

~76~

I've cried plenty of times. But never like this. All my magnified emotions ripping out in one sitting. But, like other times in my life, when the world crumbles under my feet I brush off the dust and keep moving. *This will not break me.* It is going to freeze me, though. According to the clock on the fancy screen, I've been in the shower an hour and fifteen minutes. And since I let the warm water run over my body until it ran out, my hair gets to be washed in cold water. That's enough to shock me back into reality.

"John! I'm finished." Poor man. I hope he didn't stand at the door the entire time.

"Hi, sweetheart." He has a robe over his shoulder, towel in his hand, using his familiarity with the bathroom to navigate his way to me with closed eyes. "Did you have a nice shower?"

"Yes. Thank you for being considerate." I take the extended towel, liking that he's pretending I didn't just drain a lake.

"Of course." He holds out the robe as I dry off as quickly as I can manage. I exchange the towel for the robe. "Let me know when you've slipped that on and I'll take you out of here to get you dressed. I can help with the robe if you need me to."

I do need him to. But wish I didn't. So I'm not asking. "Ready."

"Then up you go." He opens his eyes and lifts my robed body into his arms, carrying me out of the shower and turning the cushioned chair by the sink away from the mirror. He places me gently on the seat, closing his eyes and disrobing me with a long sigh.

"Keep your eyes closed. The last thing I need is you being repulsed by my body. It's bad enough you have to look at my face."

"Your face is beautiful." He slips a t-shirt over my head, sliding my arms gently into the sleeves. "And I don't possess the ability to be repulsed by you."

"That's because you haven't seen me naked." Even the tiny bits of skin that aren't covered in bruises aren't a normal color.

"I'm going to assume that wasn't an offer." His hands move to my legs, beginning to work the sweatpants over my cast.

"You assume correctly." If not for the accident, I'd probably extend the invitation.

He slides the pants into place, opening his eyes. "One day soon, you'll be back to exactly as you were before the accident."

"Until then, I get to keep enduring the humiliation of you dressing me like an invalid."

"Don't knock being an invalid." He tries not to smile. "If it ever happens to me, I hope you'll take my clothes off."

"Too bad for you that I don't know my way around a man's body as well as you very clearly know your way around a woman's."

He nods. "I've regretted a lot of things but right now, because I'm able to confidently do this knowing I'm not wandering into territory you don't want me in, I'm pretty thankful I have experience. Aren't you?"

My face burns, but he probably can't see it under the bruising so I might as well make it worse. "I am. And I'll have to get some experience of my own. You know, just in case."

"Now, that's something I can get behind." He grins. "Even though I know you're only talking this way to turn a very uncomfortable situation into something bearable for you, know that I'll let you practice on me anytime. Teasingly or otherwise."

"How about I just practice drying my hair?"

He picks up the hairdryer. "I've never used one of these before, but it can't be that hard. So I'll do this for you." His lips press to my ear. "You just sit here and mentally prepare for what you'll be practicing on me in a few minutes."

~77~

It feels good to have John dry my hair. Mainly because I don't want to lift my arms anymore. The shower was grueling. For many reasons. "You have a future in hair styling."

"As naturally beautiful as you are, you make it seem easy." He slides down in front of me, lifting my chin. "I know you don't want to hear you're exquisite because you don't feel beautiful right now, but I'm telling you the truth. And I'm worried about you. Did I make the right call earlier? Not coming in here while you were crying?"

"It was the perfect call. I needed time to myself."

His eyes study mine. "It took all I had to let you be alone through that storm. I'm trying to figure out the right things to do, and when to do them."

"You have an uncanny knack for getting it right. So keep following your instincts. Except on things like moving me into your house without asking."

"So what you really mean…" A smile breaks through his concern. "Is do the opposite of my instincts? Because my instinct earlier was to run in here and hold you until the rest of the world disappeared."

That would have been nice. And horrifying. "Then keep doing the opposite of your instincts."

"As long as you give me credit for fighting them." The concern is back. "You have no idea how badly I want to wrap you in my arms and never give you one second alone."

He has no idea how badly I'd love to be swallowed up by him. Or how badly things can turn out for us if my mind acts up again. I'm about due for a hallucination or two. "In the spirit of doing the opposite of what you want, give me a little more time alone. I want to put on everything in that makeup bag to see if I can deserve one of your compliments."

176

"You already do." He kisses my hand. "You don't need a drop of makeup."

"I'd feel better with a thousand drops."

"Hurry." He straightens, turning my chair around and removing the towel from the mirror. "Because my instinct is telling me to lay you back in the bed so I can show you just how deserving you are. And so I can see how much practice you're going to need."

"Get out!"

Leaving with a chuckle, and a warning for me not to get up on my own, he clicks the door shut. I stare into the mirror's abyss. The freshly washed hair, despite the puffier eyes, has this new creature marginally less scary than the last one. *Thank God for the trickery of makeup.* I dig into my bag, managing to fade out some of the bruising and cover a few cuts. This is as good as it's going to get.

"John." I only have to whisper his name. The door promptly swings open, a whistle on his lips.

"Stunning!"

"I'm still not in a place to hear you talk that way."

He hoists me into his arms. "If I let you have your way, you'll never be ready to hear it."

My arms slide around his neck. "If you truly love me, you're supposed to let me have my way."

"Ditto, sweetheart." He heads for the door. "So, green-light me to whatever level of loving you're comfortable with and I'll lay you in this bed and start showing you how appreciative I am of every gorgeous inch of you."

Laying me down and pulling the blankets over me with a wink, he smiles. "Do I still have permission to be next to you?"

"Yes, but…"

"I know this isn't the right time." His lips press to mine. "I just want to make sure you never forget how precious you are to me. Even if I have to embarrass you to prove the point."

"Then you don't want the green light?"

"Easy." He laughs. "Teasing me like that will get you into trouble. You already know I have a self-control problem."

All the women he's dated float through my mind. "Did you love any of them?" His brows knit. I swallow. "Your past girlfriends."

"I was young and dumb. Playing the field, not realizing I'd be cursed for eternity if I didn't take time to figure out what love is." His fingers stroke mine. "I've only been in love once. And I plan to stay this way."

~78~

John and I are in the midst of loving tranquility. Hands entwined, my head on his chest, the rest of the world a vague memory. It's the perfect setting for the best nap of my entire life. But like all our perfect days, this one is interrupted. By the ring of his phone.

If it weren't for the calls tormenting me before the accident, he wouldn't have a nice bruise on his leg from where my cast kicked him. "Sorry."

"I'm the one who's sorry." He curls me back against his chest, ignoring the phone. "I should have turned that off. Especially while all I've ever wanted is in my arms."

"It might be an important call."

"Not more important than this right here." His arms cinch tight. "One of these days I'll implement the first lesson you taught me and turn off the phone *before* it rings."

That would be nice. But he didn't. And the caller is persistent. "Answer the phone."

He lets go of me and slides away, stepping out of bed. "Try to get back to sleep while I let them know not to ever call me again."

Lifting his phone from the nightstand he heads down the hall, not wanting me to hear what he's going to say to the caller. But his voice booms. From the kitchen I hear bits of the scolding. "If I don't answer, leave a message." … "You found them?" … "How pathetic are you?" … "Don't interrupt my day again unless you have something worthwhile to report."

I know what a chucked phone sounds like. He just threw his. "John?" He rushes down the hall, relief washing over his tense body at the sight of me still in bed. "Worry much?"

"With you, I've learned I have to." He smiles. "Two-hour naps do you good, though. You look rested enough to run a marathon."

"I think I'll settle for getting up. Who was on the phone? You sounded upset."

His big hands engulf me, stopping me from moving. "You're supposed to be lying down."

"I know you believe me doing anything other than lying still is detrimental to my health, but I promise it isn't. I'll feel better if I get up."

"I'll move you up a little." He gently drags me into a half-seated position. "How's this?"

"Nothing like getting up." I bring his hands to rest in front of me. "I'll sit here like this for a little while. Now, the phone call?"

"Detective Summers says they aren't getting anywhere on your case. He thinks interviewing you will shed some light. But I don't want them overwhelming you with questions."

"I'm going to have to talk to them eventually."

"I know." He rubs his face. "But you had a hard night and a pretty tough morning, so it doesn't need to be today. We can wait as long as you need to."

"You think waiting is a good idea?"

He swallows hard, the decision weighing heavy. "The person responsible for your accident needs to be caught. And *if* them talking directly to you really is the key, it has to happen."

"Then there's no point dragging things out. I'll talk to them today. Can you drop me off at the station?"

"They can come here."

My heart sinks. I grip his hand. "It's better if I go to them."

"It's better if they come here." He asserts. "It's admirable how you're willing to rise to any occasion, but you don't need to do this. Not today."

"I'm only rising to the occasion because I literally can't rise in any other way. If my legs worked, you'd be saying something completely different right now."

"I have no doubt I would be, sweetheart." His head dips. "No doubt at all that my words would be centered around getting you to slow down long enough for me to barricade the exits."

~79~

It's nearly time for the detectives to arrive. I watch the clock, more nervous with each ticking second. The jitters aren't hiding themselves well. John takes note of every twitch. "It's too soon. We'll call this whole thing off."

"No. They're already being overly flexible, and I can't avoid them forever. But I'd like to go into the living room. I'm not comfortable with them being in my bedroom."

"It didn't take long for you to realize it's *your* bedroom." His grin grows two sizes, right along with my blush.

"You know what I mean."

"I do know what you mean." His hands slide under me. "And I seriously like it."

Placing me in a reclined position on the living room sofa, he fluffs pillows under my legs and behind my back. Grinning all the while. "Stop!"

"I'm not doing anything." He chuckles. "Except enjoying the fact that you know I built this house for you."

"House? Or is it more like a prison?"

His eyes roll. "Either way, I made it nice for you. Have you seen the bathtub? It's big enough for both of us." My face is crimson, and the doorbell is ringing. "Saved by the bell."

Having to talk to the detectives is hardly saving. Especially with him around. He lets Detective Beckley and Detective Summers inside, each of them taking seats opposite me and not wasting any time getting down to business. Beckley pulls out a small brown notebook and fires off his first question. John pumps the brakes. "Before she answers, we need to go over the ground rules."

"Ground rules for our own interview?" Summers snaps.

"Ground rules for being in *my* house, talking to *my* girlfriend." John eyes the man. "A privilege I'm *letting* you have."

Summers focuses on me. "Ma'am, do you want to talk to us?"

"She feels up to being questioned right now." John's tone is a warning. "That can change. At any point, if she feels overwhelmed or *I* think this interview needs to end, you'll leave. Immediately. Understood?"

Beckley understands the power of wealth. "We know what she's been through, and we'll respect both of you. We're just thankful she's recovered enough to speak to us today."

"Yeah, we're real thankful." Summers doesn't care how deep John's pockets are.

The older man gives him a look. "What my partner means is, this time with her is necessary. So thank you, Mr. Beller."

John tucks himself under my legs. "Necessity remains to be seen. She's still in a fragile state. I'm not as sure as she is that she's ready to talk about the accident, or to see pictures of what I saw first-hand. I want the person responsible caught more than anyone here, but I won't neglect what's in her best interest."

"I want to answer their questions." I put my hand on his arm. "So we can put this whole ordeal behind us. While I talk to them, why don't you go lie down?"

"Go ahead, detectives." His arm swings possessively across the back of the sofa. "Ask whatever it is that you so desperately need to ask her."

~80~

If I insist on being alone with the detectives, John will kick them out. Then we'd be no further than before they arrived, and part of the reason he wants me living with him is the lack of knowing who ran me off the road. If these men can figure that out, I'm one step closer to going home. Before I mar him with more than a bruise on his leg. Still, I regret letting him stay. He hangs on every syllable.

The detectives first ask me to walk them through the night of the accident, starting from the point where I drove away from his house. Then Detective Beckley hands me photographs, pointing out spots on a hunk of metal where they found mismatched paint. "This is my car?" It's inconceivable. "How on earth did I survive?"

"What's important is that you did." John takes the photographs away, shoving them into the detective's face.

"If you hadn't been there, I…"

"Shh, sweetheart." He rubs my leg. "I was there. And I always will be."

Summers clears his throat. "Ma'am, prior to the accident, did anyone ever threaten you? Or do anything that might have scared you?"

Not wanting to describe elements of my life that may or may not be real, especially in front of John, is made worse by the photographs of the horrific scene he happened upon that night. He's already been traumatized. "Um, the week before the accident was a little strange."

John's head jerks around. "Strange how?"

"The fire department was dispatched over carbon monoxide." Beckley checks his notes. "You spent a night in the hospital. Is that what you're referring to?"

"You what? When?"

"You didn't know?" Summers greets John's bewilderment with a satisfied smirk.

"I never told him."

Summers' smirk turns into a glare. "We interviewed the firemen. It was the worst leak they'd seen and she was in bad shape that night. Why didn't she call her *boyfriend?*"

John's hand slides to my shoulder. I slide mine over his knee. "He wasn't my boyfriend then. We'd only met the Saturday before, so I wasn't in a position to tell him anything."

"Weren't in a position to tell me?" John's jaw flexes, eyes leaving Summers to level on me. "How about being in a position to *want* to tell me? Did you tell Kim?"

"If I had, you would have known. Kevin would have blabbed."

Beckley watches us, scooting forward in his seat. "You two have only known each other for a month?"

"We had our first date a week before the accident." John swallows. "I didn't know her before then. It was a blind date." One he now probably wishes didn't happen.

"The carbon monoxide was weird, but the flowers I got were weirder." Nervous babble never leads to anything good.

"My flowers?" John's poor face falls by the second.

"No." I give him a reassuring smile. "Yours were the only reason I had any sanity at all that week."

Now I'm stuck explaining. "Flowers were sent to Scarlets mid-week, and one was even left on my windshield at the start of the week." Other people saw both so I can talk about them with certainty. Even if I end up being the one who sleep-shopped for them.

"Not from you?" Summers smiles as John's hand leaves my shoulder.

"They weren't from him. The ones that came to work had a mean note." My tongue feels heavy. "And after I threw away the one on my car, a note was hand-delivered to my house. With dead petals inside."

Beckley's face is as long as John's. "Tell us exactly what the note said. It's important. We need to know every detail."

<h1 style="text-align:center">~81~</h1>

Two bull-headed detectives and an upset boyfriend force me to spill details about the note and flowers. I even dreadfully mutter about the tormenting phone calls and horn blowing incidents. John listens. No eye contact. No gentle caress. Only a stiff ear tuned into my words.

"You're hesitant." Detective Beckley's eyes say he knows I'm holding back. "Is there more to this?"

"I'm not sure any of it's important." Or real.

"Tell us everything," Summers urges. "We'll decide if it's important or not."

I glance at John. His unseeing stare is fixed on the wall. "Look, that week was unnerving. But it was all random. Any one thing on its own wouldn't raise an eyebrow."

"I don't think it's as random as you think." Beckley taps his notebook. "I've been doing this a long time—"

"Even if there *was* someone out there specifically targeting me, I have an alarm system." I don't need an old detective's lecture. "If someone gets by that, I have a gun."

"You carry a weapon?" Summers smiles.

"A small pistol."

"Not anymore." John finally speaks. "It's locked in my safety deposit box."

The detectives' eyes slowly move from his unflinching form to watch my reaction. I swallow it down. Summers is already suspicious. Questioning John in front of him will only make it worse. "He did that after the accident. Before, it was on my nightstand. Which is why I never called the police. I was safe inside the house, and it would have been silly to call just because someone gave me flowers and blew their horn."

"Nothing is silly." Beckley's head shakes. "And it's in your best interest to tell us absolutely everything, whether you think it's connected or not."

"We're here to help you," Summers consoles. "Don't hold back. Nothing is going to happen to you while we're here."

I glance again at John's distant look. Nothing will happen to me even when the detectives aren't here. Not even a single kiss. "As far as actions that could be misconstrued as *against* me, I've told you all there is to tell. Sometimes I feel like someone is watching me, and following me. But everyone feels that way sometimes. Right?"

"How often do you feel like you're being watched?" Summers shifts in his seat. "Have you ever seen anyone? Even if it was only a shadow, we need to know."

I clasp my hands together to keep them from shaking. "On average, I'd say I get the feeling of being watched several times a week. It's been that way for a while now, though. But I've never seen anyone. Sometimes there are footprints in the yard or stray shadows at night, but the footprints are probably the pest control company or neighborhood kids. I check out the shadows and they're usually trees blowing in the wind or clouds, that sort of thing." John's hands drag down his face. I'm losing him with every word. "None of this is important to your case. I wish I could help you more, but I didn't see anything the night of the accident. Thank you for stopping by, though." I give them a smile.

"Here's my card." Summers stands, slipping the tan rectangle into my palm. "If you think of anything else or ever feel like something around you is amiss, and I mean you have even the slightest feeling, I want you to call me directly. I'll answer your call day or night. Understand?"

I nod, my periphery showing the jerk in John's chest, his breathing hitching as anger builds. "I'll be home later, so if you two think of anything else you'd like to ask, I'd appreciate you waiting until then."

"You'll be exactly where you are later." John yanks the card free of my fingers and flings it across the room. "If they have questions, they'll ask them now. You'll answer them now!"

"Ma'am, are you being held against your will?" Summers doesn't know when to keep his mouth shut.

John leaves my legs, towering over the man. "What did you just say to her?"

"I asked the kind of question that gets to the bottom of why she's sitting there scared to speak." Summers stretches, trying to make himself level with John. "Cracks are showing in this so-called close connection you keep telling us about. I think only one of you feels it. The one who's been in this relationship longer than she's known you existed."

~82~

John and I are the only ones who truly know how strong our feelings are despite the short acquaintance so it isn't hard to believe the detectives would question our devotion. But it's laughable to think John is the type of man to secretly follow a woman around. He doesn't exactly have a confidence problem.

"You told them to question everything." I try explaining. John's hands are balled into fists at his side, body advancing, backing Detective Summers toward the door. "That's all he's doing. And it's what you want, right? To question everything and get to the bottom of this?"

"Who, other than me, are you looking into?" John growls.

"We don't think you're responsible." Beckley elbows Summers out the door. "We do think everything she told us today is connected, though." His troubled eyes land on me. "It appears the perpetrator has been stalking you."

"Stalking?" I barely know the word.

"Most women in your situation don't realize anything is wrong until it escalates." He frowns. "I believe that's exactly what happened in this case."

The air around me grows thin. "Why? I didn't do anything."

"These men get ideas stuck in their heads that don't have anything to do with you." Summers snakes around Beckley, bypassing John and coming to kneel in front of me. "It's them pushing their own agenda. Which is why I'm worried about you."

"She doesn't need you worried about her!" John's hand closes around Summers' collar, jerking him backwards across the floor. "She needs you to find the stalker!"

"And she needs *you* arrested!" The man peels himself off the hardwood. "Thanks for the assault charge. I was having a hard time getting anything else to stick."

Beckley jumps between them. "Get outside, Summers. Now!"

"Yeah, let's take this outside so **my** girlfriend doesn't see me earn the assault charge." John pushes past him.

"No one is charging you with anything." Beckley's spry for an older man, artfully keeping John from exiting the house and Summers from coming back in it. "Everyone's emotions are running high. That's understandable."

"Stalker." John snaps. "She has a stalker and he's standing there looking at me like I'm him!"

John isn't a stalker. My alter-sleepwalking-ego might be. "This whole thing has gotten out of hand. Even if there is a *stalker*, I'm safe inside my house. With the alarm. And the gun—"

"You're safe because you're here." John's head snaps around, eyes blazing.

"He's right, ma'am," Beckley agrees. "If someone has been watching you, and for as long as you say, they're familiar with your usual surroundings. They've probably run through all the scenarios in which they could get to you. Being here will throw them off."

John's eyes dim, the fire snuffing out of them to look at me. Actually see me. "No one is getting near her again. Not while I'm here."

"We're the ones who can keep you safe," Summers bleats over Beckley's shoulder, earning himself another elbow to the gut from the older man.

"What my partner means, Mr. Beller, is that it sounds like she's had this problem for a lot longer than you've even known her. The two of you beginning to date may have only escalated the situation."

"You mean I could be responsible?" John's frame rocks. "For all of it?"

"No! He doesn't mean that at all." I protest.

"I don't." Beckley claps a hand on John's shoulder. "It would have happened sooner or later. Even if you weren't in the picture. And I'd say she's better off with you in it."

"As long as he's in it with her permission," Summers mutters.

"Say it one more time." John snaps forward. "I dare you."

~83~

Detective Summers is brave. I'll give him that. Detective Beckley is more so. He's the one jamming himself between John and his partner.

"All I'm saying is there are a lot of holes in this story." Summers holds his ground on the end of the porch. "And you've got her sitting there looking to you before she opens her mouth."

"I'm not looking to him because I'm scared!" I shout. "He didn't give me a script. And he doesn't deserve to be treated this way."

"Susan." John stops his forward pursuit, turning to stare at me, eyes wide. My heart splits in half.

"What are you saying? I'm nothing like her."

"Come with me." He grabs Beckley by the arm, dragging him out the door and shouldering past Summers, who looks at me longingly before trotting off after his partner.

The three of them disappear into the garage. I wait. Hoping John is showing them his truck. Not somehow lumping me in with the likes of his ex, twistedly relating my actions to hers. Maybe he should. The vile things she did to him were for selfish reasons. He's in this mess with me because *I've* been selfish.

This is the part where he's apologizing to the detectives, telling them he didn't know I was crazy. I strain to see out the window to where he and Beckley are shaking hands beside the man's car. He flips Detective Summers off. Their relationship didn't change in the last ten minutes.

The detectives drive away and John marches to the house. The door swings open, slamming off the doorstop, then slamming shut behind him. He storms toward me. My gut twists. He pushes his body under my legs. "Why didn't you tell me what was happening that week?"

"We just met." My heart pounds. "I didn't know how you would react to me calling you in the middle of the night to say someone was blowing their horn outside my house."

"I would have reacted by coming over and stopping them!"

"Okay. Sorry. I didn't know."

"You knew later." He tugs me to him. "You knew after I told you I loved you. And still, between then and now, you never told me anything. *Nothing.*"

"I said I was sorry."

"I don't want your apologies. I want an explanation." His chest heaves. "You said you loved me from the start and if that's true, why would you not tell me? Why didn't you say anything when we had lunch? Or that Saturday when we made our relationship official? You were in the hospital, for crying out loud! The *hospital,* and I didn't even know."

His eyes are deep, sunken pools. "You still weren't ever going to tell me. Were you?"

If it weren't for the detectives, he wouldn't know a thing. "Loving you from the start is the *reason* I didn't tell you. And everything that was happening is the *reason* I tried to get you to not date me."

"I *am* dating you. And I didn't hide how I felt about you!" he shouts. "You should have told me. I would have never let you drive home alone. And I would have slept in your driveway every night until I caught the person." His teeth grind. "I was in the store the day those flowers came, wasn't I?"

"I'm sorry." Tears fill my eyes. "I never meant to hurt you."

"You're the one who's hurt." He wrenches closer. "I could have stopped you from getting hurt. Instead I… I…"

"Were nice." I sniff. "Gave me bright spots inside the darkness."

"No, sweetheart." His grip falls away, hands slowly moving to my face. "I walked around with blinders on, trying to figure out how to make you love me instead of paying attention to what was happening in your life." He swallows. "I can't do this anymore."

"I understand." My head lowers. "And you don't have to feel guilty about breaking up with me. It's the right thing to do."

Hands cupped on my face, he raises my closed eyes to his lips, placing a gentle kiss on each lid. "What I can't do anymore is be so enamored with you that I forget to do what you need me to do most of all. Please, sweetheart, I'm begging you, tell me everything. Tell me every single thing that's happened to you in every single day of your life." His thumb caresses my cheek. "There can't be secrets between us. It's too dangerous. And I'd rather see this whole world burn than see the sun rise on a day that doesn't include you."

~84~

John's torn up over me spending the week we met suffering while he was sitting around thinking of ways to charm me. But from my side of things, that charm was a life saver. I'm only sorry I wasn't honest with him. And grateful the real blinders he wears are the ones that make me worthy of his love.

"I thought I could get better." I look away. "That I would get my head together and be good for you."

"You *are* good for me." He brings my chin around. "And I'm going to be good for you. Just as soon as you tell me all the things I know you're holding back."

"You don't understand." Tears trickle down my face.

He wipes them away. "Everything is going to be okay. You'll see."

What I see is how badly I want to spare him from knowing just how horrible the last few years have been. But he deserves to know everything, so the decisions he makes from here on out are right for him. Not centered on what he thinks is best for me. "You've pretty much nailed that I'm a nervous wreck most of the time. I hardly sleep anymore. And when I do, I sleepwalk. I…I do things."

"What kind of things?" His eyebrows wiggle. "Midnight food binging?"

"I wish my waistline was the only thing in danger."

Minutes turn into hours as the agony of my years unleash. He hangs on every word. As if committing to memory everything I've tried so hard to forget. One strange happening leaping into the next. Morphing and twisting until sobs are all that's left. Paranoid battle scars drowning me on dry ground.

"I would give anything to have been there for you." He presses tissue against my cheeks, mopping up the salty flow. "From the very start of your life, I wish I was there."

"I'm glad you weren't." It's too much. "Kim was. And even she couldn't help."

"I'm not her." His brow creases. "No offense, but I don't put a lot of stock in what she has to offer."

"You should." I sniff. "Because when I finally couldn't take it anymore, I went to her. She said to check myself in someplace and get evaluated. But...I thought..." To speculate is one thing, but to *know* you're crazy is another. "I thought she and Kevin were blowing things out of proportion, deciding I was hallucinating because I was depressed. But I didn't feel depressed. I felt afraid."

"You had a real-life, tangible reason to be." He soaks up more tears. "What exactly happened during their *mental intervention?*"

I give him the highlights. Like strangers approaching me in Scarlets about the state of my mind. How I'd deal with that all day and then go home at night and listen to what wasn't there. "It was horrible. So I started telling everyone I was okay. It was easier to go insane on my own."

"So Kim and Kevin didn't actually do anything to help you." His teeth clench. "They just blabbed around town, getting sympathy for themselves by using your situation to make them look like the poor little friends who had to deal with *so much.*"

They probably did paint themselves as caregivers who were being taxed to their limit. But they *were* worried about me. "All I know is I didn't tell you what was going on because I liked you. Liked the way you looked at me. Not like I was some pathetic thing to be pitied, but just a woman." I can't stop crying. "Sorry." I wipe my own face this time. "I've never cried so much in my life."

"Sweetheart, that's part of the problem. You're too strong. And way too hard on yourself."

"You're forgetting selfish." I take the box of tissues from him. "I really didn't plan on dating you. Not until I was better. *If* I could get better." I dab my eyes. "I was going to try to fix myself before I jumped in and messed up your life like this."

"All you've done is make my life better." He slides me onto his lap, lips gently caressing my swollen cheek. "You've gone through so much. And suffered all this time in silence."

"Yeah." I lean into him. "I've either gone through a lot, or imagined I did."

"Either way…" He smiles. "Right now, you're going through me loving you. And that's definitely real. Want me to prove it?"

~85~

There are many things I'd love John to prove, but how intently he can stare at a ringing phone isn't one of them. You'd think the devil himself lived within the contraption. "Relax, it's only Kim."

"I will relax, sweetheart. Right after I set her and her husband straight."

"You can't yell at people for coming to conclusions. Even if those conclusions are wrong." Which we're still not sure of, even though he insists I'm not crazy. "Leave the past in the past, where it belongs. You know they meant well."

"What I know is that instead of helping you, they made you feel so insecure about telling the truth it almost got you killed." His fingers tighten around the phone. "You can keep being too nice to fault them, but I'm not. They played a big part in you getting hurt."

"The person who wrecked me is the only one who played a part. As for the choices I made, I made them. You can't hold my wrong decisions over our friends."

He jams a finger against the phone, turning it off. "If you were in charge of the world, there wouldn't be a need for jails."

"And wouldn't that be a nice world?" I goad. "Think of all the innocent people who have been wrongly imprisoned."

I disagree that Kim or Kevin believing me instead of acting like I had a mental problem would have made a difference in terms of the car accident. "If what you're really mad over is Kevin not telling you about my mental state, it was *my* job to give you the details. Not his."

"I'm mad their actions directly led to a psycho getting close to you."

"You can't honestly believe I have a stalker. Who would stalk me?"

"Every man in the world." He grins. "I don't want to be arrested for it, but I was practically stalking you."

He chuckles at my expression. "Sweetheart, the only crazy around here is me being so head-over-heels I'm ready to give you everything you've never dared ask for."

"Except a pass for our friends?"

"That's something you dared ask for. A bad habit you have. Always asking for the impossible."

"You need to learn to cut people some slack. When they're trying their best, you have to."

He studies my face. Always searching. Questioning. I press my fingers against the steady thrum of his heart. "Now that you're calm, turn your phone back on. Kim is used to talking to me every day. She's probably freaking out."

"Kim who?" His lips drag over my jaw. I open my neck for them. He trails along the soft flesh above my collarbone. I can't remember who she is either. "Let's take this to the bedroom." His mouth rounds my shoulder. "Or keep it right here."

I find his neck with my own lips. "You are the most stubborn man in the world, John Beller."

"Somebody has to tame you." He moans. "Because when it comes to stubborn women, the title is all yours."

"Are you complaining?"

"No." His mouth cascades over my skin, fingers sliding my shirt aside to give him more real estate. "It's how I know I have every right in the world to be with you. Mike was way out of his league. But you and I, sweetheart, we're a match."

~86~

Nothing ends a good make-out session like the mention of a dead husband. Or the memories of Kim always rolling her eyes at Mike. She never respected him. He was happy to do whatever I said, however I said. She saw that as weakness. I saw it as love. And it wasn't like I bossed him around. He just preferred to defer all decisions to me. He was busy with the charities he worked for.

Apparently, John doesn't get that concept either. Rather than having another impassioned argument he left me alone in his living room, opting to go out to his workshop to *check on things.* Only, he picked up his phone before he left, and I'm not stupid. He's out there reading Kim and Kevin the riot act while I flip through television channels to distract my mind. I pause on the local news, the unfolding scene captivating. They're at the spot where I wrecked. *Police still aren't giving any information on the fiery crash that sent a local woman to the hospital. The woman, whose identity is being withheld, is said to be recovering at home.* The footage shows skid marks and debris still littering the embankment. The worst night of my life being analyzed for entertainment.

"Hey." John slips back into the room. "I like the obedient side of you. It's nice to know I actually *can* leave you alone for a few minutes."

"Finding out I'm prime time news has me riveted to my seat."

He picks up the remote. "Did they mention your name?"

"No. Thankfully."

"More than thankfully." He flips the television off. "I told the police *and* the hospital to keep your name private. If it leaks, heads are going to roll."

198

Sitting beside me, he takes my hand. "In my family, we keep our personal business private. You being my girlfriend, that extends to you. Tabloid reporters would have swarmed to get a good story, had someone spotted me."

"Everyone at the hospital knew your name."

"And they knew no outsiders were allowed to hover anywhere near your room." His head dips. "I protected your identity so reporters wouldn't follow you around later, trying to get a shot of me because people are obsessed with money and for some reason think those of us who have it are interesting. Knowing what I know now, I'm glad I had the foresight even though it wasn't for the right reason. You don't need reporters peeking through your windows too."

"No one was peeking through my windows before. It was the pest control people."

"Is being naïve a coping mechanism? You don't want to face what's really going on, so you rationalize an explanation to ignore the problem?"

That's exactly what I do. "First of all, I can't be naïve *and* stubborn. Pick one. Second, even if someone did press their nose to my glass, I'd bore them enough they'd only do it once. As for you being an important enough man to get my name buried, thank you. But now, Mr. Important, tell me what kind of damage you did to our friends. I saw you take your phone, and I'm not so naïve that I can't guess why."

"The only important thing about me, is you." He grins. "Which is why I went easy on those so-called friends. I want you to know I'll do anything for you. Even go against what I really, *really* want to do."

"If that were true, you wouldn't have talked to them at all."

"See? Stubborn." His thumb traces the back of my hand. "You're one of a kind. No one can pull off naïve stubbornness like you."

I open my mouth to protest. He kisses it. "And…" He kisses me again. "Compromising is hitting somewhere in the middle of what we both want. Which is what I just did. You didn't want me to yell at them. I wanted to put new holes in their bodies. So I compromised and only slapped their hands. Then gave them a nice update on how you're doing." His eyes twinkle. "How *are* you doing now that I've swallowed my egotistical stubborn pride?"

"I'll be better if you add gloater to your list of character traits."

His laughter warms me through. "Sweetheart, I'm working on my flaws. I'm even willing to be a little naïve for you, and whole lot gullible. But every man has his limits."

"Good." I bring his face to mine. "Because I don't need you gullible or naïve. I only need you to be the sweet man I fell in love with."

"Then you're in luck." He swings me into his arms. "You bring out the sweet in me."

Laying me down in the soft sheets of his bed, his lips move over mine. "I have the sweetest dreams about placing you here under different circumstances."

"Stop harassing people over me and maybe the circumstances will be the kind of different you want."

~87~

John and I are one gloriously entwined mess. Life hums along in sweet melody, the rhythm and harmony of two souls united in symphony. This level of understanding is something Mike and I never achieved. We had fun together and were great friends, but intimacy turned us into bumbling fools. So we mainly avoided it. We barely managed to blunder our way through losing our virginity, and not because of how sick he was. Now I wake up in the arms of a man who's the polar opposite.

These past two mornings have found our arms and legs tangled together under the cool sheets, our bodies piled in the middle of John's big bed. I'm inclined to stay right here, where he wants me. In part because the fact that I'm finally sleeping without nightmares has him relaxed and content. "Do you realize that since you've been sleeping in the bed with me, I've not had a single nightmare?"

"You barely move a muscle these days." He kisses me in the soft glow of dawn.

"Solid proof you're the only medicine I need."

"Flattering me so I don't give you any real medication?" He chuckles. "Nice move."

"No, seriously." I nestle into his chest, immune to the bite of pain when cloaked in his embrace. "I'm so calm when you hold me it makes me not want to move at all."

"Then don't." His fingers run through my hair. "We'll stay like this all day. Just you and me, cozy in *our* bed."

"Let's get up and pretend this is a normal day."

"I'd rather our normal days keep us right here." His fingers graze along my arm. "Especially when lying in bed all day is exactly what you should be doing."

"Except I'm getting up." I lift away from the comfort of his arms. "If you want me to believe that being here is what's best for me, then I need to feel like I'm returning to my ordinary self."

"Fine." He blows out his breath. "I'll get you situated in the shower, then go down the hall and take my own so we can both shower at the same time. I'll be finished long before you anyway."

Enacting his compromise, he leaves me alone as the water begins to sting its way over my body. To get through the pain, I visualize *his* body under its own cascade of water. *You have to stop using imagery.* I wash quickly. "Got to stop thinking about him in the shower."

"What, sweetheart?" The door swings open. "You ready for me?"

"No." I cringe. "Did you hear what I just said?"

"From the sound of your voice, I wish I did. Care to share?"

"Never. And I need a few more minutes."

He leaves with a chuckle that makes me think he heard every word. But now that I've called him back into the room, he isn't mentioning it. If he heard, he'd unleash it just to watch my face turn colors. Instead, he wraps me in a fluffy white robe. "I'm going to dry your hair now."

"I'll do it today." I reach for the dryer.

He yanks it away. "I insist."

"You insist on everything."

"When I'm done here, I'm going to insist you don't get up while I go make breakfast." He smiles. "And yes, I insist on making breakfast myself, so don't start arguing with me and telling me your hands aren't broken. I get it. I've heard you. But I'm still cooking." He lowers to my ear. "All by myself."

It's nice that he's skilled in domestic duties, but I can't help feeling as if our mornings will hit higher notes if we make breakfast together. So even though he made me swear fifteen times I won't get up, I'm getting up. Walking into the kitchen of my own accord will impress him. Whether he knows it or not.

<h1 style="text-align:center">~88~</h1>

Pain is subjective. The information it gives you can be used to halt progress, or the anguish can spur you to change your tactics. Of course I'm going to feel like I got hit by a truck, I basically did. But my casted leg doesn't hurt anymore and the misery in my ribcage isn't going away anytime soon. I accept both these truths and choose to focus on the former.

Finished dabbing on makeup, I press into the bathroom floor with my good foot, holding onto the sink for support. I slide my casted foot across the tile beneath me, applying weight until I'm steady and standing. My head spins, but I don't feel sick. *Moment of truth.* I take a step, jumping forward on my good foot while letting my cast graze along until it's under me and I'm steady again. I release the sink, pressing my shoulder into the wall for support.

The room spins. A slow, throbbing twirl. I spin with it, facing the door. I can still reach the chair if I need it. I can also reach the door. If I take the long way around, stay tucked against the wall and time the spin.

"Mary!" John barrels in, arms outstretched to catch my not-falling body. "Are you hurt?"

"I was only standing."

"I told you not to get up!" His face pales. "What if you fell in here? Do you see the hard surfaces? Do you see all the things that can crack your head open?"

"I see how upset you are." I run my hands over his shoulders. "I'm sorry I scared you."

"You're not scaring me, you're terrifying me." His heart pounds against mine. "I don't want any more apologies. I want your cooperation."

"I *am* cooperating." More than I should. "What else can you possibly want from me?"

"A lot." His eyes hammer mine. "Most of which I can't have right now. But I *can* have the most important one. Your safety."

"I'm *safe* simply because I'm here. Right?"

"In the grand scheme of things, yes." He swallows. "But you doing things that make me question how much I've underestimated what keeping you safe really means. You're too strong-willed for your own good. So stop already."

"You mean, do what you say."

"Yeah!" He isn't shy about admitting *anything*. "I know what's best for you, Mary. And it isn't walking around by yourself in the most dangerous room of the house."

"I wasn't walking around. I was standing. Big difference." I stare him down exactly the way he's glaring at me.

"Standing isn't the way to get you better." He shifts me closer to his body. "And I need you fully recovered because, once you are, you're going to find out what else I want from you."

I already know. So does my red face. "We're supposed to compromise. Which means you need to give me the crutches that are in the closet. And you need to stop insinuating you want to sleep with me every five seconds."

"I'm the only one who compromises around here." He hoists me into his arms. "You're the one who expects me to totally give in to you. *And* you're the one who keeps bringing up sex. When I say I want a lot from you, very little of it has to do with sex."

"You expect me to believe that?"

"Sweetheart, you have no idea what's in store for you." His devilish smile tells me it's true. "But quit trying to get yourself hurt worse and you'll find out real soon."

~89~

My moment to walk in on my own ruined, I sit where John deposited me at his dining table, toasting to starting new traditions with him. He wants to have all our meals together.

I raise my glass. "Once I'm back on my feet, we can eat together every weekend. You can come to my place one weekend, and I'll come here the next."

"We'll eat together every day." He withholds his glass. "No point in eating a meal alone when we've got each other."

"I already eat lunch with Kim on Wednesdays, and it'll be impossible to make our schedules work every single day."

"With me, everything is possible." His glass clangs against mine. "I'll even compromise and let you keep Wednesday lunch with Kim. Cheers, sweetheart."

I leave my hand hanging in the air, jiggling the glass of juice. "You're not *letting* me keep my lunch date with Kim, I'm keeping it because I can. Secondly—" A car horn blasts outside, peeling the skin from my bones. The glass slips from my fingers, crashing onto the hardwood, splattering juice and glass.

"Whoa!" He grips my shoulders. "Look at me, sweetheart. You're safe. No one is going to hurt you." His forehead rests on mine. "Take a breath for me."

"Who's out there? Who's doing that?" The horn blasts through my skull.

"I don't know. But it isn't anyone who's going to hurt you." His lips brush mine. "I'm going to go see who it is, then I'll come back and clean up the glass. Don't move. I'll be right back."

By the time he reaches the door, shouts are flying. He flings open the heavy mahogany. "Susan!"

"There you are, John Beller!" she yells. "How dare you send the police to my house because your stupid truck got scratched. I've already called my father. You'll be sorry!"

"I'll be sorry?" He storms outside. "Are you kidding me? Don't expect me to believe it's a coincidence that the very night I happen to see *you*, my truck gets keyed. Especially when you know you've stooped lower."

"You still crying over *that* spilled milk? This your way of trying to pay me back? Why don't you just get over it! We both know I was the best thing that ever happened to you."

He doesn't seem shocked. I'm not either. She's behaving exactly like the person he described her to be. "It would be extremely sad if *you* were the best thing to ever happened to me. But you weren't. You met the woman who is the night you keyed my truck. You know, the woman who isn't intimidated by you? Now, get off my property before I have you arrested."

Through the window, I see him turn, coming back inside. She follows, never taking a breath. At the threshold her eyes land on me, sitting at his table in nothing but a robe. Venom laced flames shoot from her tongue, a full verbal assault directed at me.

Until now, John's been fairly calm. "How *dare* you come onto *my* property and attack *my* girlfriend." He whirls toward her, backing her away from his door.

"John!" She's goading him. "Her words can't hurt me."

Glancing back, he hesitates. A slow smile teases the corner of his mouth. Relief and understanding wash across his brow. I'm stronger than her words and he knows it. He winks, turning back to the hiss of the snake in his ear. "My—" His cheek is met with a thunderous slap.

"Hey!" My feet hit the floor, pounding to him as he chases her fleeing form into the driveway. "You can't…" My head tilts and whirls. "You…" My leg numbs. My good leg. "Don't hurt him!" I shout, the world dimming. My face slams into something hard and cool. I taste blood. Hear the screech of tires. And greet the darkness.

<h1 style="text-align:center">~90~</h1>

New sounds beg my eyes to open. Voices wafting through the fog. Female. Not Susan. "What's wrong? Got a woman in there?"

"The smirk on your face says you know I do," John snaps. "She's sleeping."

"In the middle of the day?" A different female. An older one.

"*If* I let you two inside, you're going to your rooms and staying quiet."

"My room? I'm not a child!" the older voice snaps back. "*Good lord! Did you kill her?*"

"Be *quiet!*" he growls.

"It's kind of hard when your living room looks like a slaughterhouse." The younger gags. "Is that a drag mark? Did you drag a body through here?"

The fuzz in my head clears, a slow and steady fading buzz. Just like at the hospital. I try to speak. Force my lips to move. They push against the film of lead holding them hostage. "John," I murmur. Thick and numb. "John." Feet pound toward me. My heart races. "John!"

"I'm here." He falls into my neck. Kissing. Holding. "I should have been here when you woke up." More kisses. "Are you okay? Please tell me you're okay."

My eyes slide open. I touch his face. "What happened? Where's Susan?"

"Gone." He presses into my hand. "She's not dumb enough to come back. But Mary…" His eyes search. "Are you okay?"

Every part of me hurts. Even my non-casted foot throbs. "You drugged me."

"You what?" A woman with puffy gray-blonde hair towers behind his crouched form. "Johnathan Beller—"

"I didn't drug her." he snaps, eyes flinging to mine. "Much. I called Dr. Mansfield and he's on his way, but you were bleeding. Bad." He swallows. "I had to get the glass out. He said to give you part of a sleeping pill. I crushed it like he said and put it under your tongue."

I remember the fall. My face slamming into the floor. The glass. It burned inside my foot, scratching over the hardwood, digging deeper as I made my way toward the door. "I passed out."

"Passing out is the least of what you did." A tear slides over his cheek. I wipe it away. As bad as my foot hurts, I'm glad I wasn't awake for what he had to do.

"I'm fine. Stop crying."

"I can't take much more of this, sweetheart."

"More of what?" Katherine, his mother whose picture I've seen in the house, stands over his shoulder with an air about her that says she's not a woman to be trifled with. "Saving her? Repeatedly?" Her eyes level on me. "It must be nice to have a man constantly picking up the pieces while you—"

"Mom!" he growls.

"It's okay." I grip his hand, returning her stare—only nicer. "He's been here for me, yes. But—"

"But nothing." He squeezes my hand. "You don't owe her anything. Especially not an apology."

"Says you." Katherine shrugs. "Anyway, I have to go clean your house instead of taking the nap I thought I'd get after riding in a car with this one." She throws a hand toward her daughter, eyes leveling back on me. "You don't have any diseases, do you? I'll clean wearing gloves, but I'd like to know if I should call a fumigator instead."

"*Mom.*" John's face turns a shade of purple I never thought I'd see on him.

"Serious question, bro." Sheila's mouth twists, eyes scanning. So much like her brother. "There's murder-scene blood in there. Did all of that come out of you?"

~91~

Katherine and Sheila don't have to be in the same room to make their presence known. "Yelled at! Over a woman I just found out about today!" Katherine makes sure I can hear her from her spot in the living room. "My son, behaving like a fool. Playing nursemaid to a—"

"Mom!" His voice blasts through the open bedroom door and down the hall. "Do *not* test me!"

"The damsel in distress act has fooled better men than you!" she booms back.

My head drops. He pulls my hands into his. "Be honest with me. Are you okay? I was going to take you to the hospital, but Dr. Mansfield said if your vitals were okay that..."

"I'm fine." I meet his eyes. "Physically. But your mom hates me. She thinks I'm—"

"I don't care."

"I care! This is the worst possible way to meet her. Flat on my back, in *your* bed, wearing nothing but a robe."

He shrugs. "What we do is none of her business, and we have every right to do whatever we want."

"Every right?"

"Yes!" he snaps. "If you're going to let her make you feel guilty for doing absolutely nothing, I'm going to go get the luggage I just carried in and tell her to leave."

If they brought luggage, they intend to stay. "They're not leaving. I am." I swing my legs quickly enough to get them over the bed's edge before he wrangles me right back to where I came from. "John, this is *my* life."

209

"It's my life, too." He lies over me, blocking all escape routes. "All I want in *my* life is you. Safe. No arguing. No tears. No car accidents. No digging glass out of your feet. Just perfect, happy days where you smile and laugh and tell me you love me as much as I love you."

"No matter where I am, I'll still love you. And I'll tell you as much as you want."

I've terrified him again. The fear is written all over his face. "Your family *does* have valid reasons to dislike me. Under these circumstances, the least I owe them is an explanation."

"No one wishes the circumstances were different more than me." He presses his lips to mine. "But they're not. And that's not your fault."

"Maybe not. But you fighting with your family over me *is* my fault."

"Those two being full of opinions and unsolicited advice is the problem. I'm in no mood for it." He rolls off me, sitting up with an unexpected smile. "I *am* actually happy to have all three of my ladies under one roof, though."

"Funny, I didn't feel your happiness when we first arrived." Sheila smirks from the doorway.

"Funny, I don't remember telling you to come into my room." He smirks back.

"Things around here have been a little on edge." I squeeze his hand.

"Had they called first, they would have been greeted differently."

"Had we called first, we wouldn't be here." She pushes off the frame. "You would have made sure of that."

"Yep." He nods. "But since you *are* here, keep your thoughts to yourself and I'll let you stay. Don't, and you leave."

"Spoken like a man who doesn't have the past you have." She looks me over. He doesn't like the scrutiny.

"I'm not even remotely kidding, Sheila. I'm at my breaking point. Back. Off."

I rub his shoulder, sending every comfort I have to offer through my fingertips. "He's been through a lot lately. I'm sure you can forgive him for being short."

I give her a smile and she returns the courtesy, a twinkle in her amber eyes. "When did you two meet? Ten minutes ago?"

"All I needed was ten seconds." He grins.

"Only because those ten seconds were calm." I swallow. "They tricked him. Obviously."

"Hardly." He chuckles, passing her a sly glance. "But we can argue about that later, sweetheart. Right now, we need to celebrate. It didn't go down like I planned, but you just survived meeting my mother."

~92~

I'm not as sure as John is that I survived meeting his mother. The lump in my chest and shallow breathing say I should have taken him up on his offer to go to the hospital. But at least Sheila and I are getting along. She made the three of us sandwiches and is sitting on the bed, telling us just how *not* fine her mom is.

"She isn't going to get better anytime soon, either. Because you have him wound up tighter than a—"

"Hush!" he orders. "And stop bouncing on the bed. You're hurting her!"

"I'm only pointing out the obvious." Her dark lashes flutter. "And I barely made a single wave on your bed of indiscretion."

"We're not sleeping together." I defend. "It's like you said, we barely know each other."

"Don't." He captures my lips. "What we do is our business. They can pass all the judgement they want, but the decisions we make are ours."

Sheila watches us until his attention turns to her, arms tugging her into a playful headlock. A very loose one. She's polished. I doubt he'd do anything to mess up her look. "Apologize for making my girlfriend blush."

"Not if this is all you've got." She pushes him over. "Weak."

"I was trying to be civil in front of company." He sits up. "My sister is a lady, but only half the time."

"He's just mad I can do…well, pretty much everything better than him." She smooths down her shoulder-length hair. "We like to let him think he calls the shots, though."

She stares at him, a grin rivaling his own plastered on her face. He caves, leaning on the headboard beside me with a smile. "What exactly made you and Mom come here today?"

"I know the sight of us peeling out of my brand-new ruby-red Corvette stopped you dead." She winks at me. A *wait until you see my envy-inciting car* wink. "But we have a standing invitation to visit anytime. We chose today. Surprise!"

"That's not it." He slides an arm around me. "Tell me the truth."

"Can't a mother and sister drop in on their beloved whenever they want?" She feigns innocence.

"Sheila." The rumble is back in his throat.

"Okay, fine." She laughs. "We heard from Dr. Mansfield that the *girlfriend* we know nothing about is living with you. If you had told Mom yourself you moved a woman in here, she might have taken the news a little better. Instead, she flipped! You are in so much trouble. I can't wait!"

I've thought of a thousand reasons not to be here, but my presence upsetting his family never made the list. "This is awful."

"Mom will be fine." He pulls me in close. "And little sis here is enjoying the whole thing. Aren't you?"

"Oh yeah!" She beams. "If I can't laugh at you and Mom, what is there to live for?"

"I'm thinking dresses, parties, and cars. Isn't that how you spend your time these days?"

"Better than spending it moving strangers into my house."

"Don't knock it 'til you've tried it." He plants a kiss on my cheek. "It's working out pretty well for me."

She plunks him in the head, eyes rolling. "This is my cue to exit. But before I go, I have to know. How'd a lug like you manage to land her? Even with all that bruising, she's a doll."

"I'm charming." He slides his arm from behind me and shoots forward, wrestling her into a bear hug. "Just ask her."

With a wink, he lifts her off the bed and plops her down outside the door. "I'm also fed up." He focuses on an object down the hall. Undoubtedly Katherine is standing there. "You two had better know your place in my house."

~93~

Alone again with John, I take a deep breath. "I've been sitting around here not even thinking about your family. Call Kim. Have her come pick me up."

"No." His eyes harden. "Nothing has changed. These walls are the only ones you're going to be seeing for a good long while."

"I only agreed to stay here for one night."

"Keep going down the path you've been on and you're going to end up in a much worse place than my bedroom."

"The only place I'm going to end up is my house."

"Then that's where I'm going." His eyes challenge mine. I start to protest but his emeralds blaze. "Seeing you hurt and looking into your eyes where the suffering you're trying to hide stares back at me, I'm dying. I hurt when you hurt. I suffer when you suffer. And I don't know what to do because, no matter *what* I do, you're still hurt. Instead of getting better, you got injured again" His fingers trail over the new soreness along my nose and cheek. "Why is that every single thing you want to do makes getting hurt a matter of when, not if? Why can't you just stay safe? Warm. Here. In the house I built when I dreamed of you."

Maybe in another life. In a dream where I get what I want, too. "Why do you think your house is the only place I can possibly be safe?"

"How do you know it's not?"

"I don't." Lately, home hasn't felt safe at all. "What I *do* know is you and your mom need to make amends."

"She's fine. Just...old-fashioned."

"*That* doesn't sound like she's fine." I point toward the door where her voice breaks through, complaining loudly to Sheila.

"Apparently, Sleeping Beauty isn't just distressed, she's fragile. We can't even have a conversation with the frail thing. What on earth does he want with someone you can't talk to?"

"Give me a minute." His body moves from mine.

"No." I pull him to me. "You didn't tell her about me, so of course she's shocked to find me here. What mother wouldn't be?"

"I *did* tell her about you." He rubs his neck. "I talked to her several times while you were in the hospital. Each time I called you my girlfriend. She chose to interpret that as a girl who is a friend. And yeah, I was short with her and didn't take time to make things clear, but after you were released I *also* told her I would be out of the loop while I helped you recover. It isn't my fault she assumed that would be at your house."

"No matter what she assumed, she's here now. And she needs a chance to be alone with you so she can understand how her son went from single to living with someone in the time it took her to drive here. So let's not argue about this. Call Kim. I don't want to begin our relationship disappointing your mother."

"If she's disappointed, that's her own fault." He leans against the headboard. "If she'd stop complaining and get to know you instead, she'd love you as much as I do."

"She'll stop complaining when I'm gone."

"Before we fight *again* about how I'm not calling Kim, or anyone else, let me bring up the real reason we need to fight. *You* dragging yourself *bleeding* across the house this morning. What on earth were you thinking?"

In that moment, only one thought was present. I place my hand over the spot where Susan's blow landed, the memory flooding back in. "She hit you."

"That's why you got up? Because a girl slapped me?"

"Yes! I couldn't just sit there. What if she never stopped hitting you? I had to stop her!" He can't contain his laughter. "It isn't funny. The nerve she has to come here and yell at you after everything she's done."

"Nothing bad was going to happen this morning." His hand runs to my ribs. "Calm down before you hurt yourself for the ten millionth time."

"Something *could* have happened."

"Something *did* happen." He nods to my foot. "So no matter what, in the future, you *will* stay put when I ask you to."

His jaw tenses. "I get carried away sometimes. But if you were worried I'd hit her, please know I would never raise a hand to a woman. Not even someone as vile as Susan."

That thought never entered my mind. "I was worried about her raising her hand to you. Again."

"She could never do any real damage to me." His fingers trace up my side, rounding my shoulder, moving slowly up my neck. "But you, sweetheart, gave me a heart attack. I don't ever want to see another drop of blood leave your body." He lifts my chin, turning my face to his. "I saw the evidence of what had to be the most painful walk of your life. And as honored as I am that you'd do that for me, I'm furious over it." He leans in close. "But I understand why you did it. Because I'd do the exact same thing for you."

~94~

John's lips are tender. Sweet. All the things I want and need wrapped in the taste of his mouth and the scent of his skin. My heart has been a spillway since his first devilish grin. "Let's at least go into the living room to smooth things over with your mom, because if first impressions count for anything, I was at a huge deficit *before* she caught me in your bed. I doubt you wanted to introduce a multi-colored girlfriend with two bum legs."

"My plan was to take a very healthy you out to my family's estate on the Potomac for the introduction." He snuggles us down into the sheets. "I thought it would be the perfect setting to introduce the new lady in my life to the other two. And honestly, I couldn't wait for that day to come. It might have been where we ended up that Sunday."

If I hadn't wrecked, the next day would have been spent zipping all over the countryside in his Viper. "Estate on the Potomac?"

"It sounds pretentious." He smiles. "But it's an old family home. Mom and Sheila mainly live there full time now."

"Sounds nice."

"You'll get to spend plenty of time there." His brow knits. "I hope you didn't mind the introduction. Or me planning our first trip to see them without asking if you wanted to meet my family. In case you haven't noticed, I'm barreling down the road toward our future at a dead sprint. And I can't slow down. I got rid of the brakes a long time ago."

"I hear brakes are overrated."

"They certainly are."

He plants his hands firmly behind his head, intriguing mouth talking of buying a deserted island for us to hole up on. A plan I could get behind if there wasn't this little thing called reality. "Things don't fall apart whenever other people are around. You just need to see perfection in the imperfections because that's what normal life is. No one gets to make a plan and see it go off without a hitch."

"This someone does." He sighs. "And we *are* getting time alone. It'll be just the two of us very soon."

"But it isn't just the two of us now. So either help me up or I'll crawl myself to the closet. I need to get dressed."

"You're dressed just fine for bed."

I sit up. "You can't leave your company alone all day."

"They're big girls, they can take care of themselves."

He presses my shoulders gently back into the pillows. I cross my arms. He kisses me. "How does staying in bed sound now? And before you answer, know there's plenty more of those where that one came from."

"Then go spread some around to your family. And take me with you so I can see you charm your way back into their good graces." I eye him. "Unless you're embarrassed of me? Is that the real reason you refuse to let them get near me?"

"The only person embarrassed here is you." He jumps off the bed, disappearing into the closet, coming back out with sweatpants and a t-shirt. "If you had stayed where you were supposed to this morning, you'd have one good foot to stand on. You didn't, so I'll have to dress you while you're lying here in my bed."

"You say that like it's punishment for you."

He tugs on the robe's belt. "I was trying to hide how much I like the idea of you being naked in my bed." He unties the robe, eyes on mine. "Are you sure you don't want to stay right here and see how far my lips can get me?"

I lie back. "Enjoy dressing me, then get the crutches out of the closet."

He works the pants over my cast, keeping a sheet draped over my body. "You only get the crutches once I know you can behave. You haven't even come close to proving that to me yet."

"Good thing I don't have to prove *anything* to you."

His hands slide up my legs. "Trust me, you're going to learn to prove everything to me. And you're going to like it."

Only if it feels as good as his rough skin moving over my thighs. "I can do the rest myself." I break the course of his fingers and hike the pants into place, sitting up and clutching the sheet to my chest. He hands me the shirt. I meet his eyes. "You're going to learn to love the way I walk on those crutches."

<h1 style="text-align:center">~95~</h1>

Cradled tightly in John's arms because he insists that even if I didn't have two bum legs, the ribs would be the real obstacle to using crutches, I'm relieved to at least not be in his bed when I meet Katherine for the second time. He clears the hallway. Her eyes snap to us. "Seriously, John? There are better modes of transportation for her. For Pete's sake! Why are you carrying her?"

"I don't know who Pete is and I'm not doing anything for his sake." He settles me onto the sofa, laying me down. I push up to sit like a normal person. "Fine." He frowns. "Have it your way. Again." I roll my eyes. He smiles. "Sit still a minute."

I glance toward his mom. She's staring daggers at me. He props a stool from the corner under my legs. "How's that?"

"Fine." I look her way again, freezing under her glare. He slides next to me, cradling me in the crook of his arm. I move away from his body.

"Don't be uneasy." He tucks me back in. Closer. Lips moving to my ear. "I couldn't care less about what other people think. Even my mom."

"I care."

"And one day, I'm going to embarrass you enough that you'll stop caring." He pulls me in so tight I'm practically on his lap. "Until then…" His eyes narrow on his mom. "The best mode of transportation for my girlfriend is me. Until I decide otherwise."

"Wouldn't you like to have a wheelchair?" Her eyes are still on me. "Or crutches? So you can move about without depending on him? Or do you prefer letting him be your service animal?"

Between the beating pulse of his growl and her glare, I want to disappear. "I would love nothing more than to have a wheelchair right now, since your son refuses to let me have the crutches that are in his closet."

His flinch brings her reluctant eyes to him, finger tapping against the fabric of her chair. "Is that true?"

"Crutches and wheelchairs are unnecessary when she has me. End of subject. What else would you ladies like to talk about?"

Sheila shrugs. "Your ego?"

My laugh slipped out. Sheila's is on purpose. He isn't amused. "My ego wouldn't be a problem if you two weren't here. How long did you say you were staying? Until tomorrow morning?"

"Until we've talked sense into you." Katherine shoves a hand in my direction. "And this…this girl."

He's on his feet. Sheila heads him off, dipping down into a waving bow toward me. "What Mom means, Mary, is we'd like to stay until we've figured out why my brother moved you into his house twenty-five seconds after meeting you. May we? Please? Without having our eyes burned out for looking on your beautiful presence?"

As bad as it is, I can't help laughing again. The sound draws his attention. "Sit down, Sheila." He plops back beside me with a frown. "It hurts her to laugh. So stop trying to be funny."

"But if you address *him* as 'Your Highness', his ego will let you stay." I wink at her, patting his leg while I whisper. "Now don't you wish you'd called Kim?"

"I wish I could compromise the way you do." His eyes simmer. "But it isn't too late. We can go back to *our* room and stay there."

"Our room?" Katherine huffs. "You mean the one you paid for and she just waltzed into?"

"She didn't waltz, I carried her."

"*Wow.*" Sheila whistles. "This is going to be more fun than I thought. Who wants popcorn?"

Her lively presence is comforting, but even the bright smiles she flashes can't hide her own concern. And they certainly aren't taking the edge off Katherine's bark. "The questions you two have about me are understandable. So, go ahead. Ask. I'll answer to the best of my ability."

~96~

Mother and son are ready to do battle over me. I feel like a homewrecker. "John, please." I press a hand into his arm. "Let this happen. They need to know who I am and how I ended up here."

"I'm pretty sure the story will take longer than the actual event." Sheila glances at her unmoving mother, winking at me. "I can't wait to hear this saga."

The account *does* seem much longer than actual events. "I find this story hard to believe," Katherine challenges after I finish. "Love at first sight is rarely real. Especially when followed with distress." She focuses on her slit-eyed son. "I thought I raised you to be smarter."

"I loved her before I knew she was in distress."

"That doesn't mean you didn't sense it." she snaps, body pulling to the edge of her seat.

Her words hammer inside my brain. I've worried myself that he's only feeling how he feels about me because of guilt. "I've told him he isn't responsible for me. I've even begged to go home, but he—"

"Is taking care of his girlfriend!" he seethes. "And there are plenty of distressed women in the world. If that's what turned me on, I would have filled every room in this house with them years ago." His finger jabs at her. "That is *not* what drew me to her. If she had her way, I wouldn't even *be* dating her."

That's one way to raise eyebrows. Now they're glaring at me in defense of him. "Only because I didn't want to get involved with anyone right now." I clutch his hand. "But he wasn't easy to walk away from, and now I don't want to."

"I hear he's charming." Sheila relaxes in her chair.

222

"He's more than charming." I meet his eyes, pleading. "After what he's been through with Susan, I completely understand why the two of you are upset over me. So don't curb yourselves. I won't take offense at your questions, and he won't object to them."

"Yes, I will. I didn't bring the love of my life in here to sit her in front of a firing squad."

Even if the firing squad was shooting blanks, he'd still keep me from it. "Not everything is your call. *I'm* saying it's okay for them to fire."

"Then go ahead, Mom." He wraps a protective arm around me. "If there's something you just have to know, ask it right here in front of me. But I'm warning you, do *not* insult her again. Got it?"

"Got it." She leans forward. "Mary, my first question is, why are you not capable of thinking for yourself?"

"The end." He's on his feet, lifting me into his arms. I kick to stop him. "Are you trying to make me drop you?"

"She has every right to question her son's girlfriend. And she isn't sitting there with a butcher knife, waiting to carve up my flesh. So either you want us to get to know each other or you're embarrassed of me. Which is it?"

He sits back down. "Mom. Sheila. I'd like you to get to know Mary. My amazing *girlfriend.*"

"One who brings out the worst in you, it seems," Katherine sighs.

"And one who entered stage left only ten minutes ago," Sheila adds. "He's never been impulsive with the opposite sex before, but his new dark-haired roommate has changed that."

"Could you please knock it off?" He deflates, propping my feet back onto the stool. "Please?"

Sheila studies him. Eyes deep and questioning. Like his. Like his mother's. Even as paupers on the street, these three would be intimidating. "You filled a notebook with pros and cons before you ever asked anyone else out. I doubt you've done that for her."

"And are you being possessive with her? Or are you putty in her hands?" Katherine's gaze rests on me. "Well?" My mouth opens. No sound comes out.

"My emotions are running high, and in every direction." He rubs my knee. "And yeah, it all revolves around her. But once you spend time with her, you'll see for yourself what all the fuss is about. You'll see what I see in her."

"Fine. Leave us alone for a while." Katherine waves him away.

"Sorry, sweetheart." He meets my eyes. "This is where I draw the line. They can talk to you with me sitting right here, or not at all."

"Why? Are you not wearing your big girl panties today?" Sheila grins.

"From what I saw, she doesn't wear any kind of panties," Katherine fires. Her first round hits hard.

~97~

I'm already uncomfortable and John makes it worse by being intimately close with me in front of his mom. But his tense breathing slows with the contact, and I need this quiz to be over. Katherine's questions are eerily similar to the ones he asked the night we met. And like him, she analyzes every word out of my mouth. At least I know the punch line. Might as well get right to it.

"I'm not Susan. And as bad as I feel for saying this about another human being, the woman disgusts me. The way she behaved this morning proves her character."

Katherine nods, watching me. "John paints a stark contrast between the wrecking ball Susan and his *dear sweet Mary*."

"If I see her near him again, I doubt *sweet* will be a label I earn."

He chuckles. She manages a laugh, cold and dry. "I've said the same, but we're not barbarians. Even if my son is acting like I raised him in the wild."

"He's only worried. I've put him through a lot."

"So it seems." She sighs. "Susan is only one in a long line of many. Women like her are everywhere, and John is unfortunately in their sights."

"I'm not after his money."

"You had better not be." She sits forward. "Because if I have to, I will battle my son head-on to stop him from making a grave mistake."

"Good." I follow her lead and bend forward. "Because so will I. I will also take care of myself in every possible way, including financially. Even if your son refuses to believe I can."

"Her son knows better." He groans. "And he's tired of explaining to his girlfriend that she doesn't have to do things alone anymore."

225

Katherine takes in the show. My will pitted against his. "You're right. He doesn't appear to be open to you doing anything at all on your own."

"Because she can't do anything on her own." He stares at the room. "Am I the only one who can see her? She was in *car accident.* That nearly *killed* her."

"Case in point." Katherine shoves her hand forward. "He's completely out of control when it comes to you. You've bewitched him. Separated him from common sense. What do you expect to gain from his behavior?"

"She can have anything she wants." He secures our hands together. "I've told her that a million times already. And she knows my worth has more zeros than she's seen in her lifetime, and still, this woman who *absolutely* has me bewitched, hasn't asked for one single thing."

"That isn't entirely true." I avoid his eyes, speaking directly to her. "I've asked him repeatedly for crutches. And, if we're being really honest, I also asked him not to drug me. And well, you heard for yourself how that turned out."

"Unbelievable." He drags a hand down his face. "See what I'm dealing with here? See why I want you two to leave? I've got my hands full just trying to get her to sit still long enough to keep me from *having* to drug her."

"The problem is," I'm not concerned about what I can gain from John. I'm concerned about what I can lose. "He's too willing to put himself through *anything* for my sake."

"The woman who walks through glass to save me from nothing is saying I'm too steadfast? That's what you see. Right, Mom? Sheila?"

"He has a point." Sheila scrunches her nose.

I shake my head. "I've completely exhausted him for weeks. He's going to burn out. Then where does that leave us? Absolutely nowhere, because you could be right, Katherine." She'll agree with me. "He and I could be snowballing all because of the condition I'm in."

"No!" He turns my face to his. "The car accident has nothing to do with the depth of my love for you."

"Does it have something to do with your love for him?" Katherine asks.

"I loved him before." I touch his face. "That's why this is so hard. I want you to have a wonderful, normal life. And you can't do that while you're in the middle of mine. You're not even working. And you love your carpentry."

"I love you more."

~98~

Out of her seat and by John's side, Katherine's arm darts possessively around his shoulder, pulling him toward her. Away from me. She hesitates, looking between us as he removes the distance she's trying to force. "If my son told you he is okay being smack in the middle of your life, then he is. So I'm willing to tolerate you. If you didn't make the decision to move in here, I might even like you."

"I didn't make the decision." I jump so hard I nearly stand. "John Beller made the decision. He didn't fill me in until I was released from the hospital and now he won't let me leave."

"Kidnapping, brother?" Sheila tsks. "I can't say I'm shocked. But you might want to keep the felonies to a minimum. We have a family reputation to uphold."

Based on the accusations of Detective Summers, he doesn't like this joke. But Sheila is having way too much fun with this topic. "Mary, did he bring you here against your will?"

"He didn't *maliciously* kidnap me."

"That makes it better then." She laughs. "It was a benevolent kidnapping. Bravo, brother. Bravo."

His jaw tenses. Katherine finally smiles. A real, genuine smile. "Looking at your physical state, and knowing what we now know about the accident, I wouldn't have let you go home either."

"Finally!" He throws his hands up in triumph. Only to be cut down again with a quick shake of her head.

"I'd have sent you to a hotel," she admits. "But my son takes things to the extreme and acts like a pure fool."

"Finally!" I throw up my hands, mocking him.

He sulks. We females laugh. I even get a wink from his mom. "From one independent woman to another, while I'm here, you *will* have an ally."

"Two!" Sheila chimes in.

He rubs his face. "You three getting along is simultaneously a relief and a curse."

"What's wrong, brother?" Sheila giggles. "Is this house only big enough for one tyrant?"

Headlights shine in the driveway. He gets up. "It's only big enough for who's in it right now. So you three keep giggling and call me anything you like, I'll take my frustration out on whoever this is." He kisses my forehead. "Sweetheart, I'll be right back. And you'd better be in this exact spot."

~

Dr. Mansfield is on the very short list of approved visitors, and John's ushering him inside so quickly I don't have time to move from this *exact* spot. "Sorry for arriving so late. My pneumonia patient isn't going to recover. I've been with his family."

"Of course. And I'm doing fine. My checkup can wait if you need to go back to them."

"No, it can't." John's eyes bug out. "I'm sorry the man is sick, and I know what it's like to lose someone, but you're still in need of getting checked out."

"He's right." Mansfield gives a soft smile. "I've been worried about you. I'll go right back to the others once I put my mind at ease over you. Now, would you like me to examine you here or someplace more private?"

"Private." John lifts me into his arms.

"Oh!" Sheila fans her face. "If only we all had a big strong man to tell us what we want. After all, we're only mere women."

"I can answer for her because I know what she wants." He stomps down the hall. "This is me making sure she gets it."

<h1 style="text-align:center">~99~</h1>

John was right about me wanting privacy for Dr. Mansfield's thorough examination. Once we got into the bedroom he tucked me under the sheets and undressed me, per the doctor's instruction. Then he made a request. "At the hospital, I never stayed in the room for your exams. Most of the time you weren't awake, and when you were I didn't think you were clear-headed enough to make the decision about me being there." He swallows. "Because of your injuries, you may have to be *exposed*. I'll turn around or flat-out leave if you get uncomfortable, but I'd like to be here if I can."

I always wondered why he left. The hospital staff could have practiced modesty and we certainly can here. He's already proven that. I grip his hand. "Thank you for being considerate. I want you to stay. Even if I'm unconscious, always stay."

"You've got it." He nods to the doctor. "See if I have a future in glass removal."

I dig my fingers into the sheet as Mansfield approaches my foot, keep my face a neutral mask as he probes the gash. "Should I have brought her in for stitches?" Johns asks when Mansfield assures him every sliver was removed.

"The foot can be a tricky place for stitches." He cleans the wound, applying a clean dressing and uncovering my leg to mid-thigh. He presses on the discolored flesh. "Especially when young ladies won't stay off their feet."

"Tell me about it," John grumbles.

"Sometimes ladies have things to do." My teeth clench when Mansfield pushes on a particularly sore spot.

"Any pain here?" he asks. I shake my head and he moves on to my other leg, inspecting the cast and the bruising covering my thigh. "The swelling is down. On a scale of one to ten, how's your pain level overall?"

"One."

"Ten," John corrects. "Did you see her clutching the bedsheet before you even touched her foot?"

"My foot throbs." I avoid his knowing eyes. "But I'm not in excruciating pain."

"She wouldn't tell us if she was."

"She's a feisty one." Mansfield chuckles. "But young lady, I've known this one since he was born. He's something north of feisty. So you'll want to start cooperating with him."

"Look at that." John whistles. "Doc, that stare right there says she's not going to. Just to prove she doesn't have to. Compliments of a willful child growing up without parents." My eyes go wide. He smiles. "But I'm not her dad. And if my mom wasn't in the house right now, I'd be proving a few things of my own."

When he can't kiss my mouth shut, he embarrasses my tongue down my throat. "Can I walk on crutches now?"

"No, ma'am." Mansfield shoots the idea down, carefully checking the bruising for more tender spots, which are everywhere. John gloats until Mansfield hands me the robe to cover my bust and slides the sheet away from my torso. "You're certainly better than the last time I saw you, but it's going to take some time to get you to a place where you can move about as freely as you'd like. Which is why you're going to take it easy. Right? You realize you're running out of body parts to injure?"

"I've heard." I watch John's fixated face. He's glued to my abdomen, the entirety of it is one deep-black bruise. From what I've seen in the mirror, it wraps around my back, crawls over my shoulder, and reaches up my neck. The very neck he's kissed in pleasure.

"How's the pain here?" Mansfield presses along the third rib on my left side.

"Fine." I lie.

"Good." Mansfield smiles. "You've been lucky one too many times already."

"I know." I swallow down the horror on John's face, tugging up the sheet to hide the gross visual. He keeps staring, as if he can see through the linen. "How do house calls work, Doctor? Do you bill my insurance or do I need to make other arrangements to pay you?"

"It's all taken care of." He glances at John.

"No, it isn't." I sigh. "Whatever he's told you, ignore it. I'm the one who will be paying you."

"I'll let you discuss that with Mr. Beller." He gathers his bag. "After he walks me out."

"I'll be right back, sweetheart." John finally moves, leaving my forehead with the memory of his kiss.

~100~

John's lack of reaction to me daring to ask Dr. Mansfield about his bill is concerning. I shouldn't have let him see my body. While he's gone, I slide my pants on, exhaling the agony. Sitting up, I tug the t-shirt over my head and push my arms into the sleeves. It might be painful, but mostly because I'm stiff and sore. I *need* to start doing things for myself.

"Did you not hear what the doctor just said? The part about taking it easy?" John stomps down the hall, past the questions of his mom and sister.

"Sitting up isn't strenuous."

"Everything is!" he roars. "You're *hurt*!"

Katherine and Sheila barrel down the hall in response to his booming voice. He slams the door on them. "Open that door right now!" I demand. He clicks it locked. Ice rushes through my veins. "What's wrong with you? Did Dr. Mansfield tell you I'm dying?"

"No." He thuds down beside me. "And I don't ever want to hear those words again."

"Then stop acting like I'm fragile. And unlock the door so I can tell them I'm fine."

"She's fine!" he yells.

"I'll unlock it myself."

My muscles flinch in the right direction before he secures me in the center of the bed. "I'm not *acting* like you're fragile. You *are* fragile." Anguish rushes his face. "I just saw how much."

The bruising. It's upsetting him as much as it did me the first time I saw the whole of it. "I'm not fragile. I'm human. And you're the one who keeps reminding me the flesh will heal."

"I know." His hand curls around the hem of my shirt. He swallows. "May I?"

"Take your own advice." I rest my hand along his jaw. "Look all you want but know it *will* heal. So don't fixate on it."

He slides the cloth to my bust, fingers running along my ribs, gliding over discolored skin as if his touch can erase the vulgar display. "I had no idea it was this bad. No wonder you're in so much pain."

"I'm not. It looks worse than it is. You know how bruises are."

"I know how you are." His voice is heavy, eyes studying each patch of flesh as his hand slowly moves over my torso.

"I shouldn't have let you stay." I remove his hand, lowering my shirt. "I didn't want you to see me like this until I was healed."

His eyes close. "You were planning on letting me see you shirtless after you healed?"

"I...meant that if you happened to...I mean, if it happened...a while from now..."

"Don't worry, sweetheart." His eyes open, big hands sliding under me, lifting me onto his lap. "I've been planning on happening to since day one."

"Then should I be nervous about being locked in a room with you?"

"Very." His lips rest on my neck. "Unless this hurts?"

"It doesn't."

"You wouldn't tell me if it did."

"True."

After the shock of seeing the whole condition of my body, he needs this time with me. Holding me. Kissing me. But as much as I want to tuck under the blankets with him, I can't. "Not staying locked in here all night might make your mom and sister hate me slightly less."

"You've already won them over." He sighs. "Me, on the other hand? I might have lost their favor."

~101~

Two seconds after leaving the sanctuary of John's bedroom, Sheila snaps, "Aww, Mary, how nice of the warden to finally let you out."

"The doctor said you're healing well." Katherine pushes a cold stare our way. "I called him for an update, since the details around here were vague."

"Sorry about that." I swallow. "I'm fine."

"No, Mary. You're not fine." John sits down, keeping me cradled on his lap against my will. Katherine and Sheila observe me with twisted expressions. He glances up. "She's red faced because she doesn't want to be perched on my lap in front of you. But I don't care, because I like her on my lap."

"Why?" Katherine asks. "Is she not capable of sitting beside you like a grown-up?"

"I wouldn't know." He holds me in place as I try to slide away. "I do like it when she squirms though, so keep—"

"John!" I choke.

Katherine isn't impressed with my ability to turn colors. "You're in front of company."

"I saw you sit on Dad's lap more than once, so don't preach to me."

"But our parents were married when they acted all scandalous." Sheila grins.

His shoulders bob. "My feelings for her are the same as theirs were for each other."

"You've known her for less time than it took your dad and me to kiss for the first time."

"Unlike my father, I don't drag my feet."

His dig wasn't meant to insult his dad. It was covering the way his blood boils anytime someone brings up the short length of our relationship. "He's sorry."

"What I am, is a man who gets to make points. I love her. She loves me. We're both adults. And we're not asking for opinions from the peanut gallery."

"Lov—"

"Don't you dare saw we haven't known each other long enough." He cuts his mom off. "And don't say I don't understand what love is because I do. Yes, Mary is gorgeous and that attracted me to her at first. I felt a spark, like nothing I've ever felt before. But it was the hours we spent together afterward that knocked me off my feet." His big hand covers my cheek. "I could have filled a thousand notebooks full of dreams and still fallen short of how wonderful you are."

My watery eyes rest on his. His mouth moves for mine. "For Pete's sake!" Katherine nips. "Love or not, was what I was going to say, she's still a grown woman. Stop carrying her around. Let her move! You don't have to smother the girl."

"Listen to your mother." I move away from his lips. "Do it for Pete, and his sake."

"Do it for all of mankind." Sheila places a hand on her heart. "Show us men *can* think with their *other* brain. Get your wonderful, beautiful, sweet Mary a wheelchair."

"I'm tired of the women's coalition you're trying to form in my house when the only thing I'm doing is what's best for *my* girlfriend."

"Is she a girlfriend? Or your possession?" Sheila glares. "Or should I just be apologizing for the fact that we females have opinions?"

"Have as many opinions as you want. Just keep them to yourself." He looks up at me. "And you need to kiss me whenever you feel like it. Mom, Pete, or the Pope himself watching. If they don't like it, they don't have to look."

I glance at Katherine. She shrugs, waving a dismissive hand. She can't reason with him and neither can I. A yawn escapes my lips. He stands. "This must be her bedtime," Sheila snarks.

"If she's yawning, it means she's tired. Since she needs as much rest as she can get, yes, it's her bedtime."

"Goodnight, Mary." Katherine's metallic voice shivers down my spine. "I'm glad you have John to tell you what you need and when you need it."

"He means well, and I really am tired. So I'll see you in the morning." My hand tightens on his bicep. "When I'll be sitting in a chair all on my own. And we'll pick up where we left off. Even if you decide to switch from blanks to live rounds."

~102~

Our bedroom door shut and locked, John slips me into the sheets. "I'm telling you now, if you so much as look at the edge of this bed, you'll wish me holding you on my lap was the only thing you had to worry about." He places a kiss on my forehead and disappears into the bathroom.

I count while he's gone, reaching fifty before he comes back out. Shirtless. "Showing off since you aren't covered in bruises? That's meaner than insulting your family a hundred different ways."

"They wouldn't be getting insulted if they weren't here aggravating me." He moves into the moonlight. My eyes roam over his flesh. He smiles. "All in due time, sweetheart."

"Not what I was thinking."

He slides into the bed next to me. "Prove it."

His hand lies softly across my stomach, fingers finding their way under the cotton of my shirt and stroking along my side. My arms wrap around his neck. "The way you're babying me is silly, and it makes me feel lazy. You're not catering to me anymore."

He studies the lines of my face in the dimness, the only light the full moon shining across the patio and through the glass doors. "If you're telling me to back off, you still don't fully comprehend what you mean to me."

"I do, because you mean the same to me." I press my lips to his. "But I can't sit around all the time. So ease up."

His eyes rest on my lips. "Everything you want is intangible. And it breaks my heart I can't give it to you."

"You're giving me some of it right now." I smile. "And for the rest, you don't have to *do* anything. Just let me do for myself."

"There isn't much you *can* or *need* to do right now." He sighs. "But I'll *try* to let you do more on your own."

"See, that wasn't so hard."

"It was agony." He grins. "I don't want to make promises I can't keep. I'd rather be honest and tell you I'll struggle to do what you're asking. But I've heard you." His lips brush mine. "Can we do something other than talk now?"

"Soon." I remove my arms from his neck. "Nosy or not, the people in your living room right now love you. They came all this way to make sure you're okay. Go talk to them. And enjoy them instead of being caught up in worrying about what might happen if I blink too hard. Do you know what I'd give to have my mom back for just one minute? I wouldn't care if she called me names or made fun of me. I'd just love her."

"Remind me not to ever do business with you." he mutters. "Promise not to move, and I'll go smooth things over with our uninvited, nosy, and annoying company."

"There's the charm I know and love." I pat his cheek.

"Your heart exists to make me a better man." He kisses my forehead, getting off the bed. "They're going to know you're the only reason I'm apologizing. So brace yourself, sweetheart. You think one Beller loving you is bad? Wait until those two latch on."

~103~

I would have *talked* to John all night but in his arms, sleep beckons. I can't refuse it. Especially when no nightmares dare cross his peaceful embrace. The only thing that ever breaks through is daylight. And this morning, noise drifting in from the kitchen. Noise I'm not imagining. I haven't had one of those *episodes* since before waking up in the hospital. *Maybe the accident knocked the crazy out of me.*

"Good morning, sweetheart." John kisses my head where it rests on his chest.

"Good morning." I don't want to shift away from him. "Time to get up."

"If you say so." He rolls out of bed without a fight. My eyes roam over his barely clad body. He crosses to the closet, glancing back.

I blush. "Show-off."

"Feel free to show off all you want." He smiles. "*Any*time you want."

"So you keep reminding me."

I wait for him to disappear inside the closet and slide my legs off the side of the bed, noting the dull throb coming from the gash. "You did say you spoke to Pam, right? She knows I'll be back soon?"

"Yes." He groans, both at my question and the fact that I moved without him. "I vaguely remember something about you having a life before we met." He crosses back to me with my robe over his shoulder. "I talked to her. Everything is taken care of. Except you staying put."

"I hardly ever take days off so I have plenty of time built up to cover the days I've missed." I latch on to the bed for effect. He rolls his eyes. "I just hope it isn't putting her in a bind. Did she say how she's doing?"

"In light of the situation, I doubt she'd complain to me about her workload." He unfurls the robe and drapes it over me so I can take off my shirt. "Need help?"

"No." Every time I do this, the pain seems a little less. "I've been trying to think of what orders we had coming in, but I'm too mixed up on time."

"Pam seems capable. I'm sure she can handle Scarlets." He hoists me into his arms. "Let's get you in the shower. When you're done, I'll jump in. Unless you're still thinking about us showering together?"

"I knew you heard me!"

He chuckles. "I've just been waiting for the right time to use it."

His moment is well chosen. Now that I'm sitting with his mom and sister at the bar in the kitchen while he's off on his solo shower, the movie of us showering together plays in my head like I'm there running my hands over his soapy chest. Digging fingers into his strong back as he lifts me into the warm cascade. "You okay, sweetheart?" He saves me from drooling in my eggs.

"We waited for you." I swallow, heart pounding over the sight of his wet hair. "I know you said not to, but we wanted to."

"Thank you." His lips caress mine, eyes settling in like they know my thoughts. "I could hear laughing. I'm glad all my favorite ladies are enjoying themselves."

"We're glad you're smiling." Sheila forces me to remember we're not alone. "It's nice to see last night's sudden change remains intact."

"I'm sure you've already thanked her for that." He kisses me again. "Her extra glow apparently has something to do with having you two here to socialize with. It occurred to me last night that even though she doesn't go out much, she does work in a store full of women, that caters to women." He meets my eyes. "So you socialize a lot in that way."

"I've never thought about it like that." I pick up his plate to fill it.

"You're busy thinking about *other* things."

With a grin and a wink, he takes the plate. "I also realized this is the perfect time for me to go out and run some errands. You'll be in…decent hands with Mom and Sheila."

"Aww. He's sharing his doll." Sheila piles scrambled eggs onto his china.

"I haven't left yet." He slides most of the amassed food onto her plate.

"I knew it." She sticks out her lip. "He's already mad we looked at his doll."

"And we didn't even mess up one strand of her lovely hair." Katherine shrugs. "She can go back on the shelf. Just like new."

"Now, Mom." Sheila grins. "You know he doesn't keep her on a shelf. I just hope having a doll in his bed hasn't tempted him to open the box. I hear playing with them ruins their value."

I'm fifteen shades of red. He sits back, arms crossed. "Happy? They're only here because you won't let me kick them out."

~104~

The moment John announced he was leaving, icy fingers began to trace along my ankles, crawling up my body. Not even his banter with Sheila stops the chilly ascent. "Why don't you make good on your promise to leave." She mocks his posture. "Because at this point, Mom and I aren't going anywhere. We can't in good conscience leave a fragile doll alone with a big bad wolf."

"Wolf?" He smirks. "My reputation is getting weak."

"Ha!" Katherine folds her hands. "Since when do you care about your reputation?"

"Since about…" He looks at his wrist. "Never. That's why you had Sheila. She's the good one who upholds the family name."

My family didn't banter like this, but even so, John's family makes me realize how much I miss being a part of one. Kim's family always included me, but I never stopped feeling like an outsider. This morning, watching *this* family, faint memories float from the dimmest recess of my mind. Moments of laughter shared over plates of food. Days spent happily enjoying each other's company. Then, they were gone. Mom. Dad. And all my happiness. "John." I lay my hand over his. "Are you really leaving?"

"For a little while." He smiles. "Is that okay with you?"

"Yeah." My gut churns. "You need to get out of here and enjoy the day for a change."

"I'll enjoy the day when you're out in it with me." He lifts our hands, bringing mine to his lips. "Not a moment sooner."

Sheila grins. "Mom, that's the charming side she was telling us about. He really does have one."

"Shh," he admonishes. "You'll ruin my reputation."

"No worries." Katherine looks between us. "Despite her affinity for you, your reputation isn't likely to change. From what I've seen thus far, it's likely to get worse."

~

It's true that I've turned John into a monster. Still, Katherine and Sheila are trying to accept me. Or at least tolerate me. For his sake. But I'm going to lose ground with them if he doesn't leave soon. Despite the fear lurking on my fringes, he can't stay here running through scenarios as if his sister sneezing too hard will somehow lead to my death.

"I understand they aren't strong enough to hold me up. I'm not planning on asking them to carry me around."

"No, you'll just get up all on your own." He kneels in front of where I'm safely secured on the sofa with enough pillows, blankets, and snacks to wait out a six-month blizzard. "The two of them together won't be able to catch you if you fall. So absolutely promise not to move from this spot."

Worry traces the creases of his face. But there's a twinkle in his eye that says if I agree, and he leaves, he'll use this later to say he's doing *all* the compromising. "You shouldn't gloat. It takes away from what you're doing to prove yourself."

"I'll only be gone a few hours." He straightens, scanning the three of us. "I think I made myself abundantly clear yesterday on what I expect—"

"YOU DID!" we agree. His lips brush my forehead, his growl vibrating into my skull.

His teeth bite down, hand hastily snatching up his keys. "I'm only saying this once. *All* of you *will* stay in your seats. Not just Mary. All three of you." The door slams behind him. We watch it. Transfixed. His truck peels down the driveway. Our breaths catch. For all we know, he's going to park at the end of the driveway and walk back up just to see if we're following orders.

"Do you think he actually left?" I swallow.

Sheila shrugs. "Want to get up?"

"Yes!" If he wants someone to obey him, he needs to get a dog. "Once he sees me making it on my own, he'll forgive me. Right?"

"John certainly needs to know his way is not the only way." Katherine eyes me. "But if by making it on your own you mean leave this property, you are not. *If* I allow you to get up, it will only be to go out to the patio." She stands. "Even if I did still want you gone with *every* fiber of my being rather than just half of them, I would never cross my son that way. I'd have you removed in front of him. Not behind his back."

"But we're inclined to think we don't need to have you removed." Sheila plops a towel and roll of duct tape in front of my cut foot.

"Not yet, anyway." Katherine exhales. "I would like to see you in a different room, though."

"Good luck with that." I watch Sheila securing the towel to my foot with the silver tape. "I've already tried. He refuses."

"No worries." Sheila grins. "We're getting ready to find out if you *can* walk on crutches. And, to thwart the monster he's going to be over it, we're going to spruce you up for him."

"Unless he's into things that are bigger than a breadbox and black-and-blue all over, there's not much hope for me looking better, but I'm confident I can use the crutches. I think John *told* Dr. Mansfield to insist otherwise."

"He probably did." Katherine places a hand on my shoulder. "I doubt a manicure will make a difference if our scheme gets you hurt, but I'll go get my bag."

~105~

Even with all the padding from the towel my slashed foot still hurts, and the pain of the crutches putting pressure on my ribs made every step to the patio grueling. I took each one by myself. Scared to let Katherine and Sheila near me in case I fell. *On* them.

"I'm afraid you weren't ready for this." Katherine lowers my freshly manicured hands. "You're still shaking."

"I'm just weak." And have crippling fear scratching up my spine. Ever since John first uttered he was leaving, the paranoia has been steadily growing. I even think I just heard a door slam. "I'm eating better, so my strength is coming back. I should be full force in a couple of days."

"Maybe we'll take you for a drive then." Sheila lowers the curling iron she used on my hair. "Unfortunately, the only way I can use you today to tick my brother off is already done."

"Glad to help." I bite my lip. "The way he's behaving…" The only thing worse than an impending mental episode is having my insides ache with jealousy. "Did he try to *overly* fix the problems of all his exes?"

"Exes?" Katherine's eyes roll. "He doesn't have what I would consider *exes*, as much as dates gone wrong. No one ever made the cut for long. Until Susan. And now you."

"And he never hesitated to leave us alone with Susan." Sheila grins. "Does that answer your *real* question?"

"Um…"

"Never once did he ask me to curb my opinion of her." Katherine sighs. "Other than not taking my advice, he never had a problem with my objections. *Now* are you satisfied?"

Being the exception to his rule *is* satisfying. But I'm not sure how much he told them about the accident. Katherine could still be right. Pure guilt could be driving him. "The night I wrecked, he wanted to drive me home but I refused. Later…we kind of have this joke about me not calling him. So when I didn't, he…ended up being the one who found my car. It was on fire and… That night was pretty traumatic for him."

"Traumatic for *him*?" Sheila's brow hitches. "Didn't you nearly die?"

"I might have. If he didn't show up." I shrug. "But I was unconscious, and then in a medically induced coma, so he's the one who had to live through it. I was just sleeping."

There it is again. The door. Slamming. Closer this time than before. "Did you hear that?"

"What?" Sheila looks around. "Your fire lighting for my brother?"

"That ignited a long time ago."

"You haven't known each other for a *long* time." Katherine studies me. "Are you okay?"

I clasp my hands together to stop the visible shaking, and do my best to ignore the footfall beginning to hammer my brain. "I never tried to *hook* John. He actually thought I wasn't interested in him. Something that didn't go over too well."

"Mystery solved." Sheila's hands plant on her slender waist. "He's attracted to the fact that you didn't chase him."

"It appears so." Katherine nods. "The question is, how is he going to feel now that you're not putting up a fight."

"She's outside after I specifically told her not to move." John slips through the glass door. "I don't think we'll ever have a shortage of fights."

It's him. The doors. The footfall. It wasn't me, it was him. A smile splits my face. "Imagine the fight we'd be having right now if they let me make the type of prison break I wanted."

"I believe they did imagine it." He drops a kiss on his mom's cheek, handing her a flower bouquet. "Which is why you're still here, sweetheart." He repeats his actions to his sister, then hands me the third and largest bouquet.

"Breadboxes," Sheila mutters under her breath.

"What?" He pulls a chair in front of me. "Do I want to know what she's talking about?"

"You missed a lot."

"Apparently." He inspects my hands, not missing the fact that I've had a manicure. "I got you something."

"That figures." Sheila huffs. "Give gifts to the breadbox. The rest of us don't deserve anything. All we've done is keep your doll company while you gallivanted all over the city."

"If you're referring to my *girlfriend* as a breadbox, then yes, I did bring a gift for *only* her." I tap his hand. He sighs. "She started it."

"How grown-up of you."

"Leave it to me." His lips seek mine. "I'll start some grown-up things. I *really* missed you."

"I really missed you, too." I take comfort in his lips.

"We get it. You love each other." Sheila stomps her foot. "Now, let us see what the prince brought his breadbox."

<h1 style="text-align:center">~106~</h1>

Amidst Katherine's threat to sew us together and John's attempt to make her do it, he places the small blue bag in my lap. "This isn't really a gift, but it's something you need."

"Needed things make the best gifts." I shake the bag. "Thank you. I'm touched you're thoughtful enough to buy me anything."

"You're killing me." Sheila melts into her chair. "Just *open* it."

Not keeping her in suspense any longer, I pull out the object. "A cell phone!"

"It's nice you're so easy to please." John's finger runs along the curve of my smile. "But I don't intend to take the easy road. You're in for the spoiling of your life."

"I don't need to be spoiled. I need—" His kiss stops the flow of words.

"Your phone was damaged so I went to your carrier and they replaced it. I had them give you an upgraded version of the one you had, but I left the plan the same."

"How did you…? Never mind. I'm sure the phone company was happy to do your bidding."

"Without hesitation." His grin snakes high. "Is that okay with you?"

"Yes," Sheila answers for me. "Now she can call her dad. That poor man! Had I known Mary before, I wouldn't have done what you made me do to him."

"What did he make you do?" I glare at him.

"I *asked* her to make your dad sign over his right to make decisions about your medical care, and he didn't put up much of a fight. He gave the power of attorney to me pretty quickly."

"It isn't like he had a choice." Sheila frowns. "John called in a panic and said it was life and death, so I went in fully loaded. It was sign or—"

"Sign." His tone tells her to shut up. "Your stupid little smug doctor friend is the one you should be mad at. He made a point of having your dad contacted."

"Because it's the law." Katherine blares. "Had I known what Sheila was up to, I would have stopped this whole charade. Honey, have you even talked to your father since John locked you up?"

"She doesn't have a father." John snaps. "She has a sperm donor. Tell them, sweetheart. Tell them *all* about dear old Dad."

There's nothing to tell. Only something to know. Which will say more than I ever could. "Did he come to the hospital?"

"I offered to let him." John swallows. "But no, he didn't."

"It's true," Sheila confirms. "Part of my instruction was to let him know he was welcome at the hospital. John only wanted the power of attorney. I made it *very* clear he was welcome anytime."

"I just didn't want him being the one calling the shots for you." John searches my reaction.

"I don't blame you." I rub his arm. John's even a better choice than Kim and Kevin combined. "I would be more shocked to hear Dad did come. But I'm sorry the burden fell on you."

"You know I like making decisions for you." He grins. "And I wish you'd be a burden. I'd like a nice long list of demands, followed with an even longer list of desires."

"I'd like an explanation of why your dad isn't involved in your life." Katherine sits forward.

"My mom died, my dad walked out, my husband died, I drove off a cliff. And that's how John got stuck with me." I give the abridged version of my life story. But John's determined to give his misguided interpretation.

"His new wife doesn't like Mary being around. Probably because she knows she'll never be half the woman. And Mary doesn't want to cause *discord* in anyone's life, so she lets it all slide because she thinks he has a responsibility to his wife and *their* kids. Not her. His first and only child from a wife he supposedly loved so much he dumped her kid six months after she died." His jaw sets. "It's probably a good thing he didn't come to the hospital."

"I wish *I* had come to the hospital." Katherine sighs.

"Me too." Sheila frowns. "We just thought…well, John's never serious about anyone."

"Plus, we never like anyone he pretends to be serious about." Katherine throws him a look. "I lit a candle for you but figured that more than covered my responsibility to his *friend.*"

"It did. Thank you for being so sweet."

"They're not sweet." His eyes narrow. "Neither of them understands the word."

"Now we do." Sheila grins. "Your sweet breadbox has schooled us both. We've learned our lesson. Mom and I will behave from this day forward." Their hands fly to their hearts. "We solemnly swear."

~107~

If you want to be a part of someone's life, you are. You make time for them. Consider their feelings. And in a case like mine where the door only swings one way in regard to my dad, you wish them well and give them exactly what they want. Your absence. As for Katherine and Sheila, they didn't know me. They had no obligation to me. And John barely tolerated Kim and Kevin's presence, so I'm not sure them being at the hospital on his account would have helped.

"None of us wants someone in our lives who doesn't want to be there. Or someone whose life is worse off for being part of ours."

"There are a hundred people my life would be better off without, but that hasn't stopped them from intruding." Sheila's nose wrinkles.

"In relation to my dad, I'm a constant reminder of what he lost. I understand that more now, having lost my own husband. Grief does terrible things to a person." I grip John's hand. "And to the people who choose to love us in the wake of that grief."

"In spite of all the things that could have soured your sweet soul, you keep a positive outlook." Katherine smiles. "I respect that."

"Me, too." Sheila's amused at my lame attempt to fend off John's engulfing arms. "I'm glad Mom dragged me up here."

"I don't recall having to do much dragging." She laughs. "If memory serves, your bag was packed just as quickly as mine."

"The sense you came to talk into me isn't necessary." John's body shifts. "But since you're here and there's a fifty-fifty shot on her reaction to what I'm getting ready to tell her, the two of you can save me if her positive outlook wears off."

"It's wearing off." I glare at him.

"Now, sweetheart." He chuckles. "All I did was go by Scarlets and walk through the store. Everything looked to be in order, and Pam said to tell you everything is running smoothly. Except your runway? She laughed at that, so I guess it's an inside joke?"

"Her joke." I'm glad she didn't elaborate. "You didn't have to go there."

"I wanted to ease your mind." His lips find my cheek. "I dropped by your house, too. Picked up your mail and did a general check of the place. Everything inside looks fine and I made arrangements for the yard and landscaping to be kept up. I can't believe you did that yourself anyway."

I can't believe he spent his day running my errands. "I thought you were out taking care of your own business, not mine."

"Your business *is* my business."

"Not exactly." I drag in a breath. "I'm not ungrateful. It's just…I should have been thinking about my house and the yard…and checking the mail. All of those things instead of being here like I'm on vacation."

"I *want* you to feel like you're on vacation. Which you can't do if things aren't taken care of. I finally understood that last night. Now you're all set." He grins. "There's nothing else to worry about."

"How did you get into my house?"

"Kim." His hand slides over my knee." Now tell me about this duct tape. It looks like something Sheila had a hand in."

I wait on the edge of John's bed while he ducks into the closet. He says he can come up with a better solution for my foot than duct tape and a rolled-up towel. A solution I didn't have to fight with him to get, he offered. He's even altering the crutches so they'll fit more comfortably under my arms. "Do you mind if I make a few adjustments to these?" He holds up a pair of black wedge sandals.

"Where did you get those?" The seasonal box they were in is stuffed into the back of my closet.

"Kim must have thought you would need them." He plops down across the room. "What were you asking about a minute ago?"

"Nothing." I pick up the new phone, avoiding trying to nonchalantly ask him again if he saw anyone in the house when he came home. I'm fairly certain the noises I heard earlier were him, and he's fairly certain I'm not crazy. I'd like to keep it that way. "I should check my voicemail."

"You have quite a few messages." He nods. "Mostly from Kim's family and the people you work with."

"You listened to them?"

"For Detective Beckley. He wondered if you had any more strange calls."

"How did you know my password?"

"One, two, three, five isn't very creative." He meets my eyes. "Especially when it's the same code you use for your house alarm."

"You know they're the same because of Kim?"

"Yep." He swallows. "I hate to bring this up, but you weren't exactly careful when you entered your alarm code in front of me. I had to intentionally look away. Someone else might not have."

It's true. I'm not used to having people in my house so I wasn't careful in concealing my alarm code. But the implication that the handful of people who *have* been in my house would break in to turn off my lights is ludicrous. "I'll change the code. And I'll be very careful with the keypad from here on out."

"Sweetheart." He leaves the spot where he's working on the shoe and kneels in front of me. "I'm not scolding you. I'm just scared. Detective Beckley thinks the stalker is someone you know."

"*I'm* someone I know."

"You're not crazy." His hands engulf my face. "We *know* someone else wrecked you. We *know* someone else sent you flowers."

"We only *know* someone wrecked me." I remove his hands, holding them in my lap. "Were there any strange voicemails?"

"A few silent messages. No breathing. No anything. I deleted them."

That's the way the harassing phone calls were. "Thanks for getting rid of those."

"I took care of returning George's calls, too." He goes back to his shoe station across the room. "I left his messages, but you don't need to call him back. He knows you're doing just fine. With me."

"John!"

He shrugs. "Somewhere around call number eight I decided he needed a black eye. But because I didn't want you mad at me today, I gave him a ring instead, thanking him for being so concerned about *my* girlfriend."

"That's all?"

"That. And I let him know you no longer need his mechanic services." His eyes meet mine. "We can fight about it. Or I can fix your shoe."

"Fix the shoe."

I can't scold him when I have my own jealous urges. Ones that might have me dishing out black eyes if I ever see Susan again. "Hey, Pam, it's me." She's the first call I return after listening to the voicemails. A call John interrupts me through, making working out a timeline for my return to Scarlets difficult.

"Pam said to tell you goodbye." I pat his head when he kneels in front of me again. "And now you have my undivided attention."

"Just the way I like it." He smiles. "How does the shoe feel?"

He's added cushion and raised the straps, as if he's always been a cobbler. "I have no idea how you did it, but it still fits."

"Now, for the real test." He stands, gently bringing me upright, letting my weight press down on the cut foot. "What do you think?"

"I think all I do is thank you, John Beller." My lips land on his. "You are absolutely amazing."

"I'd be happy to tear up all your shoes for another kiss." He grins. I move my lips to his. The doorbell rings. My legs give out.

"Exhibit A on why you can't be standing up without me around." He holds me tight against him. "No more falling."

"Who's at the door?"

"Trust me when I say there will be no more unexpected visitors." He cups my face, checking my eyes for the fear I know is there. "Kim and Kevin are here. I invited them to have dinner with us tonight, thinking you're as anxious to see them as they are to see you?"

Relief floods through me. "I don't know what's gotten into you today, but thank you."

"I told them to come as soon as they wanted but I didn't know they'd show up when I was getting kisses out of you. How about I send them away and we get back to making out?"

"How about you get another kiss when you get the crutches? I want to walk into the living room on my own."

~109~

With one of John's hands on my arm and one on my back, I hobble down the hall on the crutches. My foot hurts but not as bad as earlier. And thanks to John's handiwork the rib pain is downgraded enough I can actually breathe while I walk.

"I don't like this." He groans over the sounds of amazement from Kim and Kevin. "You're in pain, and making me just stand here when there's a way to ease it is killing me."

"Just relax." I use his catchphrase as Kim bolts toward me. He stops our forward progress, body pivoting in front of mine to head off the impending collision.

"Watch out!" Sheila belts. "The warden is particular about who can touch his breadbox."

The cords of his neck are as tight as his breathing. "She's wobbly. I don't want her getting accidentally knocked down." He pivots back to my side. "Here, Kim. Full access granted. Just be careful. And that includes squeezing her too tight."

"Says the anaconda." Sheila smirks.

Kim and I exchange a tearful hug, and Kevin takes John's spot at my side. Not because John is willingly moving aside. He's moving for the same reason he left the house today. And I can't help but feel a little guilty over how compliant he's being. A sentiment soon forgotten. Compliments of Kevin.

"What did you think of the picture?"

"What picture?"

"One I'll show you later," John growls, a warning to Kevin.

"It's just a blurry traffic camera picture." Kim rolls her eyes at Kevin. "I don't know why you're making such a big deal over it."

"Oh, I don't know…" He shrugs. "Maybe it's a big deal because it could be the person who wrecked her."

"I can't believe they actually found someone!" Kim puts a palm to her throat. "I thought she just—"

"That's the problem." John moves both of them away from me. "You *think*."

He sends an elbow toward Kevin as we pass by. "Sorry, sweetheart. I already told him we're not discussing the picture tonight."

"Why?" From the looks of everyone in this room, they've all seen this photograph. Save for me. "Where did it come from? And why do you have it?"

Inky blackness twists up from my depths as John explains the photograph. He met with the detectives while he was out today. They've scoured hours of footage from every traffic and security camera between my house and his, and think they found a car following me that morning. A car that could have waited for me to leave here. "I sent a copy to everyone, even Mom and Sheila, in case someone recognized it."

"Did they?"

"No, sweetheart." He sighs. "And I didn't tell you about it because I was trying to give you a perfect day. We can deal with the photo tomorrow. Okay?"

"I need to see it." My stomach flips. "There's no one better to recognize the car than me."

"It's poor quality." His jaw ticks. "It's not like I'm hiding a smoking gun from you. The driver is just a blur, and the car isn't much clearer."

"He's right, it's a dead end." Kim sighs. "But clear enough to know it wasn't George. I was starting to worry." John's cold eyes turn on her. She swallows. "He drives a pickup. Not a sedan."

"A mechanic has access to all sorts of cars." He stands, face flushed as he meets Sheila's stare. "That's why no one saw a particular vehicle lurking around her house."

"On it." Sheila's phone is out. "Kim, sweetie, where is your brother?"

~110~

Nothing ruins dinner like the host threatening to kill a guest's brother. Kim is in tears. Kevin is ineffectively consoling her. Sheila is on the phone with Detective Summers, and Katherine's the epitome of calm while John paces the room, ready to explode. He's angry at himself for not putting the clues together sooner, and at George who he's unfairly accusing.

"Shouldn't I at least see the photograph before anyone's arrested?"

"Too late," Sheila reports with a satisfied smirk. "George is in custody."

"John!" I glare at him. "He has a family."

"They didn't *arrest* him." Sheila waves me off. "They asked him to come in and he willingly went to the station."

I look to Katherine for help. She shrugs, the billionaire entitlement showing in all three of them. "I doubt any of you would be this calm if you were the one being *asked* to come in. He didn't wreck me. He would never do that."

"If he's innocent, he should have no problem proving it." John nods to his mom, who produces a blurry black-and-white photograph.

"This is nothing. Not even *I* can be ruled out as the driver." No one on planet Earth can. "What else do the police have?"

"They confirmed the horn-blowing incidents were real." John's hand runs down his face. "The neighbors all described seeing a small dark sedan, which seems to match the car in the photograph."

"Why didn't the neighbors call the police?" Katherine asks.

"I should have called them." My heart aches for George. "It was *my* responsibility to handle what was happening. I chose not to."

"You had reasons not to call." John's eyes slam into Kim and Kevin. "Your idiot neighbors didn't. You've been completely surrounded by nothing but worthless people this whole time."

"Put the blame where it belongs." I glare at him. "No one *needed* to do anything for me, I needed to do it for myself."

His eyes flash. "The only place the blame doesn't belong is on you."

"He's right, Mary." Kevin's voice is small. "Kim and I wish we had believed you."

"You two are good friends. Nothing that's happened is your fault."

"It's all our faults!" John roars.

Catching himself, he takes a deep breath and sits beside me. "If George is cleared beyond a shadow of any doubt, I'll be the first to shake the man's hand for cooperating. But I'm not sorry he's being questioned right now. Someone *wrecked* you. You didn't make it up or hallucinate a second car. It happened, Mary."

"It wasn't George. Have him released." I clasp his hand. "Please? For me?"

A breathless hush falls over the room. John gets up. "I'll be right back." He kisses my forehead and strolls outside. Katherine and Sheila stare at me, those ever-questioning Beller eyes deciphering what kind of power I wield over him. Considering he had George arrested in the first place, not much.

"He's out." John shuts the door behind him.

"Really?" Kim sniffs. "He's innocent?"

"You seem to think he's not." John sits beside me. "Something you're not saying?"

"She's just upset." I draw him close. "Thank you."

"He has an alibi that checks out, and let Summers access his credit card statement to prove he was in the next county that night. They haven't reviewed hotel footage yet, obviously, but while we wait I told them to let him go." His teeth grind. "If he's lying, I'll know soon enough."

"He isn't." I sigh. "So thank you for having him cleared so quickly."

"This is all so hard." Kim cries into Kevin's shoulder. "I don't know how I'm going to get through this."

Multiply John's angry face by three, that's how many Bellers are glaring at my friends right now. "It's been a long day for all of us." I save the room from seeing another bloodbath. "Our appetites are ruined, so let's cut the night short and try it again some other time."

~111~

"You really don't think this George character has anything to do with your accident?" Katherine questions as soon as Kevin's taillights fade away.

"He wouldn't hurt me."

"One thing is for sure." Sheila rubs her hands together. "He won't need to work on your new car. I added a few of my own choices to your list!"

"List?" I turn to John's tight face. "What list?"

"Let's take a walk." He reaches for me, eyes firing warning shots across his sister's bow.

Me in his arms, he heads for the glass doors behind the dining table, maneuvering us outside and across the patio to where a chair waits just beyond the glass doors that lead into the master suite. "Spill," I order as he settles with me on his lap.

"Why not?" He sighs. "This night is already blown all to heck."

"Stop deflecting."

"My family has a process when we buy new vehicles. We choose what we want to test drive, and have those vehicles sent to a local dealer who coordinates the transaction so we only have to go to one place. The list Sheila didn't keep her mouth shut about is one I made for you. Mom and Sheila are leaving after lunch tomorrow and since my hands are full here, I asked Sheila to place the order when she gets home."

"You're overestimating the amount of insurance money I'm going to get. I'll be lucky to afford a used version of the car I had. Special orders are out of the question."

"You aren't buying the car."

"No, *you* aren't buying the car."

"Sweetheart." He sighs. "The last thing I want to do tonight is fight about money."

"So stop trying to spend all of yours on me."

"I have plenty for the both of us." His head rests on my shoulder. "And since everything is being put on the table, in addition to buying *all* your future vehicles, I'll be paying your medical bills, utilities and, as of this morning, your mortgage. In full."

"What?" I can't breathe.

"I canceled your dingy little alarm system, too. If you want to argue about finances, let's fight about how that thing wasn't worth the money you forked out every month. I tested it ten times and it only worked right three of those."

I'm numb. And he isn't finished. "I hired private security to keep an eye on your house. Real flesh and blood men watching and recording every single person within ten miles of the place."

"My alarm was fine." My voice shakes. "It's had a glitch lately, but I was going to call—"

"Shh." His finger presses against my lips. "The men I hired won't glitch out. And I hired them in case the lunatic stalker who ran you off the road thinks he's going to get close to you again. I'm sending a message."

I remove his finger. "I don't need you to send messages. And I certainly don't need you going behind my back to orchestrate major changes in my life."

His hand slides under my chin. "I go behind your back to avoid the tension of you denying me the chance to help you. I'd rather get busted and try my luck at getting you to forgive me than sit by and not do every single thing that's in my heart to do." His voice grows low. "Will you forgive me, sweetheart? Please?"

"Innocently making a mistake is one thing. But calculating and banking on me not being able to stay angry is manipulation. I can't live like this."

"I'm not trying to manipulate you. I'm trying to give you a good life but you won't let me." The warmth of his body reaches for me, calling me to his chest.

"You being in my life makes it good. This. Right now. These moments. Not new cars, bill paying, parties… None of that adds up to anything."

"Agreed." His mouth comes closer. "If I promise to do better, can you find it in your heart to forgive me?"

"Are you really going to try? Or are you only using the draw of your lips to manipulate me?"

"I left today, didn't I?" He grins. "Against all my better judgment, and knowing full well you wouldn't be anywhere near that sofa when I came back."

"You're seriously going to gloat again?"

"I'll stop if you forgive me." His jaw brushes over mine, mouth on my ear. "Will you?"

"I have to." I bring his lips to mine. "You aren't prepared for me not to."

~112~

Nestled on John's lap, cuddled together watching the soft glow of the moon overtake the sky between light kisses and teasing that sends his chuckles dancing over the tranquil hillsides, I'm at peace. Head on his shoulder, the feel of him vibrating through me. One day he'll know I love the man, not the money. That day might be the one when I pay back every dollar he's spent on me.

"Do you like it here?" His fingers brush along my arm.

"There's nothing *not* to like."

"But are you happy here?" He tilts my face to his. "I need to know because I want you to be happy, and I'll take you anywhere to make sure you are."

"Location doesn't matter." I smile. "My happiness comes from being with you."

"Truly?"

I place reassuring lips to his. "Truly."

He enjoys kissing so much more when I initiate it. But he isn't satisfied with my answer. "I'd like to hear you say you're happy in this house."

"You're here." He needs the exact words. "Therefore, I'm completely happy in this house. Because it's all about you."

"No, sweetheart. It's all about you." His hands cup my face. "Allow me to prove that to you."

The air cools, the dark of night swallowing us as his lips devour mine, cutting off all ability to feel anything other than the heat of desire coursing through every tiny vein. I ache to be with him. And the way he moans every time I move across his lap tells me he wants it, too. His fingers wrap in my hair, urging my head back. My own groans unleash,

265

his lips taking siege of my neck, tasting every inch of flesh. "Maybe we're both wrong," I breathe. "This is about *us.*"

"Not even close." He stands, keeping me pressed against him, lips latching on to mine and diving deep. He carries me through the doors, into his room, kicking shut the hallway door and masterfully locking it without losing his grip or the momentum in our kiss.

Placing me on the bed, he slides down my dangling legs. My eyes close. Body ready for the feel of his mouth against my thighs. "Look at me, sweetheart." My heavy lids open. Heart pounding.

"John!" He's on his knee. Hand outstretched. Holding a diamond ring. Tears stream down my face.

"Mary." He smiles. "My sweet lady who holds all of me in her hands. My life is, and will always be, completely about you. I've loved you my whole life. In dreams I never thought would come true. Now you're here. And I'm even more obsessed with you." Light dances across his emeralds. "Will you please do me the great honor of becoming my wife?"

Shock muffles my answer. He slips the ring onto my finger. "I hope that was a yes. Because I'm not prepared for no." His lips press against my knuckles. "Wear my ring, Mrs. Beller. And marry me quickly so I don't have to feel guilty about kissing you the way I'm getting ready to."

~113~

John's holding back. Keeping us from sex. He wants to wait for the day when I become his wife. Even after I told him I've completely about-faced on the no-sex-until-marriage position.

"You're going to have to stop." He swallows back another groan. "The look in your eyes is driving me wild. And I'm not even sure you said yes."

"You could keep kissing me until you hear the three-letter-word loud and clear."

His face buries in my neck, a grueling moan vibrating against me. "If my lips get started on you again, I'm liable to not care about breaking promises."

"Then our first night as an engaged couple is going to be a long one."

"Sweetheart, it's already been a long night." He nods toward the window. "Good thing it's morning. The sun might just save us both."

Dawn is breaking. "It's hardly felt like an hour."

"It's this little thing called chemistry." His body moves over mine. "We've got it in spades. Now, tell me you said yes."

"I definitely said yes."

He launches off the bed, yanking the sliding glass doors open. "She said yes! I'm the luckiest man in the world!"

"I'm the lucky one." I sit up, kicking my legs over the side of the bed. "You did ask me to marry you, right?"

"If I thought you would have said yes, I would have asked that first night." He sits beside me, pulling my newly frosted hand to his chest. "I knew you were the one the instant I saw you. I felt it right here."

"I did, too." Tears fill my eyes. "I just thought I was crazy."

He chuckles, offering to take me into the closet so I can choose my own clothes. More so, he's the one who actually wants to get out of bed this time. "Engagement has changed you."

"Whoa!" He grabs me as I push myself upright. "It hasn't changed me that much. You're not getting up on your own."

"A girl can try," I sigh.

"And a woman can listen to common sense." He swings me into his arms. "Against doctor's orders I let you use the crutches yesterday. And I'm willing to keep that up. But you have to ease back into walking and you also have to start being honest with me about your levels of pain. You don't look as tormented as you were, but I still catch glimpses of what you're trying to hide."

I would tell him to stop looking but his oversized closet has seized my senses. It's just as large as the bathroom, and my clothes are neatly hung around me. All of them. No boxes with seasons marked. Everything on display. Even my shoes and accessories fill the shelves. "What do you think?" he asks.

I reel up my jaw. "I think I can't believe you did this."

"I was being presumptuous." He grins. "Now that you've agreed to be my wife, I'll be holding your clothes hostage to make sure you keep your promise to marry me quickly."

"Did I promise that?"

"I want you to." He takes me closer to the rack I reach for. "And I don't take no for an answer."

Choosing a sundress, I meet his eyes. "I really wish I could stay mad at you."

"Why? Last night you said you want to be with me. And I want to be with you. So let's always be together."

"I'll need that blue sweater from over there." I sigh. "And a minute to process what's happening. Which isn't a no to marrying you quickly, but it's definitely a brake check."

~114~

Slipping into a sundress is a lot easier than fighting sweatpants and a t-shirt. Two things I'm *not* wearing on the first day of my engagement to the ever-handsome John Beller. Having the bruises is bad enough. I'm a rainbow of colors. And not the pretty kind.

I'm also taking off his ring. "Your family will flip if they see this. It's way too soon. They still don't like me being here."

"You already said yes." He clasps my hand, stopping me from fidgeting with the ring. "It stays where it's at."

"No." I point to the crutches he retrieved while I showered. "I'm taking the ring off, for now. And I'm walking on my own, so put me down."

He slides me down and fits the crutches under my arms. "You're not taking the ring off. I put it on your finger for a reason and I don't care what anyone else has to say about it. I love you. And you love me. That's all that matters."

"That. And other people's feelings." I sigh. "When we've been together longer, we'll tell them about the engagement."

"Nope." He opens the bedroom door, guiding me forward. "If they haven't already heard me shouting that you're going to be my wife, they're getting ready to."

I dig in outside his door. "Taking the ring off doesn't change how we feel, it only changes how they'll feel."

"Sheila adores you." He pulls me forward. "And Mom gave me her blessing. So I pretty much know what their feelings on the subject are going to be."

"Your mom knew you were proposing?"

"She knew I would someday." He grins. "Even if she thinks this day is too soon, she absolutely approves of you being my wife." He urges me forward another step. "Stop worrying."

The only thing I manage to stop are my feet. He chuckles, lips pressing to the soft flesh below my ear. "Is the ring on your finger finally tipping you off to just how crazy I am about you?"

"It's giving me a little hint." Tears sting the back of my lids. "I feel like I never know what's going to happen next. I barely have a chance to get used to one element of our relationship before the whole thing goes in a completely new direction."

"After we're married, life is going to slow way down." His hands cup my face. "I intend to soak in every second of every day we have together. I'm only moving fast now to secure what I know is going to be a good life for both of us. Is that okay?"

I can't deny how nice it is to be with a man so proactive. So forthcoming. Someone who stills the chaos in my head. "Tell me we're not getting caught up in the moment and making a mistake."

"If your feelings are as solid as mine, we're not." He chucks the crutches and lifts me to his chest. "I'll be a good husband. I'll love and protect you with every ounce of myself. I'll obey, as much as I can. And we'll be happier than any two people have ever dared to be." His grin grows two sizes. "I'll be showing my love by doing things that will look a whole lot like spoiling. But if you don't let me love you that way, it will break my heart. So I know you'll let me. And in time, you'll be as used to the lap of luxury as you are to *my* lap." He nods to the kitchen. "Now, choose. Either we go announce our engagement, or I take you back to bed to see just how bad I am at keeping promises."

His lap is all the luxury I need. "I'm not going to lie around and let you feed me grapes."

"The only time I've seen you still was while you were in a coma, and I don't care to relive anything even close to that." He holds me tight. "I'm not going to be overbearing. I swear. All I'm going to do is love you."

"Which is going to feel a whole lot like you being overbearing." His long legs deposit us in the kitchen. Sheila and Katherine stare at me. My lips fly to his ear. "Bedroom! I choose the bedroom!"

~115~

The sound of sausage sizzling bleeds into my skull. Katherine and Sheila's frozen faces stare at my hand. Cold sweat beads against my flesh. John backs away. Sheila approaches, lifting my hand. "You said yes?" I nod. Her mouth turns up. "Congratulations. Grandmother's ring is beautiful on you."

"Grandmother?" I gape. "I didn't know. He didn't tell me..."

"Grandmother gave me the ring before she died." He accepts a hug from his mom. "And there was no resizing needed. Yet another sign you *are* my lady."

"It appears so." Katherine wipes her eyes. "Congratulations. You two are both stubborn. You're perfect for one another."

I stare at the ring, seeing now the round halo design with one half-carat diamond in the center flanked by smaller diamonds running down the sides of the band is antique. "It's beautiful."

"It's been in the family a long time." His hand runs down my arm. "And in my possession all these years. You're the only woman I've ever considered giving it to."

"Thank you." He never defiled it with Susan. "I'll cherish it always. Just like I'll always cherish you."

"You'd better." Katherine scoops up my free hand. "But I already know you will. His choice was well worth the wait. I'll be proud to call you my daughter."

Tears fall from the three of us while he watches our girlish embrace, *I told you so* thick in his eyes. "I'll be proud to call you sister." Sheila smiles. "But I have to say, I'm actually starting to question your sanity, too. I mean, my brother? Seriously? You can't do any better?"

"Even if I could, I wouldn't want to."

"I'm going to make sure you never regret those words." He nudges his way into our circle. "Now it's on Sheila to keep our legacy. I've done my part to thwart the curse."

"Let's not dampen your happy day by talking about the fact that there isn't a man on this planet good enough for me." She winks. "Instead, let Mom and me go unpack. Now that there's a wedding to plan, we'll be staying a few more days."

"Nope." He swings me into his arms. "Now that we're engaged, we have adult things to attend to. And my offer for the two of you to visit anytime you want is hereby revoked. See yourselves out."

They see themselves into the living room, where I make him take me. The bombardment of wedding questions begins in earnest. My answers are all the same. "I have no idea… I haven't thought about it… I'm barely over the shock of him asking me to marry him." Still, they ask about venues, flowers, and dresses. Dominating our entire conversation all the way through a lunch I never thought I'd be this glad to see the end of.

"After the engagement sinks in and I have time to talk with John about the wedding, I'll call you two and we'll get together to plan things." I glance out the door. He's loading their bags into Sheila's Corvette. "I think he's just about got you ready."

"Uh-huh." Sheila studies me. "Are you sure you want to be his prisoner for life?"

"My wife won't be any more of a prisoner than my fiancée is." He grabs her hand, motioning for his mom's. "Say goodbye, ladies."

"Very well." Katherine waves off his hand. "I need to get home and start on the nursery anyway. I think I'll do two." She glances back at me. "Just in case you have twins."

"I'm not pregnant!"

He grins at me from the door. "As red as her face is right now, I won't ever have a problem getting her to let me kick you two out again. Thanks for that."

~116~

Lowering me onto the blanket at our picnic spot, John explains his mom doesn't think I'm pregnant. "She's just busting my chops for moving so fast with you."

"A speed easily explained if I'm pregnant."

"She's just excited." He smiles. "Everyone was pretty sure I was staying a bachelor forever. Even me. But now I get to add my own love story to the mix."

"Does your love story have kids?"

"It would be nice to have a few." His eyes roam over the view. "But if you don't want kids, I still want you for my wife. So there's no pressure. Mom will accept whatever we decide."

"I've always wanted kids." But I can't have a child if my mental disorder will hurt them. "I don't want anyone to think I'm pulling a Susan. I'm already in a position easily taken as me weaseling my way into your life, so even talking about kids is like I'm hurrying to pull the wool over your eyes."

"My eyes are wide open." He winks. "And since we both want kids, allow me to put you into another position."

We make out like we did the first time we came here. Only deeper. Until nothing exists outside of us. Hours go by without notice, our bodies pressed together in one glorious mess.

He lifts my hand, the ring sparkling in the sunlight. "I took this out of my safety deposit box yesterday with the intention of bringing you up here today to pop the question. But I couldn't wait. The diamond burned a hole in my pocket."

"It wanted to be on my finger."

"It was made for your finger." He presses close. "I'm sorry the proposal wasn't romantic. I had a plan, just failed to execute. As usual. Where you're concerned, I have a lack of control."

"You're doing a pretty good job." Our clothes are still on. "Every single second of last night was wonderful. Now I get to lie here with my fiancé, sharing what I hope is only one of *many* days like this."

"This view is yours now." He sits us up. "And there's so much more on our property I want to show you."

Our property. "It's so beautiful, being a prisoner here won't be much like prison at all."

"Since meeting you, I've laid everything on the line. That comes off as aggressive sometimes, but my heart belongs to you." He opens his palms. "These hands will never harm you. Ever. I promise."

"I know." I place my palms over his. "Having a warden for a husband won't be so bad. Now, help me up. I'm making my fiancé a nice dinner tonight. My treat. While he sits and watches me do *all* the work."

He hoists me up, steadying me on my feet. "I'll help you cook. Because even if I were the type of man who wanted his woman to do it all, you're on crutches. You're not ready for solo kitchen duty."

"Sounds like an excuse. You've been against me taking a single step this whole time."

"Not anymore." He grins. "This walking thing suits me."

"Oh, really?"

"Really." He slides down my body. Onto one knee. "Because I have a feeling you won't get married until you can walk on your own. And sweetheart, I want us to get married two weeks from today. That's when Dr. Mansfield says this cast will be off. So, will you? Will you *please* marry me in two weeks?"

~117~

With every promise he's ever made whispered again against my ear, I lie in John's bed imagining how this night will be different from the last. This is the first time I've worn a nightshirt to bed. It will be so easy for his hand to keep sliding down my thigh. Then back up. Underneath my clothing to the place I know it wants to go.

"You're testing how much of a gentleman I am." He groans, fingers resting on the hem of my shirt, moving it up a slow and steady inch. "I promise you I'm not as much of one as you think." I pull away. He stops. "Sorry. I wasn't going to…I was only talking. I can wait two more weeks."

"Really?" I wasn't going to stop him. Not for that reason.

He wipes sweat from his brow. "Yes, really."

"I feel different with you than I imagined I would ever feel with anyone. And now that we're engaged, I don't think I'd feel guilty later."

"I would." His finger traces my jaw. "As hard as it is to wait, I want *that* to be the one promise I manage to keep. I know in the end it's what you really want."

"That's not the only thing I really want."

"I'm not understating how hard it is to keep from ravishing you." His throat bobs. "If you green-light me, and I start kissing you—"

"I'm not giving you the go-ahead." I turn away, truth settling into my veins. "If we get married in two weeks, I'll still be bruised. A big blob of ugly colors. It'll ruin our wedding night. All you'll remember is how horrible I looked."

My disfigured image reflects in my mind. He turns my chin back to him. "All I'm going to remember is how good it feels to be the luckiest man alive."

"What if I'm still in pain and I can't…"

"Then we wait." He smiles. "We have the rest of our lives. We'll get around to doing everything. Eventually."

Mike and I barely got around to doing anything. Especially *it*. "How do you know? What if—"

"Mary, stop." He lies beside me, rolling me against his chest. "Trust me, sweetheart. We've had all the bad we're going to have. There's nothing but smooth sailing and blue skies from here. So let's get some sleep. Tomorrow's a big day."

"My first day out in the world since you brought me here." Two months ago, if anyone had suggested I'd be in a serious relationship, I would have laughed them to shame. "You're sure we're doing the right thing? Going from meeting to married in the blink of an eye?"

"Our life together is going to be long and full." He kisses my hand. "Of that, I'm certain."

"Even if…"

"Even if you *are* crazy." His lips rest on my temple. "I love you no matter what. Remember that. Because I think you're still holding back."

"I'm just scared we're setting ourselves up for heartache and loss."

"After the life you've lived, I'd be astounded if you *weren't* scared." His arms cinch tight. "But you're worth every risk. So all we really need is for you to wear another sundress for our day out on the town tomorrow. Have I told you yet that I loved the one you had on today?"

"About thirty-five times." I smile.

"Is that all?" He tastes the skin at the base of my neck. "I've always been better with action. I'll just have to show you how much I liked it."

~118~

Riding shotgun in John's Viper, I'm fully aware of his admiration. He likes today's dress more than yesterday's.

"After I feed my hungry lady some lunch, what's next on the agenda?"

I study my to-do list as he pulls into a roadside café. "Figuring out how lavish our wedding *can't* be in two weeks."

He opens my door. "It can be anything you want it to be."

We claim a table in a sunny spot, deciding we'd both rather have a simple ceremony. He even wants to wear jeans. "You were in an old stained pair of work jeans the night you won my heart, so I think a clean pair will be fine for our wedding." I give his hand a squeeze. "What about my dress? I'll have limited options since there isn't time for alterations. And this is my second wedding, that usually means wearing something basic. But it's your first so I don't want to shortchange you." My first dress was plain. White satin. No lace. No beads. No frills. "If you want to see your bride in the extravagant kind of dress indicative of billionaires, we had better be able to find one that fits off the rack."

He wipes ketchup from the corner of my mouth. "I'll hire a seamstress. A team of them if need be. But if you want to wear jeans too, you can. I like the way you look in everything."

"Uh-huh, which is why you've been bug-eyed seeing me in a dress instead of sweatpants."

"Only because you look like you feel better."

"Right." I sigh. "We'll go to the mall next, and after I check on Scarlets we'll go to the bridal boutique so you can show me what styles of dress you like best."

"I don't care." He drags a hand down his face. "The only thing I care about is ending that day with you being my wife."

"And I care about my husband ending that day with not only a wife, but with having had exactly what he expected to have. I don't want to disappoint you on our wedding day, and you can't tell me you haven't dreamed of your wedding day and what it would be like because I already know you have, Mr. Plan Everything."

He moves closer, the small booth barely containing us already. "Sweetheart, it's impossible to ever disappoint me. Especially with clothing. If you want ten dresses, we'll buy ten dresses and I'll marry you ten times. Just plan it out exactly as your heart desires and I *promise* I'll love every single second, because I'm already getting more than my dreams ever promised." His lips graze mine. "The scenery and show surrounding the wedding don't interest me. Only walking away with you as my wife does. So I'll go to the boutique, but trust me when I say every dress will be perfect because the lady inside the dress is perfect. And she's mine."

"Good, because I'm walking down the aisle in a t-shirt that says 'Property of John Beller'."

"I was hoping to have that tattooed on you." His chuckle fills the café. "Possible?"

"Over my dead body. And since I'm still breathing, just pay the bill and let's get out of here." I place a twenty on the table, part of the cash I picked up at the bank earlier when dropping in to order my new debit card. "Don't say a word. Just pay the bill and leave my tip exactly where it is."

~119~

The mall housing Scarlets is up ahead. Seeing it makes me long for the normalcy of work. "How long will our honeymoon be?"

"As long as you want it to be." John caresses my knee. "A week, a month, a year…it's your call."

"Be sensible. I've missed a lot of work already, and if we're getting married in two weeks that means I'll only be back for one before I'm off again. I need to let Pam know our plans. And honestly, after I check my time today, I may only be able to take a week."

"You'll be able to take as much time as you like." He pulls into the turning lane, hands tightening on the steering wheel.

If only all of us were our own bosses. "I can't just take off and not expect to lose my job."

"You're not losing your job." His knuckles turn white. "You're handing in your resignation today."

"Excuse me?"

"You're not working at Scarlets anymore." He slams the blinker. "Say your goodbyes today because you're not ever coming back."

"You're not *allowing* me to work at Scarlets anymore?" The words slap across my face. "You think the only reason we're here is so I can resign?"

"Yeah, we're getting married," he points out like it matters.

"I'm not your actual property. You can't tell me what to do." Worry builds in my gut. "You have money but choose to work. Why would you expect me to be any different?"

"Your circumstances are different than mine."

"I'm not marrying you for money. What you have is yours, I'll make my own."

A growl starts low in his chest, vibrating up his throat and over his lips. "Once we're married, my wealth is *ours*. And I never said you were marrying me for money, because if that were true, we wouldn't be getting married."

"Yet you still assumed I'd up and quit my job as soon as you put a ring on my finger? I'm keeping my job."

"Get the facts straight, sweetheart." He whips through the mall lot. "I never said you couldn't work. Only that you don't have to. And with everything that's happened, you are *not* working at Scarlets."

"What else have you decided for me?" I cross my arms. "Will I have to ask for permission every time I want to sneeze? I'm an adult who can make her own decisions!"

"The police haven't caught the guy who tried to *kill* you, so *yes*, you have to ask me before you do things. Since *everything* you want to do puts you in danger!"

"What danger?" My hands thrust forward. "Where do you see danger outside of your own mirror?"

"Don't start that crap again," he snaps. "You're the one who thought someone was watching you here. So you're not coming back and that's final."

"Final? You don't get to decide this, or *anything else!*"

"Whether you like it or not, you don't have to work anymore." He sighs. "I don't understand why you've got a problem with that."

"Of course you don't." I fling the door open, not waiting for him to stop.

He shoves the gearshift into park and scrambles to catch me. I already have the crutches pulled from behind the seat and propped under my arms by the time he grabs my shoulders. "Get away from me!"

"I'm not trying to upset you." He doesn't let go. "But I am firm on this. You're not working here anymore. Please understand why."

"No!"

"Put yourself in my shoes. What would you do if it were me in danger?"

"Stop making up excuses just to control me. My life isn't in danger every second of every day. And if it were, it wouldn't be stemming from Scarlets!"

"You don't know that!" he roars. "No one knows that because no one knows anything! Except you feel like someone watches you *and* follows you here. So why would I let you work here?"

"Because you don't have a choice to *not* let me!" I jerk free. "You can't stop me. I'm not a possession you *let* do things."

His growl sends the amassing bystanders heading for cover. "Don't get mad at them when they wouldn't be here if you weren't being a jerk. Now move! I'm going to Scarlets. Alone!"

He holds on to me, hands retaking control of my shoulders. I meet his eyes. He swallows. "I see the hurt in your eyes and I'm sorry for being the one who put it there. But this is something I can't bend on. You're going to have to understand my position."

"I don't *have* to do anything." My teeth grind.

"Sweetheart, please." His hands reluctantly fall away. "I don't want us to fight."

"I'm not Susan. Or any of the other *many* women you've dated. I don't spend nights in your bed dreaming of how it gets me closer to your money!"

I shoulder past him. He follows me. My turn to growl. A sound paralleling what he's accustomed to dishing out. He stops dead. "I know who you are. And who you're not. Which is why I love you so much that every moment of every day, every decision I make, is for you. For what's *best* for you." I keep moving, beyond insulted he thinks a proposal is an automatic resignation. "Go on inside. I'll check on you in half an hour."

"Thanks for your permission." I put distance between us. "Permission I don't need!"

John

Mary brings out the best in me. And the absolute worst. Two extremes I haven't yet learned to temper because I've never had to navigate these waters before. Watching her hobble away, the very thing I want slipping out of my hands, physically hurts. One way or another, I have to make her see I'm not the unreasonable one in this relationship. Not always.

I check my watch, setting the timer. She gets thirty minutes. Not a second more. "What?" I growl at the gawkers. "Never seen a couple argue before?" I slam my door and peel out, leaving marks on the pavement for them to stare at.

Circling around and picking a spot close to the door she disappeared through, I slam the gear into park and look at the time. What am I going to do for twenty-eight minutes and thirty-nine seconds? The only thing of interest to me is the dark-haired beauty who needs time to cool off.

I get out and pace around the car. Kick the tires. Check my watch. Scratch at a dead bug on the windshield. Check my watch. Fifteen minutes in and I'm fully descending into madness. It was definitely better when I carried her everywhere.

The phone saves me from barging into the mall like a bull. "Yeah?" Detective Beckley's call isn't only distracting, it's rewarding. In more ways than one. "You've narrowed down a list of suspects?" A list she needs to see as soon as possible. She'll just have to get over being mad that I'm cutting her alone time short. "We're at Scarlets. I'll round her up now and we'll head your way."

I don't feel a bit guilty about dragging her out of here. We need to finish our *discussion* anyway. "Where's Mary?" I ask the first sales associate I encounter in Scarlets.

"I haven't seen her in a while." The girl shrugs. "She was in a car accident."

"I know." I rub my face. "I'm her fiancé."

"Mary's engaged?" She gasps. "Can I see the ring?"

"It's on her finger." I snap. "Page her, *please.* It's important. She's here today and you should know that."

I take note of the time while she makes the page. Mary will get mad if the freckle-faced girl tells her I snapped. "Sorry, I'm just having a bad day."

"It's okay." She smiles, the telltale sign of a flirt rounding her shoulders and moving down until her entire body is poised for my advantage. "If Mary's marrying you, you must be quite the catch."

"I doubt she'd say the same right now." And for good reason. I've been idiot ground zero since that first smile in the Charleston Club. "I'm the lucky one in our relationship. She's more than a catch. She's everything."

"That she is." Pam strolls up. "It's good to see you again. Is there something I can help you with?"

"He's engaged to Mary!" the girl squeals.

"Engaged!" Pam's hand slams over her heart. "Oh, my word!"

"She didn't tell you?"

A knife twists in my gut. Even leaving things the way we did, I'm still anxious to shout from the mountaintop that Mary's going to be my wife. "She didn't show you the ring?"

"That sly little thing." She looks around. "She was going to surprise me. Show up just happening to have a diamond. I bet you got her a big one, didn't you?"

"You haven't seen her?" My vision dims. "Is that what you're telling me?"

Her brow knits. "She isn't supposed to be back at work until next week."

"Stop it!" I warn, teeth grinding. "This is not a joke. I don't care what she told you to say. Tell me where she is right now."

"We haven't seen her." She steps away, glancing at the shivering girl. "If Mary *was* here, she would have answered the page."

Earth heaves under my feet, sweat beading over my body. I reach for the wall. "Mr. Beller?" Pam's voice is distant. "You don't look good. Do you need to sit down?"

"Lock the doors." I stumble toward the entrance.

"What?"

"Lock down! Now!" I yank out my phone. Detective Beckley picks up on the second ring. "Come to the mall." I scan the corridor, scouring every visible corner. "Bring an army. Mary is missing."

~121~

I force my legs to run from store to store. Push my mouth to order managers and security guards to lock down the entire mall. "No one leaves!" repeats hard and loud until everyone complies. Guards lie in wait at exits. Managers at entrances. Security footage is cued up and employees and customers alike sit ready to give an account of all they've seen today. Even my sister is on alert. Waiting to handle what I miss. What I can't focus on. Like news vans piling up outside.

"When I say get here, I mean get here!" I snap at Detective Beckley. "Go! Send men to question every single person."

"Wait just a minute." He puts his hands up. "Tell me what happened. Have you looked for her? There are a lot of stores in here—"

"I've run through this entire place ten times over waiting for you." I lean into his face. "I've personally checked every nook, cranny, and bathroom stall. She's gone!"

"Okay." He turns, issuing orders to the handful of officers beside him before facing me again. "Is there any chance she left on her own?"

"She wouldn't do that." I lead him in the direction of the small security office, nodding to the weasel of a guard in the corner. "Play the footage." A cough behind me warrants a look. Detective Summers. Notebook in hand.

"Where were you when she went *missing*, Mr. Beller?"

"Go to hell."

"Did things go too far? Get out of hand?" The tap of his pen echoes through the room. "Is this charade of you looking for her part of your elaborate cover-up?" My hand goes for his throat.

"Enough!" Beckley barrels through me, shoving his partner out the door. "I told you to wait outside!"

"I told you he's a liar!" Summers shouts. "I don't care how much money he has. Half a dozen people just attested to him screaming at her right outside this building." His eyes flame. "Did the fight go too far, *Mr. Beller?* Did you hurt her? Again?"

"Let him in." I sling Beckley aside.

"It's her!" The security guard's squeal draws me to the screen.

"Mary." I press in. She's hobbling all alone across the slick floor, bystanders admiring her, glancing, smiling…everything but helping. Same as me. "I did this to her." My heart drops. "Summers is right. I…"

"This footage backs up your story." Beckley sighs. "She came in here alone. I'm not seeing anyone that looks out of place around her. Do you?"

I track her path, scanning those around her while feeling every drop of the scowl on her face. I put it there. "All I see is my heart breaking." She comes to an abrupt stop. "Wait, someone called her name." She waves, the scowl giving way to a smile. A genuine one. "You were right. She knows the attacker."

"How do you know she was attacked?" Summers snaps.

"Can anyone see who she's waving at?" Beckley writes down the time stamp.

"What cameras pick up that angle?" I ask the guard, blocking Summers out. "We need to see that corridor."

The weasel's face turns red. Purple blotches bubble under his flesh. "Um…we don't have cameras in that hallway."

"You what?" Air exits my lungs. I grab the screen, jabbing a finger at the corridor she disappeared down. "Can you exit that way?"

"Um, yeah. But not many people do."

Beckley diverts my fist. It smashes into the cinderblock wall instead of the guard's face. "It isn't his fault! And you can see he's scared to death!"

"He should be!" The remnants of my composure burst into flames.

"Is this what happened to her?" Summers snarls. "Lose your cool one too—"

"You're not helping!" Beckley lunges at Summers. I go for the guard.

"Don't!" He cowers. "I'm a friend of hers. Mary and I are buddies!"

I freeze. Beckley said her stalker would be someone close to her. "What's your name?"

"Andy."

"The Andy who told her people with black hair are crazy?" My hand tightens around his shirt collar.

"Not her." He swallows. "I told her she wasn't. It's just something I heard my uncle say once."

"He's as dumb as you." I press him into the wall. "Where is Mary? Lie to me, and I'll snap your neck."

~122~

Andy's alibi checks out. He was smoking by a dumpster he scratched his name on the side of. A jewelry store clerk was with him. She describes him as sweet, albeit two shades shy of bright.

"There's blood by the door at the end of the corridor." An officer rushes into the room, handing Detective Beckley an evidence bag. "And this. We found it about twenty feet from the exit."

"With the blood?" Beckley eyes the ring.

"This is hers." I yank it from the bag, knees going slack.

"Um…" The officer turns to Beckley. "There's only a smattering of blood, but the ring was in it."

"Only…" A smattering. One drop is too much. "She's gone." I hit the floor. She'd never take this off. Never throw it on the ground. Someone made her.

I heave, falling forward. Beckley orders everyone out of the room, giving me time to collapse. Despair. But I don't need time. I need Mary. "You said you have a list of suspects." I latch onto his arm, dragging myself off the floor under his strength while mine fails. "Show me. If she knew…knows the person, maybe I'll recognize them."

It's a long shot with the little time I've actually known her. But he has the photos with him. I stand against the wall as he spreads them across the desk, my body unable to bear the weight of my mistakes. Each one clenches my chest. From not driving her home that terrible night to letting her walk into this mall on her own today. I should have never given her space. Never decided to wait for facts to prove my instincts right or wrong. I should have bent a knee at the Charleston Club and never let her out of my sight again.

I wipe my face, pushing off the wall and sliding her ring into my pocket. The memory of placing it onto her delicate finger burns in my mind. George's photo is in the lineup, but it's the second picture from the right that jumps out. My hand slides over the glossy paper, truth bubbling alongside rage. "Son of a—"

"Him?" Beckley half laughs. "I put him in as a filler. There's an old sedan titled to him and we questioned him about it, but he said it hasn't run in years."

"What did you think he was going to say?" I crush the picture in my fist. "He looked me dead in the eye, said he cared about her, when this whole time it was *him* going after her."

"You need to calm down!" Summers rushes in, the sound of me ripping the monitor from one wall and smashing it against the other too much for him.

"He's been right in front of you!" I toss the wadded-up picture in his face. "Hiding in plain sight because you *asked* if he wrecked her. Like he'd confess if you said please!" He unfurls the paper, shock streaking across his face.

"He's serious." Beckley waves Summers back into the hall. "Take a few officers and go to his house. His job. Wherever. Just find him."

"I'm going to kill him." I toss what's left of the room. "I'm going to rip out his heart and shove it up his—"

"No one is killing anyone!" Beckley shouts. "Not on my watch."

"This isn't your watch anymore!" I take her ring out of my pocket. "I'm coming for you, sweetheart. I *will* find you." My eyes close, the smiling photograph of a wolf in friend's clothing flashing against my lids. "I'm coming for him, too."

~123~

"We need to go!" Detective Beckley shouts from the other side of the mall. I left him half an hour ago. Going back to question everyone as to whether or not they saw the snazzily dressed, lower-than-dirt, soon-to-be-dead Dr. Carlos Redmond today.

"You found Mary?" I run toward the detective.

"No." He sprints to catch up as I bypass him, heading for the exit he's parked outside. "It's Dr. Redmond's house." He pants. "She's not there, but from what I've heard that's a good thing."

"Not finding her is *not* good."

"You were right about him. And he planned to take her to his house." He unlocks his car. "The fact that he didn't means he's adjusting on the fly. Which means mistakes. Not well-thought-out plans he was working on long before you came along."

Running scared also means more danger to Mary. I dial Sheila. She's already on her way to the mall. "Call the governor. I want choppers in the sky and a lid on this so tight the Jolly Green Giant can't pry it open. Redmond is on the run, and the closer he thinks we are the worse Mary's chances are." I hang up, considering it done. People think I'm bossy, but my little sister isn't a force you want to mess with. She's just wrapped in a dainty package so, unlike me, you don't see her coming until she owns you.

"Hurry up!" I brace against the detective's dash. Sirens on, he weaves through traffic fast enough it would scare me if I'd never ridden with Sheila before. Too bad I've had the experience.

~

"This looks like him." I smirk as we roll through the posh community where Dr. Redmond's stately house stands tall. Police have the entire place roped off. Uniforms swarm the grounds, searching for

290

signs of the doctor or Mary. Neighbors buzz. Wanting to know what's going on at the extravagantly landscaped home of the wealthy doctor. His yard even has marble statues and cascading water features. The high-dollar version of a lawn full of pink flamingos.

I get out of the car. "Have every single one of these people thoroughly questioned. Then have the crowd dispersed. No one is to take pictures, videos, or recordings of any kind. Understand?"

"I already told them to confiscate everything." Beckley nods. "You just make sure the governor backs us on this."

"He will." I enter the gleaming pearl doors of the four-story brick house. It's just as lavish inside as out. Elegant furniture, works of art, and more marble statues adorn our path.

"This way." Beckley ushers me to the top floor. "This is where the investigation is focused."

Detective Summers stands just outside the door to the second room on the left, head jerking up with wide eyes, glancing between Beckley and myself. "Mr. Beller," he whispers, "are you sure you're up to being here? What's inside this room is…" He swallows. "Disturbing."

"I'm up to finding my fiancée." I shove him aside, eyes darting from one side of the room to the other. Bile rises in my throat. Photographs of Mary jump from every corner. Walls. Ceiling. Even the furniture is painted with them. Some so small they fill tiny cracks. Others large and framed. Some with Redmond cropped into them. Pictures covering years of her life. Taken from every angle and location. I see her at work, home, restaurants, and even sitting by a grave. "He's been everywhere."

"Those are the most recent." Summers points to the rickety gold-knobbed daybed where photos are strewn about. "Like you said, he's been *everywhere*."

Avoiding the life-size cutout slumped over the headboard, I pick up the first picture my fingers reach. Her. In a little black dress. My head spins. I grab the next one. Then the next. Our entire first date, from the time she got into Kim's car to standing on the porch with me the next morning immortalized among others on this scratchy floral bedspread. "I never had the slightest clue he was there."

"He's been doing this for a long time." Beckley cups my shoulder. "Redmond knows how to go unnoticed."

My thoughts race to that morning, when I knew she was lying after I found her at the back door. I was so caught up in my own feelings I decided to let her lie to me. Willing to buy whatever she sold. "All this time trying to win her heart, and I failed to do the one thing she actually needed me to do." I sort the pictures. Her smiling face. Her hand on my arm. Big, uncertain eyes nearly looking straight into the camera while I stand there with a goofy grin on my face. "She's paying the price for my mistakes."

"You couldn't have predicted the danger." Beckley sighs. "With all that's in this room, he had a plan before he grabbed her. We'll figure it out. And we'll find her."

A photograph in the next pile catches my attention. My truck. At Marsalas. "Yep." Summers uses his gloved hand to pull out another one. "He's the one who keyed your truck. Warning *you* to stay away from *her.*"

"I should have known." I'm an idiot. Worse. "I missed every single sign. Allowed him to get close to her. Over and over again."

"All of us did." Summers points to a different stack. My stomach revolts. I've barely lifted the top picture and already know what this is.

Vomit rushes up my throat. Beckley pushes a bag under my nose. The last thing I have of her, our lunch, pours into the crinkly sack. Photographs of an unconscious, bloody body dangling upside down assault my eyes. Images already forever burned into my skull. My legs give out, my stomach not allowing me to hold onto one tiny morsel of her. I don't deserve to. I let him wreck her. And when she didn't die, I let him keep her sedated at the hospital, playing out any sick fantasy he wanted while I stood feet away. "I let him put his hands on her." Faucets break open inside me.

Beckley hands me another stack of photos. "If you're done puking, get off the floor and look at these. You need the whole picture, Mr. Beller. Once you have it, you'll know there's nothing you could have done to prevent this. You hear me? Nothing."

He's wrong. I could have followed my instincts and beat Carlos Redmond to death the first day I met him. The day I stood in the emergency room covered in Mary's blood.

~124~

I wish I'd planned to sequester Mary on a yacht in the middle of the Pacific for her recovery instead of taking her to my house. She and I tucked away where no one could get to us. Where despair couldn't find us. An island fortress where shadowy lined photographs don't prove the noises under her house were not only real, but were compliments of Carlos Redmond. "The animal put cameras in her floor vents?"

"He made sure he was watching her from every angle." Detective Summers nods toward the walk-in closet where two officers catalogue contents. "You're going to want to look in there while you're here."

The closet is filled to the brim with oddities. Everywhere I look, bizarre items stare out from the clothing. Dolls, boxes of shredded paper that appear to be blank, makeup, wooden blocks, whips, rows of empty coffee cans, and containers of balloons. "Someone explain this to me." I rub my neck. "Why am I in the twilight zone?"

"We're not sure yet." Beckley studies the room. "Men like this never make much sense to the rest of us."

"He isn't a man." I yank a wedding dress from the rack. Mary's face is plastered to cardboard sticking out of the neck. Behind it, a tuxedo with Redmond's picture. I toss both to the floor, crushing them under my feet. "He's a monster. And the psycho is going to regret ever laying eyes on her. I don't care what it takes, find her. Now!"

My voice echoes through the house, silencing everyone except Summers. He clears his throat. "You probably need to come with me."

"You probably need to do your job!" If he accuses me again of hurting her, he's going to be the first person I hurt.

"I…" He wipes his brow. "I'm sorry. But there's something else you need to see."

293

"What more can there possibly be?" I push past him. "Look around. How much worse can this get?"

He swallows. "For starters, I can show you the bomb he's been building."

"Bomb?" I pale.

"It has your name on it." He sighs. "Literally."

The contents of the adjoining room are a different level of disturbing than anything I've seen in this house so far. One of the empty coffee cans has been converted into the beginnings of a shrapnel bomb. My name is etched into the side of the can. Beside the makeshift workbench is a diagram of my truck. "He was going to blow up my truck?"

"Probably with you in it." Beckley turns on the television beside me, showing me a horror worse than a bomb intended to end my life. Redmond had Mary under *full* surveillance. The movie playing on the screen stars my beautiful lady. "Oh, sweetheart." I sink in front of the screen as her form sneaks along the wall of her house, turning on lights. Her shaky voice calls out, asking if anyone is there. She goes to the alarm pad. Punches in the code with fingers trembling so hard I can't see how she managed to hit the buttons. I jump when her scream rips out, horror crawling out of the screen to roll over me. Lights flash around her. The alarm shouts warnings. There's banging in the background. It has to be the door she said smashed against its frame. "I'm so sorry." I touch the screen, fingers sliding gently over her tear-soaked cheek. "So, so sorry."

"She never had a chance," Summers mumbles.

"She has one now." I wipe my face. "You finally know who you're looking for. So *find him*!"

~125~

Mary's been gone one hundred sixty-eight minutes. Every second with the demented man putting her life in greater danger. I pace the police station, rolling Grandmother's ring in my fingers to quell the flesh-melting rage boiling inside. Occasionally I glance at Sheila. She's here spearheading the joining of forces between FBI and state police. Together we're making sure every effort is exhausted. A lot of that depends on our deep pockets, especially considering the FBI usually doesn't get involved with missing adult cases. But our hefty *donations* ensure everyone's cooperation. Cooperation Mary's life depends on.

"Have Mom call our Realtor." I stare at the investigation board I've been staring at for an hour. "Mary always wanted her own boutique. It's time she has one."

"John," Sheila whispers.

"A self-standing building downtown. No store fronts unless the entire building is available." I shouldn't have demanded she quit Scarlets. "Have the lawyers check into buying Scarlets, too. In case she'd rather have it."

"Take a breath." Sheila wraps her arms around me.

"Mary deserves a future!" I pull away. I know the look in her eye. The same one everyone in this room is getting. "She *has* a future." The lump presses hard in my throat. "We're going to find her. And she's going to be okay. So you make the calls."

Now I know why Mary doesn't like to be looked on with pity. It's demoralizing. I may be a moron, but I know every ticking minute with the madman lowers the odds of finding her alive. They don't have to spell it out with their sad puppy faces. "We have to know something by now." The pressure of constantly thinking about what's happening to her buckles my legs. I spin toward the room. "One of you has to know something! Instead of staring at me, tell me where she is!"

Loud silence answers me. Sheila taps on her phone, texting Mom. Others make calls, type away on keyboards, and huddle in small groups. None look at me. None offer answers. "Pathetic."

"Oh my God," Sheila gasps, staring at her phone.

"What?" I barely hear my voice over the fear of my heart. "Is it Mary?" Tears slip from my swollen lids. Mom's been at the hospital for the last hour, greasing palms for information and talking more candidly with the employees than any faction of law enforcement can. "Just tell me. Where's Mary?"

"It's not her. It's…"

"What? Just tell me!"

"Redmond killed Mary's husband."

The words hang in the air. Thick and choking. Beckley closes in, Summers trailing him. Sheila hands me her phone, an email on display. "John, Mom got an administrator to squeal. Redmond administered a lethal dose of morphine. A nurse witnessed him leave the room and reported he was acting strange, and the patient had been fine directly before." Words jump off the screen. Euthanasia. Malpractice. Public scrutiny.

"What's this about an audio file?" My tongue is lead.

"Mom recorded the conversation with the administrator. Secretly." Sheila sighs. "The woman admits they *did* determine Redmond's guilt, but chose to reprimand him in-house rather than face lawsuits from the masses who would use the incident to attack the hospital's patient care."

"They let him get away with murder?"

"He told them he was a personal friend of the patient, carrying out Mike's dying wish." She takes back the phone. "He played it off as benevolence."

Summers crosses his arms. "And because of how your mom got the information, our hands are tied."

"Your hands haven't been tied this entire time!" I yell. "Yet you still never caught him! And you're *still* walking around stupefied. Find. My. Fiancée!"

I don't care how she got the information, Mom accomplished more in an hour than these detectives did in weeks. They're out of excuses. "There's no red tape, people!" I shout to the room. "You work for *me*. Now do what you've got to do and *find Mary!*"

Now that I know Redmond has killed before, the fear is greater. All I can hope is his sick fascination with Mary will keep her safe. "He's not MacGyver. He's *one* man!" One stubby legged little man whose limbs I'm going to rip off and shove down his throat. "What's his 'Plan B'? If not his house, what are his other options?"

~126~

When Mary wasn't on social media, I should have hired a private investigator. A sleuth might have found the threat, then I wouldn't be in the dark right now. "News? Anybody?"

Sheila straightens from the makeshift desk of a puffy-faced man whose blue tie is pinned tight against his starched white shirt. His chunky fingers jab into keys on his laptop. "Mom sent us a lead. About a farmhouse."

"Where?" My heart drops.

"All we know right now is a nurse remembered him talking about the place last year. He'd just bought it and told her it was an hour outside of Huntington."

"North, south, east or west? Which way out of town?"

"He's almost got the property record." She places a hand on the man's shoulder, smiling encouragingly at his sweat-soaked face. Playing him. Like a cat with a mouse. "We never thought to check names of Redmond's dead relatives, but Doyle here is getting the job done."

"We should have thought about it! Someone in this room should have thought about it three hours ago! Why *wouldn't* the psycho buy land in a dead person's name?"

"Why did the lawyer doing the paperwork let him?" Detective Beckley scratches his chin, moving into position to watch the screen over Sheila's shoulder.

Redmond had a sister. She's been dead for fifteen years. That much I know. Finding next of kin was high priority. "Money," I mutter, catching Sheila's frown. We know all too well what kind of luxuries printed paper can buy. Redmond's lawyer didn't care *why* his client wanted to use a dead woman's name, he only cared about the extra paycheck. A decision I'll make him regret.

"Got it!" Doyle sends his screen to the printer. "This has to be where he went. It's secluded."

"Let's go." I map the property on my phone. "Now, people!"

"It's not only secluded." Summers hesitates. "In that area, it's defensible. We need to formulate a—"

"Cowards can stay behind." I lead a stream of officers outside. "I'm getting her back. And I'm not asking nicely." I nod to Beckley. "Choppers in the air. Dogs on the ground. An army at my back."

"Done." Sheila answers for him, a grin on her face. If I weren't frantic to get this procession moving, I'd take time to both fear and admire her. "Drive like the wind, Beckley. I'll take care of the rest." She opens his car door. "Just get my brother to his breadbox as fast as possible. I'm not ready for Armageddon. And if his lady isn't found, he'll bring the sky down. Block by beautiful block."

If I thought it would help, I'd blast the stars right out of heaven. For now, I'll settle for the sky being filled with the thump of helicopters. The banging in my ears is only dulled by the pounding of my heart. I sit on the edge of Beckley's seat, the entire police force behind us, racing toward the farm. My ribs ache, lungs pushing hard against their cage. Exhilarating breaths at the hope of finding Mary, agonizing puffs of fear over the condition she'll be in. She's been locked up with the monster for five hours. "Faster!" My fist smashes the dashboard. "Either step on it, or let me drive!"

"You're in no condition to ride shotgun." Beckley pushes the pedal to the floor. "Let alone drive."

~127~

Mary

My fight with John seems so small now. If I could take back my words, compromise with him, understand how his own fear drives him, I'd gladly be standing next to him at Scarlets handing in my resignation. But my whole life is a mountain of regrets. While I hold my head high and pretend I'm okay on my own, all I'm really doing is avoiding feeling like an outsider by making myself one. Always the interloper in Kim's borrowed family, the intruder in my dad's, the girl who married a man who didn't have a family so she didn't have to try to fit in. And the woman too convinced of her own paltriness to believe a stalker could be real.

I watch Carlos pacing, dust rustling to float through the beam of light shining through a crack in the drapes shading the window. He doesn't know I'm awake yet. He's mumbling to himself, reaching out every so often to slice the air with his knife. The silver blade gleams each time he turns left, into the stream of light that's my only gauge on how long I've been here. *If* today is still today. For all I know, the cloth he put over my mouth held a drug that knocked me out for days.

"I warned you!" His blade stabs the emptiness in front of him. I dig my fingers into the bed I just woke up on, trying to keep my eyes only slits and my breathing steady. As long as he isn't coming at me, I can just lie here. *John will look for me.* My heart aches. *He will.*

John was conflicted the last time I saw him. I was angry. Then Carlos lured me away. "Mary!" he called my name from a darkened hallway in the mall. I went to him, eager to make amends. He accepted my apology and asked for a favor in return. "Since leaving the hospital against my wishes seems to agree with you, how about coming out to my

300

car? I just bought a new suit but no one has an eye like you. And I have a very important date that I'm trying to make everything just right for."

"Is the special *date* with your girlfriend? The surprise trip you told me about?"

"Oh yes, it's a surprise. She's been wanting this for a very long time." His eyes gleamed, an excitement I've never seen on him animating his features. "I'm parked right back here, by the door."

Standing beside his car, he unlocked the rear door and asked me to grab the shoes off of the floorboard while he retrieved the suit from the trunk. I leaned in, maneuvering the crutches out of my way so I could reach the bag. A blow landed against the back of my skull. I fell onto the seat. His weight fell over me. I screamed, trying to thrash him off me, but he was too heavy. His hand snaked around my throat and up over my mouth. "Sleep, my lamb." His voice croaked against my ear. "I'll shear you soon."

The memory brings tears. I try to stop the flow but they leak from my eyes, wash down my cheeks and soak the bed beneath me. A reflexive sniff releases, the sound turning Carlos's attention to me. "There you are." He stomps toward me. "I want you awake for this."

"No," I cry. "Carlos, don't do this."

"I did everything for you." He seethes, spit dribbling off his lip. "*Everything.*"

"I know." I raise onto my elbows. "You did. And I'm grateful. But what you're doing now…is this because I didn't stay at the hospital?"

"It's because you're a harlot." He leans toward me. "John Beller's strumpet. And now you're mine."

He presses the flat of the blade to my neck, eyes dilating. "That's my girl. Cry for me, Mary. Scream." He smooths the blade down my neck, fingers resting on the collar of my dress. "I love it when you scream. The sound…" His mouth parts. "Oh that sound."

I hold my breath and still my chest. His breath is sour. Familiar. A spray of odor from my dreams. He angles the blade, slicing through the seam in the fabric at my neck. "Don't worry, you'll scream."

"Don't do this." Tears blur my vision. "Please, don't do this."

"That's right. Beg." The knife raises over his head. "You want this."

"I don't!" I scream, his arms coming down, plunging the knife into the bed beside my head.

His fist balls in my hair, yanking my face to his. "You want me. You've always wanted me. Not that pathetic slug of a husband whose bedside you cried at every day. Me!" He yanks my head to the right. "See that? You get to stay with me, Mary. As soon as I have my fill of you, I'll slice open your veins and drain every last drop of you into that bucket." His mouth presses into my neck, his tongue sticky and wet. Like the racoon under my house. It was him.

"Please don't." Sobs shake out of me, hands fighting against his chest, but the more I struggle the more he groans, his body stiff with pleasure. I stop fighting. He takes his mouth from me.

"I'm going to paint the walls with you. Keep you. Forever entombed in this room with me." His face hardens. "I should have taken you after I put that slug out of his misery. Then you wouldn't have to die today." His hand closes around my throat. "Then we could be home, putting you in a new outfit. You should see all the things I had ready for you, pet. Especially the chains." His chest expands, ecstasy thick in air around him as he presses against me. "Scream, Mary." His hand tightens. "Scream!"

~128~

I hold my tongue. Swallow my screams until Carlos throws my body over and yanks up my dress, the fabric ripping under his grip. "No!" I fight for space. Drag myself across the bed and kick out with my legs.

He flips me back over, hands groping for flesh. "Those eyes." His own are dilated, my fear feeding his fantasy. I go for the knife. He yanks it from the sheets and unbuttons his pants. "I'll bring you John Beller's head before I kill you. Would you like that, pet? A chance to stare into the cold dead eyes of the devil who ruined you?"

"Don't touch him." My teeth grind.

"First I touch you. Then I kill him." He smiles. "And while his head bleeds beside you, I'll have you again. I'll have you until there's nothing left of you." His pants fall to his ankles, spittle slicking his lips. *John.* His voice mocks me. *John, help me.*

"It was you." Anger rises inside me. "You were in the smoke, watching me die."

His lip curls. "I warned you both."

Reality floods in. Mike died sooner than expected because Carlos killed him. The sadistic man destroyed me. Emotionally. Mentally. Physically. And now he's going to kill John.

Fear binds to anger, fueling a power I've never had. Carlos moves forward and with all the strength I have, I lift my casted leg and plant it in his groin. He howls, stumbling backward. The pants catch, tripping him sideways. His head hits the corner of the stone hearth sprawled along the wall of the nearly empty room.

I push off the bed, cast and bare foot hitting the scratched planks of the floor. Stumbling forward, momentum propelling me toward the door, I fall against it, twist the knob and push over the threshold. I glance

303

at Carlos. His body isn't moving and blood is seeping down his face. The knife is sprawled across his open palms. "Carlos," I whisper. There's no movement. I killed him.

Shaking too badly to stand, unaware of any pain—only fear—I lower myself to the floor and crawl to him. I slip the knife from his hand, curling it in my own. "Carlos." He doesn't move. I lean over him, applying pressure to his scalp. He's losing too much blood, but he still has a pulse. "Carlos." Tears stream down my face. I think of the man I've known, his smiling face and kind words.

"Mary!" I hear John's voice as clear as if he's standing next to me. My head snaps to the door. I have to get out of here. Find a phone. Call an ambulance. Save John. No one can hurt him. No one. Carlos's fingers twitch. I recoil, hands slick with his blood. I drop the knife and wipe them on my dress, crawling over the dusty floor until I reach the safety of the threshold. Glancing back at Carlos, he's still down. I move forward, crawling through the unfamiliar hall toward the light of the fading day. I round the corner and don't try to stand.

My dress rips under my knees as I scurry over the floor, crossing the freshly drywalled room to the outside door. Pulling myself up by the handle, I swing the door open and press my unsteady body against the frame. There's nothing here. Only acres of grass.

Carlos's car is off to the right, parked in the grass beside the porch. Behind it is a dirt road. I hobble forward, putting most of my weight on the casted leg to ease the throb I now feel in the bare foot. My only hope is reaching his car and finding the keys still in it.

Gripping the porch railing, I lower onto the first step. My dress catches under the cast. I fall forward, tumbling down the remaining three steps to land with a thud in the dirt below. I drag my body forward, toward the car, fingers digging into the dirt. Maybe if I'd stood I wouldn't have noticed, but down here in the dirt it's obvious—John's ring is gone.

Hysteria is akin to insanity. I frantically search the dirt path I just crawled, looking for the diamond John gave me. Part of my brain tells me to run, flee, get as far from this dilapidated, once-white farmhouse as I can. The other part says I have to find the ring. *His* ring. The only thing I have left of him.

Wind kicks up, enclosing me in a cyclone of dust. My hair beats against my face. I squint through the debris, eyes on the steps as the drum of helicopter blades beat the sky. John's ring has to be inside. I head for the steps. "Mary!" I hear his voice again, muddy and drowned by the growing roar of sounds behind me. I move faster, I have to get the ring.

"Mary!" John's clearer now, ringing out among a blaze of sirens. I spin around, holding onto the corner of the steps. Cars speed toward me, fanning out from the road to swarm the lawn around me. In the middle of them all is John, feet digging up earth as he runs toward me. He calls my name again and I reach for the lattice covering the bottom of the porch. Every muscle in my body burns as I pull myself upright. He yells for me to stop. Officers pile out of their cars, guns trained on me.

Detective Beckley drives around John, cutting off his path. John slides overtop the hood, his stride steady and strong. The door of the house rattles. Officers start shouting. A demonic yell rips from a throat behind me. I turn slowly. Carlos staggers onto the porch, the knife I dropped by his side clutched in his fist. Officers order him to drop the weapon. He does, relief washing through me when the knife clangs over the porch's wooden planks. Then his hand swirls behind his belted waist, coming back around with a gun. I follow the trajectory of his aim. He's trained on John. "No!" The shot drowns my scream.

John

The sound of gunfire still echoing across the field, I lunge forward, catching Mary's tumbling body in my crushing arms. I drag her to my chest, collapsing in sobs as her nails dig into my flesh, her life clinging to mine. "I'm sorry, sweetheart." My tears wash over her bloody cheeks. "I'm so, so sorry."

Beckley drops beside us. I pry myself from her and glance to the porch. Carlos Redmond's blood oozes from the hole in his head. I tuck her deeper into my chest, she doesn't need to see his lifeless body. "I've got to get her out of here."

"Is she okay?"

"She will be." I hoist her sobbing frame up with me, burrowing my face into her neck and carrying her away from the grisly scene amid a myriad of emotions. They swim in an endless abyss. I need to soothe her while making sure an ocean of terror clings to my soul so I never fail her again. I'll keep her safe. And I'll remember nothing I feel compares to what she's been through.

Hurrying to the car farthest from the farmhouse, I drop into the passenger seat. Legs sprawled outside the vehicle so she has more real estate on my lap. "Sweetheart." I press against her ear. "On my life, you *will* be safe for the rest of yours." She presses against me with force matching the strength I hold her with. Too tight. But we don't need to breathe. We need to do what my instincts have always told me to do. Lock her in my arms and force the rest of the world away. Starting with Detective Summers. He should have heard enough of my bark today to know my bite will be worse. "Leave."

"I just want to check on her." He keeps his distance. "There's a lot of blood in the house. Is it hers?"

I've been looking for damage but her nails are so entrenched it's hard to move. There's a nasty knot on her head and I can see blood, but some of it is Redmond's. Spraying over her when Detective Beckley's bullet crushed his skull. She definitely isn't bleeding out, though. She's only trembling. So hard I can feel the car move beneath us. "Sweetheart," I whisper, "how badly are you hurt? Do you need a hospital?"

Her dress hangs in tatters. A shred of what was once a sundress that lay beautifully against her olive skin. Dirt mats her hair. Filth and blood cover her from head to toe. Still, all she whispers is, "Home."

I glide delicate fingers along her back. Holding her tighter with each small stroke. I lift her face. She slams it back to my chest. "I'm going to take you home, sweetheart." I glance at Summers. He scratches his neck.

"I really need to know about that blood. Especially if it's hers."

"I kicked him." Her nails pulse inside my flesh, blood quivering under her chipped polish. The sweetest pain I've ever felt. "It isn't my blood. I kicked him!"

This isn't the time or place to laugh, but I'm ready to full-belly howl. "You kicked him?"

"And he hit the fireplace." Defiant eyes lift to mine, face transplanting mud from her cheeks onto my shirt. "That's what he gets for threatening to do to you what he did to Mike."

If he wasn't already lying in a pool of his own blood, I'd rip Redmond's throat out. "He only said that to hurt you." She doesn't need to live with the knowledge of him preying on her husband. "He was trying to break you. But he can't, sweetheart." I rest my forehead on hers. "We won't let him."

I wish she'd gutted him. Only, she'd end up feeling bad for hurting him. Even though he tormented her, led her like a lamb to slaughter. Used smoke and mirrors to make her think she was going insane so he could swoop in and lock her up, drug her and keep her hostage in his house, surrounded by clueless neighbors who would shake his hand and feel sorry for him because he had such a madwoman to care for. And her imbecile friends helped perpetuate the glamour. "I'm sorry I didn't get here sooner." Sorry I forced him into plan B. "I'm sorry I made you deal with him alone."

I'll track her via satellite before I lose her again. "I'm sorry I can't erase every terrible second you've ever had." I lower to her ear. "I *can* make sure you never have another. I *will* make sure."

~130~

Mary's poised to burrow into my flesh. I won't mind if she does. I'm not a spineless coward like Redmond. I don't hurt women. Prey on them for my own pleasure. Filth like him should never be allowed to look on any of them. Especially Mary. But he did. And now he's going to rot in hell. Where I'll put anyone else who ever *thinks* they have the right to touch her. I'm the new monster lurking in the shadows. Ready. Waiting to tear apart anyone who threatens her.

I blew Redmond's plans to pieces from the first date, but he adapted. He didn't just coincidentally show up at the mall today and capitalize on an opportunity. He followed us. And I not only paid zero attention to the traffic around us, I offered her up on a silver platter. He must have been in the café. In disguise. Listening to our plans.

"It's over, sweetheart." I move us into the cruiser's backseat. "They're going to get whoever drives this car, and they're taking us home." My house. The one that's more hers than mine. Because I'll die before I take her back into the tiny home where a tormentor drove her mad. I'll move out if I have to. Build her fifty new houses. Take her to Mars. Anything but return her to the place he watched her every move. I only hope she forgives me for not asking what *home* she wants to go to. For now, there is only one choice.

Beckley stands nearby, watching Mary's sobbing form cling to me while he chats with the officer getting ready to drive us away from this place. "I'll never let my guard down again, sweetheart."

"Carlos said I'd never leave here." Her soft syllables roll over me like knives. Every beating inch of my heart raw. "He said my blood would paint the walls."

309

"You *are* leaving here, and I'm going to burn the walls down." I meet Beckley's eyes. "There won't be a single speck left. Not so much as an ash." Beckley nods, knowing arson is the least of the crimes I could be committing right now. Had he not got to Redmond before me, I'd be the one covered in the man's blood. Not Mary.

A young paramedic approaches. I move Mary's hair away from her ear, lowering my lips. "There's a paramedic here for you. Can he check you over before we leave?" Her legs jerk up onto the seat, knees bending in a protective shell. I wrap my arms around the ball she's made and shoot the man a warning look.

"Procedure—"

"I don't care about procedure." Her physical damage is concerning, but that's not what's hurting her most. And I can't force her go to a hospital when a doctor just tortured her. "I'll tend to her."

"But—"

"She doesn't want you touching her, so you're not!"

"I don't have to touch her to see she needs to go to the hospital." He points to her leg.

I hadn't noticed the crack running the length of her cast. But it doesn't change anything. "No hospitals." I rub her back for assurance. "I'll make arrangements with my doctor and have her treated at home." I focus on Beckley. There's one last thing I need to do before we leave: extend a hand to the man who placed a perfect shot between Redmond's eyes. One second later and the monster might have been the one to pull the trigger. "Thank you, I'm forever in your debt."

~131~

Officer Smith is polite enough not to speak. He drives Mary and me home in silence. The only sound is the soft fall of her tears. I hold her. Let her cling to me. And sit quietly. Because nothing I say can take away her pain. Or erase the mistakes I made that led to it.

"Thanks." I give Smith a grateful nod and carry Mary to the house. She's still in turtle position, legs tucked tight against her body. "Are you hungry, sweetheart?" I take her to the bedroom and lower us to a chair. Her nails remain attached to my flesh, silent sobs wetting my shirt. "Is there anything I can get you?" I press my lips to her temple. "Do for you?"

Nothing comes out of her but the steady fall of tears. "May I look at your leg? To check the cast?" Make sure I'm not being an idiot, denying her medical attention right away. "Sweetheart?"

The faintest hint of a nod. "Okay. Here we go." I slide her off my lap, repositioning her to the chair and letting her bloody nails dig into my shoulders. I slide to my knees, scrunching the filthy tatters of her dress to see the split in the cast. It's in two at the bottom and a crack runs from there, all the way to the top. "It's not safe for this to be on you. I can take it off for the night. Would you like that?" A tiny dip of approval brings a cascade of tears falling over her cheeks. I wipe them away. "I need a tool from my workshop. Let's go get it."

Finding my Dremel is easy. Everything in my workshop has a place, and everything stays in its place. The time spent keeping it orderly has never been more rewarding than right now. Mary secured against me, I pick up the saw case and head back to the house. We bypass the bed. I deposit her in a chair on the patio. The very chair we made out in the night I asked her to marry me. "Sweetheart." I remove her nails from my shoulders, kissing her knuckles and moving down to give attention to each tiny blood-soaked finger. "I'm going to go back in the house now. You're perfectly safe, and I'll be back in thirty seconds." After the cast comes off, she needs a bath. "Do you trust me?" She stares at her fingers. The blood. And nods. I kiss her forehead. "Thirty seconds."

Dashing to the bathroom, I turn the tub faucet on and pour in soap. This won't be the bubble bath I've teased her about, but necessity demands we use this tub tonight. "I hope you like lavender." I leave the tub to fill and rush back to her, doing my best to smile. She's vacant, eyes unseeing while tears slide over every cut and bruise along their path to her chin. "When I had Kim bring your things here, she stopped and bought some lavender bubble bath." Nothing. Not even a blink. "Is it okay if I start on the cast now?" Her hands reach out. I lean closer. She crumples my shirt in her fists. "All right, sweetheart." I slide down her leg, moving the saw into place. "This little tool is noisy. I'm going to start it up now. Just hold still for me."

I flip the switch, firing up the blade well away from her body. She doesn't flinch. "Ready?" She nods, holding perfectly still. "Here we go." Carefully, I let the blade make contact with the cast. It slides through the plaster. I guide it along the crack. The cast gives way, tumbling onto the patio. "All done, sweetheart." I turn the saw off and rub her long leg. "Is there any pain?"

"No," she whispers, definitely lying. Her leg could be cut off and she'd try to convince me it didn't hurt. All because she doesn't want to *put me out* by having me care.

"Let's get you cleaned up."

Cradling her in my arms, I take her through the double doors of the bathroom. A thick layer of bubbles crusts the water. I sit her in the chair by the sink and turn off the faucet. "I'll buy you a new one, sweetheart." I rip what's left of the dress off her body, making my hands as gentle as my voice. I have no idea what she endured today, but this has to be done. I snap the threads of her soiled panties and unfasten her bra, sliding it carefully down her arms. It's going straight in the trash with the rest. I can't remove the memory of what happened, but I sure as heck can make sure she doesn't have mementos.

Shedding my own clothes, which I'm also trashing, I hoist her back into my arms. Something as trivial as modesty doesn't matter right now. She needs me. And I definitely need her. I need to wash the filth from skin so pure evil should have never been able to look upon it.

We slide down, warm water rushing over us. I settle her against me. Hard sobs jerk from her depths. I let mine loose, sobbing right along with her. Relieved. Guilty. "Never again, sweetheart." Images of Redmond's house flick through my mind. The photographs. Videos. The complete control he had over her. "Never, *ever* again." She won't just live, she's going to thrive. She's going to do everything she's ever wanted. Have everything she's ever dreamed of. The treasures she's never thought to dream of. No evil will dare cross her path. Because what lives within me now is far worse. "I absolutely promise. You *are* safe."

$\sim$132$\sim$

Mary and I cried until long after the bubbles were gone from our bath. The water surrounding us is cold. I'm still running the sponge over her body, gently scrubbing away the grime and tears that have added to the list of visions I'll never get out of my head. From her bloodied body at the car crash and watching her unconscious form lying in a hospital bed afterward, to lifting her from the muck of the farmhouse. I'll hold these images close to me. Let them guide every decision I make.

"I must have been really dirty." Her soft voice breaks into my thoughts. "That, or you like aging us fifty years." Her pruney hand rises from the water, reminding me of who she is. A woman too strong-willed to let evil destroy her.

"You weren't a bit dirty." I press my face against her shoulder. "I've just been looking for an excuse to get you in here. And now that I've got you where I want you, I'm not letting you go."

"But I'm cold."

If I could kick myself, I would. "Sorry, sweetheart." I meant to turn the hot on again when the water cooled, but we've been in the tub entirely too long now anyway. "Sit tight and I'll go get us some clothes." I slide her forward and raise myself up from behind her, grabbing a towel. "I'll be right back to get you out." And I'll have a heater installed on the tub so I don't nearly freeze her to death again. Because I'm clearly doomed to keep being a moron. Here I am ready to leave her in ice cold water after she just said she was cold. "How's this?" I turn the water on, adjusting it fairly hot. She moves into the stream with the faintest hint of a smile. It breaks my heart. She's way too resilient. I admire that about her. But I don't know if it's healthy. "I'll be right back, sweetheart."

Running to the closet I tug on a pair of sweatpants and grab one of her nightshirts. Dashing back, I grab her towel. She moves to the edge of the tub, kneeling, trying to push up and get out on her own. "I've got you." I lift her, steady against my chest, and wrap the soft cotton around her shoulders. There's no point lecturing on the many reasons she shouldn't move around in this slick-tiled room. I've covered the facts before and she didn't listen to me then, either.

Sitting her on the countertop this time, instead of the chair where her dirt-stained remnants still cover the seat, I work a second towel over her hair with quick gentleness. "Feel better?" A faint nod sends tendrils cascading over her back. I run the towel over her body. She sits unmoving, not so much as a flinch over my touch on her bare skin. I assess the still-fading bruises from the car wreck, the cuts and new scrapes mixed into the damage covering her beautiful form. I'm so glad the man who did this to her is dead.

"Do you think you could eat something now?" I slide the nightshirt over her head, feeding her arms through the openings.

"No," she whispers.

"Not even crackers?" I cradle her in my arms.

"My stomach is a knot. But you should eat."

Here she goes again. Worrying about me instead of herself. "I'll get us some crackers." I tuck her into our warm bed and pull the covers up tight, pressing my lips to her forehead. "Then we'll see if we can work out those knots."

I dash to the kitchen and arm myself with crackers and a small can of ginger ale. "I keep these on hand because some days I get lost in a project and forget to eat until my stomach starts getting queasy," I explain when I return, carefully climbing onto the bed and sliding under the blankets. "Here, take a sip." I hold the can to her lips. "Do you want a straw?"

"No." Her trembling hand takes the can. I steady it as she tastes her first small sip.

"Have you…" He probably starved her. "Is this the first food you've had since…" Her eyes close. Affirmation. The last meal she had was our lunch. "I'm sorry."

"So am I." Her head rests against my shoulder. "Do you still want to marry me?"

"With every fiber of my being."

Since she first walked away from me at the mall, I've wanted to know her feelings on allowing me to be her husband. "After everything I did, do you still want to marry me?" I swallow. Her silence gives no confidence. "You're pretty torn up emotionally. You don't need to make a decision or even talk about it tonight." I can beg later. Let her heal before putting a full-court press on her that would make the Lakers jealous. "I love you."

"I'm going to throw up." She lurches forward. I scoop her into my arms and run for the bathroom.

~133~

I hold Mary's freshly washed locks out of the vomit. Seeing the child whose mother died, the little girl left alone when her deadbeat dad decided he didn't want the responsibility of being a parent anymore. The young woman devastated by the loss of a husband. And the woman tormented by a man who claimed to be a friend while I stood by and let it happen. "I'm so sorry, sweetheart." If I could express the depth of my sorrow, she'd be certain of my vigilance to never fail her again. But I can't express what's limitless. And I can't stand the thought that talking about marrying me is what's causing her ginger ale to make a reappearance.

"Do you feel better now?" My throat is on fire, choking to hold back tears she doesn't need to be burdened with. I wonder if anyone has ever been there to care for her like this. If when curled over a toilet, anyone has ever even been there to check on her. I kiss the crown of her head. "I'm going to get you a washcloth."

I lift her away from the toilet, running the cool cloth over her forehead and cheeks. "Do you think you're done?"

"I think I'm a terrible breadbox."

"You're a good everything." I'm going to kill my sister for this stupid nickname. "Want to get back in bed now?"

"I…" She inspects her nails. Broken and jagged. "When you showed up, I was on my way back into the house."

"Why?" Air sucks from my lungs. Blobs of water pool in her swollen eyes, tears running loose down her face. I can't wipe them away fast enough.

She bats my hand away. "It's gone, John. The ring. I searched…in the dirt outside. It wasn't there."

317

A tremor starts in my feet and worms up my spine. She was going back inside the house to look for the engagement ring. "Mary, don't you *ever* put yourself in danger. Not for anything. You hear me? *Nothing* is worth your life. Especially a ring!"

"It was your grandmother's." Her tears fall harder. "I promised to take care of it."

"I don't care." I grip her shoulder. "Break a million promises, Mary. Break me! Rip my heart out and stomp on it. But don't ever, for **any** reason, put yourself in the line of fire."

I sit her on the countertop and yank my stained jeans from where our dirty clothes are strewn on the floor. I turn the pockets inside out. "This ring?" I hold it up. "Without you, it's a hunk of junk taking up space."

"You have it?" She slumps. "You have it."

"I have you." I stroke her raven hair. "I love *you*. So wipe away the part of your brain that tells you locking yourself back up with a madman is an option. It isn't. I—" Her lips hit mine. Hard. Fast. Hungry. My arms swarm her. I lift her onto my hips. Mouth greedy. Hot. Wanting.

The taste of her drips down my throat. I groan. This woman is sugar sweet and blazing spice. Her hands run down my body. This isn't the time. It can't be what she wants. "Mary?"

"It's mine," she whispers against my ear, peeling the ring from my hand and slipping it onto her finger. "This is where it belongs."

I swallow. "Did you just use my own tactic against me?" She's better at kissing to distraction than I am. I've never deployed anything like what she just laid on me.

She looks at the ring on her finger. "Don't ever yell at me again."

"Don't ever let one single tiny thought cross this beautiful head of yours that sounds even remotely close to you risking your life again." I caress her cheek. "Yes, sweetheart. The ring is yours. Like I'm yours. Always."

"Then I'll marry you." I catch a grin before her head tucks against my chest. "If you forgive me for kissing you before I brushed my teeth."

"The only thing I won't forgive is you not saving your life every time you get the chance." I cradle her in my arms. "The fact that you don't already know to do that terrifies me."

"Do you already know to do it?" Her doe eyes look up to mine. "If you ever put yourself in harm's way again, I promise I'll yell louder than you've ever dared to." Her chest heaves. "I've already been the reason one husband was killed. I'll die before I let you sacrifice yourself for me, John Beller. You hear me? No more *you* protecting *me*. Carlos was coming after *you*. He pointed his gun at *you*."

~134~

Mike is dead because of cancer. He died a few months sooner than expected because of Carlos Redmond. Mary isn't responsible. She didn't trigger Redmond's sickness, and I'm not going to let her blame herself for his actions. "Nothing that happened is your fault. Not what happened to Mike. And certainly not what happened to you." I tuck her back into bed. "You didn't *do* anything."

I lie beside her, lifting her chin. "Not even your tender heart is your fault. You see the best in everyone. Even when there's nothing good to see. It's part of what makes you a truly amazing person. But every once in a while you have to see people for what they are." Even me. "I'm sorry for the way I've treated you. And I'm really, really sorry I didn't stop him."

"I should have stopped him." She wipes tears from her lashes. "He got to do what he did because I *chose* to be oblivious. I just…couldn't imagine having a stalker."

I can't imagine her not having a hundred of them. Not psychotic ones like Redmond, but lovesick dopes like me. "Your heart doesn't want to let you see how cruel the world is."

"It lets me see how prideful I am." She sniffs. "You were right about me. I go around thinking I can handle everything on my own and refuse to let anyone help me. And it nearly got you killed."

"It nearly got *you* killed." She still won't feel sorry for herself. "But I was wrong, sweetheart. Pride isn't your issue." I run my hand along her cheek. "You've been let down so much you stopped expecting anything from anyone. Self-preservation. And after the way I let you down…" She should hate me. "I've learned my lesson. I swear you'll never again feel how you felt in the hands of that monster."

Her eyes close. "I should have listened when you said it wasn't safe to go to Scarlets."

If I let her, she'll fall on her sword and take every ounce of guilt away from the monster responsible for her pain. But she can't spin this. She can't do what people have always let her do. "All you're guilty of is choosing to live your life the way you want to live it, despite what the rest of us idiots say about it." I place a gentle kiss on each closed lid. "I didn't realize I was an ogre until you were gone. It nearly cost me what I want most in this world." I drop my mouth to her ear. "You. Safe and happy. For all eternity."

I wish I could take away the guilt she feels over circumstances beyond her control. Nix the strength she puts into looking for a way to blame herself. She was the victim of a deranged man's fantasy. Victim. Not the cause. "I love you." I tilt her face to mine, coaxing her thick lashes open. "I'm sorry for the many things I've done to hurt you."

"I'm sorry I got angry." She sighs. "If I hadn't stormed away like...like..."

"Like a woman who had a right to be mad." I smile. "I didn't even come close to handling that situation right, and you let me know."

"It was a stupid argument." She presses into me. "One I thought would be your last memory of me."

I thought the same thing. "I couldn't see then how my words came across. But I see it now. I had no right to demand you quit your job."

"I had no right to act the way I did."

"Sweetheart, you acted exactly the way a woman being ordered around by a man *should* act." She was too nice, actually. "My intention was to keep you safe. But it backfired because I forgot to also keep you happy." I let my arms hold her as tight as they want. "From now on, I'm going to be supportive in every possible way, in whatever you want to do. As long as it isn't dangerous." I lower to a whisper. "There's always going to be that one catch. And my knuckles might keep dragging for a while, but I'm trying to pick them up. So next time I do the stupid thing I'm bound to do, don't walk away. Stay. And beat some sense into me."

"How about I just give you credit for trying not to be a chauvinist?" She spins inside the cocoon of my arms. "You were all I could think about today. I'd rather lose my job than lose you."

"Try to get rid of me." I grin. "It won't go well for you."

A laugh slips out of her, tickling my ribs. I stroke her hair. "Brace yourself, sweetheart. You haven't seen egotistical tyrant yet."

~135~

I'm not sure what time I fell asleep this morning. After Mary entered dreamland I slipped out of bed and called Sheila, giving her and mom an update. They expected to be meeting us at a hospital and bashed me about not insisting Mary get treated right away, but the purpose of this new life of mine is to toe the line between doing exactly what Mary wants and what's best for her. Outside of some expected tossing and turning she slept solidly while I whispered my defense, and after I climbed back into bed she curled against me and didn't move.

The calm of those early hours lured me into another mistake. I let exhaustion take me. It buried me so deep I never felt Mary rip from my arms. Now I'm awake, and she's gone. Again.

"Mary!" Time and heart stand still. There's no sound but the beat of my feet over hardwood floors. Mary isn't here. The bedroom, bathroom, closet, and kitchen are all empty. I search the spare rooms. "Mary?" Her absence sends wild horses stampeding through my chest. I fling the front door open. "Mary!" Her name ripples across the lawn, echoes back to me in shocking silence. There's no way someone got to her. Not here.

"Mary!" I run toward the garage, hating myself for sleeping so deeply. My truck is here. She didn't leave me, run from my smothering arms in the middle of the night. "Mary!" I scan the yard. A distant murmur catches my ear. I dart around the garage. It's coming from the tree line. "Mary?"

"John!"

My legs go airborne, branches tearing at my face, ripping my clothes. The smallness of her voice answers me each time I yell. I run harder. Faster. She's close. "Mary!" Her hands are up. I crash through them. Pushing my body over hers. Covering. Swarming. Protecting.

322

"John! Stop!" She reels against my grip.

"Who brought you here?" I hold tighter. "Where are they? Stop moving!"

"I'm alone." She grips my face, forcing me to focus on her. "I came here alone."

"Alone?" Her words shake loose a different kind of fear. "You came out here alone? Just up and decided to take a leisurely stroll on two bum legs through woods you don't know? *Without telling me!*"

"I didn't want to wake you." She smiles. "I wanted to explore *our* land."

She's testing my patience. And looks sexy doing it. Especially when she calls this *our* land. "Don't ever do this to me again." I fill my lungs with the scent of her hair. "Not knowing where you are petrifies me."

"I didn't mean to scare you." Her hands slide to my beating chest. "I'll tell you next time."

"Putting a GPS on you will take care of the problem." I nuzzle into her neck. "You want it inserted under this patch of skin." I kiss the hollow of her collarbone. "Or maybe down here?" I bring her wrist to my lips. "Or someplace more creative?"

"Nowhere." She grins. "I'll just be sure to tell you every time I'm going for a walk."

"But you nearly gave me *another* heart attack." I look deep into her pools, frowning for effect. "That wouldn't happen if you were wired. And you want me to be happy. Right?"

"Right." She presses her lips to mine. "I want us both to be happy."

"Then your walking privileges are revoked and you're being fitted with the latest technology."

"Neither of those are happening." Her arms slide around my neck. "But I will let you carry me back to bed."

I'll never turn down a chance to get her in my arms. She's up and cradled to me before her breath cools. And I can always install trackers in all her shoes. "Wait." I set her on her feet. She stands in front of me. Proud and tall. "Mary, you're...you *walked* out here? Without crutches?"

"I was wondering how long it would take you to notice." She steps closer. Unsteady but strong.

"Sorry. I was a little distracted by the terror of you disappearing again." She laughs at me. "It's not funny." I swing her back into my arms. "And you're supposed to be... I don't know. Distraught or something."

"Is that what you want me to be?"

"No." I tuck her against my chest and head for the house. "It took me half the night to convince Mom and Sheila you're okay. They're worried. And think I should take you to talk to someone."

"I only want to talk to you." Her hand rests on my shoulder. "Besides, we'll see them tomorrow and they can judge for themselves that I'm okay."

"Tomorrow?" I was hoping this time around she and I would be alone for a while. "They'll be happy to get the invitation."

"I'm sure they will be." She grins. "It isn't every day the infamous John Beller gets married."

~136~

A man can get used to the way Mary makes her points. She barely lets go of my lips long enough for me to breathe. Then there's the wiggling around on my lap. Every little move drives me wild. Normally, she innocently has no idea of the effect she has on me. She simply is. And it's sexy. Today, she intentionally has me on fire. The woman wants to get married tomorrow and doesn't care what I have to say about it. Unless what I have to say is yes.

"Sweetheart." I pull her off me. "You've been through a lot." Forced to look evil in the eye. Watch it seethe and fester all around her. "We can wait. For as long as you need. I'm not going to rush you. And I don't want you to rush yourself." I trace her jaw. Her perfect jaw. "I love you. And I'm not going anywhere."

"Neither am I." She exposes a neck begging to be kissed. "I want this." Her hands run under my shirt. "And you said I can have anything I want." Her body molds to mine. So perfectly I couldn't have crafted a better fit.

I take the bait, lips trailing softly against the delicate skin beneath her ear. Pulse quickening. Wishing we were free of these last weeks. Free to explore every tiny crevice. Free to bask in our pleasure. But the last weeks *did* happen. And, more than anything, I don't want her to have regrets. Not about me. This. Us.

"We have a lifetime together." I force my lips to heel. "We'll make it official one day. Until then we—"

"He said I'm a whore." She jerks away, arms folding, eyes blazing. "He said he was going to treat me like one until there was nothing left of me."

Bile loosens in my gut. "You should have never been put in that kind of position."

"I don't care about the position!" She bites. "I care that he wins! Because you, Mr. Pushy, all of a sudden don't want to rush me down the aisle! You've pushed me from the second I met you. Now that I actually want to run with you, you don't want me!"

"I want every single inch of you. In a thousand different ways." I pry her arms apart, putting them back around my neck. "What we just went through was traumatizing for me. For you, it was a million times worse. And while I admire what you're trying to do, I don't want to brush this under the rug. I want to make sure you're okay. Because you're not what he called you. And if he touched you like that and I—"

"If he wanted to rape me, he should have waited to say he was going to kill you." She climbs off my lap. "Then maybe he could have done more than just claw at me before I buried my foot in him so hard that, even if he wasn't dead, he wouldn't be able to use his loins! And you're not burning that farmhouse down!" She jabs a finger into her chest. "*I'm* the one lighting the match."

This side of her petrifies me. The delicate butterfly willing to attempt beating someone to death with her paper wings. No hesitation. And she's propping most of her weight on her formerly casted leg. It either doesn't hurt, or it hurts less than the gashed open foot. Either way, she's standing of her own accord and blowing what's left of my mind. "I'll stand beside you while you set the blaze. But, though you're good at finding hope in despair, and one day you'll tuck all of this away where not even the memories can hurt you, that day isn't today."

"It isn't any day." She hardens. "Because I don't want to forget. I want these memories front and center. So I don't ever get anyone I care about hurt again."

"You didn't—"

"He nearly killed you!" She yells. "And me! We could both be dead right now but we're not. And you said you wanted to marry me as soon as I could walk on my own." She takes a step. "I can. So if you don't want to marry me just say it. Don't blame it on what happened to me. You can blame it on what happened to you *because* of me, but don't act like I'm some poor, fragile—"

"I can't ever act like you're fragile. Because even though every fiber of you is the most precious and fragile thing I've ever seen, you're too stubborn to appreciate my admiration." I drag her into my arms, lips falling on her soft skin, starting at the crown of her head and working over her cheeks. "The only thing I'm guilty of is not sticking to my decisions." I hoist her onto my hips. "Trying to be nice. Pliable. So you don't get mad and slip through my bullheaded fingers." I lay her on the bed. "But you stay mad at me anyway." I tug off my shirt. "And you never listen to me. If you did, you'd know that without you, my world doesn't just crumble. It disappears." I lie over her. "I'm going to marry you. If you want that to be tomorrow, fine by me."

"Really?" Light dances in her eyes.

"I already have your wedding gift." I tug at the hem of her shirt. "Sort of."

Her big eyes dilate as I work my mouth over her, her breathing rapid. "This isn't my gift to you." Though it's definitely her gift to me. "I'm buying my bride a store so she can open the boutique she's always dreamed of."

She gasps. "Seriously?"

"My first act as your husband is to prove I support anything you want to do." I hold tight to this moment. Etching her into my mind. Her hands run down my back, giving my aching heart assurance. "Don't think I'm too sweet before I tell you the catch. There's a security plan."

"An armed guard following me around twenty-four seven?"

"Don't be silly, I'll be the one following you around." I grin. "The armed guards will only patrol the perimeter."

"Then my gift, husband," she smiles, "is making the boutique so successful I have my own millions. To pay you back." Her lips raise to mine. "And so I can be on equal footing. Because I'm going to be just as protective and overbearing with you as you've been with me. You are *not* leaving my sight, John Beller."

"I'm going to make you swear to that in our wedding vows."

Keeping an eye on her won't be hard if she stays close enough to keep an eye on me. "I'm a lucky man to have a wife who doubles as my bodyguard." I drag her ear to my mouth. "Millions are good and all, but I'm a billionaire. And in twenty-four hours, so are you."

A NOTE FROM THE AUTHOR

When you start living the life of your dreams, there will always be obstacles, doubters, mistakes and setbacks along the way. But with hard work, perseverance and self-belief there is no limit to what you can achieve.

— **Roy T. Bennett, The Light in the Heart**

The journey from rough draft to published novel has been arduous, fraught with missteps and uncertainty. Without the support of my friends, family, and colleagues I would not have picked myself up after each fall because I never would have attempted the climb. For each of you, I am grateful.

Among the many whose names won't fit on the page below, I'd like to first thank my husband Joe. He is the constant wind in my sail, the strength at my back and the hand in mine. Without his unwavering belief, I wouldn't have penned the first word.

As strongly encouraging as his father, my son Derek never failed to give me the tough love I needed to leap into the abyss of publishing. My fear was real, but he reminded me the only way through it was to do it. His feedback is inestimable in all parts of my life.

A huge warm hug to my amazing sister-in-law Billie, who read this manuscript when it was somewhere below rough draft status, and to Aunt Kathy for bringing me flowers and cards of encouragement.

A deep and profound bow to Arielle Eckstut of The Book Doctors, whose guidance is invaluable. Eighteen cheers for my editors, Kim Huther of Wordsmith Proofreading and Anita Stratos of Proof Positive. I assure you any mistakes within these pages are solely mine, for all these wonderful women did their best to right my path.

I mention with reverence, Marianne Nowicki of Premade Ebook Cover Design. The magic she possesses to see inside my mind is to be awed. I dream, she creates, and it's perfect! Many thanks to Lloyd Lens Photography for providing a photo of a West Virginia backroad to incorporate on the cover, and for the author photo.

If you've ever given me so much as a kind smile, *thank you.* This book exists because of you.

The next title in this four book romantic thriller set releases September 1, 2021! Read on for a preview! And join my mailing list at LeeDawnaBooks.com to be among the first to receive news and information about the release.

September 1, 2021
Book Release Preview

~1~

I'm photogenic. Or so say the stack of surveillance photos in my hand. They were undoubtedly taken by some creepy dude holed up in a rusty sedan, his telescopic lens clicking away trying to catch me in the *act*. But just like the jerk who followed me around in Europe, the cheater-catching private eye providing these headshots is going to be disappointed. My days of being dumb enough to bury my sorrows in a woman are long gone.

To this buffoon's credit, while he wasted time snapping photos of my lone face peering out of my third-floor bedroom window, he made the building I'm living in look a lot nicer than it actually is. The whole three-floor structure is dusty and dated, with doors falling off hinges and carpets stained any place they aren't torn. But from these photographs, you'd never know the ruin surrounding me.

Working out of an office on the first floor of the same building compounds my dismal living situation. Knowing who's behind these impressive photographs is equally repulsive. I wish I could divorce her. But my overpaid lawyer says I'm not getting out of this marriage without opening my wallet, so we're staying hitched. Whether Cassie likes it or not.

"Shred these for me." I hand the flattering mail to the clerk and walk out of the cramped post office. I didn't notice anyone tailing me earlier and I don't see anyone now, but I'm new in this quaint city so unless the voyeur is openly pointing a camera at me, I'm not going to spot them.

I don't want to have to move again. I'd rather stay here pretending to be blissfully ignorant of Cassie's existence because Huntington, with its colonial architecture and small-town feel despite being a bustling metropolis, beats the heck out of being exiled in Europe. A man can only endure cookies masquerading as biscuits for so long. Three days ago, my first meal back in the States was a big fat plate of buttermilk biscuits doused in sausage gravy, with a side oath to never drink tea again.

Hopping into my Land Rover, I shoot Cassie a text. *Nice try, but I've avoided giving you a single cent for over seven years. I'm not going to cave now. Especially over more stupid photos.*

What are you talking about? Her words ping my screen. *What photos?*

Playing stupid doesn't mean you are, I type back. *Stop trying to harass me. And leave my family alone while you're at it!*

You leave them alone. And sign the divorce papers while you're at it!

If she wants me to sign a single piece of paper relating to our marriage, she knows my terms. And since she'll never agree to them, she can go to her grave still being my wife. *Just go away, Cassie. Never hearing from you again is too soon.*

~2~

Dad only gave me the East Coast operation of Kingwood Properties to get rid of me again. I'm well aware that his dabbling in Huntington hasn't led to anything more than a lone secretary set up in a single office. But just like the Kingwood family built their fortune in commercial real estate along the west coast, I'll prove I can build mine here. Plus, Dad and I get along about as well as Cassie and I do, so moving across the country is the only option that lets me be *home* without actually being home.

My brother is the one who actually gets to stay home in California. It isn't fair, but Curtis has always been Dad's clone so he's the one inheriting the keys to the kingdom while I'm shuffled off to every dark corner they think my name can be buried in. Too bad for them I figured out the game. Just like in Europe, I intend to capitalize on my time in Huntington. The properties Dad and his perfect son don't want will be added to *my* company's holdings. And once A.K. Investments rivals Kingwood Properties, they'll see I know the business of buying, renting and selling better than Curtis, and certainly better than my sister's podgy husband.

The first order of business is attending a charity event being held at one of the dozen properties Dad *did* manage to acquire during his brief interest in this side of the continent. The flat-roofed banquet hall adjoins a golf course, butting up to the overgrown fifth hole. Driving around the tan-sided venue I park in the back, in front of a row of ground-level windows. From what I recall of my one and only tour of the place two days ago, these two-foot-tall panes lining the wall provide light to a hallway that slopes down to the basement.

Behind me, draped over my backseat, is a slim-notched single-breasted suit. After three sleepless nights I considered not attending tonight's Veterans' Banquet, but it's a toss-up as to what will make the vein in Dad's neck bulge more, and I'm banking on my presence here doing more damage than skipping.

In case he's the one bankrolling Cassie's voyeurism, he can also choke on this. I throw open my door and step out onto the scorching pavement, dropping my drawers. If they're watching, Cassie can eat her heart out over what she can't have, and Dad can stroke out over the surfer's body he's always complaining I spend too much time on. Which is a joke, because I spend zero minutes on my physique. He'd know that if he actually cared to ever talk to me.

Conversation with me doesn't interest him. All he's ever done is declare me to be a long line of grief and screwups. So now he has something new to add to his list because stripping down to my birthday suit in a public spot even makes *my* dumb moments list. Still not the dumbest thing I've ever done, though. Marrying Cassie without a pre-nup is.

Snatching my baggy shorts and t-shirt from the pavement, I toss them into the Rover and look around. The golf course is rundown, the dozens of cars around me appear empty, and the row of windows is only two feet tall, so I doubt anyone passing through the hallway would bother glancing out to the parking lot. But the longer I stand here naked, the dumber I feel. Plus, I'm trying to get back into the Kingwood fold, not confirm their every judgment. They may be the reason my life is a cesspool of oozing agony, but that doesn't mean I have to make them look at my dangling jewels.

Leaning toward the backseat, movement draws my eyes to the right. There's a shadow silhouetted in one of the windows. I face the glass. If someone's in there, they better enjoy the show. I only make mistakes once. And sooner or later the people exploiting those mistakes will pay for every moment of anguish they've inflicted. "Eat your heart out. Literally."

Growing up in a family like mine means wearing suits more often than not, but being worse than a black sheep means not being forced to attend events. At twenty-nine and not really part of my family anyway, I need to force myself to, at the very least, attend charity banquets. I'm just not sure I got tonight's timing right.

Lack of sleep keeps my days mixed up. The insomnia started right after my very short marriage imploded. I was a naïve twenty-one then. Now, my weeks all run together and when the battery on my phone dies, I lose all hope of even knowing what decade I'm in. I'd put myself out of this misery if the witch I'm hitched to wouldn't get all my money after I died.

Sun blazing its last rays of day, I yank on the suit pants and drag the crisp white button-up over my bronze arms while imagining Cassie burning through my bank account before my body is even cold.

Sliding the last button into place, I shrug into the suit jacket and smooth my hair in the side mirror. I didn't bring a tie. The only one I own I was wearing my first day in town, when I met with Joan, the tight-laced lady who runs the nonprofit hosting tonight's event. While she explained her organization's work in helping veterans return to civilian life, I sat in front of her with gravy splotched on my shirt like a toddler. After she left, Gladys, the brave lone secretary keeping my family's affairs organized, informed me Joan has connections with deeper pockets than my own. Her point was to inform me of the need to make better impressions. Another reason I decided to attend tonight. But if the shadow I saw earlier belonged to Joan, I can only hope she liked the show, otherwise a gravy-stained tie is the least of my problems.

Rounding the banquet hall, I regret letting my temper get the best of me. Joan is already on her way into the foyer. I reach for the handle of the exterior door, gut somersaulting. "Good to see you again." I step inside and take the hand she's extending, a brief firm shake and then palms at my sides. No need to acknowledge me stripping for her. "How are tonight's final preparations coming along?"

"They're fine, but I didn't expect to see you." Her head tilts. "Is everything okay? We're still permitted to use the building, I hope?"

"Of course." I stumble over my tongue and avert my eyes from the all-smiles woman strolling toward us. The curve of her swaying hips draws me back in, and now that she's standing next to Joan I can't help but *know* her skin smells as delectable as she looks. A flash of me digging my fingers into her shoulder-length honey hair and kissing every bit of that red lipstick off her hits my frontal cortex. I clear my throat, pinning my hands together. "I'm just stopping by to make sure you have everything you need for tonight's dinner."

I've sworn off women. I've even sworn off alcohol to make sure I rid myself of all female mistakes. I'd rather stay celibate than get mixed up with another Cassie. "You mentioned always needing help, so I'm at your service, Joan. And don't let the suit fool you, I'm not above emptying the trash." Sweat builds under my collar as the unidentified drink of dead and bitter dreams on Joan's left provides the answer.

"We never turn away volunteers. Especially tall, dark, and stallion ones."

I force my eyes off her lips again, staring directly at Joan. I'm not here to flirt. No matter how much the luscious woman strokes my ego.

Joan saves me from having to launch a response. "Mr. Kingwood, allow me to introduce you to the person solely responsible for making tonight's event happen. She isn't tall, dark, or stallion, but she's equally impressive. In many ways." Her narrow blue eyes twinkle. "This young lady is *the* Miss Sheila Beller."

"Beller?" Moisture breaks out across my entire body. "Of the John Beller family?"

"Guilty." Sheila laughs, the sound tickling over my ears like quenching rain. "But I don't want to know what you've heard about my family, particularly my brother, unless you're willing to give me the chance to dispute it over dinner. Say, next Thursday at six?"

About the Author

Lee Dawna is a romantic thriller author living in the rolling mountains of West Virginia. An avid traveler and outdoorswoman, you may bump into her along a remote trail where a meandering stream whispers her next story. Connect with her on:

Instagram https://www.instagram.com/leedawna_author/,

Twitter https://twitter.com/LeeDawna_Author,

Facebook https://www.facebook.com/leedawnabooks

Goodreads https://www.goodreads.com/user/show/77747080-lee-dawna